## THE HEAT OF DESIRE

"Are you really trying to clear my father's name?" Cedar cried. "Or are you simply looking for a juicy bit of scandal to emblazon on the front page of the *Sun*?" She glared at him, daring him to deny it all, knowing, even before he spoke, that it would all be lies.

"Is that what you think I'm doing?" Guy demanded.

"Well, isn't it?" she retorted. "Why else did you come here, if not to get a story?"

He reached for her, pulling her close to him. "I'm here for this," he said, and he kissed her.

Once his lips touched hers, it didn't seem to matter that what they'd both felt the instant before was anger. Once his lips touched hers, nothing else mattered at all.

For Cedar, everything was spinning, all was confusion. She felt safe with his arms around her, for the first time in what seemed an endless age. Not even the unaccountable liquid heat that filled her at the touch of his lips frightened her now . . .

# SUSAN SACKETT

# A TASTE OF PASSION

**ZEBRA BOOKS**
**KENSINGTON PUBLISHING CORP.**

ZEBRA BOOKS

are published by

Kensington Publishing Corp.
475 Park Avenue South
New York, NY 10016

First printing: July, 1992

Printed in the United States of America

# Chapter One

"It was a wonderful speech, Papa."

Cedar Rushton quite literally glowed with pride as she watched her father step off the podium. She gave him a clean hand towel as soon as he was out of the sight of the cheering crowd he'd left behind him in the longshoremen's hall proper.

Magnus Rushton took it thankfully. The night air was thick and sultry, the sort only New York summers seem capable of spawning. But it was late September, no longer summer, and nights of this sort ought to have rightly been abandoned for more pleasing weather. In the heat that persisted despite the calendar, and after the exertion of an impassioned political address, Magnus was thankful for his daughter's offering. He immediately brought the towel to his face, using it to mop up the drops of perspiration that coated his forehead and cheeks as he looked down at her beaming face.

He returned Cedar's smile. Her expression, and especially the clearly evident pride in him it unabashedly displayed, left him with a feeling of satisfaction nearly as great as the one he had felt when the crowd in the hall had first begun their enthusiastic applause. But as the pounding roar began to fade and his audience stood and began to stream from the hall, his sense of pleasure faded. In its wake the uncertainty he'd felt since the start of the campaign returned.

"Do you think they'll act?" he asked her. "Do you think they really understood how necessary it is that there be change?"

He turned and peered past the curtain to the thick stream of humanity that was massed in the aisles and moving out of the hall. He screwed up his nose at the moist, tobacco- and sweat-laden air that stirred in their wake and wondered why he hadn't noticed that particularly unpleasant bouquet while he'd been speaking.

"Of course they did, Papa," Cedar quickly assured him. "There are, after all, a great many people in this city who are not in the pocket of William Marcy Tweed. And they'll vote for an honest government, one that considers the poor and the working class, if they're given the chance."

Magnus smiled warily. He was beginning to doubt the wisdom he'd shown in allowing Cedar to become so thoroughly drawn into his political campaign. Surely, he thought, it wasn't quite natural for a young woman to have such adamant views of political matters. She ought to be home, tending to the darning or reading an uplifting book. Or better yet, she ought to be in her own home, with a husband and children to occupy her thoughts. Instead she was here, in this smelly, smoke-filled, dirty hall, waiting dutifully to buoy his spirits and encourage him, to spout at him all the words he no longer had the patience to say to himself.

He realized that if he weren't quite so dependent upon the feeling of pleasure the sight of her smile gave him, if she didn't ease the sense of loneliness that had filled him since his wife's death the previous year, he'd do what he ought to do and keep her safely away from the far less than pleasant details that seemed to dominate a political campaign. But he was, he realized, as weak as the next man, and only too willing to have her there to assure him when he most needed assurance that what he was doing was right.

"I'm not trying to take on Boss Tweed nor Tammany Hall just yet, Cedar," he chided her mildly. He couldn't help but smile, however, inwardly pleased that she thought him capable of that far from meager feat. "I'm only making an attempt to wrest one small commission out of their greedy hands."

Cedar pursed her lips. She was not at all pleased with her father's determination to belittle what he was doing.

"An important commission, Papa," she told him firmly. "Reforming the city's Department of Municipal Properties is the first step in clearing out the likes of Tweed and his cronies."

"She's right, Magnus. And if any man in this city can do it, you're that man."

Chester Bowles was storming towards them, his short, thick body thrusting forward with the sort of determination a locomotive under full steam suggested. Cedar stared at him, wondering why he made such slow and plodding progress even while giving the impression of such forceful movement.

Bowles waved a thick, half-smoked cigar in his beefy right hand as he spoke. When he came to an abrupt stop at Magnus's side, he heartily slapped Magnus's shoulder with his free hand while he returned the thick tube of tobacco to his mouth.

Magnus scowled, but stifled his dislike of his major political supporter, reminding himself that politics does, indeed, make strange bedfellows and that he needed Bowles not only for his organizational skills but also for the hefty contribution he had made to the campaign coffers.

"Well, let's see if we can clear out Michael McNaughton before we take on Tweed, shall we?" Magnus suggested with a wan smile.

"A year or two of your running the department without graft might just embarrass Tweed into retirement," Cedar told him.

"First I have to get elected, Cedar," Magnus reminded her. "After that we can talk about embarrassing Boss Tweed."

"And a few more speeches like the one you gave tonight should be enough to turn out McNaughton on election day," Bowles told him, his thick body shaking with jovial intensity. "Apropos of your speech, there were a few points I thought of that you might want to consider . . ."

Magnus lifted a restraining hand to him, stopping the flow of his words before it had the opportunity to grow to so great a torrent that nothing would dam it.

7

"I don't think we need bother Cedar with the postmortem, Chester," he said. "If you'll excuse us, I'll see her into a hansom and be back in a few moments."

Bowles nodded a round head. His thick mustache seemed to stir up the air like oars pushing seawater.

"I think we should review your speech for the rally tomorrow as well," he said. He didn't notice Magnus's grimace at the prospect as he turned to face Cedar, lifting her right hand in his and planting a thickly damp kiss on it. "As always, it is a great pleasure to find such a beautiful flower blooming in these bleakly unadorned halls, my dear," he told her. "Will we have the pleasure of your company tomorrow?" He pressed her hand with his and smiled at her, baring a row of large, tobacco-stained teeth.

"I'm not sure Cedar will be able to attend tomorrow's festivities," Magnus replied before Cedar had the chance. "I think she's been spending a good deal too much time hearing speeches in hiring halls and at political rallies."

Bowles grinned. "But this is democracy, my dear Magnus," he objected. "What could be more wholesome than watching it in action?"

"For a young woman, just about anything," Magnus replied in a dry, completely unamused tone.

Bowles's smile vanished. "I shall be heartbroken to miss you," he said to Cedar. His expression did, indeed, show disappointment at the prospect of this deprivation.

Cedar pulled her hand gingerly from his. She heartily disliked the hot, damp, soft feel of his flesh touching hers, and she disliked even more the look that he always seemed to have when he stared at her, a look very much like that she'd seen in his eyes one evening at dinner as he'd surveyed an enormous cut of beef on his plate just before he'd smacked his lips with anticipation of the first bite.

"And I should hate to miss Papa's speech," she told him tersely. "Good evening, Mr. Bowles."

Bowles bobbed in a clumsy imitation of a courtly bow. "Good evening, Miss Rushton."

The niceties obviously concluded, Magnus took Cedar's

arm and escorted her past the podium and through the now deserted hall.

"How do you tolerate that man, Papa?" Cedar asked when they were well out of Bowles's earshot. "He's so, so . . ."

"*Unpleasant* will serve, Cedar," Magnus told her.

"I can think of quite a few more fitting words, Papa," she said.

"I'm sure you can, Cedar, but we neither of us need speak nor hear them just now. And I shouldn't need to remind you that Chester Bowles is an unfortunate necessity. We may not like him, but he wants to see McNaughton out of the chair of that commission and me in it. What's more, he's shown his support in a most material and, I hardly need add, welcome manner to that end. For now, that is enough to make me overlook a few deficiencies in his personality."

Cedar scowled, not in the least placated by Magnus's words.

"He wants McNaughton out so that he can make a bigger profit on his city contracts," she told him firmly. "He's hoping that his help will mean that you'll see that he gets a larger share of the pie."

"I suppose he probably does, Cedar."

She was shocked at the way he calmly admitted what ought to be an odious thought to him.

"But that's just the sort of thing you want to stop, Papa."

"And if I'm elected, Cedar, I assure you, just as I've assured those voters who take the time to listen to me, that I will. Bowles may not realize it yet, but he will simply have to be satisfied with pocketing the graft he's had to pay to McNaughton in the past."

"Still, I don't like your having a man like him involved in your campaign. His only reason for backing you is to line his own pockets. He's no better than McNaughton."

"He's a businessman, Cedar," Magnus reminded her. "The profit motive is what makes business run."

"The same can be said of Tammany Hall, Papa," Cedar replied.

Magnus shrugged, but made no reply as he pushed open

the door to the street. For a moment Cedar stood in the doorway, savoring the relatively clean and cool air outside the hall, ridding her lungs of the smoke-and-perspiration-laden air she'd been breathing for the previous three hours.

Her relief was short-lived. A tall figure, that of what appeared to be an idler whiling away the last of the evening leaning against a light post and contemplating the passing traffic, darted a quick glance at Magnus, a slightly longer one at Cedar, then disengaged itself from its support and ambled toward them.

"Impressive speech, Mr. Rushton," the man said as he approached Magnus. "Did you mean any of it?"

Magnus ceased his consideration of the street and the possibility of finding an available hansom for hire, and turned to the tall, lanky young man who addressed him.

"Every word, young man," he snapped angrily, his tone clearly saying that he resented the implication that he hadn't.

"Then I can quote you in the *Sun?*" the stranger asked.

Magnus's cheeks darkened slightly. His eyes narrowed as he considered the stranger's face.

"You can, but you won't," he said finally. "Or am I to assume the *Sun* has suddenly changed its leanings, climbed out of Tammany's pocket, and now aligns itself on the side of political reform?"

"I write the truth, Mr. Rushton," the reporter replied sharply. "Editorial leanings do not interest me, nor do I take them into account in what I write."

Cedar was surprised to see that her father's words made the stranger's cheeks color in anger just as his had ired Magnus. The glow from the street lamp cast a pale, golden light that just barely showed the darkened flush in his well-chiseled cheeks. From them, her glance drifted to his other features — a long but straight nose, firm, thin lips, dark blond hair brushed back and away from his face. And a pair of deep blue eyes that she found, much to her surprise, had turned away from Magnus and were now staring back at her. She quickly looked away, embarrassed by the unladylike interest she'd shown in him and even more so by the fact that he

10

seemed amused at having caught her staring at him.

Guy Marler *was* amused by Cedar's rushed survey, and once he'd recovered from Magnus's accusation, he repaid the compliment with a rather more intent inspection of his own. He considered the halo of pale golden hair that framed her face, the wide, high cheekbones, and large, thickly lashed eyes that seemed impossibly green in the lamplight. But more than any of that, he considered her lips, slightly larger than fashion dictated and, like her cheeks, flushed red. Guy found himself wondering what it would be like to kiss those lips, and had to force himself to turn his attention away from that consideration and back to Cedar's father.

Who, at that moment, was becoming decidedly antagonistic at what he considered the undue attention Guy had shown his daughter.

"I'll believe that, young man, if and when I see some honest reporting about this campaign, if and when I see the *Sun* pose the question of why the city paid nearly three times as much to build a small schoolhouse on Horatio Street as a private citizen spent to build a house nearly twice the size only a few blocks away. If you want me to believe you write the truth, and not what you're told to write, you'll find out why the city has spent more of the citizens' money on municipal building under McNaughton's leadership of the department, with less result, than it ever has before, while what little relief there was for the poor has dwindled until it is nonexistent."

Guy held up a hand and grinned as Magnus paused for breath.

"I've already admitted that your campaign rhetoric is convincing, Mr. Rushton," he replied. "But McNaughton has given valid reasons for the growing expenses of his department."

Cedar nearly choked at his words.

"The only real reason is the greed of Tammany," she retorted.

She was angry—angry that this man could stand there so calmly and ignore what her father was saying, angry that he seemed not to believe or, even worse in her eyes, not to care.

11

She stared at him. He seemed bemused by her outburst, even mildly amused, and that only made her angrier.

"Accusations without proof are of little value, miss," he told her.

"I don't know why my father bothers talking to the likes of you. Tweed's friends control your paper, just as they control all the others in the city." Her eyes narrowed and she leaned toward Guy. "But there are still honest citizens left in New York. And with their help, my father will be elected despite anything Tammany can do."

Magnus put his hand on her arm and drew her away, urging her toward the curb.

"That's enough, Cedar," he told her calmly. "It's not worth either of us wasting our breath."

He darted an angry glance at Guy, then turned his back to him and motioned to a hansom that was turning onto the far end of the block.

Despite the obvious dismissal, Guy made no move to leave them. He found himself intrigued by what he'd heard Magnus say that evening and was beginning to think he might look a bit more seriously into the possibility that the sort of malfeasance that Magnus had implied riddled the city's government might actually exist. But more than that, he realized he was intrigued by Magnus's daughter's vehemence. Or was it, he wondered idly, not her political views, but perhaps simply the thought of those impossibly inviting lips of hers? He sighed, and told himself those particular thoughts would lead him nowhere, or if they did, it would only be to the sort of trouble he'd avoid if he had half an ounce of common sense.

"Bring me some proof that McNaughton is milking his department for Tammany, and I'll see that it gets onto the *Sun's* front page," he found himself saying.

The words surprised him. He hadn't thought about them. They just seemed to slip out.

In any event, they had the effect he wanted them to have. Both Magnus and Cedar turned back to face him.

"If I had absolute proof," Magnus replied, "this city

12

wouldn't need me. McNaughton and his friends would be in jail, Mr. . . ."

"Marler," Guy told him. He let his glance drift once more from Magnus's face to Cedar's and he found himself smiling. "Guy Marler."

"And if you were half so intent upon printing the truth as you say you are, Mr. Marler," Cedar broke in, "you'd look for some proof yourself and not wait for it to come to you."

Guy's expression sobered as he saw the passion in her eyes as she spoke. There was no real reason why he ought to believe what Rushton and his group of crackpot reformers were spouting about McNaughton, but for some reason when he looked into Cedar's eyes, he found that he wanted desperately to believe, or at least to make her believe he did.

"I might just do that, Miss Rushton," he said as the cab Magnus had hailed pulled up to the curb beside them. He reached forward and opened the door for her.

She stared back at him for a moment.

"I wish I believed you, Mr. Marler," she said.

Then she turned back to her father, took the arm he offered her, and climbed up into the cab.

"Don't wait up for me, Cedar," Magnus told her. "I'll probably be late." He closed the door and called up to the driver, "Eighty Thompson, driver."

Magnus turned and walked back into the hall, completely ignoring Guy as he passed him. But his indifference made no impression on Guy whatsoever.

The fact was, Guy was far too preoccupied with the pair of green eyes that stared out of the cab at him before it pulled away. He stood on the curb and watched the cab move along the nearly empty street, staring after it for a long while before he turned and began to walk slowly back to the *Sun's* offices.

It was a long while before he could force his mind to think of something other than Magnus Rushton's daughter, and what it would be like to press his lips to hers.

Cedar's expression was entirely sober as she considered her

reflection and dutifully pulled her brush through her hair.

It was not her usual habit to bother with the contemplation of her physical charms, nor to waste time mourning whatever deficiencies such a survey might expose. But for some reason, on this particular night, she found herself unable to simply brush her hundred strokes, turn out the light, and climb into bed.

Instead she peered with a critical eye at the image in her glass. Not an altogether unpleasant face, she decided after due consideration. Admittedly, hers was not exactly a face that met the strict dictates of fashion. Her nose was a bit too long, and was stubbornly straight rather than smartly up-turned. An honest evaluation forced her to admit that her lips were much too full, and in no way could they be described as anything like the neat little bows that the idealized faces of the fashionable ladies pictured in *Godey's Magazine* wore. Nor could she claim even the remotest kinship to their magnifi-cently endowed and corseted forms. Her own body was un-fashionably slender and absolutely without need of confining stays or lacings.

But if she had no need to prop up her bosom or lace in her waist, she told herself she could certainly count a lithe and graceful body to her credit. And to her list of assets she added high cheekbones, bright, wide eyes, and blond hair that was a perfect foil for flawless skin.

Unfortunately, she'd allowed that flawless skin to take on a bit too much color from the sun during the summer month she'd spent in Saratoga with her aunt and uncle. She smiled as she thought of her Aunt Felicia continually rushing after her with a forgotten parasol or bonnet and the admonition that "young gentlemen aren't interested in ladies who look as though they tend crops in the fields."

Not that Cedar ever considered any young gentleman's in-terest or its lack as a guide by which to judge her actions. The time she spent with her uncle's thoroughbreds—riding, talk-ing with the trainers, and mostly watching the horses being put through their paces—left her with a firm grasp of Sarato-ga's most famous pastime, and as a result she was never at a loss for company nor for a partner at the dances at the fashionable Pump House spa.

Her aunt's depression at the fact that none of those gentlemen callers went on to the critical stage of presenting her with a proposal of marriage was something Cedar considered more amusing than anything else. She was far too interested in the handsome thoroughbred racehorses her uncle raised and her father's upcoming political campaign to waste very much time mourning the nebulous loss of a suitor whose attractions, in her estimation, paled beside those far more intriguing subjects.

True, she had heard one or two of those young men refer to her in rather deprecating tones as the "serious one," but that fact did not unduly disturb her. And when her aunt gently suggested she try to be a bit less intense, she replied that she'd rather be thought serious than dull-witted, and then went off to watch her uncle's favorite roan being taken through his paces on the practice track, purposely forgetting both bonnet and parasol and returning later in the afternoon with cheeks turned decidedly red from too much sun.

It wasn't that she considered offensive her aunt's innocent scheming to see her married. It was just that she wasn't ready to find herself tied to a house and a life of afternoon teas and counting invitations to dinner parties. There were too many far more important matters to which she would rather apply her attention, most importantly her father's decision to leave his law practice and run for public office.

But for just a few moments on that particular evening, she seemed to have forgotten that determination and instead found herself wondering just what a specific young man, Guy Marler to be precise, had thought of her. When it occurred to her that she'd been staring at her reflection but thinking about him, she suddenly pushed herself away from her dressing table, dropping her brush among the clutter, and turned away, telling herself that he was hardly worth the time she'd already wasted on him. After all, her father had dismissed him as nothing more than one of Tammany's paid underlings, and that made him at best an adversary and at worst as corrupt as Tweed himself.

She blew out her lamp and climbed into bed. She spent a moment pushing away the blankets and trying to make herself comfortable despite the hot, still night air. But once she'd settled herself, she found Guy Marler's face creeping back to steal her attention, and his words—that he wrote the truth, not what he was told to write—kept returning to her mind.

She fell asleep wondering if she could believe him, and more, if she could, where that belief might lead her.

Cedar opened her eyes and stared at the finger of moonlight that streamed into her room. She let her thoughts drift for a few moments back to those she had had just before she'd fallen asleep, back to thoughts of Guy Marler. She remembered the way his eyes had found hers, the way they had seemed to speak to her just before her carriage had driven off, and she remembered the way she'd wanted to believe him, the way some part deep inside her wished that she might have reason to see him again.

It had been pleasant to fall asleep thinking of him, but now thoughts of him faded and were supplanted by a feeling of discomfort that completely bewildered her. The house was quiet around her, and she ought to have simply turned over and gone back to sleep. But something seemed wrong to her, although she wasn't quite sure what it could be. She sat up, lifted the small clock on the bedside table, and squinted in the dim light to see the hands.

"Three-thirty," she murmured half aloud, startling herself with the sound of her own voice.

She sat still and tense for a moment, listening for some sound, something to explain the odd feeling she had, but heard nothing. Still, she realized she was far too edgy to try to go back to sleep. She replaced the clock on her bedside table, swung her legs out of the bed, and felt along the floor for her slippers. Then she carefully lit her lamp, adjusting the flame so that it made a small orb of light.

She stood, lifted the lamp, and crossed her room to the

door, stepping softly out into the silent and empty hall. There was no sound in the house, no noise whatever, not even a stirring of the leaves in the trees outside the window that stood open at the far end of the hall to catch whatever stray breeze might happen to find its way there.

Her father's room was at the opposite end of the hall from her own, and Cedar crossed to it quickly, before she had the time to consider that she was behaving foolishly, that she ought to simply go back to her own room and try to sleep. Surely it must be the heat, she told herself, the unseasonable, thick, muggy night that had unnerved her.

She tapped softly at the door, then pushed it open and darted a look inside. One quick glance at the neatly turned down and undisturbed bed confirmed her feeling of discomfort.

She walked into the empty room, stopping only to consider the fact that her father's nightshirt was neatly laid, untouched since the housekeeper, Mrs. Kneely, had left it there six hours before, just as she had every night in Cedar's memory.

"Papa," she called out softly, but she knew there would be no answer, that her father certainly wasn't hiding in the closet or beneath the bed. She took one last look around, then left the room and returned to her own.

She reminded herself that Magnus had warned her that he would be late, reminded herself that the evenings he spent in the company of Chester Bowles often extended well into the morning and, despite Magnus's attempts to hide it from her, more often than not led to the consumption of a goodly amount of alcoholic beverages. Not that she had ever seen her father actually inebriated. Magnus was far too controlled a person to allow himself to become drunk. But she had no doubt but that as the hour grew late, Bowles would press a whiskey or two on him, and Magnus would not decline.

She told herself that that was probably all there was to his being so late, the two of them going over Magnus's speech for the rally and then relaxing with a glass or two of whiskey, Bowles talking loudly and at great length as he smoked his smelly cigar, and the two of them forgetting the time. But de-

17

spite the fact that she told herself there was really no reason for her to worry, she realized she would not sleep until she knew Magnus was finally safely home.

She found her dressing gown and pulled it on, then stepped out to the empty hall once again, this time walking its length to the stairs and then silently descending to the parlor floor below. She walked through the dark and empty parlor, then turned to the door to her father's study, pulled it open, and entered.

She had no idea why she liked this particular room of the house so much. It was hardly what could be considered a feminine room, with the walls lined with dark, leather-covered books, the great, usually untidy desk that dominated the room's center, the two wide, leather-covered wing chairs, and the sofa that surrounded the fireplace. The single window faced north, and the room was usually dark and certainly never cheery, despite her conscientious efforts to ensure there was a bowl of fresh flowers always on the table and another on the desk.

Still, it was to this room that she invariably gravitated when she was troubled or simply depressed. Perhaps that was because as a child she'd been able to come to find Magnus here and always know he would calm her fears. Perhaps it was simply that since her mother's death the previous year she and Magnus had grown so close to one another, so dependent upon one another. Whatever the reason, she told herself as she set down the lamp on the desk and seated herself in Magnus's well-worn wing chair, she would not worry so much about him if she just sat there to wait for his return.

Out of habit and lack of any other occupation, she absently began to neaten the disorganized heap of papers that littered the surface of the desk. First she gathered up the pile of foolscap on which Magnus wrote out the first drafts of his speeches, the ink-covered surface of the pages completely filled with Magnus's handwriting, the cross outs and corrections looking out of place beside the lines of his painstakingly neat script. It was the near emptiness of one page that caught her eye, the few words *Pennsylvania Railroad — real estate sale —*

*McNaughton* sitting alone in the center of the otherwise blank sheet. She told herself it was some note Magnus had written to himself, and dismissed it as unimportant, dropping the page onto the pile with the rest and covering it with a half dozen others. Then she addressed herself to the pile of newspapers that were the majority of the remaining litter on the desk.

Magnus took all the city's major papers, the *Herald,* the *Observer,* the *Sun,* even the *Truth Teller,* which was well known to be little more than the Tammany Hall house organ. When she'd asked why he wasted his time and money on it, Magnus had told her that it was best to know what the opposition was saying in order to know what to say in rebuttal, and she'd been unable to deny the wisdom in this argument.

The latest edition of *Truth Teller,* she noted with a wave of disgust, would leave Magnus with a good deal to rebut. The front page was emblazoned with Tammany rhetoric, damning the "hollier-than-thou politics of the reform movement." Although Magnus was not mentioned by name, there was distinct reference to him, and the suggestion that even the "purer-than-snow" reform candidate might have a few skeletons in his own closet that he might not wish to come to public light.

Cedar pushed the *Truth Teller* aside after giving vent to a few decidedly uncomplimentary thoughts concerning its misnomer. Ordinarily she would simply have gathered up the heap of papers and disposed of them, but for some reason she found herself leafing through them until she reached the *Sun* and began scanning its front page.

She told herself that the few moments she'd spent in the company of Guy Marler that evening had no bearing on her sudden interest in the unsavory headlines the *Sun* sported, but her conviction was shaken a bit when her glance fell on the byline of one G. Marler.

The article detailed a rather gory murder and the subsequent trial of the purported perpetrator, the more unpleasant particulars reported with what she could only consider unnatural relish, the whole obviously intended to appeal to the commonest taste for sensationalism. She was disgusted that earlier that evening she had found herself preoccupied with thoughts of the man who was capable of writing such an article, and even more so that this was the reporter the *Sun* had seen fit to send to cover her father's campaign speeches. She balled up the paper, telling herself that she could expect nothing from the sort of man who would write such articles as the one she'd just read, certainly not the fairness or honesty he'd promised.

Guy Marler, she told herself firmly, was the enemy, and any thoughts she might have expended on him were thoughts that were flagrantly wasted. She blushed and told herself she was a fool as she recalled the sort of thoughts she'd harbored about him earlier that evening, then told herself she would not allow herself to make any such mistake ever again.

Her thoughts were abruptly interrupted by the shrill sound of the front doorbell. She quickly decided that Magnus had forgotten to take his latchkey, for surely no one else would be at the door at that hour. Hoping that the noise hadn't wakened Mrs. Kneely, she dropped the newspaper that was still in her hands and bolted through the library to the front entrance.

"Really, Papa," she said as she pulled the door open, "you should be more careful about taking your . . ."

The words died in her throat as she realized it wasn't Magnus standing on the stoop facing her. She brought her hand to the neck of her dressing gown, uncomfortable and confused in the short instant before anger superseded all other emotions.

"Miss Rushton."

"Go back to your paper, Mr. Marler," she hissed at him as she started to close the door. "Ask them to teach you enough manners so that you know what appropriate calling hours are."

He put his hand against the door, preventing her from shutting it firmly in his face.

"This isn't exactly a social call, Miss Rushton," he told her firmly. "I only wanted to arrive before the police."

"Police?"

Bewildered, Cedar ceased struggling against the force he was exerting on the door and let it fall once again open.

Guy nodded grimly.

"Your father has been shot, Miss Rushton," he told her without preamble.

"Shot?" she gasped.

Guy gave her no time to consider what that fact might entail.

"His wound is not serious," he assured her. He raised his eyes from hers, not wanting to feel responsible for the pain he saw in them, not wanting to see the far sharper pain he knew the words he was about to speak would cause her. "As soon as he's been treated, he's to be arrested for the murder of a whore at a bordello on Water Street."

Cedar felt suddenly dizzy, totally disoriented. She took a step backward, away from him, not sure if he'd gone mad, or if she had.

# Chapter Two

"Perhaps we should step inside, Miss Rushton."

Cedar moved away from the door as Guy stepped inside. She was too dazed to protest or try to bar his entry, too confused to consider that she was admitting a virtual stranger into the house in the middle of the night.

Guy pushed the door closed behind him. He put his hand on her arm. The touch of it surprised him, the realization that her skin had gone cold despite the warmth of the night air. When he touched her she began to tremble.

He peered into the darkened parlor beyond the entrance hall, found himself just able to make out the shapes of chairs and tables in the dim glow of moonlight that edged in through the large, heavily draped windows. He gently steered her into the room, then pushed her into the nearest chair before he made his way slowly in the darkness to the mantle and found matches with which to light a lamp.

Cedar stared at him in a dazed silence as he fumbled about in the unfamiliar room. Until he had pushed her into the chair, she had been unable to think of anything but what he had said about Magnus, but now she found herself unable to so much as consider the thought, as though her mind had decided what he had told her must be a lie and now refused to give credence to that lie by honoring it with her attention. Instead, she watched him light a match and lift the globe of a large oil lamp, giving those simple tasks an attention they hardly deserved. The flame caught and there was a sudden, bright glow that stung her eyes.

By the time he'd adjusted the flame, however, her eyes had adjusted to the light. Now that he was bathed in the light, she realized he was disheveled, that his clothing was wrinkled and his tie loosened. It occurred to her that he had about him the appearance of a man who had been drinking. She began to wonder if everything he'd told her was nothing more than some ugly, drunken joke.

"The police will be here soon," he told her when he had adjusted the flame of the lamp to his satisfaction. He lifted it and brought it to the table beside the chair where she sat. "I thought it would be better if you knew what to expect before they arrived."

She stared at him, quickly realizing that his eyes were clear and his hands steady. Whatever it was he was trying to do, she decided, it was not the result of some inebriated whim.

"Why?" she asked abruptly.

She was still looking up at him, and Guy found her open stare more than a little disquieting. He turned away from it as he found a chair near hers and seated himself.

"Why what, Miss Rushton?" he asked.

"Why have you come here with this preposterous story of yours?" She found she had regained her self-control, and now was more curious than anything else as to why he had done what he had. "Surely," she added, "you don't expect anyone to believe any of the nonsense you've spouted."

Why *had* he come, he wondered. He realized he'd been asking himself precisely that same question since he'd decided to leave what he ought to have done that evening and instead come to find her. He'd abandoned his chance of writing a lead story, one that would have given him the front page for certain and most probably a long-deserved raise in salary as well. Instead, he'd come to find her, to try to protect her from the worst of what he knew was going to follow. And for the life of him, he didn't know why.

"Look, you're going to hear things, accusations, decidedly unpleasant things," he told her. He realized he was trying to explain as much to himself as he was to her. "I thought it would be easier for you if you knew what was coming."

She shook her head. "This is all nonsense," she told him firmly. "My father couldn't possibly have been shot. He spent the evening discussing his speech for tomorrow's rally with Chester Bowles, and he will be home at any minute." Her eyes grew sharp and her voice began to rise as she spoke. "He would not go near any bordello, and he most certainly could not be arrested for anything, let alone the murder of some . . . some whore."

Cedar realized she was nearly shouting as she began the last sentence, and that there had been a note of hysteria in her voice before she'd completed it. She didn't care. Even the thought that Magnus might have done what Guy had told her he'd done was sheer insanity, and she had no intention of believing even a single word of it. She stood abruptly.

"I don't know why you've come here with this ridiculous story, Mr. Marler," she told him, "nor do I care. I think you should go."

Guy didn't move.

"I can appreciate your shock, Miss Rushton," he told her. "And I can understand your natural reluctance to believe what I've told you. But the fact is, quite simply, that your father was found, bleeding and unconscious, in a whorehouse. He was holding a pistol in his hand, and a young woman was found in the room with him, a young woman who happened to be quite dead."

"That is not true," Cedar shouted at him.

"I'm very much afraid it is true, Miss Rushton," Guy told her calmly.

He refrained from mentioning that he had seen the scene he'd just described to her, that he'd been at the police station when the report of the shooting had come in, that he'd

24

stopped by there on his way home on the off chance of finding a story after having closed a saloon with two other reporters. He'd followed the police to the whorehouse, wandering into the room where the murdered woman lay before anyone had thought to see him unceremoniously to the door. Actually the scene had been a good deal grislier than he'd described, blood everywhere, the woman on the bed in a pool of it, and Magnus Rushton liberally stained by the flow from a hole in his shoulder and a gash on his forehead.

"I don't believe you," Cedar told him.

But in part she did, she realized. She was still staring at him, her eyes meeting his. However reluctant she was to accept it, she somehow knew he was telling her the truth, or what he believed to be the truth. Still, she could not simply accept what he'd said. It was a mistake, she told herself firmly, some horrible, ugly mistake.

"And I suggest that you reconsider, Miss Rushton," Guy replied, "because it's true, every word. Considering who your father is and the fact that he is currently engaged in a loudly contested political campaign, I sincerely doubt that either you or he will be able to manage to avoid a good deal of unpleasant publicity. It won't be long before the police arrive here, and I can assure you there will be reporters on their heels, hungry for all the unsavory details."

"Is that why you're here, Mr. Marler?" she demanded. "Have you come looking for ugly details?"

Cedar's eyes narrowed. So that was why he was here, she thought. He'd fabricated the story about Magnus in order to get into the house, in order to sneak around, find something . . . But what? It made no more sense to her than the story he'd told her.

"Cedar, what are you doing up at this hour? What will your father say . . ."

Mrs. Kneely's voice faded away as she walked into the room and saw Cedar, clad in nightgown and thin linen dressing gown, standing facing a slightly rumpled but intense-looking young man. The sound of her sharply indrawn breath spoke more clearly than words could have of her shock at that particularly inappropriate scene.

"What is this—this person doing in the house at such an hour, Cedar?" she demanded in a sharp voice. "I've half a mind to go wake your father and have him throw this ruffian out on his ear."

Cedar turned to face her. Under any other circumstances she would most likely have smiled at the sight of the middle-aged housekeeper. Mrs. Kneely was clad in a gray wool dressing gown that was firmly buttoned up to her neck despite the heat, and half a dozen disorderly tufts of unmanageable gray hair poked stubbornly out from beneath a ridiculously frilly white nightcap. The circumstances, however, precluded a smile, and Cedar could only muster a forlorn and bewildered glance.

"Papa's not in his room, Mrs. Kneely," she said softly. "He hasn't come home yet."

The housekeeper's gray eyes grew sharp as she turned them back to Guy. A look of stubborn distrust settled over her features.

"Not home yet?" she repeated. "Nonsense. It's past four in the morning. Where would he be at this hour if not home in his bed?"

"At the police station," Guy told her. "Being arrested for murder."

Mrs. Kneely's normally bright pink cheeks faded to a dull, pasty white. She placed one hand over a decidedly ample bosom, used the other to grasp the back of a chair to steady herself, and then slowly worked her way around the chair so that she could sit. She'd been with the Rushtons since she was widowed nearly thirty years before, and never once had she lost her composure until that moment.

She looked up at Cedar.

"I don't understand," she said in a ragged whisper.

"This man is a reporter, Mrs. Kneely," Cedar replied

after a moment's hesitation. "He says Papa has been hurt, that he's in some sort of trouble."

" 'Murder,' he said," the housekeeper barely managed to croak. "Murder!"

"There must be some mistake," Cedar assured her. She put a comforting hand on the older woman's shoulder, taking a measure of comfort herself from the firm solidity and familiarity of the touch. She looked back at Guy. "I'm willing to give you the benefit of the doubt, Mr. Marler, of accepting that you've made an honest mistake, and that your motives for coming here with this preposterous story were purely innocent. But I must insist that you not repeat this nonsense lest someone actually accept it as truth. Now will you kindly leave?"

Guy considered her superior expression as she spoke, an expression that told him she had drawn a line and considered herself on one side of it while he remained firmly rooted on the far side. He shrugged and pushed himself to his feet. He'd been a fool to come here, he told himself. He was far too old to allow himself to be influenced by a pretty face and yet that was precisely what he'd done. And he'd also wasted an opportunity to be first on the scene of a decidedly sensational story. He'd regret it in the morning. Damn, he thought angrily, he regretted it already.

"As you like, Miss Rushton," he told her. "It would seem my attempt to emulate the good Samaritan was ill conceived, however well intended."

As he started for the door, the bell sounded for the second time that night, the noise this time shrill and prolonged. Cedar froze as Guy turned back to face her.

A loud voice called from outside, "Open up. Police."

Cedar turned terrified eyes to Guy.

"It wasn't a mistake, was it?" she whispered.

He shook his head. "I'm afraid not, Miss Rushton," he told her.

She looked suddenly fragile to him, As though she might break were he to touch her. Her eyes filled with liquid, and he knew she was fighting to contain the tears.

He felt an unprecedented urge to put his arms around her. Whatever distance he'd thought she'd put between them a moment before suddenly disappeared. He wanted to hold her, to comfort her, but that, he knew, was decidedly out of the question.

"Perhaps you'd better dress," he told her, aware that she needed to do something to distract herself, at least for the next few moments, until the shock of the situation settled into her and dulled a bit.

She nodded and, with the housekeeper trailing after her, obediently started for the stairs. She hesitated, stopping with her hand resting on the newel post, then started to climb as the bell rang again. Loud voices outside the door continued to announce the unpleasant presence of the police.

"They'll wake the whole street," Mrs. Kneely muttered angrily. She was obviously beginning to regain her composure, for the fear was gone from her eyes, replaced now by a look of distaste.

"You'd best let them in," Cedar told her. "I'll be only a moment." She started up the stairs, but stopped after she'd climbed only a few, and turned to let her eyes find Guy's. "Will you stay?" she asked him.

She had no idea why she asked and even less as to why she wanted him there. She reminded herself that only a few moments before, she had determined he was her father's adversary, perhaps worse. In any event, he was the least likely person to come to her or Magnus's aid. Still, she knew that alone she would not be able to get through what was to come, and the thought of him being there seemed to steady her.

He nodded.

"Yes," he told her. "I'll stay."

She nodded at him, then turned back and ran up the

stairs as Mrs. Kneely reluctantly started to open the door.

Cedar sat on the hard bench, uncomfortable and ill at ease, trying to pretend interest in the bleak walls of the police station. Everything in the place was a drab, dirty beige—the wooden benches, the walls that might once have been white but had aged unpleasantly, the huge desk and low wooden rail that separated the waiting area where she sat from the more ominously mysterious closed off area beyond. Her father was somewhere back there, she realized, and that thought left her miserably weak and shaking.

The police officers that passed by her paused only long enough to give her a smilingly knowing glance before moving on. She could almost see their thoughts in those brief glances, the smug certainty that told her they were indifferent to her misery, that they considered her father guilty and her, by extension, unworthy of consideration.

She'd given them her statement, told them about the speech at the dock workers' hiring hall, insisted her father had spent the remainder of the evening discussing his upcoming speech. They'd seemed unimpressed by what she had to say, and tried to dismiss her requests to see Magnus, telling her to come back the next day.

But Guy had promised to talk to a friend he hoped could help, and he'd disappeared after the uniformed officers into that mysterious maze to the rear of the desk. For some reason the police seemed to ignore his presence, or, more generally, to treat him with good-humored acceptance. She was almost beginning to think of him as one of them.

It seemed to her that he'd been gone an awfully long time. She hadn't thought to wear her own watch, and she couldn't bring herself to ask any of the police officers the time. Her only clue as to the hour was that the morning sunlight she remembered had barely managed to struggle past the grime that coated the windows above her head had now grown bright enough to overpower the layer of dirt. It must be somewhere near midmorning, she decided, and with that decision came the realization that she was exhausted. She felt abandoned in this awful place, and she had no idea what she ought to do.

When Guy finally reappeared a few minutes later, she sprang to her feet as soon as she saw him.

"Is he all right?" she demanded as she started forward to him. "Did you convince them to let me see him?"

"Just for a few minutes," he told her as he took her arm and turned her toward the desk. "It's against regulations."

"Regulations?" Her voice rose as a wave of anger swept over her. "They've arrested my father when he's done nothing, kept him in this horrible place, and now they're saying it's against regulations to let me see him?"

Cedar realized she was becoming a bit hysterical, but she was too tired and too distracted to care. All she wanted was to see Magnus, to have him assure her that it was all a terrible mistake, that it would be straightened out soon and he would be home before she knew it.

"Look," Guy told her, a note of displeasure creeping into his voice when he saw the look of disgust the desk sergeant gave her as they passed him, "I've convinced a sergeant friend of mine to tell the guard to look the other way for a little while. If you insist on behaving as though there were a conspiracy against your father, he's more apt than not to change his mind. Now quiet down, and try to be circumspect."

Cedar stared up at him, surprised by his expression even more than by the sharpness of his words. He was right, she realized. She was behaving badly, and she ought to thank him for trying to help her, not act as though it was all his fault.

They'd stopped just short of the door of the guarded area where prisoners were held. She looked at the guard, then back at Guy.

"I'm sorry," she murmured. "I'm just worried about my father."

He nodded. "I know," he told her as he nodded to the guard who unbarred the door and moved aside to let them pass. "But you won't do him any good by behaving like a hysterical schoolgirl."

She nodded, accepting the criticism silently, aware that it was probably warranted. He led her on, past a half dozen empty cells, and another four that contained rumpled looking men sprawled over the bare mattresses on narrow cots, apparently sleeping off the previous night's drunk. The smell of the place, one of carbolic overlaid with vomit and urine, was appalling.

Guy hurried her past the drunks, down to the end of the hall. He stopped for a moment by way of telling her that this was where she would find her father, then moved aside. Cedar gripped the bars and stared into the bare little cell at Magnus.

He was sitting on a cot with his back resting against the wall, his head back and his eyes closed. A dark red welt on his forehead seemed all the more angry against a face entirely drained of color. There were stains of blood and dirt on his shirt, which had been left half unbuttoned to reveal a mass of white bandage encircling his chest and shoulder.

"Papa?" Cedar whispered tentatively. "Papa, are you all right?"

She realized that until that moment she hadn't really believed she'd find him here, that deep inside she'd been convinced that she'd go home and find him there waiting breakfast for her.

But now she realized only too painfully that there was no way to avoid accepting what Guy had told her. The bandages and the bloodstains on Magnus's shirt attested to the fact that he had been shot, and his presence in this horrible place was finally real and undisputable.

Magnus opened his eyes slowly. He seemed disoriented, as though he could not quite place himself and was wondering at the strangeness of the surroundings. Finally his expression settled itself and he turned his eyes slowly to her.

31

"Cedar?" he asked as he pushed himself to his feet and crossed the cell to her. "Cedar, what are you doing here?"

"Mr. Marler convinced them to let me see you, Papa," she replied. She took the hand he reached through the bars to her and pressed it against her cheek. "Are you badly hurt, Papa?" she asked, her eyes falling once again to the bloodstains on his shirt. Magnus slipped his hand to her chin and lifted her face so that she was no longer staring at the ugly stains.

"It looks much worse than it is, Cedar," he told her. "The doctor who bandaged me said it was just a scratch."

"It doesn't look like a scratch, Papa," she said.

Magnus drew a deep breath and released it slowly.

"You shouldn't be here, Cedar," he told her.

She shook her head. "It's all a mistake, isn't it, Papa? You must tell them you weren't ever at that . . . that place, that you couldn't have killed that woman. You must tell them that you were with Mr. Bowles. They'll have to let you go then."

"I've told them I didn't kill anyone, Cedar," he said. "They don't believe me."

"But they have to believe you," she insisted. "You couldn't have killed anyone. You wouldn't have gone to a place like that and you didn't know that woman. It's all preposterous."

Magnus darted a glance at Guy, who had backed away to allow them some small measure of privacy. Then he brought his eyes back to find his daughter's. He seemed to be struggling with himself, part of him wanting to keep from telling her what he knew she would learn eventually in any event, part of him wanting finally to put an end to the lie that lay so glaringly between them.

"I was there, Cedar," he finally told her, saying the words very slowly. "I knew the woman who died."

Cedar gasped and stepped back and away from him. She could feel the blood pounding in her cheeks, could hear it in her ears. She'd heard wrong, she told herself. She knew him, knew the sort of man he was. He couldn't have gone

32

to a place like that, couldn't have known that kind of a woman.

"I don't believe you," she said in a hoarse whisper.

"I said I was there, that I knew her," Magnus told her hastily as he saw the look of shock and disappointment wash over her features. "But I did not kill her. I liked her. I certainly had no reason to want her dead."


Cedar felt her father's eyes on her. She forced herself to look at him, and when she did she saw fear in his eyes, something she'd never seen there before. That couldn't be her father, she told herself, standing there telling her he'd gone to a house of prostitution. But more shocking to her than what he'd said, she realized, was what she saw in his eyes. It was as though Magnus had turned old in the hours since she'd last seen him, old and tired and afraid.

And with her recognition of his fear came the realization that she had no right to condemn him. He was her father and she loved him. Whatever had happened, whatever he had done, however distasteful to her, nothing could change that.

"What happened last night, Papa?" she asked him softly.

Magnus glanced up at Guy, obviously reluctant to speak in front of a reporter, wondering if he'd spoken too freely already, if what he'd said would appear the following morning emblazoned on the front page of the *Sun*. Guy saw the look of distrust on his face and took a step forward.

"I told you last night I write the truth, Mr. Rushton," he told Magnus. "If you didn't kill that woman—"

"I didn't," Magnus interrupted in a harsh tone.

"Then the truth can only help you," Guy replied. "Trust me."

"Trust you?" Magnus asked in a voice that intimated the prospect was as likely as the possibility of him turning into a dove and flying out of the cell.

"You really don't have many choices," Guy told him.

33

"You know as well as I do that Tammany will be pushing the mayor's office to bring this to trial quickly, hoping to sweep the election before your reform people can muster some sort of response. And frankly, I wouldn't be surprised if your holier-than-thou reform friends washed their hands of you as soon as the particulars of the situation are made public, and, believe me, they will be made public. If that's not bad enough, from what I've seen, the police seem to think they've found their murderer. You were found in a locked room with a murdered prostitute and a gun in your hand. Frankly, I very well may be your only hope."

"It's true, Papa," Cedar murmured. "I could tell from the way the officers out there acted. They think you killed that woman."

Magnus's expression slowly turned to one of resignation. He lowered his head and stared at his hands for a moment. Then he looked back at Guy.

"She had a name," he said. "Mary. Mary Farren." He turned his gaze to meet Cedar's. "I make no excuses for what she did to survive. I don't suppose she had very many choices. She was a plain, honest girl, one who didn't ask for anything she hadn't earned."

Cedar was bewildered by the tenderness she heard in his tone when he spoke of the murdered prostitute. He'd known the woman, she realized. It wasn't simply that he'd gone to her that once, that he'd simply gotten drunk with Chester Bowles and gone in search of a prostitute. It had been more than that, much more.

Her throat constricted, and when she spoke, she had to force the words out.

"You . . . you've known her for a while?"

Magnus nodded. He'd said more than enough to damn himself in his daughter's eyes, he realized. He realized that he felt relieved that the time had finally come for him to tell her all of it.

"For more than a year and a half," he said. "Since shortly after the time your mother fell ill."

Cedar gasped. She didn't want to hear these things, she didn't want to hear any of it. She told herself she could come to accept the fact that her father had had dealings with this woman. After all, he was a man, and not so old as to be without certain needs. But the thought that he had taken up with a prostitute while her mother was still alive was unthinkable.

Magnus needed no words to convey to him what she was thinking. He reached out to her, trying to touch her, to make her understand.

But she backed away from him, and he gave up the attempt.

"She was a kind and generous person, Cedar," Magnus said. "I have no need to apologize to you for my actions."

Cedar swallowed the lump in her throat.

"No, Papa," she agreed. "You don't."

Magnus looked up at Guy. "I didn't kill her," he said. "And she didn't deserve to die."

"Well someone damn well killed her," Guy said.

Magnus seemed startled by the coldness of Guy's tone. He shuddered, remembering when he'd wakened in the room to the sight of her bloodied body.

"Yes," he agreed. "Someone killed her."

Guy stared at him a moment, expecting him to go on. "What happened?" he asked when Magnus remained mute.

Magnus shook his head. "I don't know," he replied. "I remember being with her, then getting dressed. And then everything went black. When I woke there were people all around, and Mary was dead. All I know is that I didn't kill her."

"Oh, God," Cedar murmured.

Guy scowled. " 'Oh, God' is right," he said.


Cedar's mind was still reeling when she found herself standing on the sidewalk, feeling the mid-morning sunshine warm on her face. Guy was talking to her, and she had to settle herself, to force herself to listen to what he was saying.

"Wait here. I'll find a carriage and take you home."

She shook her head. "You needn't bother, Mr. Marler. I can see myself home alone."

He turned and stared at her in silence for a moment. Then he put his hand on her arm.

"Cedar, you're going to need some help. You'll have to find your father a good criminal lawyer, and I'm probably more suited to advise you in that matter than any of your father's lawyer friends who spend their days writing wills and filing suits for contested property. With any luck, a good criminal lawyer might be able to save his neck."

She jerked her arm from his grasp. She realized he had begun to call her by her given name, although she certainly hadn't given him leave to do so. But she had other matters to consider just then, far more important matters.

"You're talking as though you think he's guilty," she snapped.

"You heard what he said," Guy told her.

"I heard him say he didn't know what happened," she countered.

Guy gritted his teeth. It occurred to him for perhaps the hundredth time that morning that he should just turn his back on the whole situation. It was obvious that she didn't want him there, that she didn't want his advice or his help. And he could think of at least a hundred things he might be doing that would prove more profitable than trying to prove Magnus Rushton innocent.

"He was found alone with the body in a locked room, Cedar," he told her, aware that his patience was wearing thin and that that fact had become more than apparent in his tone. "He had the murder weapon in his hand. And he can't come up with an explanation for any of it. I don't suppose you would care to find one that sounds even remotely plausible?"

Cedar felt a wave of anger for him, a wave that swept

away the last of the pain caused by what her father had told her.

"He was shot," she hissed through tight teeth. "He was hit on the head."

Guy nodded. "Yes, he was shot," he agreed. "Half a dozen people heard the shots, two of them. One that wounded him, and another, a minute later, that killed her."

"Well, someone else fired them."

"Not according to the police. They think the two of them fought, the woman pulled the gun, wounding him, and he wrestled it away from her and shot and killed her."

"And the blow to his head?" Cedar demanded.

"He became faint from the wound, fell, hitting his head on a table."

"I don't believe it, not any of it," she snapped.

"Then you come up with a better explanation," he suggested. "The door was locked from the inside. And no one else was there."

Cedar bit her lips and forced herself to swallow the thick ball that seemed to have filled her throat. Everything he said was logical, entirely too logical. And she could think of no alternatives that were even remotely possible. All she did have was the knowledge that despite the pain she felt at that moment, the thought of losing her father was more than she could bear. Magnus had told her he was innocent and she believed him. She had no alternative but to believe him.

"He said he didn't do it," she said finally. "And if he said he didn't kill her, that means he didn't."

"You're so terribly sure, are you?" Guy asked.

She nodded. "Yes, I'm sure. I know my father."

"From what I saw and heard a few months ago, I'd say there were a few things you didn't know about your father, Cedar. Perhaps you don't know him as well as you think you do."

Cedar gritted her teeth and narrowed her eyes. "I said I was sure," she snapped. But once the words were out, she seemed to collapse inside. What he said was true, there were things she hadn't known about Magnus, things she never would have thought possible. She felt the tears biting at her eyes and she began to tremble. She turned away.

Guy put his hands on her arms and turned her back to face him. When he saw the tears in her eyes, he felt something inside himself begin to melt.

"It doesn't matter what you believe," he told her softly. "What does matter is what a jury believes. A good lawyer can make a case for self-defense, and that could save your father's life."

Cedar shook her head. "He didn't kill her," she insisted.

She believed, she told herself, she had to believe. And she had to make others believe as well. Because even if some lawyer could make a jury accept that Magnus had killed in self defense, he would still be branded a murderer. And that, she knew, would kill him. Not physically, perhaps, but it would still kill him.

"He's innocent and I intend to prove it," she said. The sound of her own voice startled her. It was sure and sharp, and the quiver of impending tears was gone. She looked up at Guy. "Even," she added, "if I have to do it alone."

# Chapter Three

Cedar felt numb, almost stiff, with disbelief. Guy was forced to propel her forward, his firm hand on her arm guiding her past the door and into the kitchen. He followed her, then quickly shut the door behind them and bolted it.

Mrs. Kneely slowly rose from the hard, straight-backed chair where she'd been sitting, taking what little solace she could from a cup of tea. She needed nothing more than a glance at Cedar's face to realize that there was little chance that any comforting news would be forthcoming.

"How long have they been out there?" Guy demanded, purposely ignoring the housekeeper's dazed expression and forcing her to turn her attention away from Cedar's shock glazed eyes.

"For an hour or more," Mrs. Kneely replied. "I locked the door, drew all the curtains, and came back here where I couldn't hear them." She motioned to the single cup and the teapot that stood on the otherwise empty kitchen table, witness to her vigil.

Guy nodded. "Good. They'll go away eventually if they're ignored, but give them anything to chew on and they'll make a circus out of this."

"This?" Mrs. Kneely asked. "Just what is *this?*"

"Papa's been arrested for the murder of a prostitute," Cedar said.

The words seemed almost to surprise her, the sound of her own voice distant and weak, almost as if she were not quite aware of what it was she was saying. She took a step forward, moving with slow deliberation toward the table, stepping hesitantly, as a blind man might move in a strange place.

"Then it's all true," Mrs. Kneely gasped. She put a pale, shaking hand to her lips.

"Yes, it's true," Guy told her. He put his hand on Cedar's arm and guided her to one of the heavy wooden chairs, then turned back to face the housekeeper. "Could you get her a cup? I think she could use some of that tea."

His suggestion roused the older woman, returning her to her usual practical frame of mind. As long as she had been alone in the house, she had been totally paralyzed by the thought of the scandal that had descended upon the household, but now that she was needed, she seemed to forget all that in the press of more mundane matters. She bustled forward to the stove.

"I'll make a fresh pot," she said as she lifted the kettle.

Guy pushed Cedar down onto the chair. She turned to look up at him as she sat.

"Those men out there," she asked, "they were waiting for me, weren't they?"

He nodded. "Reporters. They'd try to get you to say something about your father, hopefully something incriminating, before you had the chance to consider what your words might mean."

"Incriminating?" The thought sent a spark of anger through her. "What could I possibly say about Papa that would be incriminating?"

Guy shrugged. "Anything can sound any way you want it to, given the proper context, Cedar," he told her.

She shivered at his words and thought of the dozen or more reporters they'd seen lounging around the front stoop. If Guy hadn't been with her, if he hadn't realized who the men were and told the driver to continue on around the corner, she would have gotten out of the carriage and found herself face to face with them. It would never have occurred to her to try to avoid them, to come in by the back way. She had never been forced to sneak into her own home before. She swallowed the lump in her throat as she realized there had never before been the need. After all, Magnus had never before been arrested. There had never before been mention of that . . . that person, the one he was supposed to have killed.

She darted a sharp glance at Guy. Those men outside her door were his fellows. She wondered if under other circumstances he'd be one of them, if he'd be standing outside her door with them, hoping to get her to say something awful about her own father, something that could be used to make it seem that she believed in the guilt of her own father.

"I suppose you'd know all about that," she murmured. "About making words sound some way they were never meant to sound."

There was a bitter note of accusation in her voice, and Guy realized that he had nothing to offer to refute it. She was right, he told himself. He made his living by making things sound as sensational as possible, and more often than not the speaker's intent got lost in the shuffle. It was the game they played, he and his fellows, the game that earned their bread and sold newspapers, skirting the fine line between exaggeration and libel. Always, before, the defense that he never lied had been enough to him to justify what he did. At that moment, however, with Cedar's wide green eyes staring up at him, it seemed weak and unworthy, and he didn't even bother with it.

He took his hand away from her arm. "I suppose I do, Cedar," he agreed with a note of reluctance.

He turned away from the disgust that crept into her eyes, surprised that it hurt him to see it there, wondering why he even cared as he pretended interest in watching Mrs. Kneely place plates, cups, a platter of muffins, and a pot of tea on the table in front of them. Now that her attention was centered on familiar matters, he noted, the

41

housekeeper seemed a good deal more settled.

"You eat something, Cedar," Mrs. Kneely directed, her tone firmly motherly, as she filled the cups with still steaming tea.

"I couldn't, Mrs. Kneely," Cedar replied.

"Try," Guy told her firmly. "Starving yourself won't do your father any good." He put one of the muffins on a plate and pushed it towards her. Then he took one himself and gnawed hungrily at it.

He could sense Mrs. Kneely warming to him. Perhaps it was because he was making the attempt to bully Cedar into eating, he mused. Or perhaps it was just that he was there, filling the void, the lack of a masculine presence in the house, that Magnus's arrest had left behind. In any event, she seemed to have lost all the antipathy she'd shown him the night before, and now behaved toward him as though she considered him a welcome visitor. There was no question, Guy realized as he swallowed a bite of muffin, she was the sort who would appreciate a man who appreciated her cooking.

"Excellent, Mrs. Kneely," he told the housekeeper when he'd swallowed the last of the muffin and reached for another. He smiled up at the older woman with crumb-specked lips, feeling not the least hint of guilt in the knowledge that he was trying to manipulate her.

"Thank you, young man," she told him, and rewarded him for the compliment with a broad smile. "Cinnamon raisin, my mother's recipe. Fresh ground cinnamon, that's the secret."

Guy took another bite. "Delicious," he muttered through the crumbs.

He failed to add that he was starving, that just about anything would have tasted palatable to him at that moment, and that a couple of fried eggs and a rasher of bacon washed down with a few cups of strong coffee would have been considerably more to his liking than tea and muffins. Instead, he smiled his most winsome smile at the housekeeper, determined to make friends with her, to win himself an ally in the house, even as he ruefully considered the far more productive use to which he'd put that boyishly charming smile in the past.

"Which reminds me," Mrs. Kneely went on. "I usually do my marketing Saturday morning. There's next to nothing left in the house. But with those men out there . . ."

Guy nodded in commiseration. "I know. It can't have been pleasant for you. But it's best if you just go about your usual business. Only I think you'd better leave by the back way." He nodded toward the door by which he and Cedar had entered.

"Of course, of course," she agreed, and began bustling about the kitchen. She had transformed from the huddled mass of inert fear she'd seemed when he and Cedar had entered the house. Now she was suddenly a bundle of energy, removing her apron and reaching for her coat and putting on her bonnet.

Cedar couldn't believe the two of them, their everyday conversation about fresh ground cinnamon, the mundane consideration of the state of the larder. She pushed away the plate Guy had placed in front of her and turned angry eyes to him.

"How can you sit there, calmly eating, when my father, my father . . ."

Her voice broke, and the sobs she'd been holding back since she'd spoken with Magnus suddenly filled her throat, choking her.

"Look, Cedar," Guy began as he pushed his chair back from the table and turned to face her. He didn't get any further. One glance at her quivering lower lip and he knew she was slowly beginning to crumble inside.

He was right. The tears welled up in her eyes and then started to pour out, making thick rivulets as they ran down her cheeks. She was shaking with the sobs, unable to control them, suddenly not caring if he saw her this way, not caring about anything. He leaned forward to her, reaching his arms out to hold her.

For an instant Cedar tried to pull away from the arms he wrapped around her, and a fleeting thought swept through her, that she really didn't know this man, that she shouldn't let him hold her. But the thought was gone as quickly as it had come. She let herself fall against him, aware that she was thankful for the comfort the feel of his arms gave her.

"It's all right, Cedar," he told her. "Just let it out." He looked up at Mrs. Kneely, who was standing now, half in and half out of her coat and with her bonnet askew. "Perhaps a sip of brandy," he suggested.

The housekeeper nodded and hurried off to fetch it.

Alone with Cedar, with his arms around her, Guy told himself he should be thinking just about anything but the thoughts that were creeping into his mind. No matter how hard he tried—and he made a concerted effort for a few seconds before he gave up the attempt as useless—he could not force away the desire to kiss her, the consideration of what those beautiful, full lips would feel like were they to be pressed against his own.

She lifted her face, turning tear-stained eyes up to meet his, and he would have satisfied his curiosity at that moment but for the return of Mrs. Kneely.

Instead, he took the bottle of brandy the distracted housekeeper held out to him, poured a healthy portion into Cedar's cup of tea, and then pressed the cup into her hands.

"Drink some of this," he told her.

She looked down at the amber liquid in her cup. "I can't just leave him in that place," she murmured. She turned her eyes back to meet his. "It's horrible and it's all wrong. He didn't do it. I can't just leave him there."

"We won't, Cedar," Guy told her gently. "I promise you, we won't."

He meant it, he realized. He wasn't quite sure why, but he did know that at that moment he meant every word.

Cedar sniffed loudly, took a long swallow of the brandy-laced tea, then sat for an instant with her eyes closed as the heat of the alcohol spread through her. She was far from accustomed to strong drink and found the tingling, heated sensation decidedly startling. But the feeling was not at all unpleasant, she decided, and it wasn't long before she realized that the brandy had somewhat calmed her.

She opened her eyes to find Guy staring at her.

"Better?" he asked.

She nodded, and sniffed again, and wiped her cheek with the heel of her hand. She was beginning to feel more than a little embarrassed by her outburst. After all, she told herself, she wasn't the useless sort of female who resorted to paroxysms of tears because reason and plain common sense failed her. She'd always been proud that she possessed more of those two qualities than was commonly considered fashionable or even useful for a young woman. And now when she needed both, she was behaving as though she had neither.

Guy removed a slightly crumpled but clean handkerchief from his pocket and silently handed it to her.

"Thank you," she murmured as she took it and began to wipe her damp cheeks. "This is foolish," she said. "I never act like this. I don't cry." And as though to prove her own unemotional, practical nature, she blew her nose noisily, making no attempt to minimize the sound.

He smiled. "I believe you," he told her.

Mrs. Kneely tugged nervously at the ribbons of her bonnet. "Perhaps I ought not to go," she suggested.

Cedar looked up at her concerned face.

"No, Mr. Marler is right. You should go about your usual routine, Mrs. Kneely," she insisted. "It won't do Papa any good for us to sit around in a dark house, crying and behaving like hopelessly dull-witted females. You must go about your marketing, and I have a bit of thinking to do."

Mrs. Kneely cast a bewildered glance at Cedar, but quickly resigned herself to doing as she'd been instructed. The truth was, she felt far more comfortable occupying herself with those things she was accustomed to doing, less prone to think about those things she found far too disconcerting to consider.

"You'll be all right here?" she asked Cedar as she finally settled her bonnet squarely on her head.

"Certainly. Why shouldn't I?" Cedar demanded. She took another swallow of her tea.

The matter settled, the housekeeper pulled on her gloves, took up her purse, and opened the door. She stood for a moment, staring out into the empty back alley, assuring herself there was no one there to spy on her. She turned to Guy.

"It's safe," she whispered.

Then she slipped out of the house, pulling the door silently closed behind her, acting as though she were a thief making a daring escape from the law.


Cedar actually found herself suddenly laughing. For some unaccountable reason, she was beginning to feel just a tiny bit giddy.

"She'll never admit it, but I really think Mrs. Kneely would make an excellent conspirator," she told Guy in a decidedly conspiratorial whisper of her own.

He reached for the teacup she was still holding in her hand.

"I think you've done with that, Cedar," he told her.

"Oh, no, I haven't," she said, pulling the cup back and away from his reach, then lifting it to her lips and swallowing the remaining liquid.

Guy scowled. "You shouldn't have done that," he told her.

"Oh?" Cedar dropped the cup onto its saucer, then pushed her chair back from the table. "And why not?"

"Because I may have been a bit too generous with the brandy I poured into it."

"Well, no matter. No harm done," she told him and stood.

And immediately realized that there had most decidedly been some harm done. She tottered dizzily, and would have fallen had Guy not caught her arm and steadied her.

"Too much alcohol too quickly ingested," Guy diagnosed in a voice that suggested intimate knowledge of the malady. "The usual prescription is a few hours rest followed by a cup of strong coffee." He began to propel her across the kitchen to the door he'd seen the housekeeper take on her quest for the brandy. It would, he surmised, lead him to the front of the house.

But Cedar was hardly disposed to sleep at that moment. She pulled her arm free of his grasp.

"I am quite capable of making my own way, Mr. Marler," she told him. "And I have no intention of wasting the day when I could be doing something to help Papa."

"And just what is it you intend to do, Miss Rushton?" he asked in a tone as sharply acid as hers had been.

She pulled back, temporarily bewildered. She had thought of something, she remembered, but it seemed just on the edge of her memory at that moment, just beyond her grasp. She shook her head as though she were trying to shake the thought loose, and was instead rewarded with a dull, throbbing pain. It took all her energy to keep from showing it to him.

"The papers," she said after a moment, in a sudden burst of enlightenment. "I read something last night. I can't remember what it was, but I'm sure it had something to do with Papa."

Guy shrugged. "The papers," he repeated, his words dull with doubt.

"Yes, the papers," she insisted. "The newspapers. It's a good thing Mrs. Kneely was intimidated by those reporters outside. Otherwise she'd have cleared them all away by this time."

Cedar steadied herself, then began to march along the passageway to her father's study, taking great care not to let Guy see just how uncertain her progress seemed to her, nor

47

how close she was to walking a decidedly crooked line. But somehow she reached her destination without mishap, and pointed to the heavy mahogany doors. Guy dutifully pulled them open.

She let him enter first, deciding that she couldn't reveal anything if he couldn't watch her and he couldn't watch her if she was behind him. Once inside the room, however, her preoccupation with Guy vanished. She felt a stab of loss, as though Magnus was being torn away from her, as though he was leaving her alone and completely without direction. Her father seemed so close to her in this room, and the knowledge that he wasn't there, that he might not be there for a long time to come, was suffocating and terrifying.

The pain that had overwhelmed her while she sat at the kitchen table threatened to claim her once more, but she forced down the constriction in her throat and the dull throb of loneliness and disappointment that filled her. She couldn't let go in front of Guy, she told herself. Not now, not again.

Guy had started forward, to Magnus's desk, and suddenly Cedar saw his intrusion into her father's private realm as a desecration, an invasion. She darted forward, passing by him and reaching for the heap of newsprint she'd looked through the night before. The *Truth Teller* was on the top of the pile.

"Here it is," she said, pointing to the article she'd read the previous night, remembering now that she saw in it what had been nagging the edge of her consciousness. "Look at what they say about Papa, about his having things he'd rather keep secret."

Guy scanned the article, then looked back at her and shrugged.

"Well, for once it seems the name of this rag is apt," he said. "There was a small secret in your father's closet, now, wasn't there? One even you didn't have any idea was there."

Cedar felt herself blushing, even as a wave of anger washed over her at his mention of her father's whore. But

48

anger wouldn't explain anything, she told herself. And she refused to be cowed by his insinuation.

"Don't you see?" she demanded, perturbed with his seeming lack of perception. "If they knew about that—that woman, then they could have arranged what happened in order to show Papa in the worst possible light. They could have had that woman killed so that he would be discredited. And this article proves that they knew."

Guy scowled. "No, Cedar," he told her. "This article proves nothing. It could be nothing more than a handful of mud meant to dirty a political opponent. It's not an uncommon practice, you know—throw a little dirt, and see if some sticks."

She shook her head. "Not to my father," she insisted. "They knew."

*"They,* Cedar?" he asked.

She mimicked his scowl. "Tammany, of course," she nearly shouted. She couldn't understand why he was pretending to be so purposefully obtuse. It was all completely apparent to her. Surely he could not help but see that Tammany was behind what had happened to her father. "This newspaper is a Tammany organ, everyone knows that."

Guy met her impatient stare with an unimpressed glance.

"And so what you're saying is that Tweed had this extremely prophetic article written, ordered the murder of Mary Farren, and arranged matters so that your father was inextricably implicated. And he went to these extremes all to secure the election of a commissioner of a small department that his ward politicians have probably already assured him?"

Even before he finished speaking, she felt the certainty of her conviction beginning to leak away. But she refused to give it up entirely.

"Yes," she replied, "that's precisely what I'm saying." She started to turn away, not wanting to allow him to dissuade her.

Guy shook his head. "Don't you think it's all a bit too contrived?" he asked her, his tone demanding that she return her attention to him. "Why should Tweed go to that much effort, or, for that matter, take that much risk? For the few thousand that would make their way back through the grapevine to his own coffers? Don't you think that a bit farfetched? And if he were planning such a thing, why would he practically announce it in his own newspaper like this? What you're suggesting simply doesn't make any sense, Cedar."

"It does," she insisted. "It has to."

"No, Cedar, it doesn't."

She wanted to argue with him, but he seemed so certain, and she couldn't think of anything to say that sounded nearly as rational as his argument sounded. He was right, she realized. It all did sound too contrived. She began to waver. Maybe he was right, she thought, maybe Tammany had nothing to do with Mary Farren's death.

But she quickly banished the possibility. Tammany simply had to be behind what had happened to Magnus. There just wasn't anyone else. If there was no one else, then that would mean her father was guilty. And she knew her father could not possibly have done what they said he had done.

She shook her head, trying to settle her thoughts, and only succeeded in disturbing the precarious equilibrium she'd established. Her head began to throb again, and she began to wish she hadn't drunk all the brandy Guy had poured into her cup.

Whatever her thoughts, they didn't seem to concern Guy. He'd already dropped the newspaper and turned his attention to the heap of Magnus's notes Cedar had straightened and left in an orderly pile at the side of the desk the night before. Before he had the chance to begin to search through the sheaf of notes, however, Cedar managed to settle the throbbing in her head. She stared at him as he put his hand to the pile of papers, and then lurched forward, leaning past him and putting her hand on the heap.

"What are you doing?" she demanded.

"Looking," he replied.

"Looking for what?"

He shrugged. "I'll know when I find it," he told her.

"There's nothing there that could have any bearing on the situation," she retorted. "Those are my father's private papers."

Now it was Guy's turn to feel exasperation. "Look, Cedar," he told her. "Neither of us knows what might have bearing and what's trivial. The only way to find out what's important is to consider everything."

"Not that," she insisted. "You have no right to paw through my father's things."

"Cedar, I think I have a little more experience in this sort of thing than you do," he told her. "I've reported a good number of murders, and I have a far better idea than you could possibly have as to what might be useful."

His words reminded Cedar of the article he'd written, the one she'd read the night before. It had been filled with gruesome details, a sensationalistic article that had completely revolted her. A wave of disgust filled her at the memory of it. That was the sort of thing those men lounging around the front of her house were intending to write about her father. Her eyes narrowed as she considered Guy, as she began to see him in an entirely different light than that in which she'd considered him during those horrible hours since the police had appeared at the door.

"Yes," she agreed through tight lips. "I'm sure you have a much better grasp of the situation than I."

"Good," he said, and he turned his attention back to the pile of Magnus's notes.

She didn't move her hand. "You will leave my father's things alone," she hissed.

He looked up at her again, and this time he made no attempt to hide his irritation with her.

"I thought you were the one who wanted to get to the bottom of this, the one who wanted to clear your father's name?"

She couldn't understand why he was being so insistent, why he couldn't respect Magnus's privacy. The ugly doubt that had edged its way into her grew darker and more insistent. And the stronger it grew, the more clearly she found herself answering the questions that had plagued her about him since he'd appeared the night before. She suddenly knew why he'd come to the house, why he was there, why he was being so helpful.

"Is that what you're doing?" she demanded. "Trying to clear my father's name? Or are you simply doing what your comrades outside my front door are doing, looking for a juicy bit of scandal to emblazon on the front page of the *Sun?*" She glared at him, feeling the heat of her anger surge through her, daring him to deny it all, knowing, even before he tried, that it would all be lies.

Guy stared at her in silence a moment. His expression hardened into one of anger before he responded to the attack.

"Is that what you think I'm doing?" he demanded.

"Well, isn't it?" she retorted. "Why else did you come here, if not to get a story?"

Guy was again silent for a moment, and he found himself asking himself the same question she'd asked him as he stared at her.

"Damned if I know," he finally hissed between clenched teeth. He began to turn away from her, but then stopped and turned back to face her. "Yes, I do know," he said slowly.

Cedar realized as soon as she saw his expression that it had changed, that there was something strange in it now, something hard and certain, something that frightened her just a little. She tried to step back, away from him, but he reached out for her, putting his hands on her arms and pulling her close to him.

"I'm here for this," he said, and he pressed his lips to hers.

* * *

It wasn't happening the way he'd thought it would happen. Before, in the kitchen, when she'd seemed so vulnerable and lost, that would have been more to his liking, for it would have pleased him to be able to comfort her, to have her think of him as a pillar of strength on which she might lean in her own moment of need and confusion.

But once his lips touched hers, it didn't seem to matter that what they'd both felt the instant before was anger. Once his lips touched hers, nothing else mattered at all.

The spark of anger was drowned by something far stronger, something blinding and sharp and searing. It surprised Guy, for he'd never felt anything like it, despite the fact that she certainly wasn't the first woman he'd ever kissed. All he knew was that the touch of her lips, the feel of her in his arms, left him filled with a hunger that was like nothing he'd ever felt before.

If the effect of that contact was bewildering to Guy, it was a revelation to Cedar. Nothing could have prepared her for the thick surge of liquid heat that filled her at his first touch, for the waves of sweet fire she felt coursing through her veins. It swept away everything in front of it, the anger she'd felt with him, her doubts, even her fears for her father. She tentatively brought her hands to his shoulders, and then they seemed to move of their own volition, one hand flirting with the tip of his ear before both hands fled to the nape of his neck and locked themselves there.

She felt dizzy and giddy and light-headed, and wondered if it was the effects of the brandy that made her feel that way. She fell against him, pressing herself close to him, thinking that if he released her she would surely fall. She closed her eyes and let herself drift with the tides that filled her, not questioning where they might take her, not even capable of telling herself that it might be to a place where reason would tell her she ought not trespass.

Her reaction surprised Guy almost as much as his own.

If anything, he'd expected her anger. He'd been prepared to face that, he realized, in return for having had his curiosity satisfied. But instead he felt the warmth fill her, the same heat he felt growing within himself. More than anything, it pleased him to know that he had been its cause.

He wrapped his arms around her, holding her close, not wanting to chance losing her when he lifted his lips from hers. And when he did, when he stood staring down at her, he watched her slowly open her eyes and saw the look of confusion in them. He realized then that what had happened in that instant when their lips had touched was even a greater mystery to her than it had been to him, that whatever urge had pushed her to return his embrace had come from something deep inside her, something that had pushed her without need of thought or reason to guide her.

He brought his hand to her cheek, pushing away a lock of hair that had come loose and allowing his fingers the sweet sensation they found as they explored the feel of her skin.

For Cedar, everything was spinning, all was confusion. She felt safe with his arms around her, and for the first time in what seemed an endless age since she'd learned that Magnus had been arrested, she was not afraid. Not even the unaccountable liquid heat that filled her at the touch of his lips to hers seemed frightening now. However strange it might be, something deep within her told her that it was nothing to fear. She could only think that she did not want to lose that feeling, that she did not want to lose the feeling of safety she felt with his arms enfolding her.

And then an ugly edge of doubt began to bite at the edge of her conscious once again.

"That's not why you're here, is it?" she begged him softly, terrified that he might say that it was, that she might be forced to pull herself from the safe circle of his arms. "You didn't come just to spy, just to write some horrible story about Papa?"

He shook his head. "I swear to you, Cedar, I only want

to help. I only want you to want me to help."

A wave of relief filled her. "I do," she murmured.

It was true, she told herself. She had no idea what to do now, no idea where she ought to go or to whom she ought to talk if she intended to do something more than sit and wait for fate to enfold her father in a web from which he would be powerless to escape. She felt a thickness form in her throat as she realized how helpless she would be alone.

"I need you," she told him.

And as though to prove what she'd said, she pulled herself to him and pressed her lips once more to his.

# Chapter Four

It had been fated, Guy realized. From the instant he turned to watch Magnus leave the union hall and saw Cedar walking toward the street on her father's arm, this moment had been predestined. One glance at her and he should have known that there was no doubt that it would happen, that somehow he would make it happen.

That was the reason, he realized, that he'd come to this house the night before rather than keeping his mind on business, rather than staying at that bordello and finding the details of what he knew would be a sensational story. Instead, he'd left the place, well aware when he did that he'd lose his best chance at that story.

He'd told himself that he could use her, that with her he could learn more than he could alone, but even before he'd knocked on the door, he'd known he was lying to himself. He'd come here to find her, it was as simple as that. Even if he hadn't been quite sure why he was being drawn to her, he'd been unable to resist whatever power it was that pulled him to her.

Now he knew why he'd behaved as he had. This was the reason, what he felt when he wrapped his arms around her, when he pressed his lips to hers.

He could think of a hundred reasons why he ought to leave before he became too obsessed with the feeling. His conscience told him that he'd given her too much brandy, that she was not entirely in control of herself, that fear and worry for her father clouded her judgment at that moment. None of those rational arguments seemed to have much effect on him, however. His arms refused to release their hold of her.

For an instant a voice inside him told him that she was certainly not the sort of woman who would treat this type of thing lightly, that she would have expectations. He had always taken care to avoid ties in the past, a fact of which he found himself reminding himself even as he pulled her close. This was not the kind of game it was safe to play, he told himself. Pursuing her was nothing less than sheer folly.

He knew he ought to leave. A voice inside him told him to go now, before it was too late.

But he realized he had less choice in the matter than she did at that moment. He knew that if she'd pushed him away, if she'd told him to go, he would have had no choice but to do as she asked. He freely admitted to more than his share of things of which he was less than proud—he'd lied, even stolen, to get material for a good story—but he'd never forced himself on a woman or taken advantage of one who was not in a position to defend herself. If he had somewhere traded the right to think of himself as a gentleman in order to succeed at his job, at least he had always clung to the knowledge that he was basically decent. But when he felt Cedar press herself to him and kiss him, he knew he couldn't turn away if he wanted to. And he knew more than anything else that he certainly didn't want to.

Cedar felt a sharp lurch within herself when he pulled her close and returned her kiss, as he let his tongue play over her lips and then become a gentle, tentative probe. She had never felt anything like this before and was confused at first, but she did not pull away. She realized that she didn't want to free herself from him, that she didn't want to leave the circle of his arms. If he asked something of her that seemed strange to her, well . . . everything had grown strange in the previous twenty-four hours. This at least brought her pleasure.

She parted her lips to admit him, bewildered at the sensation that filled her, at the wave of liquid heat that began to run in thick rivulets through her veins. When he lifted his lips from hers, she was breathless, and the sound of her heartbeat filled her ears.

"Send me away, Cedar," he told her in a hoarse whisper. "Tell me to go. Now."

They both knew that he was warning her, that he was telling her that in a moment or two more there would be no turning back. Even as he spoke, he wondered if it wasn't already too late, wondered what he would do if she ordered him to leave.

Cedar stared up into his eyes, asking herself what it was she saw in them, wondering if she was a fool to believe him, to trust him. But she banished her own doubt, telling herself that she needed him, that without his help she would have no chance to clear her father's name. More than that, she knew that if she did not trust him, she would have to force herself to leave the feeling of safety she found in the circle of his arms.

At that moment, more than anything else, she knew she needed that sense of security, needed some refuge from the terror she'd felt as she'd watched her whole world begin to crumble around her. She had no choice but to trust him, she realized, no choice whatsoever.

"Please stay," she murmured softly. "Don't leave me alone. Not now."

He put his hands on her cheeks and stared into her upturned eyes. Fool, a voice inside him screamed. Get out now, before it's too late.

Instead he leaned forward to her once more, pressing his lips to her eyes, closing them with his kiss.

Cedar gave herself up to the feel of his lips as he lowered them to her neck, freeing herself of thought, simply letting herself drift. Nothing had ever been like this, nothing had prepared her for the shivering heat his touch released within her. There had never been anything to make her suspect she had held hidden somewhere within her the capacity to feel like this. Somehow part of her had lain her whole life still and secret inside her, waiting for his touch to be freed.

And as this strange creature within her came to life, it was able to push away everything in its path. The churning, endless thoughts that had been haunting her grew fainter and fainter until finally they disappeared entirely. She had no thoughts during those moments for Magnus, for the murder, for anything except the feeling of Guy's arms around her and his lips against her skin.

She barely noticed his fingers as they expertly unfastened her buttons. All that was real to her was the feel of his lips as they followed close behind his hands, which bared first her shoulders and then her breasts. It was only when he'd pulled away the bodice of her dress that she realized she was standing in front of him wearing little more than her shift.

If she'd allowed it, her conscience would have insisted that what was happening was wrong, that she was about to give away something that a well-bred woman of her age and class guarded assiduously until her wedding night. Everything in her background, every tenet by which she'd been raised, would have branded what she was doing as a sin.

But she had no intention to listen to her conscience. She allowed herself to heed only one voice, the thick, pounding call that filled her veins at Guy's touch, the voice of her own suddenly wakened passion. She was dizzy with the feel of it, weak and lost, and sure of only one thing, and that was that she didn't want the feeling to end.

For an instant she wondered why she felt this way, why this man held such a strange power over her when no one before had ever been able to affect her. Perhaps it was that he seemed to have expectations of her, seemed to think her capable of thought even if he disagreed with her. Or perhaps it had nothing to do with him at all. Perhaps she simply had been freed by the confession Magnus had made to

59

her that morning. Whatever the reason, she realized she had made her decision the moment he'd taken her into his arms and kissed her.

It was like some cloudy, mist-filled dream. One moment she was standing with him holding her, the next they were lying on the thick carpet in front of the fireplace. In between there was only the sense of floating, the gauzy mist that made the world beyond them disappear, and the insistent, throbbing pounding of the strange, unknown sea that had sprung up to fill her at his first touch.

And the tides of that sea, she realized, were growing steadily stronger. As he pressed his lips to her naked breasts, as his hands stroked her belly and her thighs, the waves seemed to grow ever higher within her, snatching her up and tossing her. She felt herself powerless in their grasp, but she realized she didn't care. She had no desire to struggle against the pounding of the tides within her, no thought to extricate herself from their powerful hold. This force, this alien stranger that had lain hidden within her for her whole life, may have been a mystery to her, but she had no fear of it, only a hunger to go wherever it might lead her.

When Guy parted her legs with his own, she readily complied, without any thought save that she wanted to go wherever it was he was taking her, eager for the feel of him, for the knowledge of what it meant to be a woman. And when he kissed her and then pressed himself to her, that first sweet thrust was a revelation to her, like a shaft of light within her that shimmered and spread itself through every cell in her body.

She found herself clinging to him, her hands at the back of his neck, holding herself close, so close to him that she wasn't sure where her own body ended and his began. The sensation of flesh against flesh, the taste of his tongue on hers, of his lips pressed to hers, and the feel of him, deep within her, all this seemed to her as though it was a previously missing part of her, as though she had been created for this moment, had lived her whole life with the expectation that it would come to her exactly as it had.

He began to move inside her, at first guiding her movements with his hands until she realized that some part deep within her already knew this dance, that it was something she had no need to be taught. Her body accepted his, welcomed his with an inborn knowledge that sprang from some deep well inside her that had been the bequest of her mother and her mother's mother and back for a hundred hundred generations before her.

It terrified her when it came to her, that first, shattering release. If what had come before had mystified and intrigued her, this powerful explosion that filled her frightened her, for it robbed her of the last of her control, of her own feeling that she ruled her body. She felt lost within herself, felt that her body had shattered and dissolved, had melted and become merged with his.

She pressed herself to him, unaware that she was trembling uncontrollably. She heard a sound, something far away, a deep, low moan, and didn't realize that she had uttered it.

Guy felt her trembling release. Somehow the knowledge that he had brought her this pleasure was a greater spur to his own passion than anything he had ever felt before. It shattered his own control, leaving him bewildered at the power of her effect on him even as he gave himself up to the sweet wave of rapture that carried him with her.

They lay together, arms and legs still entwined, breathless and spent, both rapt in their own thoughts of bewildered wonder. Cedar was still confused by the knowledge of what had been freed inside her, by the awareness that she was capable of feeling such things as he had released within her. And Guy, whose experience certainly far outweighed hers, found himself lost in the realization that he had never before felt anything quite so intense, quite so shattering, as what he'd felt with her.

"I'm lost," she murmured groggily, and she pressed her

61

lips against his chest, absently wondering at the sweet, salty taste of his flesh.

"Don't worry," he whispered. "I'll find you."

"I hope so," she murmured. "If not, I'll never find my way back."

She curled herself up, comfortably spent and close in his arms. She was confused, she realized, and her mind filled with questions, questions she was sure he would be able to answer. But the words, she found when she tried to frame them in her mind, became muddled and murky. Her eyelids had grown unaccountably heavy. She quickly realized that struggling to remain awake was useless. Once she had accepted the necessity of sleep, it quickly claimed her.

Guy leaned forward to her head, letting his lips brush against the thick cloud of her hair. Freed of its pins, it lay spread across his arm and shoulder and down onto the thick wool of the carpet beneath them. A pale golden shimmer, it felt like silk where it touched his skin.

The scent of those golden curls, her scent, filled his nostrils, softly floral, like crushed rose petals. He lifted a handful of her hair and let it slip slowly between his fingers, thoughtfully considering the feel of it, the glimmer it cast in the narrow finger of sunlight that managed to snake its way past the drawn draperies.

He stared at the strands as he let them fall, idly wondering what had happened to him in the previous twenty-four hours, what change she'd somehow managed to precipitate within him. For he was changed, he realized, although he didn't quite know how or why. It bewildered him to realize that she'd done this thing to him, that in the few hours since he'd met her, she'd somehow touched some part of him that had never been touched before.

He held her for a while, watching her sleep, oddly at peace with himself and thinking how much he would like to lie there with her, wondering how it would feel to have her wake in his arms. But eventually he accepted the fact that he could not afford to allow himself that luxury, and he reluctantly rose, carefully extricating himself from her.

He took a cushion from the sofa and placed it beneath her head, making a small effort to make her as comfortable as he could. Then he quickly gathered up his scattered clothing, pulling them on and darting an occasional glance at Cedar, all the while feeling guilty for leaving her there, and yet aware that he had no choice, that it was best that he leave like this, before there were explanations to be made, promises extracted that he would most probably be unable to keep.

Before he left, he went to Magnus's desk and penned a quick note to leave for her. Once there, however, he found his reporter's curiosity roused as he eyed the heap of notes she had refused to let him read. Some instinct told him that there was something of importance there, and he reached for the pile without remorse or the slightest pang of conscience.

As he skimmed through the pile of notes, he felt a growing pang of disappointment. The notes seemed to be nothing more than early drafts of political speeches, relatively bland and boring. But he found himself confused by the words scrawled on one of the sheets, and this he pulled from the pile, folded, and slipped into his breast pocket before he turned away. Stopping on his way to the door only to leave the note he'd written on the floor beside Cedar's pillow, he slipped silently out of the room.

He made his way back to the kitchen and glanced quickly outside before letting himself out of the house. He'd no sooner pulled the door closed behind him when a peal of thunder shook the humid, too warm air. A moment later, just as he made his way out to the street, the downpour began, a heavy, drenching squall that he knew would soon soak him to the skin.

He turned back to stare down the street at the front of her house, grimly satisfied as he saw the crowd of reporters who had been lazing by the stoop take to their heels. He turned up his collar, resigning himself to the soaking, then turned on his heel and began to walk through the downpour.

The first thing Cedar noticed when she wakened was that the air no longer seemed so heavy and ominous, that the heat had somehow magically lifted. But that thought was quickly superseded by the realization that she was lying, naked, on the floor of her father's study.

There was a moment of confusion that was worsened by a sharp throbbing in her head as she pushed herself up to a sitting position, then replaced by a wave of remorse as she remembered how she had gotten where she was.

And with the memory came a wash of hurt as she realized she was alone, that Guy had left her there and sneaked away. He'd not even had the courage to face her, she realized, to say something to her before he left.

She berated herself, telling herself she was a fool to have let it happen, especially there, in her father's study. That part seemed the worst to her, that she had somehow defiled the place, soiled it in a way that could never be washed clean. She stared at the chair where Magnus would sit by the fire, and she could almost picture him there, staring at her, his expression filled with shock and disappointment.

She shivered and began to gather up her clothes, even as she futilely tried to remember how they'd gotten where she found them. As she hastily pulled them on, she found herself blaming Guy, telling herself that he had taken advantage of her, that she had been drunk from the brandy, that worry for Magnus had clouded her judgment. But deep inside she knew all that was nothing more than an attempt to excuse what she'd done. If she must blame someone, she told herself, then the blame was her own. Still, she could not forgive Guy for leaving, for not having the courage to face her before he fled.

It was only when she lifted the cushion to return it to its

place on the sofa that she found the hastily scribbled note. She must have shifted the cushion as she slept, and covered the piece of foolscap. It was wrinkled from the weight of the cushion and her head.

If she hoped for words of tenderness from him, her hopes were quickly dashed. There was only a single line: *Must go—much to be done still.* He hadn't even bothered to sign it.

She stood staring at the words in mute disappointment, then shifted her glance to Magnus's favorite chair, to the image of his disapproval. But the image quickly faded as she reminded herself that her father was in no position to dispense guilt, that he'd confessed as much to her only a few hours before. She looked down at Guy's note again and told herself there was only responsibility—hers, Guy's, Magnus's—and that guilt had no bearing on what had happened to any of them in the previous twenty-four hours.

Magnus had faced that responsibility. She was sure that telling her what he had told her about himself and Mary Farren had been the hardest thing he'd ever done in his life. And she told herself she was willing to face her responsibility for what had happened between her and Guy, just as her father seemed willing to face his. A wave of anger and remorse drifted through her as she realized that Guy had run off, that he'd left her to face it alone. She crumpled the note angrily, dropping it into the wastebasket, telling herself she was a fool to expect anything more from him.

The sound of the kitchen door opening and then closing alerted her to Mrs. Kneely's return. Despite the fact that she was dressed now, the room set back to rights, and despite the fact that she'd told herself she had done nothing for which she need feel guilt, still somehow the thought of the housekeeper finding her where she was seemed indecent to her. She realized she could no sooner face Mrs. Kneely than she could have faced the lords of the Inquisition.

She fled from her father's study, leaving his image behind her, running to the hall and then up the stairs and to her own room.

Once there she closed and locked the door behind her, then paced for a few minutes, trying unsuccessfully to ignore the pounding in her temples, the bequest, she realized, of the brandy. Finally she turned to her bath, telling herself there was no way she could simply wash herself clean, but unable to think of anything else to do but to try.

"What do you mean you don't have anything? The biggest story in months, and you come in here and tell me you don't have anything?"

Granger Nichols stared at Guy with the sort of cold anger that was clearly intended to intimidate. His dark, decidedly myopic eyes grew glassy and sharp with implied accusation behind the protection of the thick spectacles that covered them, and his chin seemed sharp even beneath the thick covering of a slightly grizzled, prematurely graying beard.

Whatever Nichols's intent, Guy was unmoved. He'd seen the editor leave less experienced men cowed and shaking often enough to know that weakness was the least advantageous position from which to bargain, and he also knew that Nichols was inclined to use bluster when he found himself on less than solid ground.

He stirred slightly in his chair, aware that he was uncomfortable in his still-damp clothing. He felt a hint of amusement when he realized Nichols assumed the movement was due to something else altogether and a satisfied smirk appeared on the editor's face.

"Well?" Nichols demanded.

Guy shrugged. "I told you, I don't have anything. If you want the more lurid details, you'll have to read them in the *Truth Teller*. You can get McBride to do a rewrite if you're so desperate for a story. I don't want to have anything to do with it."

The satisfied smirk disappeared as Guy spoke. It was

66

more than obvious that Nichols was not pleased with the response.

"Don't give me that, Guy. You were there. And you were with the daughter at the station house this morning. You have something to do with it whether you want to or not."

Guy's eyes narrowed. "Do you have a spy network out there, Granger?" he demanded. "Or are you just having me followed?"

"Don't underestimate the power of your editor, Guy," Nichols replied. "He sees everything, hears everything, knows everything. And perhaps more importantly, he has the power to fire you in his hands."

Nichols spoke in a terse, hard tone, but despite that, Guy could see a hint of amusement begin to work its way into the editor's eyes. It occurred to him that Nichols enjoyed his moments of omnipotence, however brief or delusional they might be.

"So you already put McBride onto this one," Guy ventured, noting by the way Nichols's expression deflated that his guess was correct.

The editor shrugged, then nodded.

"You weren't around," he admitted. "I sent McBride off to the station house, where they seemed surprised to see him. Your friend Sergeant Shehan told him you were already on the story, that you were there when the body was found at Madame Blanche's. McBride returned decidedly put off, Guy. He's wondering how you can afford to patronize one of the city's most expensive bordellos. He was about to ask me for a raise when I threw him out of here."

Guy laughed. "Wise move," he said.

Nichols's eyes narrowed. "Still, I find myself wondering the same thing."

"What if I were to tell you the ladies at Madame Blanche's pay me?" Guy asked with a grin.

Nichols shook his head. "I'd either call you a liar or have you committed," he replied, but he finally smiled.

Guy shrugged. "And you'd be right," he admitted. "Truth

is, after that fine speech of Rushton's you sent me to cover, I stopped by the station just to see if anything really interesting was happening. Shehan was about to give me the boot, but then fate proved once again that my timing is perfect. I visited Madame Blanche's last night courtesy of the New York City Police Department." His smile disappeared. "And from the moment I saw Magnus Rushton there, I've found myself wondering just why you decided to send your best crime reporter to cover a decidedly dull political rally." He leaned forward toward Nichols. "I don't suppose someone over at Tammany let slip to you that something unpleasant just might happen to the thorn the reform movement stuck in Tweed's side?"

Nichols's smile vanished. "You aren't my best anything," he retorted.

"But you will admit my expertise is not precisely in the area of politics, won't you, Granger?" he prodded. "Care to tell me why you sent me to Rushton's rally?"

Guy watched Nichols look away, no longer willing to meet his glance, and realized he'd guessed correctly a second time. He couldn't believe it, but from the way Nichols was acting, he could only surmise that at least some part of Cedar's bizarre suspicions must have some small seed of truth in them after all.

"Well, Granger?"

"You should know by now, Guy, that publishers have friends and those friends have friends," he said. He let his gaze drift slowly back to meet Guy's. "Look, I live by one hard and fast rule—never argue with the publisher. And if you want to go on eating in this town, I'd suggest you learn to do the same thing."

"Your concern for my continued well-being is overwhelming, Granger." Guy made no attempt to keep the sarcasm from his tone. He pushed himself to his feet and stood leaning over Nichols's desk, staring down at the older man.

Nichols stared up at him through the thick glass of his

spectacles. "You're good, Guy," he said slowly. "But don't mistake a little talent for power. You and me, we're the same. We do what we do, better than some, certainly, but that's all. If we keep our noses clean, we get to live a comfortable life. But let yourself stick that nose where it doesn't belong, and I assure you, you'll find someone happy to cut it off. Keep your nose clean, Guy. Don't go pushing it places where it doesn't belong."

"I asked you a question, Granger," Guy said. "Avoiding an answer only makes my curiosity itch."

"And I gave you an answer," Nichols answered sharply. "The only answer you're going to get. I suggest you go out and get me a story I can put on the front page—a nice, juicily titillating story about the murder Magnus Rushton committed at Madame Blanche's house—and forget about your damned itch."

Guy straightened up and stood silent for a moment, staring at Nichols.

"I think I'll do just that, Granger," he said finally. "I think I'll go and look for a real story about that murder. And when I come back with it, I intend to bring the truth."

Nichols's lips twisted into a crooked smile. "Who's truth, Guy?" he asked. "Rushton's? Or that poor, dead whore's? Or maybe that pretty daughter of Rushton's, maybe her truth is the one you want. McBride tells me he heard you and she were pretty friendly for strangers."

Guy felt a flush of anger wash over him at the mention of Cedar.

"Leave Rushton's daughter out of this, Granger," he said sharply.

Nichols shook his head at Guy's reaction. "So that's what this is all about," he mused. "Coldhearted reporter, finally finding he's not without his own weaknesses after all. I suppose a pretty face can melt any man's defenses. But take my advice, Guy, find a better target for your affections. Word is, this one is going to get messy, and there's no way Rushton's daughter won't be touched by it. Just write the story."

"And keep my nose clean?"

Nichols nodded. "And keep your nose clean."

"And to hell with whoever gets hurt?" Guy demanded.

"I learned a long time ago to leave morality to the preachers, Guy. You should do the same thing."

Guy slowly shook his head. "How much did you get when you sold your soul, Granger?" he asked slowly. "Or didn't you ever have one to begin with?"

"A reporter can't afford one, Guy," Nichols replied. There was a hint of regret in his tone, and more than a hint of resignation. "Stick around a little longer and you'll understand that."

Guy put his hand on the doorknob, but paused before he turned it. "I hope I don't last that long, Granger," he said.

The pale skin of Granger's cheeks flushed suddenly red with anger. "Don't preach to me, Guy," he hissed. "You're in no position, the way I see it. I know for a fact you've used just about every lousy trick there is to get a story, so don't preach to me. I'm no dirtier than you are. I've just survived longer."

"I've no objection to surviving," Guy told him. "I just don't want to get to the point where I don't recognize that what I'm doing is dirty."

Before Nichols could say anything more, Guy pulled open the door and left.

# Chapter Five

Cedar stood on the curb and stared up at the enormous building in front of her. William Marcy Tweed's house was large, nearly three times the size of the house on Thompson Street she shared with her father and Mrs. Kneely. Just the sight of it was enough to make her wonder just what it was she had hoped to accomplish by coming here. With all the money and influence Tweed had at his command, she began to wonder if perhaps he really was above both morality and the law.

Suddenly feeling more than a little intimidated, and aware that the sinking feeling in her stomach was her determination slowly leaking away, she had to force herself to put her foot on the first of the front steps. With every step she climbed, she felt another wave of uncertainty wash over her. Had there been many more than a dozen of them, she never would have even reached the front door.

She had to force herself to think about Magnus, to remind herself that at that very moment he was sitting in a bare, ugly jail cell, and that his being there was almost certainly the fault of the man who lived in this impressive house. It was that, and not the indignant thought that this mansion had most likely been paid for by money that had come from the pockets of the poorer citizens of New York, people whose need far exceeded Tweed's, that gave her the courage to put her hand on the ornate brass knocker, lift it, and bring it down smartly.

The door was opened quickly, almost as if the liveried butler who opened it and stood facing her had been waiting there in the entranceway for her, as if she had been expected. He was very tall, and the imperious look he leveled down at her was clearly evaluating, as though he were judging her by considering what possible reason a young woman could possibly have to appear unescorted at a gentleman's door at such a late hour.

"I'd like to see Mr. Tweed, please," Cedar told him.

The butler's look didn't change. "Have you an appointment?" he asked in a startlingly deep basso.

Cedar glanced at his expression and quickly decided he was the sort who would send her packing if she admitted to the truth.

"Yes, I have," she found herself lying without rousing so much as a twinge of conscience.

He still didn't change his expression, despite the fact that he probably recognized the lie, as he mutely stepped back to allow her entry into the house.

Cedar stepped inside and glanced around. It was a huge entrance hall, marble-floored, boasting elaborately carved paneling on the walls and an equally impressive staircase. The center was dominated by an enormous ebony table holding a large flower-filled and gilt-decorated porcelain vase. Cedar dully noted that the entrance hall to Tweed's home was larger and far more elaborately decorated than the whole of her father's study.

"Whom may I say is calling, miss?"

"Cedar Rushton," she replied.

For the first time the butler's emotionless expression faltered and a hint of curiosity crept into his eyes. Cedar noticed the change and wondered what he could have overheard about her father in the previous days. She wished she had the power to unlock the man's memories, sure they would explain the mystery of what had happened to her father.

She had begun to unbutton her coat, but as the butler

made no motion that indicated he intended to help her off with it, she left it as it was. She wasn't there, after all, for a social call. Perhaps it would be best to retain what little armor she had available to her.

"Wait here, please," he told her in a tone that suggested that, unwarned, she might be expected to go wandering. He turned sharply around, crossed the hall quickly to a paneled door at the far end, knocked, and waited a moment before he pushed the door open and entered the room. Cedar stared after him as he pulled the door closed behind himself, and she was left with a vague impression of a large, chandelier-lit dining room.

The first minute she waited alone in the hall dragged slowly into two and then several, and the indecision that had assailed Cedar while she stood on the street and stared up at Tweed's impressive house began to return. She eyed the front door, contemplating the possibility of fleeing now, before the butler returned. It probably wouldn't matter even if she did, she told herself. Tweed probably wouldn't agree to see her after all.

The thought that she'd be pushed out without so much as the chance to say what she had come to say had, if nothing more, the positive effect of reinforcing her determination. She had come here to tell Tweed that she knew what he'd done, that if he did not see that her father was immediately released from jail and cleared of the charges against him, she would somehow see that his part in the death of Mary Farren was brought to light. She wasn't really sure how much good it would do, but she remembered hearing Magnus once mention that bluster was a good approach when dealing from weakness, and it seemed the only path open to her. At worst, she thought, Tweed might inadvertently reveal something to her, something she might use.

Once again feeling the strength of determination, she gave up her contemplation of flight and turned back to the door through which the butler had disappeared. Just as she did, it opened. He stood, framed by the impressive carved portal and the far more impressive room behind him.

"This way, miss," he intoned.

Cedar crossed the hall, and as she neared him, he stood back, letting her pass. She walked into an enormous dining room with ornately framed mirrors on the walls, three enormous chandeliers hanging from the ceiling, and a table large enough to easily seat twenty that was surrounded by heavily carved and upholstered chairs. The brilliance of candlelight glinted off sharp white linen, the welter of silver serving pieces, and a crystal-and-silver epergne in the center of the table. Trays of fruits and cakes, as well as a crystal decanter, snifters, and a humidor, indicated that she had come just as the meal was about to be concluded.

Three men sat at the far end of the table. At its head, seated in an armchair easily twice the size of the other decidedly ample chairs, and staring up at her was, unmistakably, William Marcy Tweed. Two men flanked him, two who, unlike Tweed, had, to Cedar's knowledge, avoided being characterized by the press. Neither was even vaguely familiar to her. The man on Tweed's left, a hefty, red-haired man with fair skin and freckles, dropped a fork onto a plate littered with cake crumbs and lifted his napkin to wipe his lips before he turned to face her.

Tweed leaned forward, put his hands on the table, and pushed himself to his feet.

"Miss Rushton?" he asked. "May I assume that you are Magnus Rushton's daughter? It took me a moment to place the name when Bailor announced you."

Cedar nodded. "Yes," she replied, "Magnus Rushton is my father."

Tweed pushed his chair aside and started around the table toward her.

"This is, indeed, a surprise, Miss Rushton. A pleasant surprise, certainly, as I must admit the sight of a handsome young woman always delights me. But I must tell you how shocked we were at the news of your father. As you must be, I am sure. I had always thought of Magnus Rushton as

74

a sober and decidedly upstanding man. This whole nasty business quite unsettles me." He was standing beside her now, and he extended his hand to her. "Is there some way I might be of help to you, my dear?"

Cedar darted a glance at the hand he held out to her, and pointedly ignored it.

"I wonder if we might speak in private, Mr. Tweed?" she asked.

It was quite obvious that she had refused to take his hand, and Tweed dropped it, recovering quickly, even smiling at her as he motioned to the two men seated at the table.

"But these are my closest friends and associates, Miss Rushton," he told her firmly. "Anything you might wish to say to me you can most certainly say with absolute confidence in their presence." He turned to face them. "Mr. Michael Dodd, the publisher of the *Truth Teller*, and Mr. James Connolly, my personal assistant." The two men nodded as they were introduced. "Now please, tell us all what you've come to tell me."

Cedar darted a quick glance at the two men still seated at the table, then one at Tweed. She'd not expected to find him like this, at his table, in the presence of others. Now that she thought about it, she really hadn't thought about what she ought to expect. Not that any of that mattered.

She cleared her throat quietly. "I've come to tell you, Mr. Tweed, that my father is innocent, and stands unfairly accused."

Tweed nodded his head as he turned back to her. Despite the thick camouflage of beard that obscured his cheeks and lips, Cedar had the distinct feeling he found her statement more than a little amusing.

"A most commendable attitude, I'm sure, my dear. A man could wish for no more than a daughter's trust," he said. He turned to the others. "Don't you agree, gentlemen?"

"Certainly," the red-haired man, the one Tweed had introduced as James Connolly, murmured. Then he grinned across the table at Dodd.

Tweed turned back to Cedar. "But I'm afraid your pleading your father's cause to me is of little value, Miss Rushton. I have no influence with either the police or the judges in this fine city."

Cedar replied to his falsely sympathetic smile with a sharply tight smile of her own. "Haven't you, Mr. Tweed?" she asked. "I would have thought otherwise. In that case, however, perhaps I should go elsewhere with my information."

"Information?"

Tweed lost his grin, and both Connolly and Dodd stared up at her with rather more interest than they'd shown her until then.

"Yes," Cedar replied. "Perhaps there will be others more interested in the fact that you and"—she paused and nodded to Dodd—"your associate printed an article that practically predicted the murder my father is accused of committing fully two days before it happened."

Tweed turned away, addressing his attention to the crystal decanter which he leaned across the table to retrieve, along with a snifter, from its tray.

"Would you care for a bit of brandy, my dear?" he asked as he poured a healthy tot into the snifter. Then, before she could decline, he answered his own offer for her. "Of course not," he said with a small flourish of his hand. "A refined young woman like yourself wouldn't drink brandy, would she?"

Cedar felt a guilty wash of embarrassment, and with it the flush it brought to her cheeks. She found herself irrationally wondering how he could possibly know what had happened that afternoon, for why else, she asked herself, would he mention brandy that way? But then she told herself she was behaving foolishly, that he couldn't know anything about her or about what had happened between her and Guy. Still, an uncomfortable edge of guilt refused to be entirely banished and she found herself feeling warily on edge.

Tweed returned the decanter to the table. "I'm not quite sure I understand what it is you're saying, Miss Rushton," he went on thoughtfully. He turned his back on her then, dropping all pretext of acting the gracious host as he returned to his place at the far end of the table. "Am I to understand that you have come to my home to tell me I've predicted a murder?"

"You and your friend, Mr. Dodd," Cedar replied. "And you made the mistake of putting your prediction into print for all the city to read."

Tweed shook his head as though he were trying to settle something inside it. "Are you saying you think I had some knowledge of this murder even before it was committed, Miss Rushton?"

"Yes, Mr. Tweed," Cedar replied evenly. "That is what I am saying."

"We had received information that your father was a regular customer at Madame Blanche's bordello, Miss Rushton," Dodd interjected, "hardly what would be expected from a candidate who preaches a doctrine of moral rectitude. That is all that article was referring to."

"Is it, Mr. Dodd?" she demanded. "I think not."

"I fail to see what any of this has to do with me, Miss Rushton," Tweed said as he settled his considerable bulk into the chair he'd vacated when she'd entered the room. He swallowed his brandy meditatively, all the while staring at her.

"It is well known that the *Truth Teller* is the Tammany house organ, Mr. Tweed," Cedar responded. "And that makes any hint of conspiracy in its pages point back to you."

Tweed leaned forward to the humidor, opened it, and slowly selected a cigar. He held it beneath his nose, inhaling thoughtfully before he let his eyes find hers again.

"Am I to believe you have come here to accuse me of

having somehow arranged for this murder and then implicating your father, Miss Rushton?" he asked after a moment's silence.

"That is precisely why I've come here, Mr. Tweed," she replied.

"And would you care to explain why I'd do such a foolish, not to mention illegal, thing?"

"To insure the election of the candidate backed by you and Tammany, of course," Cedar replied.

Tweed laughed. It wasn't much of a laugh, as it was short and didn't convey any real sense of amusement, but still he laughed.

"Surely you don't believe that, Miss Rushton. I will admit that it would not especially please me to see a candidate backed by the Tammany Society lose an election, but these things are, after all, the vagaries of politics. Now murder and the deliberate implication of an innocent man . . ." He let his words trail off as he shook his head in apparent dismay at the mere suggestion, then lifted his glass and drained the brandy that remained in it.

Cedar ignored his speech and the suggestion of shock. He was, she mused, a very good actor, or perhaps just a convincing liar.

"I believe you would most certainly do those things, Mr. Tweed," she said, "were your candidate's loss to mean the start of a movement to reform what Tammany has done to politics in this city. And that is just what it would have done. If my father wins this election, the Reform party will end up sweeping you and yours out of City Hall in the next few years and you know it."

Cedar couldn't believe she was saying these things, couldn't believe she had actually spoken until she heard her own words. But once she had, once she saw the looks Connolly and Dodd exchanged, she knew she was right. There was no longer any hint of amusement in either of their expressions, and Connolly's pale complexion had turned an unbecomingly bright red.

Tweed, too, darted a glance at the two other men. Then he removed a small silver device from his pocket and busied himself clipping off the end of his cigar. Bailor moved forward with a lighted taper as Tweed put the cigar to his mouth, but pulled it away when his employer withdrew the cigar before it was lit and waved the butler back.

"And just what do you intend to do with these decidedly bizarre fantasies of yours, Miss Rushton?" he asked.

Cedar didn't answer immediately. Instead, she smiled at him, delighted at the thought that she had managed to unsettle him. Had it been enough, she wondered, for him to do what she asked and see that her father was cleared of the murder charges against him?

"I've come here to tell you that if you don't see that my father is cleared of the charges against him, I will see that proof of those facts are brought to light."

Tweed considered her expression, then motioned to Bailor to return the flame. He put his cigar in his mouth, slowly drawing on it as he put the end to the flame, taking almost ritualistic care to light it evenly as a round disk of ash appeared at the end.

"Oh, forgive me." Tweed withdrew the cigar and looked up at her. "You don't object, do you, Miss Rushton?" he asked in a falsely concerned tone.

"Would it matter if I did, Mr. Tweed?" Cedar asked.

He smiled then, finally dropping all pretext. "No," he replied. "It wouldn't. Especially as you are about to leave. I'm afraid I must admit that I seem to have lost whatever interest I might have had in listening to your preposterous tales, Miss Rushton. I must ask you to go." He motioned to the butler. "Be so kind as to show Miss Rushton to the door, Bailor. And find her a cab. It isn't safe for a young woman to be out alone on the streets at this hour."

"Is that a threat, Mr. Tweed?" Cedar demanded.

"It is an observation, Miss Rushton," he replied. "And now I must wish you good night."

Bailor rounded the table and approached her. "This way,

miss," he said and nodded toward the door.

Cedar glared at Tweed. "You haven't heard the last of me, Mr. Tweed. That I promise you," she said.

"I wish I could say it has been a pleasure, Miss Rushton," Tweed responded. He nodded to the butler and waved them to the door.

Cedar didn't fight when Bailor put his hand on her arm. It wouldn't do any good, she told herself. But as he escorted her to the door, she felt all sense of hope fade. For a moment she'd been sure that she'd said something that disturbed Tweed, perhaps even enough to spur him to see her father freed and his name cleared. Instead, he was showing her the door without letting a single scrap of information slip.

The three men sat in silence as they watched Bailor escort her from the room. When the door was closed behind them, Tweed motioned to the decanter.

"Pass that bottle, Jimmy." He nodded toward the now closed door. "Damn shame. God never should have given pretty women tongues or thoughts to put words to. A plain woman, now, a man can turn his back on and ignore, but it hurts a man's soul to think of the waste of a pretty woman like that one."

Tweed had lost the carefully studied manner of speech he'd used when Cedar had been in the room. Now that he was no longer taking pains to control it, his accent had lost its gloss and pointed to his rather ordinary origins.

Connolly put his hand on the decanter, but before he lifted it, he turned to Tweed.

"If you will remember, Bill, I warned you about McNaughton," he said. "He's gotten too greedy, lets too much stick to his fingers. I told you as soon as the Reformers got a bead on him that we should wash our hands of him and find someone else. I told you there'd be trouble."

"It has nothing to do with us," Tweed replied. "No one's going to believe her stories. She doesn't have any proof linking me with that whore's murder because there is none."

"But she may have something linking McNaughton," Connolly insisted.

Tweed shook his head. "She wasn't a good enough actress to convince me of that, Jimmy. She came here hoping we'd tell her something, that's all."

"So what do we do now?"

Tweed smiled. "Why, you, me, and Mike, here, we write a little editorial for the next edition of the *Truth Teller*, and we point to our reform opposition with their lily-white hands that are stained with blood."

"You don't mean we're going on with McNaughton?"

Tweed's expression hardened. "We haven't any choice now. If we don't give every appearance of outraged innocence, we'll be doing the same thing as admitting to that crazy girl's accusations." He grinned suddenly. "And since Magnus Rushton has already given us the ammunition, we'd be fools not to use it. Now hand me that bottle. I never could do any work worth a damn with my throat dry."

Cedar remembered to glance out at the front of her house as the cab turned down Thompson Street. The reporters were there, fruitlessly waiting for whatever it was they hoped to gain by finding her. She told the driver to go on around the next corner rather than stopping in front of the house, wondering as she did how she had come so quickly to accept the fact that it was necessary for her to sneak into and out of her own home.

She settled back on the seat of the cab and sat hunched and brooding. She never should have gone to see Tweed, she told herself. The excursion had been as useless as everything else she'd done lately, and only proved to make her feel incompetent and foolish.

It was little comfort for her to remember the worried looks Tweed's guests had exchanged when she'd suggested she could prove their host was tied to Mary Farren's murder. She had no such proof beyond their expressions, and that was hardly going to prove her father's innocence in a court of law.

It might have been easier for her if she had some clear idea of how to go about finding some more useful proof. But for the moment her mind was clouded with the knowledge that she was floundering, and there was no one to whom she could turn to find help.

It was only too clear to her that unless she intended to let other people determine her father's fate to suit themselves, she had to gather together the wits God had given her and begin to use them. There simply was no one else on whom she could depend. If nothing else, her experience with Guy Marler had taught her the folly of placing her trust in the wrong hands.

The cab drew to a stop and she stepped out, handing the fare up to the driver, then turning to eye the long, dark line of carriage houses that backed the houses of her block. The prospect of walking alone along those deserted buildings in the dark was hardly appealing, but she marshaled her courage, telling herself it could hardly be worse than facing Boss Tweed and his cronies.

As she walked along the dimly lit row of carriage houses, she reviewed the alternatives that remained open to her. Proof of her father's innocence, she mused, that was what she needed. And to be honest with herself, she had to admit that she had no idea what it was for which she should be looking. The only thing she did know was that there was only one place she could go to find what Magnus needed — to the bordello where Mary Farren had been killed.

The prospect was hardly appealing. The thought of going to that place, especially knowing that Magnus had gone there, that he'd looked to a whore to take the place her mother's illness had forced her to abdicate, quite simply revolted Cedar. But she reminded herself that she was no longer in a position to make moral judgments. Her own standards, it seemed, were as flawed as her father's, or perhaps more so. In any case, they were not above censure.

After all, it was a woman's duty to safeguard her innocence. Men, on the other hand, were never burdened with such a responsibility.

She ducked down the alley between two carriage houses, taking the route to her own back garden that she and Guy had followed earlier that day. It hardly seemed possible that that had only been a few hours before. She'd been lost then, completely unable to cope with what had happened, with what she'd been forced to accept. By comparison she felt strong now. If she wasn't entirely sure about how she was going to do it, at least she knew for certain that she would find some way of proving Magnus innocent. One way or another, she promised herself, she would do it.

She slipped her key into the latch and then let herself silently into the darkened house, feeling much like a thief as she closed the door behind her and then stood in the darkened room. Not even bothering to light a lamp, she moved through the still house to the front parlor. Once there, she lifted the edge of a drapery and darted a glance out at the disconsolate group that leaned against the rail of her front stoop. It was late now, nearly midnight, and she wondered how much longer they would remain. They'd have to give up soon, she told herself. It couldn't be soon enough to suit her.

She turned away and returned to the hall, then slowly climbed the stairs. She was exhausted, she realized, far beyond merely tired. That was a better thing than not, she decided. Maybe she was tired enough to sleep despite the images of Magnus in that horrible jail cell that had slipped in and out of her mind constantly all through that day. For she certainly needed some rest, she knew. The following day would come far too soon, and with it a whole new set of unpleasant circumstances with which she must cope.

"He's been transferred to the Tombs."

The desk sergeant hadn't even bothered to look up at her.

Cedar stood for a moment staring dumbly at him, as though she hadn't understood the words, then turned and walked out of the station house.

She was beginning to feel numb again, the same way she'd felt the previous day, despite the fact that she was well aware the feeling could only serve to make her useless. She tried to shake the feeling, but she couldn't entirely rid herself of it. The thought of her father in that horrible place was almost worse than the realization that he'd been arrested in the first place.

She couldn't rid herself of the feeling, not all through the ride across town. It was still there when she climbed out of the cab and stared up at the forbiddingly ugly gray stone that fronted the Tombs. And she still had not managed to quite shed it when she found herself seated on the opposite side of a sturdy oak table from Magnus.

"Papa," she said softly. She tried to look at his eyes but found she couldn't. Instead her eyes drifted slowly downward, to the dirty gray color of the coverall he was now wearing, to the dark four-digit number that was clearly marked on its breast pocket. A voice inside her told her that this man sitting across from her in that ugly coverall could not possibly be her fastidious father.

Magnus saw the dismay in her eyes. "It's better than a bloodstained shirt with a bullet hole in it, Cedar," he told her.

The words startled her and she finally lifted her eyes to meet his squarely.

"I could have brought you something," she murmured, but stopped when she saw him shake his head. "I suppose they won't let you wear your own things," she finished weakly.

"I'm afraid not," he replied, then dismissed the matter with a wave of his hand. "But no matter. I have more pressing things to consider. I saw a criminal lawyer yesterday afternoon—"

"Lawyer?" Cedar interrupted. "But I haven't spoken to

anyone yet. I'd wanted to talk with you first—"

"Your friend Marler sent James Wyatt to see me," Magnus said, cutting her off. "I'd heard a good deal of him. He has an excellent reputation. I didn't precisely find him a pleasant man, but I need a lawyer, not a friend. I've decided to retain him."

"Oh," Cedar murmured, feeling a little out of her depth. She'd certainly had no idea Guy had sent a lawyer to see her father. She began to wonder what else he had done after he'd left her the previous afternoon.

"He thinks there is a good case for self defense," Magnus went on, ignoring her bewildered expression, "and advised me to make that plea. In his opinion, that may be the only way I'll avoid spending the remainder of my life in jail."

"But you didn't kill her!" Cedar exclaimed.

Magnus opened his mouth to speak, but then closed it, swallowed and shrugged. He looked down to where his hands, clasped together, rested on the rough top of the table.

"I haven't decided yet," he said finally. He looked back up at her. "I don't want to die in prison, Cedar," he said softly.

"There must be another way, Papa," she insisted. "You can't agree to accept the responsibility for a murder you didn't commit."

"I don't know that I'll have much choice, Cedar," Magnus told her. "At least I'll be free."

"But your political career?" she countered.

Magnus shook his head. "Is already over before it's begun," he told her. His tone was thick with regret and resignation. "The Reform Party has washed their hands of me. One of the guards very kindly showed me this morning's *Chronicle*. I assume they'll eventually get around to sending someone to tell me personally," he added with a tinge of bitterness.

"They can't," she murmured.

"They have," Magnus told her firmly. "It seems I am suddenly a pariah. Which leads me to the subject of a decision

85

I made last night—I don't want you to come here again."

Cedar stared at him a moment, completely dumfounded.

"You can't be serious, Papa. Of course I'll come to visit you," she insisted.

"No you won't," he told her. "If you do, I won't agree to see you. I don't want you to be subjected to this place again. I think you should go to stay with your Aunt Felicia until all this is over and settled."

Cedar shook her head. "No, Papa," she told him. "I'm sure I can help. I can find something, some proof, something—"

Magnus slammed his hand down on the table. "No. I don't want you involved in this any more than you already are, Cedar. If I can't do anything else, at least I can see that your life is not ruined because of what I've done."

"But you haven't done anything, Papa," she insisted.

"Haven't I, Cedar?" he asked. "The look on your face yesterday when I told you about Mary told me something entirely different."

Cedar swallowed. She wanted to tell him that it didn't matter, that she understood now, that what he'd done with Mary Farren didn't matter. But somehow she couldn't. It did matter. It seemed to darken her memory of her mother, to turn the wake of hurt Cedar had felt at her death bitter. Even what had happened with Guy Marler still couldn't wash away that pain.

She realized that Magnus was staring at her and still she couldn't meet his eyes. She looked down, at her hands.

"I was wrong yesterday, Papa," she said softly.

"But what about right now, Cedar?" he demanded. "Are you wrong now?"

She couldn't answer. After a moment Magnus stood, darted a quick look at the guard who stood at the side of the room, then leaned across the table and kissed her quickly on the cheek.

She looked up at him.

"Papa . . ."

"Don't come back, Cedar," he told her. "When this is over and I'm home, we'll have time to talk about it."

Then he turned away from her and motioned to the guard that he was ready to leave.

Cedar sat, feeling numb and lost as she watched the guard open the door for Magnus, then close and lock it behind him. She couldn't let this happen, she told herself, couldn't let him bear the guilt for a crime he hadn't committed. She had to find some way to clear his name.

And that meant she had to get some answers to questions, answers she could only find at the bordello where Mary Farren had been killed.

# Chapter Six

Cedar rang the bell and waited. It seemed forever before she heard the sound of footsteps approaching the door, and all the time she waited, she wondered what she was going to say when she was faced with the necessity of explaining why she wanted to be admitted to a bordello.

For the truth, she realized, would hardly be appropriate under the circumstances. Her father and Mary Farren's body had been found in a locked room. Unless she was to accept the official version of what had happened—that Magnus and Mary had entered the room, locked it, then proceeded to those events that led to the prostitute's death— she had to believe that the scene had been arranged with the connivance of someone who lived in this house. And that someone might very well be the person who had actually murdered Mary Farren. Whoever it was, it was not beyond possibility that that person might decide the best way to end any unwanted inquiry would be to dispatch her as well. She would have to be circumspect if she was to have any hope of finding some answers, and she would also have to be very careful.

She needed a lie, then, one that would sound plausible, and the only reasonable one that sprang to mind was the most obvious, that she was in search of a job. The prospect of pretending she was a whore was far from appealing to her, but she told herself that she need only act the part for a few hours, until she could ask a few questions and get a few answers. The problem was to broach the subject in a way that would not rouse any suspicion. Then she could leave and no one would be the wiser.

When the door was finally pulled opened, she found herself facing a tall and extremely powerful looking black man. His smooth shaved head made his eyes seem even more piercing than they might otherwise appear, the nearly black irises surrounded by white made even whiter by the contrast with his dark skin. He seemed distracted, for he was mumbling softly, to himself apparently, something about how he wasn't used to admitting visitors so early in the day, which completely confused Cedar, for it was nearly noon.

Cedar screwed up her courage and was about to say she had come in search of work. She looked up at him, saw the way he was considering her, and for some reason her mouth felt as though it were filled with cotton wool and the words remained unsaid. But after making a cursory inspection of her, he stepped back and let her in without uttering so much as a word.

"You don't have the look of one in need of an abortion, so I s'pose you've come lookin' for a place," he said once he'd closed the door behind her.

Cedar had heard whispers to the effect that madames often supplemented their incomes by providing ladies with the means of ridding themselves of the results of an imprudent act, and now she realized this was true. She nodded her head, feeling dull and miserable, wondering if in a month's time she might be faced with the prospect of presenting herself once again at the door of a bordello, in need of that very service, the result of her decidedly imprudent act with Guy Marler.

"Yes, a place," she murmured. She found she had to force out the words, and they sounded as frightened and uncertain as she felt.

He laughed softly, apparently amused by her apparent discomfort. He quickly looked her over, this time with a knowing and obviously experienced eye. Once his inspection was complete, he offered her an encouraging smile.

"Don't you worry none," he told her. "Miz Blanche won't be turnin' you away."

With that pronouncement, he motioned her to follow him. She trailed along behind him, slightly dazed at how easy it had been to make her way inside Madame Blanche's establishment, especially when she'd anticipated just the opposite. She didn't let herself stop to consider just what someone who was "lookin' for a place" would be expected to do, sure that if she did, she'd simply turn tail and run.

"Wait here," her guide told her once they were in a large front parlor. "You kin sit."

Having uttered the invitation, he turned and crossed to the far side of the room. He looked back when he'd reached the door, nodded to her, then knocked and entered, pulling the door firmly shut behind him.

Cedar looked around. The house seemed oddly quiet around her. Not a sound emanated either from the room into which the porter had gone or from the floors above. She could not pretend that she was disinterested in her surroundings. Some perverse part of her had wondered, ever since she'd been old enough to know that such places existed, just what the inside of a bordello could possibly be like.

And with respect to its decor, at least, she had to admit that Madame Blanche's establishment certainly did not in any way miss measuring up to her wildest expectations.

The parlor was generously furnished with a matched suite of carved rosewood furniture, all upholstered in thick red velvet, and all sporting a wealth of small, naked figures, tiny naked cupids, in their decoration. Heavy velvet draperies, also red, hung at the windows, and thick Turkish carpets covered the floors. There was a large chandelier hanging from the ceiling, and a half dozen ornate girandoles, all gilt embellished and with a wealth of hanging crystals, on the mantle as well as small tables set near the walls. The decorations of Madame Blanche's house, Cedar decided, like Tweed's, spoke of affluence and a briskly profitable trade.

She was wandering about the room, staring at the furnishings, when she realized she was idly fingering a small gold locket that hung on a chain from her neck. Her fingers suddenly froze. The locket contained pictures of her parents inside. Best, she thought, if it were not seen, for someone might recognize the likeness of her father. She removed it and dropped it into her purse.

Cedar had just seated herself on the edge of a small settee when a tall, generously endowed woman stormed through the same door by which the porter had left. Half a dozen improbably red curls poked out from under a red and gold brocade turban that matched the thick folds of fabric of the flowing robe she wore. Or almost wore. The front was extremely low cut, and exposed a wealth of pale pink flesh that was only partially obscured by the thin wisps of the robe's marabou trim.

Cedar decided immediately that Madame Blanche was probably a good business woman. Her face, although showing the signs of age, was still handsome and boasted dark, exceedingly intelligent eyes. There was a brisk air about her that seemed to say that this woman had made her own way in a world that did little to ease the passage of a woman alone, and she was more than content with what success she'd made.

Cedar quickly realized she'd interrupted Blanche's stint at her books, for she held a long quill pen in her hand and waved it, motioning Cedar to her feet. The madame's fingers were freshly stained with bright blue ink.

"You're the one looking for a place?" Blanche demanded. She stared at Cedar with those dark, knowing eyes, and spoke with a sharp, no-nonsense tone.

Cedar quickly stood up. "Yes, ma'am," she replied.

She was nervous, she realized. Madame Blanche was far more imposing even than William Marcy Tweed had seemed to her. She felt almost as if Blanche could use those sharp eyes of hers to look inside, to search out a lie. Cedar felt herself cringe internally, sure she would not like to face Madame Blanche's wrath.

Despite her fear of discovery, Cedar still couldn't keep herself from staring at the madame. Everything about Blanche completely fascinated her, from the tinges of the previous evening's rouge that still clung to her otherwise pale cheeks to the half dozen large rings that decorated the long, carefully manicured fingers of her hands. There was a thin fog of scent surrounding her, richly floral but laced with a sharp overtone of strong coffee.

"Well, don't just stand there," Blanche told her in a tone that had quickly grown shrill with impatience. "Take off your coat."

Cedar quickly unbuttoned her coat and shed it. She returned her gaze to Blanche and found the older woman not at all satisfied.

"Lift your skirts and turn around," Blanche directed as she stared at Cedar with an evaluating look, the sort a butcher might give to a prize cow he was considering purchasing.

Cedar gathered up the fabric of her skirt and petticoat, each second feeling markedly less comfortable as she bared her legs and did a slow pirouette. For some reason she couldn't fathom, she found herself wanting desperately to measure up to Blanche's requirements, hoping that those fiercely sharp eyes would find no grave flaw in her, even as she felt a wave of revulsion at the thought of being considered nothing more than a piece of goods to be offered for sale.

To her relief, Blanche seemed satisfied with what she found in the course of the inspection. She was nodding her acceptance when Cedar had completed the three hundred and sixty degree turn and once again stood facing her.

"All right, you'll do," Blanche told her. "You have a name?"

"Cedar," Cedar replied. She hesitated only an instant before she went on. "Cedar Ashton," she added, giving Blanche the only name other than her own that sprang immediately to mind—her mother's maiden name. Once she'd uttered it, however, she felt guilty, as though by using the name in this place she was despoiling her mother's memory.

"Family?" Blanche demanded in the same half-interested tone.

Cedar nodded. "Just my father," she said, deciding that the fewer lies she need tell, the better. After all, the circumstances she found herself facing at that moment might very well be the sort that would force a woman to find what means she could to support herself. "He's in prison—"

She got no further.

"I don't want to hear your story," Blanche interrupted. "Everyone's got one, and they all end up the same. You came here because you have no place else, and you have to eat." She waved the quill pen at Cedar. "I'm only interested in brothers or a husband, someone who might come bursting in, making a scene. It's bad for business."

"No," Cedar replied, feeling a thick, uncomfortable feeling in the pit of her stomach at the realization that there really was no one. "No one would care."

"Just as well," Blanche pronounced. "You're lucky you came to me. Life on the street is damn hard. But this is an honest house, clean and safe. If any client tries to hurt you, I personally see he's thrown out. You'll be treated decently, and I don't cheat you. In return for security and a fair wage, you live by my rules as long as you're under my roof. You understand?"

Cedar nodded. "Yes, ma'am."

It was, apparently, the right answer.

"You don't drink except what you're given of the champagne the clients buy," Blanche enumerated. "Try to steal from a client and you'll be out on the street before you take your hand from his pocket. If a gentleman offers you something extra, fine and good, but ask for it and I consider it the same as stealing. No squabbling with the other girls. If you have a problem, you find a quiet, peaceful solution. Twenty-five dollars a month, plus your room and board. Any questions?"

"No, ma'am."

"You bring any clothes besides what you're wearing?" Blanche made a vague motion with the quill towards Cedar's outfit.

Cedar looked down. She was wearing a perfectly acceptable morning dress, navy blue with red piping, but she had to admit it was hardly what she would have imagined would be appropriate working attire for an aspiring whore.

She shook hear head. "No," she admitted with a tinge of real regret.

"I'll have Sally fix you up. The cost of it comes out of your first month's pay." Blanche turned her head toward the room from which she'd come, but didn't lower the hand holding the pen that was pointed at Cedar. "Sally!" she cried in a voice loud enough to make the cut-glass crystals hanging from the girandoles shake and sway. They hit one another, the tiny impacts making a soft tinkling sound completely at odds with the sound of the cry that had caused them.

Almost before the echo of the cry had died away, a small, round, gray-haired woman wearing a maid's black and a large apron came huffing into the room. She leveled a look in Madame Blanche's direction that said she wasn't at all delighted to be summoned at that moment, but settled her expression before she spoke.

"You called, ma'am?"

Blanche turned the quill pen toward the newcomer.

"We have a new girl, Sally. You'll have to see about some clothes for her."

"Yes, ma'am," the maid replied.

"She can have Mary's old room if it's been set to rights."

"Yes, ma'am."

"And get Addy to hurry up with breakfast. I've had four cups of coffee this morning, and no food. I'm hungry."

"Yes, ma'am."

Apparently satisfied that her presence was no longer required, Blanche swept from the room without offering Cedar another glance. In her wake she left a trail of the scent of her perfume and the even stronger reverberations of her personality.

Sally scowled at Blanche's back, then, when the madame had disappeared, turned to face Cedar.

"You might as well come along," she said, turning toward the stair hall and motioning to Cedar to follow. "I'll be showin' you to your room." She stopped and looked back at Cedar. "Hope you have better luck than the last poor soul who had it," she added.

She turned away again and, huffing all the way, made her way to the stairs. Cedar stood, slightly numb for an instant before she regained her senses, watching her. She had done what she'd intended to do, been accepted, at least conditionally, in Madame Blanche's house. Now, with a few quietly placed questions, she might find some of the answers that had eluded the police investigation of Mary Farren's murder. She wondered why she didn't feel proud of what she'd accomplished so far, why instead she felt an uncomfortable bite of fear in the pit of her stomach.

"Well, you comin'?"

Sally stood at the foot of the flight of stairs and stared back at her. Cedar collected herself and hurried after her.

By the time Cedar had reached the stairs, Sally was already halfway up them. She stared at the maid's black-draped rump moving rhythmically and put her foot on the first step.

It was only when she'd climbed several steps that she realized what it was that was bothering her. She was, she realized, about to be shown to the room where Mary Farren had been murdered.

Actually, Cedar found she had to admit that it was a

rather pretty room. There was a large bed, of course, with a shiny brass headboard and a lacy white spread that predominated, but there were also frilly white curtains at the windows, a comfortable-looking fainting couch by the far wall, a small settee at the bed's foot, and a thick Turkish rug on the floor in front of a marble faced fireplace that was still closed off for the warm months by a fancifully decorated fire screen.

Cedar stood by the door and stared in. It took only a second for her glance to be drawn to a large spot on the rug that appeared lighter than the rest, faded apparently by the scrubbing it had been given there. That, she realized, was where her father had fallen. It was the stain of his blood that had been washed away from the rug leaving that irregular, pale mark.

Sally saw her fascination with the spot on the rug. She moved to it, knelt, and patted the thick wool pile.

"It's dry. The mark will fade," she said, more to herself than Cedar, apparently taking pride in her own handiwork. "I s'pose you heard about the murder?" she asked.

Cedar nodded. "Yes," she admitted. "A little."

"Well, don't you be payin' it no mind," Sally told her. "Never anythin' like that before in this house, and there won't be again."

"Did you see it?" Cedar asked. "What happened?"

"Don't do no good gossipin' about it," Sally told her sharply. "I mind my own business, and if you're smart you'll be doin' the same."

"But was it here?" Cedar pressed. "In this room?" She looked at the spot on the rug again, and shivered.

"Don't make no difference," Sally told her. "It's all bin washed away along with the mess." She straightened up, adjusting her apron, patting it with her hands. "Madame Blanche said there won't be no more to do about it, and when she says somethin', it's usually so." That pronouncement made, Sally went on to more pressing business. "Bath and necessary are down the hall," she said briskly as she pushed back the curtains to admit some sunlight into the room. "Meals in the dinin' room, don't be expectin' to be served special other times. Your laundry's seen to, but you keep your own room." She eyed Cedar with the same sort of critical professionalism Blanche had used. "You're about Elly's size. I'll send her by with some things until I can see to gettin' the seamstress here for some of your own. Breakfast will be ready in half an hour. You need anything else?"

Cedar shook her head. "Breakfast? Isn't it nearly noon?" she asked, puzzled by the strange hours kept in the house.

Sally laughed a short, hard laugh. "You'll get used to it quick enough," she predicted. Then she left Cedar alone, pulling the door closed behind her as she left.

But Cedar knew the possibility was unlikely. She looked again at the stain on the floor, and then turned her gaze to the bed. No, she mused, she would never get used to it, not even were she to stay in this place a lifetime.

Cedar wasn't alone with her thoughts for very long. Only a few moments after Sally had left her, there was a knock on the door. Startled, she turned to find that whoever had come to see her wasn't standing on ceremony by waiting for her to admit callers. The door was pushed open and a head popped through the opening.

"Sally said there was a new girl," her visitor informed her.

The door was pushed fully open and a pretty girl with a wealth of dark curls and merry eyes entered. She was wearing a pale rose dressing gown and holding an armful of clothing.

Cedar offered her a weak smile.

"I guess that would be me," she said.

The girl crossed the room to the bed, where she deposited the armful of clothing, then turned to Cedar, right hand extended.

"I'm Elly," she said. "Well, Eglantine, actually, if you can believe a mother would actually do that to a helpless baby.

97

It was her great aunt's name, and I suppose she wasn't much of a mother, anyway, namin' me after the old witch, then leavin' me to live with her when my father left and she got tired of havin' me around to remind her she couldn't hang onto him." She paused, momentarily lost as she considered just where the thread of her logic had led her, then smiled as she remembered she was in the midst of introducing herself. "But everyone just calls me Elly, and that seems to suit well enough."

Cedar was more than a bit surprised by this guilelessly unselfconscious flow of personal revelation, but she managed a smile as she took Elly's hand. Her smile was infectious, and there was laughter in her voice, and a sultry hint to her slightly southern drawl.

"Cedar," she introduced herself. "Pleased to meet you."

"Likewise," Elly replied. She pointed to the heap she'd dumped onto the bed. "Sally said you need some workin' clothes and you were about my size." Her eyes narrowed speculatively. "I'd say you're a bit smaller, but I'm sure we can find something that'll do." She began to search through the pile. "There's a pale blue with ecru lace that's really a little too tight. You could keep it if it fits. We could go shopping together once you get your first month's wages. I know a seamstress down on Grand Street who charges a third what Blanche's seamstress who comes to the house charges." She located the blue in question, pulled it from the heap, and held it up in front of Cedar. "That should fit you fine," she pronounced after a moment's judicious consideration. "Go look in the glass."

Cedar dutifully did as she was told, holding the dress to her, turning to the tall pier glass, and staring at her reflection. It didn't take long for her to realize that the dress was extremely low cut, that it would practically bare her breasts.

She turned back to face Elly. "I don't know," she murmured, hesitating, not wanting to appear ungrateful, but unable to hide from her expression the fact that she considered the dress little less than scandalous. Her cheeks colored noticeably, and she put her hand to the bodice, as though her touch might make the fabric stretch.

Elly gave her a knowing look. "Your first time, huh?" she asked.

Cedar blushed and nodded. Her experience, in Elly's eyes, would seem woefully lacking. She couldn't keep her thoughts from drifting to what had been her single experience, with Guy, in what she was pretending was now her profession. Hardly enough to qualify her as professional, but then she presumed in this particular profession that that was not necessarily a handicap. Still, she could feel her cheeks grow redder.

"Well, don't you worry," Elly assured her. "It'll be fine, you'll see." She pushed aside the heap of clothing and dropped onto the bed, bouncing with the give of the springs. "Mary was just like you," she mused, looking around the room as though the dead prostitute might still be there, hiding in the shadows in the corners. "Poor, sweet little Mary. She was the one that got killed."

Cedar fingered the lace at the neck of the dress. There was a tightening in her throat and she could hardly get the words out. "I read about it in the papers," she admitted. "How could something like that happen?" she asked cautiously. "I mean, Madame Blanche said it was safe here."

"Damned if I know," Elly replied, and her expression grew hard. "The one they arrested, who they say done it, he was Mary's favorite. He'd come two or three times a month, always to see her, never anyone else. She thought he was kind of sweet on her, you know? I remember she once said she'd take a small place with him, if he offered. He was kind to her and she really cared for him, even if he didn't have much money. Not that she really thought he'd ever marry her, him havin' a family and all, but she said she'd be happy in a little place, with just him comin' to visit."

Cedar found herself feeling a bit queasy. Listening to this

sort of thing said about her own father seemed unnatural to her, wrong somehow. Still, she realized that the loquacious Elly might prove to be the source of the answers to her questions.

"You and she were friends, then?" Cedar asked, hoping to keep her talking, hoping to learn something that might have some bearing on what had happened that night.

"Best friends," Elly said, her expression sharply sober. It was obvious that she mourned Mary's loss. "It seems strange to have someone else in her room."

"I'm sorry," Cedar murmured. "It must be hard for you."

Elly looked up at Cedar again, and this time smiled. "None of it's your fault, certainly. If it seems strange to me to be in her room with you, don't think I blame you." She rose and crossed the room to the dresser, opening and staring into the empty top drawer. "She kept chocolates in here," she said. "You can still get a hint of the smell of them." She inhaled deeply and sighed. "I just can't get used to it, though, nothing else left but that smell, almost as though she'd never been here at all," she murmured. "Not any more than I can get used to the idea that Rushton could have killed her."

Cedar's heart leaped into her throat. She prayed there was some solid reason that Elly might have for not believing her father had killed Mary Farren.

"But the paper said the door was locked," she murmured.

Elly shrugged. "There's ways," she said, dismissing the objection. "And there was that other one, the Tammany toad, the one who Mary said couldn't keep from braggin' about all the money he was goin' to have once he sold all that land for the Pennsylvania Railroad station . . ."

Her words trailed off, and she seemed to be concerned with the inside of the empty drawer.

"Other one?" Cedar prompted softly.

This was the first mention of anyone other than Magnus in connection with the murder, and now Cedar realized she'd found someone who not only believed her father innocent, but also knew something about a member of Tammany. Could it be Tweed that Elly was referring to? she wondered. How could she ask without seeming too interested in a subject that should, by rights, mean nothing to her?

But before Cedar could frame a reasonably disinterested question, the sound of a deep, low gong filled the house. Elly looked up, pushing shut the empty drawer into which she'd been staring.

"Breakfast," she said, "finally. A person could starve to death some mornings until Addy finally gets it to the table. But the food's good," she added as she took the dress Cedar was still holding and tossed it negligently back to the pile on the bed. "You can try it on after we've eaten," she said, Mary Farren's murder apparently pushed aside by the prospect of food. Elly's mind, it seemed, could keep track of only so many matters at a time, and it was now turned to breakfast and the matter of Cedar's nonexistent wardrobe. "And I have some silk flowers we can pin in your hair. Just wait. You'll be so pretty tonight, Blanche'll have to fight them off."

"Didn't I tell you?" Elly demanded as she backed away from her handiwork to let Cedar stare at the reflection of herself in the mirror. "Just like I said, Blanche'll have to beat them off," she said. She stood behind Cedar, critically assessing her own reflection and then carefully adjusting the placement of her own ample assets to their best advantage.

Cedar tried to swallow the uncomfortable lump in her throat. She'd intended to leave long before things ever got to this point, but somehow she'd stayed just an hour longer, and then an hour longer than that, all the while hoping to turn Elly's conversation back to the matter of Mary Farren's murder. But for some reason the subject always seemed just beyond the edges of Elly's incessant chatter, and now Cedar realized she had no way to escape. She stared at her reflection in the mirror, at the hand-me-down blue dress that just barely covered her nipples and hugged her waist like a second skin. She couldn't keep herself from putting her hand to the lace trim and tugging.

"Now you stop that," Elly commanded. "You'll tear that lace." She took Cedar's hand in hers and started toward the door. "Come on, now," she said, tugging Cedar into movement. "You can't stay up here and hide all night, you know. Blanche'll be up lookin' for us before long, and she'll be mad as a wet hen for havin' to climb up the stairs. Stop worryin' an' come along."

There didn't seem to be anything to gain in fighting the inevitable, Cedar realized. Elly wasn't about to talk any more about Mary Farren's murder that evening, and that meant her little escape was at an end. She would go downstairs and leave, slip away somehow before anyone noticed. She only regretted she hadn't learned more, hadn't found out who it was that Elly referred to as the "Tammany toad."

There was already a good deal of noise from the floor below, the low rumble of masculine voices as well as the higher trill of female laughter, all of it accompanied by the sound of a thin soprano voice and a piano.

"Damn," Elly murmured as she hurried Cedar towards the stairs. "I usually sing with Maisy. Blanche will be fumin'."

Cedar turned her glance to the entrance hall below. The porter who had admitted her that morning, dressed now in perfect evening attire, was in the midst of performing a rather more formal version of that same task, taking the coats and hats from a group of three men.

Cedar would have preferred to lag behind and let the three men use up all their openly hungry glances on Elly. Unfortunately, Elly urged her forward, giving her shoulder a small nudge for good measure, and Cedar found herself descending the stairs while six very interested eyes took in her all but bared breasts.

"Ladies, ladies," one of the men called up to them, "your

timing this evening is perfect." He was tall and large, about forty, and had the air of a man who cares very little about listening to any thoughts but his own. He turned to his companions. "Now I ask you, gentlemen, could you ask for lovelier companions for the evening?" he asked his two friends. Without waiting for an answer, he moved to the foot of the stairs just as Cedar reached the next to last step and took her hand in his. "Elly, my dear," he said as he lifted Cedar's hand to his lips, ignoring the fact that she was staring at the door wondering how she might gracefully get past him, "who is your charming friend?"

"You be nice, Jonsey," Elly purred as she edged her way forward, grasping his free arm and hugging it close to her breast. "This is Cedar, and she's new, and still a little shy. Don't you go frightenin' her, now."

"Frightening her?" he asked. "I would think that's the last thing I'd care to do." He darted a glance at Elly, then turned it back to Cedar. "Cedar? Charming, charming."

"How do you do, Mr. Jonsey," Cedar murmured, and tried to gently tug her hand away from his.

He would have none of it. He held her hand firmly, putting it in the crook of his arm and then holding it there. "It's Sutton, my dear," he told her firmly, correcting her. "John Sutton." He grinned at Elly. "I think what pretty Cedar needs is a glass of champagne, eh, Elly?" He held his free arm for Elly to take, then started forward to the parlor, sweeping Cedar, mute and slightly dazed, along with him.

She darted a glance back at the door, realizing that there was no possibility of pulling away from him and bolting for it. The evening at Madame Blanche's was just getting started, she realized, as the door was once again being opened and another group of men admitted, further swelling the tide that was pushing her toward the parlor. She had little choice but to let it pull her along and wait until there was a moment when she could slip away. Besides, she told herself, as long as she was in the noisy parlor, she was certainly safe enough. It was the prospect of being alone with one of these men that she had to fear.

Sutton was calling out loudly for champagne. Almost before he'd finished his order, the bottle and a half dozen glasses appeared. He patted Cedar's hand while the bottle was being opened and the wine poured, then finally released it as he reached for two glasses.

"Now you drink this, my dear," he told her, handing her one of the glasses. "Doctor's orders. It makes all the little gremlins disappear." He drained his own glass and darted a smile at his two friends and Elly, who were laughing their agreement and sampling the champagne. But when Cedar didn't so much as lift her glass, the smile disappeared. "Go on," he told her. "You'll see. You'll like it."

Cedar shook her head. "I don't drink," she murmured, and started to return the glass to the tray. She thought of what had happened to her the last time she'd drunk alcohol, and her hand began to tremble.

Elly frowned, and edged close to her. "You're insultin' one of Blanche's best customers, Cedar," she whispered. "At least sip it."

"Is there some problem?"

Blanche was dully magnificent, swathed in heavy burgundy colored silk, her red curls carefully arranged, a wealth of jewels decorating her neck, ears, and fingers. But her smile was as warmly sincere as her painted cheeks were natural, and her eyes were hard as she turned them to meet Cedar's.

"Oh, no," Elly quickly interjected. "Cedar's just never had champagne before, that's all." It was obvious she was trying to keep Cedar from getting into trouble with the madame on her first night.

"Oh?" Blanche asked. She smiled again, this time at Cedar alone, and there was a sharp warning, not humor, in the expression. "Well, taste it, Cedar. Mr. Sutton only orders the best."

"I—I don't think I ought to drink," Cedar said. She felt

her cheeks redden as she remembered what the brandy had done to her the day before. "I get tipsy very easily."

"That's the idea," Sutton said, and the three men laughed loudly. He pushed the hand in which Cedar held the glass. "Now drink up, my dear, and we'll begin the evening early tonight."

Cedar could feel the weight of all their eyes on her. She darted a hopeless look toward the door, and then, resigned to the fact that escape was impossible for the moment, she reluctantly raised the glass to her lips.

# Chapter Seven

Cedar brought the glass to her lips and took a small sip of the champagne. It was, she found, far from unpleasant, slightly sweet to the taste, and the bubbles imparted an agreeable tingle. She was pleased when there was none of the fiery rush she recalled the brandy had left in its wake. She decided that champagne was not all that terrible a thing after all. Still, she had no intention of simply downing the whole of the glass. She was not at all sure that the wine's effect would not be more potent than its taste.

She darted a quick look at Sutton and found her efforts did not quite satisfy his expectations.

"You can do better than that," he told her firmly, and he pushed the hand holding the glass back toward her lips.

She drank a bit more, and then smiled hopefully up at him, wondering if she'd finally pleased him. She thought she might be feeling just a bit light-headed, but wasn't sure if she wasn't imagining it. The one thing she knew for certain was that she couldn't afford to lose control of herself as she had the day before when she'd been with Guy Marler.

It was probably the smile more than the progress she made with the wine that placated Sutton, for her glass was still nearly full, but he seemed satisfied. He returned her smile.

"Now that wasn't so bad, was it?" he chided.

Cedar shook her head. "No," she admitted, truthfully enough. "It's quite nice."

Pleased that her customers once again seemed happy, Blanche lost interest. "Enjoy yourselves, gentlemen," she said airily to the three men before she drifted away, intent on insuring that no other impediment to her clients' pleasure existed in her parlor.

Sutton emptied his glass and deposited it on the tray. "Do you dance, Miss Cedar?" he asked.

Before Cedar had the chance to answer, Elly replied for her. "Of course she does, Jonsey," she said, and added a small giggle as she relieved Cedar of her glass. "What sort of a lady doesn't dance?" She nudged Cedar's shoulder, urging her to take the hand Sutton had extended in invitation.

Cedar soon found herself on Sutton's arm, crossing to the far side of the room where Maisy, whose efforts were mostly lost beneath the chatter and the sound of the piano, was valiantly pretending that the man beside her who had placed his hand on her waist was interested in her singing. Several other couples had preceded them to a small cleared area set aside for dancing, and the floor was fairly crowded. This hardly seemed to indispose Sutton, who eagerly wrapped his arms around Cedar.

She found herself enclosed in his grasp, waltzing a bit leadenly to the strains of the music, musing that whatever talents Sutton might have, they certainly didn't lie in the dance.

But he seemed more than content with the ritual, and Cedar didn't protest, even though he held her rather closer and more tightly than she would have wished. If nothing else, his gropingly clumsy dancing precluded conversation and left her a chance to think. She quickly decided that her only chance to get away was by drawing the least possible attention to herself. And that meant that she had no choice, for the while at least, but to be precisely what she was expected to be. A little shy, perhaps, but definitely anxious and willing to please Blanche's customer.

When the music stopped, she looked up at Sutton and offered him what she hoped was a properly enticing smile.

"Another glass of champagne, my dear?" he asked.

She was more pleased than not that he had lost interest in dancing. "If you think it would be all right," she agreed, tilting her head and glancing up at him coquettishly. "I really don't know how much one ought to allow oneself. I shall have to depend upon your judgment."

He seemed pleased enough at the prospect of making the decision for her, and he led her to a couch at the side of the room. One of his companions was no longer there; he had taken to the floor and was dancing with Elly. The other was seated on a facing couch beside a dark-haired, rather florid girl dressed in pink with an excess of dark red ribbons who seemed to hang on his every word. Cedar remembered having seen her at breakfast, but could not remember her name.

At Sutton's order a second bottle of champagne appeared with the same speed as had the first, and along with it glasses of whiskey for the men. Before she knew it, Cedar was seated beside Sutton on the couch, holding a glass to her lips and pretending to be delighted that he was pleased enough with her to put his arm around her and stroke the bare skin of her shoulder.

She found it strange when the two men began to speak heatedly about the rising stock market even as they nuzzled their partners, pausing in their conversation occasionally to press moist lips against the soft flesh beneath an ear or let a hand fall to the smooth skin of a half-exposed breast, but obviously more interested, for the moment at least, in the subject of money than in that of passion.

That situation, however, Cedar knew would not last very long. She deftly deposited her still-half-filled wine glass on the tray, then slid it behind one of the emptied glasses. When there was a pause in the men's conversation, she put her hand on Sutton's.

"I'm sorry," she murmured. She bit her lip, pretending confusion and a bit of embarrassment.

Sutton wasn't entirely pleased with the distraction. The

whiskey, apparently, had made him irascible.

"What is it?" he demanded.

"I . . . I have to excuse myself for a moment," she told him. She motioned toward an empty glass on the tray, pretending it was hers. "All that wine. I'll be right back."

He accepted the explanation and drew back his hand. "Don't be long," he ordered.

Cedar nodded. "Just a moment," she said as she slid away from him and stood. "I promise."

She gave him a last, parting smile, but he was already returning to his conversation, apparently content that matters would progress to their natural conclusion with no further effort on his part. Cedar dismissed him from her thoughts as she crossed the room. Her only real regret, she realized as she darted a glance back to where Elly was energetically dancing with Sutton's friend, was that she had not learned any more about the "Tammany toad" and what he might have had to do with Mary Farren's murder.

As she neared the entrance hall and the front stairs, she realized that she would not be able to simply walk out the front door. More men were arriving, and the porter stood guard there, blocking her exit as effectively as he barred the entry of any unacceptable-looking potential customers. She would have to make her way to the rear of the house, somehow avoid the cook, Addy, and leave by the kitchen door.

She was just turning toward the rear of the house when she was startled by the weight of a hand on her arm.

"I decided to save you a trip and go on up with you."

She felt herself go queasy as she turned to find Sutton behind her. His discussion of the stock market apparently concluded, he seemed ready now to proceed to other diversions.

Panicked, she put her hand to her stomach, grasping for the only excuse that came to mind.

"I'm feeling a bit ill," she told him, and realized it was not all a lie.

"Don't worry," he said, dismissing the objection. "It's just the wine. You'll be fine."

He pushed her forward, toward the stairs and her bedroom.

"Sorry, friend, you'll have to wait your turn. I've already paid for the lady's services."

Cedar didn't need to turn to know it was Guy Marler. It was as if the sound of his voice was imprinted on her memory, never to be forgotten or confused with any other. A wave of relief and pleasure washed over her as she told herself he'd come here, after her, to protect her from any hurt.

She turned to face him and found her relief quickly colored by half a dozen other emotions. Guy grinned at her, then smiled pleasantly at Sutton, by all appearances a genial but stubborn and slightly drunk simpleton. If he'd come to save her, he'd first ingested a good deal of alcohol to prepare himself for that task. He'd come to the bordello for the same reason all the other men had, she realized. She filled with anger at the thought, an anger that was tinged with disgust.

"You've made a mistake," Sutton told him. "The young lady's occupied."

Guy shook his head. "No mistake," he said. "Ask our hostess if you like."

He turned and nodded toward Blanche, who was at that moment approaching with the now silent soprano, Maisy, in tow. The madame immediately began to placate Sutton while Maisy most obligingly wrapped her arms around his free one.

"I'm so sorry, John," Blanche purred, all sweetness now, with no hint of the threatening monarch she'd been to Cedar half an hour before. "You know how it is with a new girl, things get confused. But Maisy was just telling me what a pleasant time you two had last week." She flashed an effusive smile at him as she expertly removed Cedar from his grasp and substituted the smilingly accommodating

110

Maisy. The substitution completed, she nodded quickly to Guy.

As soon as she was freed, Guy put his hand firmly on Cedar's arm and pushed her toward the stairs. She could almost feel Blanche's eyes on her as Guy hurried her up the flight.

When they'd reached the top, she tried to shrug away from his grasp. He held firm.

"Let go of me," she hissed.

He darted a glance down the hall, to where a couple were just leaving one of the bedrooms.

"Be quiet," he whispered sharply, then pushed her against the wall as the couple approached, insuring her silence by pressing his lips to hers.

She struggled with him for a moment, but her protest, she realized, was halfhearted at best. The moment his lips touched hers, she realized it wasn't just the brandy that had made her act the way she had the previous afternoon. It was something far more, and whatever it was, it was a strong and potent force. There was a rush of liquid heat in her veins at the touch of his lips to hers, not so very different from the feeling she'd thought had come from the brandy. The lightheadedness she felt she knew was definitely not caused by her imagination.

Quite against her own better judgment, Cedar found herself kissing him back.

"That's better," he said when he lifted his lips from hers. "Much better."

She realized he no longer looked either as genial or as drunk as he had seemed a moment before, when he'd addressed Sutton. His eyes were disturbingly sharp now, and he was smiling down at her, clearly pleased with himself and the effect he had on her.

The smile infuriated Cedar. She darted a glance at the retreating couple, now midway down the stairs, then pushed angrily against his chest.

"Let me go," she hissed at him.

111

The force of his grasp didn't abate in the least.

"What the hell are you doing here?" he demanded.

Cedar pursed her lips. "I don't suppose I need ask the same question of you," she said tartly. She shrugged her arm again, finally succeeding in making him release her arm. "Anyway, it doesn't matter. I'm leaving."

He shook his head. "Not just yet," he told her. "We have a little searching to do first."

That pronouncement completely confused her. She'd been wrong, she realized, when she'd assumed he'd come to the bordello for the most obvious reason. But it seemed he hadn't come to save her either. She wasn't sure if she felt relieved or not.

"Searching?" she asked.

"Of Mary Farren's room," he told her. He stared down at her with a look that told her he considered that fact self evident. "Unless you've already done that?" he asked in a tone that suggested he doubted she had.

She started. How could she have been so foolish as to overlook such an obvious opportunity, she wondered. She'd been in that room the whole of the afternoon, and it had never occurred to her to search it.

"But there's nothing there," she protested, trying to defend herself from the smugly knowing look she saw in his eyes.

He raised a quizzical brow. "Are you sure of that?"

She had to admit that she wasn't—to herself, at least, if not to him.

"What is there to look for?" she demanded. "The dresser is empty, the stains washed away. There's nothing to find."

He shrugged. "When I see it, I'll know," he told her as he stepped back, releasing her from his hold. "Are you coming?"

She stood for a moment, dull and unsure, almost able to feel his eyes on her. She glanced quickly toward the stairs and thought of escape, telling herself that she certainly had no intention of going into that room alone with him. But

112

she couldn't dismiss the possibility that there was something in there that might have some bearing on the murder, that might help prove her father innocent. She could not be so great a coward as to ignore that possibility and run away like a frightened mouse.

She stalked past him, ignoring his grin, marched to the door, and opened it. He was just behind her, pressing close enough to encourage her to move quickly inside the room. He followed, closing the door firmly behind them.

"Alone again, at last," he said. He smiled, obviously amused with the situation. He reached out for her.

She slipped beyond his reach. "I think not," she told him firmly.

"Think again," he told her. "After all, this is a bordello, and I paid nearly a week's salary for the privilege."

He was grinning, quite enjoying himself, she thought.

"Ask for a refund," she told him.

His smile faded and the humor disappeared from his eyes. "I don't suppose you'd prefer your boorish companion downstairs?" he asked.

"One boor or another," she replied tartly.

"I suppose a whore can't afford to be fussy."

She colored at that and suddenly felt as though she might cry. She had played his whore the day before. No matter how hard she might wish to forget that fact, she knew she couldn't. What was worse, she couldn't even blame what had happened on him. It had been her own fault, and that was a fact she could not escape.

She bit her lower lip, bit it hard, letting the hurt supplant the ache she felt in her heart. But he seemed unaware of what she was feeling. He crossed the room and stood beside the bed, staring at the busy pattern of the paper that covered the wall, completely oblivious to her discomfort.

She watched his back for a long, silent moment, wondering what it was he seemed to think he might find. When he didn't speak, she finally found she couldn't keep still any longer.

113

"How did you know I was here?" she asked.

He continued his inspection, moving slowly as he peered at the wall. He began to tap it gently with his knuckles.

"I didn't," he told her absently.

"But you just said you paid for me."

"I paid for the room, not a particular woman," he replied. "The fact seemed to amuse Blanche, who is, it seems, ever willing to accommodate the paying clientele. She said that if she'd known that a room where a murder had been committed was such a lure, she wouldn't have had the blood washed away. A pleasant idea, don't you think?"

Cedar shivered. The thought was nothing short of sickening.

"Until Blanche pointed you out to me," Guy went on, "I had no idea you had taken up the profession." He finally turned back to face her. "Or am I to assume that you had another motive?"

"You can assume whatever you like," she told him. "I came here looking for something that might help my father."

"Then it's just as well I've saved you from a life of dishonor and degradation."

She swallowed. "Have you?" she asked.

He seemed bewildered by the intensity of her words, of her stare. It's nothing more than a game to him, she told herself, and this is just amusing banter. She turned away.

"Cedar? What is it?"

She shook her head. "Nothing," she said. "This place upsets me."

He accepted that. "Did you find anything?" he asked her, his mind once again on the matter of Mary Farren's murder.

She shook her head. "Not enough. Elly—she's the girl with the room next to this one—she was a friend of Mary Farren's. She made a reference to some Tammany person and something about a land sale and the Pennsylvania Railroad." She suddenly felt defeated.

"Not enough," she admitted.

Guy started at her mention of the railroad, but he hid his reaction well, and Cedar didn't notice. He stared silently at her for a moment longer, then turned back to his inspection of the wall. Still and mute, she watched him for a while, until her patience finally wore itself thin. He'd completed a tour of approximately half the room and was standing at the side of the empty dresser whose scent of chocolate had so intrigued Elly earlier that afternoon.

"What are you looking for?" she demanded finally.

He shrugged. "I don't know," he admitted. "A hidden entrance, something. I suppose it was . . ." He stopped midsentence and knocked several times in the same place. "What could this be?" he mused softly.

"What is it?" Cedar demanded.

"Shh," he said, waving her once again to silence. He knocked several times more, slowly inching his way along the wall.

Intrigued now, Cedar crossed to him. "Have you found something?" she asked.

He grinned, then nodded. "I think so," he replied as he fingered the narrow line where two strips of wallpaper met. He carefully slid his fingers upward, toward the ceiling, then slowly downward, kneeling, finally stopping with his hand near the baseboard. He looked up at her and smiled. "And this, I should say, is it."

With that he pressed his hand against the ornate molding of the baseboard.

There was a soft click, and the wall swung back, revealing a nearly invisible, three-foot-wide door.

Cedar stared at the opening, not quite believing what she saw. Until the panel of wall had swung back, she'd never have known the wall was not solid.

"What's back there?" she asked in a hoarse whisper.

Guy peered into the gloom behind the opening.

"Let's see, shall we?" he suggested.

He lifted the lamp from the dresser and, holding it

115

high so that it cast the most light, pushed the panel back and walked through the opening.

Cedar hesitated for only a moment before she darted after him.

Cedar stood, bewildered, and stared at the interior of the tiny room. It wasn't much larger than a good-sized closet, but it was clear that the space was certainly not used for storage. Save for a single chair that was set facing the wall, it was totally empty. The walls were blank, bare wood. At the far side, a narrow set of stairs led downward into the gloom.

"What is this?" she asked Guy in a hushed tone.

"Here," he said, ignoring her question and handing her the lamp. "Hold this."

She took it, holding it high and watching as he seated himself in the chair. He stared at the blank wall, a look of confusion on his face. After a moment he leaned forward, then whistled softly.

"Well?" she demanded. "Are you going to explain?"

He looked up at her. "I'd say Madame Blanche sells more than one kind of entertainment," he told her. He stood, took back the lamp, and motioned her to the chair.

Confused, but too curious to do anything else, Cedar sat where he had.

"There," he said, putting his hand to a narrow slit in the wall.

Cedar leaned forward and peered at the place where he pointed. She was rewarded with a narrow but clear view of the bed.

She gasped and drew back. "That—that's disgusting," she said.

Guy stepped back and turned to the stairs.

"Shall we see where that leads us?" he suggested.

She stood and, as she did, jarred the chair slightly. Its feet moved against the floor, making a rough scraping sound.

"Be careful," Guy hissed. "Don't make any noise."

She nodded, and followed him down the narrow stairs. Once at their foot, they found themselves in a tiny space, facing another apparently blank wall.

"Now what?" she whispered.

He didn't answer, but knelt as he had upstairs, feeling along the line where the wall met the floor. It took him a moment to find it, but once again he located a latch. Again there was the soft click, and the wall swung back and open.

They found themselves in a large, well-appointed room, furnished with desk and comfortable chairs and a large, decidedly impressive looking safe. When she turned back to face the stairs, Cedar realized that the opening from this room, just like the one from the room above, would be virtually invisible, hidden by the pattern of the paper that covered the walls.

"Madame Blanche's office," Guy whispered.

Cedar didn't think to ask him just how he'd come by that particular piece of information. She was too busy wondering what would happen if they were caught there. She could clearly hear the sounds of music and laughter from the parlor.

"Let's leave," she begged softly.

Guy nodded. "Good idea," he agreed, and he started back to the stairs.

She grabbed his arm. "Not that way," she protested. "Now we know what happened, how the real murderer got into and out of the room. We have to get out of here, go to the police."

He shook his head. "We know how it could have been done," he told her. "But we have no proof." He nodded toward the single door in the room, the one that led to the front parlor. "And I don't think it would be prudent to leave that way, do you?"

She had to agree that he was right. Blanche had watched them climb the stairs. Even if they managed to slip into the

117

parlor, their presence there was sure to be noticed. And she had, Cedar reminded herself, a second customer who was waiting for her attentions.

When Guy waved her back toward the narrow stairs, she didn't make any further protest, but moved as he directed her, climbing the stairs quickly, stopping only to turn back and watch him pull the wall closed behind him.

When they were back in the room with the hidden panel once more shut, Cedar found she couldn't keep herself from staring, searching the apparently solid wall for the narrow crack that would allow a voyeur to watch whatever might take place on the bed.

"Can we leave now?" she asked. The thought of remaining any longer in that room left a sick feeling in the pit of her stomach.

He nodded, and turned to the door.

But before he took a step toward it, there was a firm knock.

"Mr. Marler?"

It was Blanche's voice coming from the hall.

Cedar darted a frightened glance at Guy. He put his fingers to her lips, motioning her to be quiet.

"What is it?" he called.

"I'm afraid you're occupying a very valuable commodity this evening. The time you've paid for is up."

"Take off that dress and get into bed," Guy whispered to Cedar.

"What?"

"Just do it," he ordered.


Afraid not to do as he told her, Cedar pulled clumsily at the buttons of the dress, tearing off two as she fumbled with them, pushing the dress down to her hips and then to the floor. She climbed into the large bed, feeling intimidated by the knowledge of what had undoubtedly occurred there in the past, by the knowledge that her father had lain with a prostitute there.

Guy shed his jacket, shirt, and cravat and kicked off his shoes, letting them all lie where they fell. He strode quickly to the bed darting a disappointed look at Cedar as he hurriedly disordered the bedclothes. He pointed to her hair, motioning to her to remove the hairpins, and she did as he directed, letting it fall in thick folds to her shoulders. Guy gave her a final, critical glance, then crossed the room to the door. He put his hand on the knob, but paused for an instant to rumple his own hair and paste a self-satisfied expression on his face before he pulled the door open.

"I've decided to stay the night," he told Blanche as soon as he was facing her.

Blanche shook her head. "I told you, Mr. Marler. Only an hour. A new girl is always in demand."

"I'll pay," he insisted.

"I'm afraid that will be very expensive," she told him.

"How much?"

Blanche's eyes narrowed. She seemed to be mentally weighing his worth, considering what the contents of his purse might possibly be.

"Twenty-five dollars," she told him.

For an instant Guy thought he hadn't heard correctly. She was asking a fortune, more than most working men, himself included, earned in a month. What's more, it was all the money he'd managed to wrest from Granger Nichols's tight fist for the purpose of bribing potential informants. But he didn't have much choice, he realized. If he didn't pay, he'd be forced to leave Cedar to deal alone with Blanche's other, doubtless less accommodating, clients. He hesitated only a moment.

"All right," he agreed.

He turned back to the room, located his jacket, and removed a leather wallet from the inner breast pocket. He counted out five five-dollar certificates and handed them to the madame, who had followed him into the center of the room. She took the bills, folded them, and placed them neatly in the folds of the heavy fabric that swathed her ample breasts. Then she darted a glance at Cedar, who was cowering down beneath the covers, and smiled.

"You're quite a pleasant surprise to me, Cedar, my dear," she said.

With that she turned on her heel and left the room, pulling the door firmly shut behind her. Guy followed her to the door, then turned the key in the lock.

"What do we do now?" Cedar asked when Guy turned away from the door and faced her.

"I suppose I join you," he told her, nodding toward the bed as he returned his wallet to his jacket pocket and then dropped the jacket on a chair.

She sat up and stared wide-eyed at him. "You aren't serious."

He shrugged, then smiled at her. "I've just bankrupted myself to save you from the unwanted attentions of another man," he told her firmly as he seated himself on the side of the bed and leaned forward to her. "You might show a bit of gratitude. It's not as though we're total strangers, you and I."

Cedar swallowed uncomfortably. His face was only inches from hers, and she could feel his breath, warm against her cheek.

"That was a mistake," she told him, cringing back and away from him. "I'd never drunk brandy before. I'd never drunk anything before. You should have realized. You shouldn't have taken advantage of me."

He didn't move for a while, just sat there, staring at her. Part of him wanted to tell her how he'd felt when he'd returned to her house the previous night, and then again that morning, to find that she wasn't there. It had been painful to him to realize that she was avoiding seeing him, despite the fact that he had told himself that Granger Nichols had doubtless been right, that for his own good he should forget about her, and he'd salved his ego by telling himself that it was a mistake, that as soon as he saw her again he'd make her see what an appealing fellow he really was. But now he could see he was wrong. She really wanted nothing to do with him. He'd been a fool, he told himself, to think it would be otherwise.

He straightened, backing away from her.

"Just as you like, Cedar," he told her.

"And we certainly can't stay here any longer," she went on.

But then he put his fingers against her lips, stilling any further words. She pulled back, about to speak, but he motioned to the far wall, the one with the hidden panel. She put her hand to her lips and stared, wide-eyed and frightened, at the wall, listening for whatever sound had alerted him.

It was there, certainly, a faint scraping sound, the same noise she'd made when she'd inadvertently moved the chair.

Guy once again leaned forward to her. "Don't do anything stupid," he whispered. Then he stood and began to remove his trousers. "Just a minute, Cedar, my sweet," he said in a normal tone. "I assure you there won't be anything else to bother us tonight."

He crossed the room and turned down the lamp. Cedar watched his shadow return to the bed in the darkness, then felt the mattress shift as he climbed in beside her.

She felt trapped. Simply lying in this bed, knowing that her father had not long before come to it to make love to a whore, left her feeling miserable and her memories of her mother soiled. Even worse was the knowledge that someone was sitting on the other side of the wall, his eye to the narrow crack in the wall, waiting, watching.

Guy moved close to her. She put up her hands, trying to push him away.

"They're expecting a show, Cedar," he whispered.

"And they're not going to get one," she hissed back angrily.

"I don't mean that," he said, his tone low but sharp, angry now, too, the prospect obviously as distasteful to him as it was to her. "But I paid twenty-five dollars for this night, and they'll know something's strange if we don't pretend."

He was right, she realized. He'd paid Blanche a whole month's salary, a whore's month's salary, to spend the night with her. And it was more than possible that the man who had killed Mary Farren and arranged matters so that Magnus would be arrested for the murder might be the one who was sitting on the far side of the wall, staring in at them, watching.

She began to tremble. "What's going to happen?" she murmured.

Guy put his arms around her and drew her close.

"Nothing," he told her gently. "Whoever is there will get bored soon and lose interest. And tomorrow morning I'll get you out of here."

Suddenly all the resistance drained away from her. She felt lost now, floundering in waters far beyond her depths. She was alone and frightened and had only Guy to help her. And that thought, almost more than any other, terrified her.

She must have trembled or let a small sob escape her, although she was aware of doing neither, for he put his hand to her chin and tugged it gently until she stared up at him. His eyes were pale sparks in the darkened room.

"Think what you want of me, Cedar," he whispered softly. "But don't be afraid of me. I'm many things, but I am not a rapist."

He pressed his lips to her forehead, then lay back against the pillows, pulling her down to him, holding her close, but gently, without any sign that he expected any greater intimacy.

"Sleep, Cedar," he told her. "I have a feeling tomorrow may not be a simple day."

Cedar knew he was right. There was no such thing in her life any longer as a simple, uncomplicated day that proceeded in its rightful, orderly way. The next day, like those that had just passed, would certainly bring their own terrors to be faced. And her only escape was a few hours sleep she might find between that moment and dawn.

# Chapter Eight

When she woke the next morning, it took Cedar several moments to realize where she was. Still half-asleep, she stared dully up, forcing her eyes to focus in the dim, early-morning light, bewildered by the sight of the unfamiliar ceiling. But she came fully awake when Guy stirred, and she turned and glimpsed a naked, masculine body lying beside her.

She nearly leaped from the bed.

She stood and stared at him for a long moment as the surprise ebbed and she remembered where it was she was and what had happened the night before. Lying among the rumpled bedclothes, he seemed oddly boyish to her, his arm thrown lazily over his head, a stray, blond lock lying across his forehead and brushing his eyebrow. And as the memory returned to her, as she realized how kind he'd been to her when circumstances would certainly have allowed him to behave quite differently the previous night, she began to feel a grudging feeling of warmth for him fill her.

She bewilderedly considered the way her feelings for him shifted from one extreme to the other, from an anger that was so strong it seemed about to choke her, to this tenderness she felt growing within herself as she watched him sleep. No one had ever been able to churn her emotions in this way, and his power to affect her this way puzzled her.

But that mystery paled when she let her thoughts drift to the longing he had roused within her with a simple kiss. Just the memory of it left a pleasant, heated tingle in her veins.

Unfortunately that warmth wasn't enough to fend off the early-morning chill that had invaded the room. The unseasonably warm weather, she realized, had finally ended, and fall all too abruptly arrived. A determined wind pushed at the edge of the curtains and filled the air with a first hint that winter would arrive more quickly than would have seemed possible two days before.

She shivered, and hugged herself, then crossed the room quickly and closed the window. She paused then, and leaned her cheek against the cold of the glass. How had her neat, well-ordered life become so strange? she wondered as she stared at the sky and watched it slowly filled with a rosy dawn light. A church steeple rose, dark and solid, into the air, a comforting symbol of the security and normalcy that had been lost in her life since this whole ugly episode had begun. She watched the first rays of sunlight reflect from the gilt cross, a dazzling shaft of bright clear light, and that, too, seemed symbolic to her, as though God were telling her that if she remained strong and steady, the horrible nightmare would somehow end.

"Penny for your thoughts, miss."

She literally jumped when Guy spoke and put his hand on her naked shoulder. Her reaction left her feeling more than a little foolish. When she straightened and turned to look up at him, she had no idea that her expression still reflected sufficient fear and surprise to make him withdraw his hand and take a step backward.

"I know you're not exactly ready to swoon over me, Cedar," he said, his tone more disappointed than hurt, "but I don't think I'm so repulsive that you'd be willing to jump out the window to avoid my touch."

She looked rather sheepishly up at him. "You surprised

me, that's all," she told him. "I thought you were still asleep."

"Actually, I woke when you left the bed." He grinned, and returned his hand to her shoulder. "Without you there, somehow it no longer seemed nearly so comfortable."

"I think you are vastly overstating my influence," she told him.

He was smiling at her, and he nodded, motioning toward the bed. "We might try it again for a while," he suggested. "Just to see if it's really my imagination, or if it could possibly be something else."

He let his fingers drift slowly down her arm, leaving a small shiver trailing behind them, and a sudden wash of warmth. Cedar felt a thick lurch within herself, and she realized that she very much wanted him to put his arms around her, wanted him to hold her close and assure her that things would indeed work out, that her father would soon be free and they'd be able to forget the whole thing had ever happened. She needed that, she realized, needed the comfort of his arms and words of assurance.

And for some unaccountable reason, even beyond her need for comfort at that moment, she wished he would kiss her. Some part deep inside her reminded her of how he'd made her feel and cried out to her that she wanted to feel that way again.

She turned her eyes to the bed, and as she did she caught a glimpse of the wall that concealed the hidden opening. At the sight of it, the heat Guy's touch had generated disappeared suddenly, and she felt cold again, and completely revolted by the thought. Whoever had been there the previous night, hiding in that small space on the other side of the wall and watching them, was surely long gone by now. Still, the realization that someone had been there was more than enough to chase away any remote thought she might have had of honoring his request, even

126

of allowing herself the comfort of his arms around her.

She stepped back from him, turning away as she did and so not noticing the look of hurt that crept into his eyes when she removed herself. She stepped back, not wanting to allow herself to remain too accessible to his touch.

"I'll be glad to be away from this place," she murmured.

Guy shrugged away the dull ball of hurt he felt at the realization that she found even his touch unpleasant. He wondered why it bothered him as much as it did, wondered why he cared. He'd dealt with women's rejection in the past, not exactly cheerfully, but with the realization that there were a goodly number of other alternatives, and many who would welcome his attentions. But this time the hurt of rejection dug deep inside him. Whatever the reason, he quickly realized the feeling would not disappear simply because he wanted it to.

"You're probably right," he found himself saying as he began gathering up the clothing he had so hastily cast off the previous night. "If we're going to get you out of here, we should do it before the whole of the house is awake. I think it would be best to avoid as many of Blanche's muscular employees as possible. I'm not sure I'm exactly fit to fight the whole lot of them, even for you."

While he busied himself pulling on his trousers, she made her way to the wardrobe and removed her own dress, the dark blue she'd worn the day before when she'd arrived. Somehow that seemed months before, and the person she had been then a child compared to the way she felt at that moment.

She turned and faced Guy, and found that he hadn't begun dressing as she'd thought, but was standing, simply staring at her, his trousers in his hand. There was something in his eyes, she thought, a hint of regret and longing, and for a moment she wished she hadn't pulled away from, wished he would say something loving and hold out his arms to her. But when she looked again, whatever it was she had seen was gone and she could only wonder if it had ever been there. He was staring at her with nothing more than amused lechery.

"Still," he said, and nodded toward the bed, "it does seem a waste."

She scowled. "And this *is* a whorehouse, after all," she added, sure that was what he was thinking.

Again, the lecherous grin. "My thought precisely," he said.

"Why doesn't that surprise me?" she asked tartly.

"Just the natural progression, I suppose," he suggested. "You, me, alone in a room with a bed . . ."

"A shame," she agreed tersely, "that you have to leave."

She turned away from him and began to pull on her dress, wondering why she felt so angry at that moment. She nearly tore the seam as she pushed her sleeve through the arm hole.

Guy's grin disappeared. "*We* have to leave," he corrected.

She shook her head. "Not just yet," she told him. "I want to see if I can find out something more about Mary Farren's 'Tammany toad.' "

"I think last night overinflated your sense of adventure, Cedar," he told her. "Might I remind you that you're not exactly experienced in the fine art of investigating murders?"

Once again Cedar felt one of those sharp shifts of feeling that so puzzled her. He had no right to patronize her, she found herself fuming silently. She leveled an angry glare at him, wondering even as she did how he managed to infuriate her so easily.

"And might I remind you that you were the one who said what we found last night proves nothing, that we need something more than just a supposition of how it might have been done," she retorted. "We have to find out who Mary Farren's Tammany customer was. For all we know, it could have been Tweed himself."

128

"Even if it was, it still proves nothing," Guy told her.

"But at least it tells us where to look," she countered.

Guy was momentarily silent. She was right, of course. Without finding another man with a motive, another reason for Mary Farren's death, Magnus would be left to bear the burden of guilt for the murder. Still, the thought of leaving Cedar alone in the bordello sickened him.

"You can't stay here any longer," he told her as he pulled on his trousers. "Or need I explain to you what would have happened to you last night if I hadn't happened along? What would have happened if I hadn't bankrupted myself to stay here with you?"

"Are you really concerned, or are you simply asking me to show my appreciation in a more than verbal manner?" she demanded.

He dropped the shirt he was lifting from the floor, his interest in it lost, paled by her challenge. He crossed the room to her, put his hands on her shoulders—holding her firmly enough to make her cringe slightly—and stared into her eyes.

"And if I did?" he asked. He lowered his face until his lips were inches from hers. "What if I demanded what I've already paid for?"

"Then you can consider what happened the day before yesterday as payment on account," she hissed.

He felt her words like a hard blow in his stomach. He'd thought of little else but her since the first moment he'd seen her. That fact did not especially please him, but he was not about to pretend it wasn't so. The realization that she had absolutely no interest except to buy his help in freeing her father generated a gut wrenching hurt inside him.

"Damn you," he muttered. "Twenty-four hours in a whorehouse and you already think like a whore."

"Why are you so angry?" she asked, confused by what she saw in his expression and what she heard in his voice.

129

Then, misinterpreting his anger, she asked, "Could it possibly irk you that I might be able to discover something the great Guy Marler might have missed?"

"I'm not angry," he said. But he was, he realized, even if he wasn't sure why. It certainly wasn't jealousy, at least not the kind she suggested it might be. "You're playing a very rough game, Cedar," he warned her. "And you don't have the slightest idea what you're getting into."

"Perhaps you'd like to explain the rules," she suggested.

"Don't be a fool," he replied. "There are no rules. Murderers don't follow rules."

His words and his tone frightened her, more than she wanted to think about. She felt herself go weak inside, and the bravado she'd felt only a moment before disappeared completely.

"I'll be careful," she said, softly now, as she stared up at him. "But I can't leave without trying just once more."

"You're determined?" he asked.

She nodded. "Yes."

He let his hands drop away from her shoulders. He couldn't force her to leave. If he tried to take her away by force, he had no doubt but that he'd be stopped before he got her to the stairs. In many ways a bordello was more secure than the Bank of New York.

"Be home before dark," he warned her.

She was about to say that he wasn't her father, that he had no right to order her about. But she didn't. It wasn't anger she had seen in his eyes, she realized now, but fear for her safety.

"I will," she agreed.

He turned away, found his shirt again, and slipped it on.

"If you don't, I'm not sure I can help you here," he told her, trying to make himself sound matter-of-fact and disinterested, and not quite succeeding.

He was, in fact, sure he couldn't help her once he'd left

the house. Unless he managed somehow to squeeze some money out of Granger Nichols's discretionary funds, he mused as he pulled on his boots, the only thing he'd get for his efforts, were he to try to enter Madame Blanche's establishment again, would be an unpleasant bout with the bruiser who guarded the door and with one or two of his friends. And without evidence of a crime, he couldn't even persuade his friend at the police department, Sergeant Shehan, to forcibly enter the police commissioner's favorite bordello.

"I promise," Cedar assured him. "I'll leave by noon."

He looked at her and shook his head. "You're a fool," he told her firmly. "You can't do your father any good here."

Cedar's expression hardened. She had already made her decision and had absolutely no intention of allowing him to dissuade her.

"At any rate, I intend to try."

"Stubborn, too," Guy muttered as he lifted his jacket from where he'd left it on a chair and swung it over his shoulder. He stared at her and his blue eyes grew steely. "You are not only argumentative and completely contrary, you are by far the most stubborn woman I have ever had the unfortunate experience of meeting."

Cedar couldn't keep from smiling.

"Thank you, Mr. Marler," she intoned sweetly.

He considered her rather smug expression for a long moment, then, without allowing her a chance to protest, put his arm around her and pulled her close. He kissed her, hard, on the lips, lingering a second at the end, letting his lips soften just a bit.

When he released her, Cedar realized she felt slightly dazed—and decidedly confused.

"Why did you do that?" she asked in a bewildered whisper.

"It was a reminder," Guy told her. "We have a debt to settle. I don't intend to forget it. And I don't intend to let

131

you forget it either."

With that he turned and crossed to the door, leaving Cedar to stand staring numbly at the closed door after he'd disappeared.

Impatient to be doing something, Cedar struggled unsuccessfully to keep still and silent in her room for the next few hours. It was hard waiting until it was full morning before she attempted to go to Elly's room, even though she knew it would be useless to try to rouse her any earlier. She tried to occupy herself, removing her hastily donned dress and washing with the cold water she poured from the jug into the basin on the stand in the far corner of the room. She dressed once again, then carefully combed and arranged her hair in a sedately school marmish bun at the nape of her neck. There was something about her environment that made her want to hide her light under any available basket.

She spent some time finding the buttons that she'd inadvertently torn off the dress she'd worn the night before, and then some time more carefully sewing them back on. She shook out the dress, inspecting it for any other damage she might have done it, then folded it neatly and set it on a chair. That done, she set about making the bed, smoothing the sheets with unnecessary care, tucking in the ends, and making careful, square corners at the foot.

Unable to think of any further tasks with which to occupy herself, she finally went and stood by the window, idly watching the traffic in the street below.

Finally, after what seemed a nearly endless morning, when she saw that the sun shone bright enough to glint off the cobblestones on the sidewalk, Cedar decided it had grown late enough to suit her purposes. She gathered up the dress Elly had loaned her and stepped out into the silent hallway.

The whole of the house seemed asleep still, although Cedar did think she heard the chink of cutlery from the dining room below. She walked carefully along the hall to Elly's room, not wanting to rouse any of the others if she could avoid doing so. When she reached the door to Elly's room, she knocked softly and put her hand to the knob. When she turned it, she found the door was unlocked.

She pushed the door open carefully, not wanting to cause a stir in the event that Elly was not alone. She peeked in, completely unsure of what she might find.

Although the room was in decided disarray, Cedar saw only one head on the pillows. She stepped in, looking about first to make certain Elly was indeed alone, then closed the door gently behind her. She walked over to the bed and put her hand on Elly's shoulder.

She was greeted with a grumpy growl.

"Good morning, sleepyhead. Does everyone in this place spend the whole of the daylight hours asleep?"

Elly rubbed her eyes, then pushed herself up to a sitting position.

"Good Lord, what time is it?" Elly asked after a yawn and a stretch.

"Nearly noon, I should think," Cedar replied.

Elly's eyes narrowed and she stared up at her.

"Are you always so abysmally lively in the mornin'?" she demanded.

Cedar laughed. "Yes," she admitted.

Elly put her hands in front of her mouth and yawned again.

"Just my luck," she muttered. "Make a new friend, and then find she has simply disgustin' habits." She groaned and rubbed her eyes with the heels of her hands.

Cedar laughed again. "I brought back your dress," she said, and she placed it neatly on the only chair that was not already otherwise littered.

"Oh, I thought I told you, you could keep that," Elly

said as she gathered the pillows together, plumped them with a lazy stroke of her hand, and then leaned comfortably back against the pile.

"Oh, I couldn't," Cedar told her. She glanced at the dress, remembered how effectively it had displayed her assets, and felt a slight blush creep into her cheeks.

Elly didn't notice. "I guess you'll be wantin' things you pick out yourself," she mused. "I can't say as I blame you. Hand-me-downs are for poor children," she added in a tone that implied she'd been forced to wear her share.

"I'm afraid I tore off a few of the buttons last night," Cedar told her, "but I sewed them back on."

Elly giggled. "So your gentleman caller last night wasn't as drunk as he looked," she said. Another giggle. "I thought he was terribly handsome."

Her reference to Madame Blanche's customers as gentleman callers surprised Cedar. It was the sort of old-fashioned term her Aunt Felicia was in the habit of using, and conjured up images of sitting on a porch swing and sipping glasses of lemonade. It certainly seemed strange to Cedar in the setting of a whorehouse.

"I suppose he was," Cedar admitted, not at all liking the direction the conversation was taking. She'd come looking for information, not an unsolicited testimonial to Guy Marler's good looks. "I thought we might go shopping this afternoon," she ventured. "You mentioned a dressmaker yesterday. Remember?"

Elly was suddenly completely attentive.

"You have money?" she asked. A sly gleam shone from her eyes. "After payin' for the whole night, he gave you money?"

Cedar swallowed the uncomfortable lump that suddenly filled her throat, and nodded. "Yes," she lied.

"Oh, won't Maisy be jealous," Elly crowed. "First John Sutton takes a likin' to you, and now this. I couldn't be more delighted."

134

"I take it Maisy isn't your favorite?" Cedar asked.

Elly shrugged. "Oh, she's all right, I s'pose. It's only that lately she's been actin' like she's visitin' royalty, ever since Jonsey gave her a diamond bracelet last month. It was really a very small diamond, but she wouldn't hear any of that. Then, last night, when she saw him goin' upstairs with you, she was fit to be tied. If Blanche hadn't had that other one waitin' for your time, there would have been all hell around here today."

She smiled brightly at Cedar as she pushed away the covers and swung her legs out of bed. Apparently the prospect of someone besides Maisy doing a bit of crowing appealed to her immensely.

"It wasn't so very much money," Cedar told her. "I just thought it might be fun to go to the dressmaker's." She watched Elly cross the room to the washstand, pour some water into the bowl, and splash it on her face. It's now or never, she thought, and then went on before she had the time to consider that posing the question might reveal more about her than she wanted revealed. "It's not like he has a fortune, not like that Tammany man you mentioned yesterday, the one who called on the poor girl who had my room before me."

Elly groped for her towel and then turned a bewildered glance to Cedar before she wiped away the drips that fell from her chin.

"Oh," she said after a moment's hesitation as she thought back, "you mean Mary's toad. He didn't have a fortune. He just boasted to her that he was goin' to make one soon." She finished drying her face, dropped the towel half in, half out of the bowl of water, then turned to the mirror and lifted her brush to her hair.

Cedar pretended only passing interest.

"I didn't know that politics were so lucrative," she said.

"It wasn't politics he was goin' to make his money with," Elly replied. "At least not directly. Somethin' about the

Pennsylvania Railroad, about buyin' up land cheap and then sellin' it for a fortune. I really can't remember."

"Who was he?" Cedar asked.

Elly put down the brush and turned to face her, for the first time a hint of suspicion sneaking into her expression.

"Why are you so interested?" she demanded.

Oh, God, why did I ask like that? Cedar thought, terrified that she'd put Elly off. She shrugged.

"I don't know," she murmured. "In case he comes back. I'd like to get to know a man with a fortune."

The explanation seemed to satisfy Elly. She turned back to the mirror and once again lifted her brush.

"Well, aren't you just learnin' real fast, now?" she said. " 'Fraid we'll all have to take our chances, though," she went on. "Mary never mentioned a name, and I got the feelin' he only came a few times. It was probably just talk, anyway. You know how men talk when they're tryin' to impress a woman."

"I suppose so," Cedar agreed.

A gong sounded from the floor below. At the sound of it Elly immediately dropped her brush and reached for the robe that lay across a chair.

"Thank the good Lord," she said. "Breakfast. I'm starvin'." She glanced up at Cedar and grinned knowingly as she pulled on the robe and tied the ribbons at neck and waist. "After last night, you must be, too."

"You go on down," Cedar told her as she followed Elly to the door. "I'll be there in a moment." They walked out into the hall.

"You forget somethin'?" Elly asked as she pulled the door closed behind them.

"I . . . I just want to comb my hair," Cedar murmured, and she started back along the hall toward the door to her own room.

"Your hair is just fine," Elly called after her. "Dull lookin', but just fine."

When Cedar didn't turn back, but continued instead on down the hall, Elly shrugged and turned toward the stairs. She, at least, had no intention of missing the first, and most important, meal of the day.

Once back inside her room, Cedar went to the wardrobe and removed her coat, purse, and bonnet. She would have to wait a few moments, she told herself as she pulled on her coat and arranged her bonnet, for she could hear movement in the hallway and knew the others would be going down to breakfast just as Elly had.

She turned and scanned the room one last time, feeling oddly disjointed in it now, realizing that she had learned more about her father in the few hours she'd spent in it than she had in a whole lifetime in their own house. Not all those revelations were ones she would have wished to have experienced had she had the choice, she thought, especially those that concerned Mary Farren.

More than that, she realized, she'd learned a good number of things about Guy Marler as well. And perhaps she'd even made a few discoveries about herself, she mused. Madame Blanche's establishment seemed to have had the effect of opening her eyes to a great many things she might never have otherwise seen.

As she did a slow survey of the room, Cedar's eyes lit on the portion of wall that hid the secret panel. Rather than the wave of revulsion she'd felt the night before when she'd let herself consider what lay behind the wall, she now found herself filling with curiosity and the realization that she had the opportunity to satisfy at least a part of it. For Blanche's office, she knew, was at the other end of the stairs behind that wall. And chances were more than likely that Blanche had played at least a passive part in Mary Farren's murder. Whoever had done the actual killing would have to have gained

137

access to those steps through that office, and Blanche could not possibly have remained ignorant of that fact.

There was the possibility, no matter how slight, that there might be some evidence left in that office, something that might point to the identity of Mary Farren's "Tammany toad." However slim that chance, Cedar knew she could not leave Madame Blanche's house without searching that office.

Her mind made up, she crossed the room quickly before she had the chance to change it. She knelt and began to grope along the baseboard, cursing her own stupidity for not having watched more carefully when Guy had found the latch. It took her several minutes of searching, but her fingers finally located the narrow metal latch. She pulled it, and the panel of wall swung back. Cedar stepped through the opening, pushing the panel back into place behind her. Once inside the bare little room, she stood still for a long moment, letting her eyes accustom themselves to the near blackness. Then, moving carefully, keeping her hands on the wall and taking care to make as little noise as possible, she slowly edged her way to the stairs.

There was almost no light at all in the enclosed space, and she was forced to move very slowly to keep herself from falling, carefully finding the edge of each step with her foot before she stepped down. It was several minutes before she finally reached the bottom of the flight.

For an instant she was stricken by a feeling of panic, the fear of being in a strange, enclosed place in the near-total darkness. She could feel the walls surrounding her, almost as if they were closing in on her, trapping her. She found herself gasping for air. Her heart seemed to be beating against the wall of her chest. She had the terrifying feeling of being locked up alive in a tomb, the feeling that she could not breathe and would surely die there.

Somehow she managed to still the rising panic, however. She reminded herself that she'd been there only hours before, that there was nothing lurking in the tiny space, nothing hiding in the darkness that could hurt her except her own fear. She forced herself to kneel down and go about the task of finding the latch that would release her.

She was surprised at how quickly her fingers found the narrow metal strip. Once she had touched it, the last of the feeling of panic disappeared. Her breathing returned to normal, and the pounding in her chest faded.

She waited an instant longer, her ear to the wall, assuring herself that there was no noise in the room beyond, no sound that would mean someone was in the office. Finally satisfied that it was empty and Blanche gone to the dining room with the rest, she pulled the metal latch and felt the wall swing back beneath her hands. A narrow line of light brightened the darkness.

She moved into the room slowly, listening for the normal clamor of female voices at the breakfast table, assuring herself that there was no sound that might indicate someone was coming. She pushed the section of wall closed behind her and crossed the room to the desk.

For a moment she stood and simply stared at it. The surface of the desk was covered with papers, but they were in neat, orderly piles. She reminded herself that the day before, she'd decided Blanche was a good business woman. One glance at the desk confirmed that evaluation.

She had, she realized, absolutely no idea what she might be looking for. Something to do with Tweed and Tammany, she told herself, something to do with the purchase of land.

She put her hand to the pile of papers in the furthest corner of the desk. It consisted, she immediately saw, of nothing more interesting than butcher's and grocer's bills. The more mundane matters of running a bordello, it seemed, did not differ substantially from that of running any other household.

She returned the bills and went on to the next pile.

More bills, she found—dressmakers, milliners, laundresses—the list was enormous. Cedar flipped through them, then turned her attention instead to the large black ledger that lay in the center of the desk. She lifted it and pulled it open.

She quickly realized that Blanche kept a list of her more notable customers. They included quite a few names that Cedar immediately recognized. Among others there was the New York City chief of police, a state senator, several well-known financiers, and a good number of ward leaders and other politicians. She felt an unpleasant lurch when she saw that her father was also listed. And then one of satisfaction when she saw that William Marcy Tweed's name was there as well.

But knowing that Tweed was one of Madame Blanche's customers did not tie him to Mary Farren's murder. She quickly turned the pages of the ledger, looking for something else.

"My, aren't we busy this morning?"

Cedar's hands turned to ice. Suddenly numbed, she let the ledger fall back onto the desk.

She turned to find Blanche in the doorway, staring at her. There was no question but that she had seen Cedar looking through the ledger, for there was anger and the promise of punishment in her piercing, dark eyes.

# Chapter Nine

Cedar felt her heart leap into her throat. Her hands began to shake and she had to force them down to her sides to hold them still.

"I—I was looking for the dining room and wandered in here by mistake," she said. The lie sounded completely improbable, even in her own ears, and she hurried on, hoping a flurry of words might cloud the fact that there was very little logic in her explanation. "I drank a little too much champagne last night. It left me a bit confused—"

"Not so confused as that," Blanche interrupted, waving Cedar to silence. "Do you really consider me so great a fool as to believe that you were going to breakfast dressed in your coat, and mistook my desk for the dining room table?" Her eyes narrowed and she stared at Cedar, searching for a more acceptable answer to her question. "You were looking for something," she said flatly. "What is it?"

"I was just curious," Cedar insisted. "When I came in and saw the desk and realized where I was, and I thought of all the money that man paid last night . . ."

Blanche smiled. "And you thought you'd look through my books, just to get an idea of how much I make from the hard work you poor girls put yourselves to." She shook her head. "No, I don't believe that, either. You were looking for something. Now why don't you tell me just what it is you were looking for? Money? That's it, isn't it? You were thinking of stealing from me?" There was a hint of surprise in her tone, as though the possibility of one of her own committing so heinous a crime was simply unthinkable to Blanche.

Cedar shook her head and stared silently back at the madame. If I let her think I'm a thief, she thought, at worst she'll throw me out. She won't really hurt me.

Blanche waited for an answer to her question, saying nothing, watching Cedar grow more and more uncomfortable. After a few moments, however, apparently bored with the silence, she seated herself in her desk chair and stared up at Cedar.

"This puts me in an unpleasant position," she said thoughtfully. "I find you here, in my office, where you don't belong. You are looking through my papers, and you are dressed for the street. I don't know what you're after, but I can only assume you've come here with the intention of stealing from me and then running away." She tapped her fingers on the surface of the desk, betraying her own impatience and the anger that lie beneath her apparently still-calm demeanor. "I believe I told you yesterday what I think of girls who steal from my clients," she said, her tone suddenly hard and threatening. "I'm even less sympathetic to anyone who tries to steal from me."

Cedar swallowed uncomfortably. "I haven't stolen anything," she insisted. "I—I just decided I didn't like it here, that's all. I didn't like those men last night. I just want to leave."

"And so you came in here to write me a touching little note of farewell, eh?" Blanche shrugged. "Why don't I believe you?" She pointed to Cedar's purse. "Empty it," she ordered.

Cedar breathed a deep sigh of relief. She'll see nothing belongs to her, she told herself, and then she'll let me go. Not thinking any further than that, she quickly pulled her purse from her arm, pulled open the drawstring closure, and dumped the contents on the desk.

Blanche poked through the small heap of Cedar's belongings, idly fingering the comb, the lace handkerchief, the latchkey, the locket, then opening the change purse to find it contained about a dollar and a half in small coins.

"You, see?" Cedar told her, reaching forward to sweep the pile back into her purse. "There's nothing of yours there."

"Not quite so quickly," Blanche snapped as she grabbed Cedar's wrist and held her hand down on the surface of the desk. She pushed Cedar's hand back roughly, and returned her attention to the contents of the purse. "Innocent enough looking," Blanche said as she casually ran her fingers over the small square of white linen trimmed with lace. "But perplexing, too." She lifted the latchkey and held it up in front of Cedar's face. "I find myself wondering why someone who claims to have no place to go has one of these," she said. "You do see my point?"

Cedar fixed her eyes on the key. "It's from the place where we used to live," she said slowly. "I never gave it back to the landlord when we had to leave."

Blanche dropped the key back onto the desk. It landed with a small clatter.

"So you could go back and steal from the next tenant?" she suggested.

"No," Cedar replied. "A memento. From another lifetime. To remember the way things were. That's all."

Blanche's expression said quite plainly that she was not convinced. "You must understand that I can't allow a thief to simply walk out of here," she told Cedar slowly. "If I do, the others might think they might be able to succeed where you failed. Do you understand what I'm saying?"

Cedar nodded. She didn't need the explanation, only the tone of threat in Blanche's voice to make her understand what the madame was telling her.

"I didn't come here to steal," she insisted softly.

But Blanche was now busily inspecting Cedar's handkerchief, and seemed to find it far more interesting than Cedar's words. She shook out the square and spread it out on the surface of the desk, staring at the initials that were embroidered in the corner.

"*CR*," she said thoughtfully. "You told me your name was Ashton." She looked up at Cedar. "Unless things have changed markedly since I was in school, Ashton doesn't begin with an *R*."

"It wasn't mine," Cedar said. She was not accustomed to lying, and the words felt awkward even as she spoke them. It was becoming harder and harder for her to think of some sort of explanation for Blanche's questions. "It belonged to a friend."

"And you stole it?" Blanche suggested.

"No, she gave it to me," Cedar insisted.

"Along with this?" Blanche asked, and lifted the locket. The initials were on it, too, a tiny *CR* engraved on the back in flowery letters. "Gold. Valuable, I should think. I don't suppose your friend just gave this to you, too?"

Cedar let her eyes follow the movement of the locket swinging gently from the chain as Blanche held it up. She'd been such a fool not to return to the house after she'd seen her father in prison the day before. The key, the handkerchief, and most especially the locket — she ought to have left those things at home, where they could not possibly incriminate her. She'd been a fool to come here with them still in her possession.

She realized that Blanche was watching her, realized, suddenly, that the madame certainly knew she was lying, probably had known it from the start. She bit her lower lip, frightened now, wondering what Blanche would do to her. Her thoughts drifted to what she knew had happened to Mary Farren, and her blood ran cold with fear.

Blanche was still staring at her, still holding up the gold locket.

"Let's just open this locket, shall we?" Blanche suggested and she smiled up at the panic she saw in Cedar's eyes.

Terrified now, Cedar lunged forward, reaching for the locket, hoping to wrest it from Blanche's hand. But the madame sensed her charge even before it was started, quickly pulling back and out of the range of her grasp. The locket still securely in her hold, Blanche raised her hands and heaved at Cedar's chest, pushing her back, sending her sprawling on the floor.

"Michael!" Blanche cried out, the sound of her voice not very loud, but extremely angry.

Before Cedar could scramble back to her feet, she found herself staring up into the face of Michael McNaughton, the man whom her father opposed in the upcoming election for commissioner.

"Do you know her?"

McNaughton, seated comfortably on Blanche's couch, stared at Cedar thoughtfully. His hair was uncombed, and he was dressed in rumpled shirt sleeves. It was obvious that he was not long out of bed, Blanche's bed, presumably, given the fact that he had entered from the rear of the house, from Blanche's private apartment.

Cedar found herself wondering what bearing that fact might have had on Mary Farren's murder and her father's arrest. McNaughton close to the madame of the bordello where Magnus had come to ease his loneliness. Tweed one of her noteworthy customers. Circumstances, Cedar realized, and Boss Tweed had insured Magnus would never win the election.

She wished she had time to think, wished she could concentrate on something other than the cold look in Blanche's eyes and the hard, ungiving grip of the hands that held her still.

145

After a long moment's consideration, McNaughton shook his head.

"She looks familiar, but I can't place her," he said.

Cedar tried to move, but the black porter who had so efficiently guarded the door the evening before was holding her arms back, his grasp hurting her just enough to keep her from really struggling to free herself. She realized it was useless to try to escape his grasp, useless even to make the effort to defy Blanche.

The madame held up the locket. "I wonder if this might not give us a clue," she said before she pressed the tiny lock and opened the small, gold oval.

"Well?" McNaughton asked after a moment of silence as Blanche inspected the two pictures inside.

Blanche took one last look at the tiny face that stared up at her from the picture, and then turned her glance at Cedar. "I should have seen the resemblance," she said. She handed the locket to McNaughton. "Here. You look." Then she smiled at Cedar. "I don't suppose your real last name would be Rushton, would it?" she asked.

Cedar made a frightened effort to free herself, but it was only too clear that fighting the porter's grasp was as useful as tugging at a thick iron chain. When he pulled her arms back sharply, she uttered a small cry of pain and ceased to struggle any further.

"Rushton's daughter?" McNaughton inspected the picture and then scowled. "What the hell is she doing here?" he muttered angrily.

"Why don't we ask her?" Blanche suggested. "Well?" she demanded of Cedar. "What are you doing here, Cedar? It is Cedar, isn't it, or was that a lie as well?"

Once again Cedar found her arms being pulled painfully back, this time not to warn her, but to encourage her to answer.

"I came to find out who was really responsible for the murder they've charged my father with," she said. The hold on her arms loosened, not much, but enough to relieve the sharp pain, letting it ebb to a dull ache.

"Most commendable," Blanche said with a smile. "Giving up your precious chastity to save your father's good name."

McNaughton looked pained. "Now what do we do?" he hissed at Blanche.

"That depends on Miss Rushton," Blanche said. She took the locket back from McNaughton and stared thoughtfully at the pictures one last time. Her eyes grew sharp when she looked up at Cedar, snapping the locket shut and dropping it back to the small heap on the desk. "How did you get into this room?" she demanded.

Cedar swallowed uncomfortably. She nodded toward the door from the parlor. "How else?"

Blanche looked up at the porter. "Willy?" she asked.

The black man shook his head slowly. "No, ma'am," he said. "I was sweepin' up in there all mornin', and I didn't see her."

"Care to offer some other answer, Cedar?" Blanche asked, and as she did she nodded to Willy.

Cedar cried out in pain as the porter pulled her arms back again, this time more sharply than before. It felt as if her arms were being torn from their sockets.

"Enough, Willy," Blanche said.

The pain ebbed as he released his hold. Cedar gasped for air, then looked at Blanche's eyes, searching for a hint of compassion in them and finding none. They're going to kill me, she thought. Just like they killed Mary Farren.

"Shall I ask you again, Cedar?" Blanche pressed. "How did you get into this room?"

Cry out, a voice inside Cedar told her. Someone will hear you. Someone will come. But even as the thought occurred to her, Blanche smiled and shook her head.

"Scream if you like. No one but the people in this house will hear you, and believe me, Cedar, not one will lift a finger to help you. Now I asked you a question, and I expect an answer. How did you get into this room this morning?"

Beaten, and sure that Blanche already knew the answer to her own question in any event, Cedar nodded toward the panel of wall that hid the secret opening.

"Through there," she murmured.

Blanche paced slowly to the side of the room, then turned and started toward the other, deep in thought. McNaughton watched her, his expression becoming more and more irritated as she continued pacing and said nothing. Finally he struck the surface of the desk, and Blanche turned back and faced him.

"She knows about the passage," he hissed. "We have to get rid of her."

Cedar's eyes grew bright and round. But somehow she managed to keep from giving up to the panic that threatened to control her.

"People know I'm here," she said. "They'll come looking for me if they don't hear from me soon. They'll know if something happens to me. If you don't let me leave now, they'll know you're responsible, just as they'll know about the land sale and Mary Farren's murder."

McNaughton's head snapped back sharply, and now it was his turn to feel the grip of panic. But Blanche was not quite so easily stunned as was he.

"What land sale?" she demanded sharply.

Cedar drew in her breath sharply. She'd made a mistake, she realized, a very costly mistake.

"I don't know," she said.

"You said it," Blanche countered. "What land sale?"

Again she saw Blanche nod to Willy, and she braced herself for the pain. But no amount of preparation could equip her to deal with the wave of pain that engulfed her. She heard a scream and dully realized she had let it escape her.

148

"What land sale?" Blanche asked again when the pain had subsided and Cedar was shakily gasping for breath. "Or shall Willy offer a bit more encouragement?"

Beaten, Cedar shook her head.

"It was something someone said Mary Farren mentioned," she gasped in reply. "That's all. Something someone said."

She wouldn't settle for that, and Cedar knew it. Something someone said. Who said? What else? But there wasn't anything else, and Cedar knew that she couldn't tell Blanche it had been Elly. After all the stupid things she'd done so far, she could not be so foolish as to give up the one friend she might have in this place.

As though she had been reading Cedar's mind, Blanche demanded, "Who said?"

Cedar shook her head. "I don't remember," she said. Then, when Willy pulled her arm back, she shouted it again, this time through the pain. "I don't remember!"

She gasped for air when Willy released his hold, and stared back at Blanche, wondering why she'd been so great a fool as to think herself equipped to deal with these people. Why? she thought. Why hadn't she listened to Guy, why hadn't she left with him early that morning?

Apparently neither McNaughton nor Blanche was entirely convinced with her explanation.

"What else?" he shouted at Cedar. He pushed himself to his feet and crossed the room to where Willy was holding her. He put his hand on her chin, his fingers pressing painfully into her cheeks, and brought his face close to hers. "What else do you know?"

Cedar tried to pull her head back but was stopped by the thick wall of the porter's chest.

"Nothing else," she sobbed softly. "I don't know anything else."

McNaughton turned to Blanche. "I don't believe her," he said.

"I'm not sure I do, either," the madame agreed, "although Willy does have a way of making people tell the truth."

"We have to get rid of her," McNaughton insisted.

"Not without talking to him first," Blanche told him sharply. "And not here, in any case. If they come here, looking for her . . ."

"It's a lie," McNaughton told her. "Just another of her lies. No one knows she's here."

"That is not a chance I'm willing to take," Blanche said. She leveled a look of disgust at McNaughton. "I'm the one with the most to lose here. Have you any idea how much this place brings in a year? I'm not giving it up because you've lost your nerve. Whatever you do with her, you do it someplace away from here."

"We can't just let her go," McNaughton insisted. "We don't know how much she knows."

"Like I just told you," she replied. "We put her someplace safe, and we talk to him. We let him decide. Then, whatever happens, it'll be on his hands, not ours." She nodded toward Willy. "Put her in the basement for the time being," she directed. "And bring Elly in here. The two of them were very friendly yesterday. It would be interesting to know just what they may have talked about."

"It wasn't Elly," Cedar objected. "I don't remember who it was, but it wasn't—"

Her words were lost as Willy tugged at her arms, urging her to move toward the door. One more wave of pain and then Willy didn't have to urge her very hard, for she knew she had no chance to escape, and the thought of the hurt returning made her quick to move as he directed her.

But as she stumbled along the bare back corridor toward the basement stairs, Cedar realized that Blanche and McNaughton were most definitely responsible for Mary Farren's murder. And she was equally sure that they had done it at the orders of the man Blanche had referred to, the man who could only be William Marcy Tweed.

What she was not sure of was if she would live long enough to be able to tell anyone else what she now knew.

Cedar stood stock-still and let her eyes adjust to the darkness. The light was very dim, only the thin rays that worked their way through a dirt-encrusted and narrow grate high above her. While it managed to successfully diffuse the light almost completely, the grate still permitted the cold to fill the tiny room. She hugged herself, quickly chilled by a morning cold that was far beyond the meager protection of her thin summer coat.

When her eyes finally acclimated themselves to the dimness, she looked around the small basement room to which Willy had brought her. She'd had only a glance before he'd withdrawn, taking his lantern with him, unceremoniously leaving her alone in the darkness. Nearly blind until her eyes adjusted, she'd stood, still and afraid, listening to the dull scraping sound made when he secured the door behind him by lowering a thick board into the metal latch on the other side.

It was a more than sufficient prison, she decided—damp, empty, and grimy, and affording no means of exit save for the now firmly latched door. The grate, even were it wide enough to permit her to squeeze through, was too far above her for her to reach. With nothing on which to climb, she was completely without means of even reaching it.

For lack of any other idea, she cried out for help, thinking that perhaps a passerby on the street might hear and come to her aid. But either there was no traffic passing close to the house at that hour, or the grate and the distance muffled the sound. There was no response to her cries, and after fifteen minutes or so, already grown hoarse, she gave up the attempt as useless.

Eventually, she leaned wearily into a corner, huddling into the thin fabric of her coat, feeling miserable and lost. The misery was only intensified by what she thought was the weak sound of a scream coming from somewhere above. Blanche and McNaughton, she realized, were not just questioning Elly. They were probably punctuating their questions with enough force to convince her to tell the truth.

That thought was almost as painful to Cedar as her own situation. She knew she was as responsible for what was happening to Elly as she would have been were she the one to deliver the blows. She'd lied to Elly, using the friendship she'd been so freely offered as a means to gain information. If she'd been honest, she thought, if she'd told Elly who she was and why she was there, perhaps her guilt might have been less. As it was, it was a burden that weighed down on her and threatened to choke her.

And, much as she hated herself for the selfishness of her own thoughts, she could not help but consider what it was she was losing. Elly had been the one person in the house to whom she might have hoped to turn for help. That hope dwindled and rapidly disappeared as she listened to those muffled screams from above.

And there was, she realized, no one else who might find her. Guy had warned her he could do nothing to help her if she got herself into any further trouble. The chance that he might somehow slip past Willy at the door, make his way down into this dank basement, find her and spirit her away was improbable beyond even the most illogically wishful musings. She was alone, with no one and nothing on which to rely except her own wits, and at that moment they were dulled and completely useless. She was, she realized forlornly, without any means of getting away.

She had no idea how long she was left alone in the near darkness. It was long enough for her to become unpleasantly stiff from the cold, but not quite long enough for the thin, pale fingers of light that edged through the grate to fade entirely. No more than an hour or two, she assumed, even if it seemed far longer to her. Alone, in the darkness, she had been beginning to wonder if Blanche had decided to simply leave her to die in the basement. As she had earlier, when she had been in the darkness in the hidden passageway, she felt waves of irrational panic wash over her, leaving her filled with the feeling that she was being imprisoned alive in a tomb.

It was no surprise, then, when all she could feel was gratitude to hear footsteps approaching and see the door being drawn open. Even her fear of what was to become of her disappeared in her relief at being released from the dark, filthy place, to know that she was not being left to die there. She realized that she was even glad for the sight of Willy, despite the knowledge that he had been most willing to hurt her at Blanche's instruction. Anything, she thought, was better than being abandoned to the cold and the darkness.

Willy pushed her back up the stairs. Numbed by the cold and the sudden sharp light cast by the lantern he held, Cedar stumbled along as he directed, without any thought of trying to get away from him, intent only on keeping herself from falling.

But once she was up the stairs and Willy nudged her along the back corridor towards Blanche's office, Cedar began to feel the fear return. No one was in the hall, and she could hear no sound from anywhere in the house at an hour when there ought to have been a fair amount of activity. It occurred to her that Blanche would hardly have confined the girls to their rooms unless something was going to happen, something that they were not supposed to see.

Willy opened the door and pushed Cedar roughly into Blanche's office. Surprised when he released her, she felt her spirits soar. But they plummeted back to earth when she turned and saw Elly's face, tearstained and with a large, ugly bruise on the cheek, turned towards her.

Cedar ran to her and fell to her knees beside the chair where Elly sat.

"My God," she murmured, and she felt the fear inside her bossom and grow until it threatened to choke her. "What have they done to you?"

But when she reached for Elly's hand, she was shocked to watch the other girl's expression turn to one of disgust.

"Liar," Elly hissed at her and she drew back. "I thought you were my friend. And all you was doin' was usin' me."

"No, Elly, please listen," Cedar said.

But Elly wasn't interested in anything she had to say. She cut her off with a sharp look and an angrily muttered, "I have listened to entirely too many of your lies."

Cedar knew she could not blame her. She *had* used Elly, she knew, had tried to get information from her and in the end put her in danger. She had no words to defend herself, no way to minimize her own guilt.

Elly turned away from her, darted a look at Blanche, who was sitting behind her desk watching this scene with evident pleasure, then turned to McNaughton, who seemed to be entirely interested in the condition of his fingernails and totally oblivious to what was going on in the room. Elly trembled slightly as her glance slid over him, then turned back to Blanche.

"May I leave now?" Elly asked.

"You can go to your room, Elly," Blanche said, her tone gently, falsely solicitous. "You might want to put a cold compress on your cheek. I'm sure you'll be fine after a little rest."

Elly nodded, only too happy to agree, to do whatever she must to get away from Blanche and more of her questions.

"Yes, ma'am," she murmured, then jumped to her feet, away from Cedar, as though she were afraid any further contact would place her in danger of contagion. She didn't look back, not at Cedar nor at Blanche or McNaughton, as she darted across the room.

But when she reached the door, McNaughton looked up at her. "I may join you later, Elly," he said in a tone that implied there was no question in his mind but that he would.

Blanche darted an angry glance at him.

Elly, who didn't turn back to him but stood facing the door, her hand on the knob, murmured "Yes, sir" before she pulled the door open and fled.

"I think you should leave," Blanche hissed at McNaughton. "There's enough trouble."

He smiled at her and shook his head. "What is the good of being the silent partner of a brothel if I can't expect a few fringe benefits?" he asked. But as soon as he'd spoken, he stood and straightened his tie, apparently preparing himself to do exactly what Blanche had ordered him to do.

Cedar watched him return to the room from which he'd come earlier, into Blanche's private rooms. When she turned her glance back to Blanche, Cedar found the madame was smiling at her. She was, Cedar thought, entirely pleased with herself.

"Well, Cedar," Blanche said as she stood and started across the room to her, "it would seem that you really don't know very much about"—she paused and shrugged—"about anything. In a few weeks it won't matter any way. Under the circumstances, I think it best if you take a little trip to the country for a while." She stood over Cedar and smiled down at her, an unpleasantly humorless smile. "Don't worry, you won't have to put yourself out or worry about details. Your travel arrangements have all been made." She nodded to Willy. "You will accompany our dear Cedar, Willy," she said, "and insure that she arrives safely. After all, we wouldn't want anything untoward to happen to her, now, would we?"

With that she turned on her heel and left the room. Cedar was left staring up at the smiling face of Willy as he started toward her.

"Damn it, Granger, you told me to get you a story, and I'm doing just that. But I can't go back there with my hand empty."

Granger Nichols gave no indication of being convinced. "You could try putting your gun in it, Marler," he suggested in a dry tone. "That's what comes to the fore in a whorehouse, isn't it?"

Guy wasn't amused. "I have to go back there, Granger," he said.

Nichols's eyes narrowed and he considered Guy's expression.

"It's that woman, isn't it?" he said, finally. "All this has something to do with Magnus Rushton's daughter." This wasn't a question but a statement. Nichols needed little more than the expression on Guy's face at the mention of Cedar to know he was right.

But Guy had no intention of making any admissions. "It has to do with a story, Granger. Isn't that what you're always screaming you want? A nice, juicy, scandalous story that will sell your damn paper by the thousands."

The set of Nichols's jaw softened, and there suddenly was a look akin to pity behind the thick glass of his spectacles as he stared up at Guy.

"You try to implicate that madame in a murder and you'll find she has a good number of friends, Guy," he said. "Friends who will be willing to protect her. Starting with the chief of police."

"You don't think I know that?" Guy replied. "But there is more going on there than the murder of some whore. Give me a little time, and I promise you even the chief of police will think twice about Madame Blanche's hospitality. Especially when he learns that the good madame has the bad taste to sell tickets to the festivities to those with a bent for watching rather than participating."

Nichols's face paled, and then, once he'd considered what Guy had told him, the edges of his lips turned up in a smile that seemed almost rusted from lack of use.

"You're serious, aren't you?" he asked softly.

Guy nodded. "That unsavory little fact might convince a few of Blanche's friends to listen to other, more blatantly illegal stories about her."

Nichols leaned back in his chair and stared up at Guy, silently musing. After a long, silent moment, he nodded.

"You may be right," he said. "Embarrassment might just be a damn sight more important in their eyes than the minor matter of a whore's murder."

"Then you'll forward the funds to finance a little more looking around?" Guy asked.

Nichols grinned and nodded. "What bothers me is that what I'm financing isn't the looking, but your baser appetites," he said.

Now it was Guy's turn to smile, remembering how little of his baser appetites had been satisfied the night before.

"Believe me, Granger," he said, "I may be the only man ever to have found absolutely nothing to amuse him at Madame Blanche's establishment."

"That does bring me some small comfort," Nichols said as he leaned forward, lifted his pen, and began to write out a voucher for expense funds. "It also leads me to wonder about you, Guy."

Guy watched him, and as he did, the last trace of his smile disappeared. He considered what might have kept Cedar from meeting him that afternoon as she'd promised, and he realized that the possibilities were nothing if not unpleasant. As hard as he tried, he could not keep himself from thinking about what he'd seen in that room the night he'd gone there with the police, from picturing in his mind Magnus Rushton and Mary Farren lying surrounded by puddles of their own blood.

No, there would be little amusement for him at Madame Blanche's, he thought grimly. And it pained him to realize that at that moment all he could do was hope that he wasn't already too late.

# Chapter Ten

Cedar's head banged sharply against the rough wood of the wall behind her. A dull "Oof" escaped her lips as the air was sharply forced out of her, but the audible sound was virtually null thanks to the gag Willy had secured in her mouth, hoping, obviously, to escape the unpleasantness that would ensue were it to be discovered that he held a captive on board the train.

She struggled to change her position, to sit upright and at least be able to keep herself from the constant, jarring discomfort as the car moved along the tracks, but with her hands tied behind her and her ankles also bound, that apparently simple act became no small feat. Movement was made even more unpleasant when she discovered that her hands and feet had grown numb from the too tight bonds. And to the catalogue of her miseries, she added the dull, aching hurt in her cheeks where the gag bit too deeply into the flesh.

After a good deal of effort, she managed at least to shift her position so that she was not leaning against the side wall of the car. She counted that as a minor triumph, but hardly one about which she could become excited. She might have made herself a tiny bit more comfortable, but she had in no way changed the situation in which she found herself.

The more time she had to consider that situation, the more she considered what would happen to her once she reached the destination Blanche and McNaughton had chosen for her, the more frightened and miserable she became. She had to force herself to think of other things, telling herself that her imagined fears would only make facing whatever she would have to face that much worse.

Just then, however, she had little more than her immediate condition to occupy her. She was virtually surrounded by heaps of mailbags, bags not substantially different from the one in which she had been unceremoniously confined and brought on board the train. It seemed impossible to her, that such things could happen in the middle of New York City. But bound and gagged, she'd had no way to cry out for help, and it would seem no one had even noticed the squirming, kicking sack of mail that had been thrown on board with the rest.

She peered over the top of the heap of bags and saw Willy and the mail-car guard happily occupied with their cards, apparently oblivious to her. The glow from the lantern hanging above them swung with the train's motion, leaving groups of moving, leering shadows on the walls around them. It seemed fitting, she thought, the lurid sight of those shadows, more fitting to what they were doing than the calm normality of their card game.

She forced herself to settle her thoughts, to consider what was happening to her. And to her father, she reminded herself, because Magnus's fate was bound up in her own.

Blanche and McNaughton had put themselves to great pains to keep Magnus away from the political race and now to keep her from asking questions as to why. It was more important to them, she realized, than merely winning a minor city office. They were expecting something to happen, and happen soon—Blanche had as good as told her as much when she'd announced to Cedar that she was being sent away from the city. A few weeks, she'd said, in a few weeks it wouldn't matter what she might or might not know.

Cedar realized that she really had learned very little, that she'd traded her freedom for a few scanty facts that still left Blanche's and McNaughton's motives a mystery to her. And without some facts, without some way of tying Blanche and McNaughton to a motive for Mary Farren's murder, her father would never be able to prove his own innocence.

One thing she did know, however, and that was that she had to find some way to get someone's attention. Without help, she was completely at the mercy of Willy and whatever instructions he might have received from Blanche before their departure. If no one saw her and came to her aid, if no one stopped Willy, whatever Blanche and McNaughton were planning would surely happen. Both she and Magnus would become simply two more victims to that act, whatever it was, just as Mary Farren had been. And if she did not enlist some sort of help, there would be nothing she could do about any of it.

Eventually the train began to slow, and finally came to a bumping, jarring halt. When it did, Cedar could clearly hear the sound of voices outside the car, and that was soon followed by a scraping rattle as the side door was pulled open. There were two thick, dull thumps that she realized was the sound of two more of the heavy mailbags being thrown into the car.

Those dull thuds roused some hope in Cedar. It struck her that at each station where the train stopped it would most likely be taking on more mail. That meant that for a few moments at each stop there would be people nearby and a chance for her to find someone to help her.

"A present for ya, Harry," one of the two men outside called once they had heaved their burdens onto the train.

The guard swore under his breath, dropped his cards, and crossed to the door.

"Damned lot o' good they do me," he shouted back at the men outside.

They replied with laughter as he leaned against the door and pushed it shut.

Once more enclosed within the car, the guard lifted the bags one at a time and with a loud grunt of effort threw them onto the heap with the rest. That task accomplished, he returned to his game with Willy. A moment or two later the train started again, slowly building speed until Cedar once again felt the now familiar swaying lurch of the car beneath her.

Cedar had no idea how many more times the train would stop, or even how many stations would have mail to be taken on, but she now was quite sure that her one chance of drawing attention to herself was when it did. She would have to somehow make her way across the car and into the view of the mail clerks as they deposited their sacks on the train, she told herself. They could not possibly ignore the sight of a bound-and-gagged woman on the mail car. They would certainly come to her aid.

She began to work at her numbed limbs, flexing and straightening her hands and feet, working the numbed muscles in an attempt to speed the circulation the ropes had slowed. It was not a very rewarding task, leaving her arms and legs filled with the unpleasant sensation of pins and needles, but eventually that began to fade and she began to feel normal sensation return.

As she worked, she concentrated on the sound the wheels made against the iron rails, on the feel of the train's movement. She'd have only one chance, she knew. If she lost it, Willy would not make the mistake of leaving her to her own devices again. He would most assuredly not allow her to make a second attempt.

Eventually she felt it beneath her, the dull lurch as the engineer applied the train's brakes, the feeling of the car slowing slightly. Now, she told herself. Now, or never.

She rolled back, onto her heels and rump, bruising her shoulder against the wooden wall as she did, but too intent on what it was she was doing to really notice the hurt much beyond the sensation of a distant throb. She had given herself, she would later realize, a nasty bruise, and it would become sore and uncomfortable, but for that moment she was far too intent to pay it much mind.

Keeping her balance with her bound hands, she began to

162

edge her way to the opposite side of the car, taking care to make as little noise as possible for fear it would draw Willy's attention to her. She kept to what little protection was offered by the shadows cast by the heaps of mail sacks, all the time carefully keeping her eyes on Willy and the guard. When the hanging lamp swayed with the train's motion, she thought she saw Willy turn to her. She felt a dull thudding in her chest, and for a moment she filled with panic at the thought that he might see her, might even hear the dull thud of the beat.

But when she looked again, she realized that neither man had turned around, that it had only been the play of light caused by the shifting shadows that made it seem as though Willy had. She offered up a prayer of thanks as the two continued to play, intent on their game and the small pile of coins lying on the table between them.

And then, somehow, she felt the far wall of the car against her leg, and realized she was only a few feet from the sliding side door. She tried to make herself small, hoping the shadows in the car and their interest in the cards would keep her from the notice of the two men. It couldn't be much longer, she thought, as she felt the car draw once again to a jarring stop.

She was soon rewarded with the sound of voices outside, just as there had been at the previous station. It came to her through the wall of the car, raising her spirits as she began to think she might actually get away. Until that moment she had simply kept herself focused on the attempt, not allowing herself to consider her chances of success or failure. But now she felt close, and she began to feel herself fill with the hope she had until then not allowed herself.

Once again there was the scraping rattle as the men outside began to pull open the door. Now, a voice inside Cedar told her. Do it now.

She flung herself forward, falling roughly in front of the door where she could not be missed by the men outside as soon as the door was pulled open.

"Back again tonight?"

Blanche's voice and smile were cloyingly sweet, but not quite so sweet that Guy could not see something far less agreeable in her eyes. She's already counting the money I'll spend, he thought.

"That little green-eyed blonde certainly did take my fancy, Miss Blanche," he replied with a false smile of his own. "I came back to find out if that first taste was really as good as I remember it."

At least that much was true, he realized. The small taste he'd had of Cedar had roused something inside him, something that had dug in and begun to grow. He was not prepared to think about what that might mean, certainly not at that moment in any case, not when she was missing and, for all he knew, in danger. Tend to one matter at a time, he told himself. Once she's safe, then there'll be more than enough time to think about other matters.

He glanced quickly at the women who lounged in Blanche's parlor, hoping he might find Cedar among them, even when he knew that she would not be. If she'd been able, he knew she would have met him as they had agreed. Someone or something had stopped her, and whoever or whatever it was, was here, in this house.

Blanche shook her head, setting her mass of too red curls into tiny movements of their own that continued on for a moment even after her head had stilled.

"I regret that particular girl is unavailable this evening," she told Guy. Again she offered him the not quite convincing smile, but through the smile he could see an expression that spoke more of anger than regret, and her cheeks grew unusually dark. "But I'm sure one of my other girls will be more than willing to accommodate you."

Guy felt his stomach lurch inside him, and he felt a wrenching fear that was entirely alien to him. It had been one thing for him to suspect Cedar was in danger, but he found it was quite another to hear Blanche confirm that she was gone, to see the look of anger in her eyes and the flush of red that colored her skin enough to show through her powder at the mention of Cedar.

She knows about Cedar, Guy told himself, knows she is Magnus's daughter, knows she was here to find something that Blanche could not want found. If there had been even a hint of doubt in him before, he was sure now that Cedar had not missed their meeting of her own will.

He should never have allowed her to stay, he told himself. He should have convinced her to leave with him, or, short of that, found some way to take her out by force if that had been the only way. His intuition had told him that if she stayed, something would happen. Now that he knew he'd been right, he found little satisfaction in his prescience, only a dull, ripping feeling in his stomach at the thought that she was in danger and he had no way of helping her.

"I don't know," he told Blanche. "I wanted *her*."

And that, too, was true, he realized. At that moment he wanted her desperately, wanted to hold her in his arms, wanted to feel her safe and close to him. More than he had ever wanted anything in the whole of his life, he wanted her.

He started to turn away, trying to think what he ought to do now, how he could go about finding her.

But Blanche was not about to lose what had been a very good customer the previous night. She turned and motioned to a dark-haired, wide-eyed girl who was sitting alone on a nearby couch.

"Elly," she called, and motioned for the girl to come forward.

Guy was about to make his refusal more forceful, but then something about the look the girl gave Blanche made him pause and think. Cedar had mentioned learning something from one of the whores. And the fear he read in this girl's eyes as she glanced at Blanche made him somehow think this might be the one.

His suspicions were confirmed as Elly stepped closer and

he saw the trace of a bruise beneath the thick layer of powder and rouge that coated her cheek. He didn't know for sure if this girl had any knowledge of what had happened to Cedar, but his reporter's intuition told him that she did. In any event, he knew he could not leave without first trying to find out.

He nodded and smiled at Elly.

"Well, aren't you a pretty little thing?" he said.

Blanche finally seemed really pleased, expecting perhaps that he'd be willing to part with another twenty-five dollars as he had the previous night.

"I told you," she purred in Guy's ear. "Madame Blanche always knows how to please a man."

We'll see, Guy thought as he held his hand out to Elly.

"Would you like to dance, Miss Elly?" he asked.

Elly stared at him, and Guy wondered what it was she was thinking, wondered if she recognized him from the previous evening, wondered what Cedar might have told her about him. But she quickly threw off the pensive attitude and put her hand in his, and Guy told himself that whatever suspicions she might have about him, she was not about to reveal them in front of Blanche.

"I'd be most pleased, sir," she replied.

The two of them turned away from Blanche, but Guy could feel the madame's eyes following them as they crossed the long parlor. He wondered if she'd be quite so happy if she knew that the intimacies he intended to pursue with Elly were not quite those that Blanche was accustomed to offer for sale.


"Damn!"

Willy's shout was more surprised than angry. He dove forward, knocking his chair back and upsetting the table and the cards as he threw himself across the car. He grabbed Cedar from the rear, roughly pulling her aside and into the shadows just as the door of the car was pulled open.

166

Cedar squirmed and kicked and tried to scream, but the small noise she made through the muffle of the gag was lost in the men's banter as the guard chatted with them and took the sacks of mail. She stared out into the night view of the station that the edge of the opening afforded her, getting a blurred glimpse of a handful of people on the platform and the two men who were now hoisting the heavy sacks of mail into the car. She was, she realized, only a few feet from safety, and it might just as well have been miles for all the good it did her.

"See ya tomorrow," the guard shouted to the men outside as he pulled the door securely closed.

He stood for a moment, his hand against the door, listening as the voices outside slowly faded. Then he turned and faced Willy. There was anger in his expression, and the shadow of real fear.

"You told me there'd be no problems," he hissed at Willy. "Do you know what woulda happened to me if they'd seen her?"

Willy got to his feet and pulled Cedar roughly along with him.

"No one saw her," he said. "Nothin' happened."

"No thanks to you," the guard told him. "If anyone finds her here, I'm out on my ass. I got a wife and three brats to feed, and I can't afford to lose this job."

Willy was unimpressed. "Then ya might think about the ten-dollar gold piece you're puttin' in your pocket by havin' a few extra payin' guests this evenin'," he said. "And ya might think about all those little things ya get to buy for those brats with the gifts Mr. McNaughton pays you to do these little favors for him. Now get me a piece of rope so I can tie her to that strongbox there, and we won't have to worry about her makin' any more trouble."

Willy lifted Cedar roughly, ignoring her protesting squirming, and carried her to the far end of the car, to the heavy safe that occupied the corner. He dropped her roughly, taking pains to let her see that he was not in the least concerned with any hurt she might receive in her fall, ignoring the tears of hurt and disappointment that filled her eyes. She darted a look up at him and then started to kick his legs, venting her frustration in the act and feeling a sense of satisfaction as Willy let a curse of pain escape him.

But she knew her small triumph could be only short-lived. Willy knelt beside her and grabbed her arm.

"Now you have made me real angry with you, missy," he told her as he dug his fingers into her arm to still her.

Cedar had no choice but to quiet. Had it not been muffled by the gag, her cry of hurt would have been more than sufficient to rouse some attention from the forward cars. But as it was, there was only a thin, nearly soundless wail that seemed to amuse Willy more than upset him.

The guard handed him the piece of rope he'd demanded, and Willy secured the rope that bound Cedar's wrists to it, and that in turn to the foot of the safe. He tugged at the ropes, assuring himself that they were secure, that she could not possibly work them loose. Satisfied, he pushed himself to his feet and stood looking down at Cedar.

"You try anythin' more like that there, and I will show you just how angry I can get, missy," he told her. "You understand?"

Cedar nodded. She understood him only too clearly. And she also understood that she had lost her one chance for escape.

A few dances, a taste or two of the obligatory champagne that Guy ungrudgingly ordered (even though he did fleetingly consider Granger Nichols's less than generous attitude with regard to expenses), and then he felt he could suggest to Elly they might remove themselves to a place that afforded them a bit more privacy. More than willing to accommodate, Elly took his hand and led him through the parlor and to the flight of stairs.

She released his hand on the stairs, leaving Guy to follow

after her up the flight and along the long corridor, sure that his interest needed no further spur to keep him in tow. Had she not turned back when she had nearly reached her own room, she would not have noticed his interest in the doors along the corridor, or even that he stopped at the room before hers and put his hand on the knob.

"That room's not mine, sugar," she told him when she saw him try the knob. She retraced her steps, joining him and putting her hand on his arm.

Guy ignored her.

He was surprised to find the door unlocked, but once he'd realized that the room had been left open, he knew he would find nothing inside. He pushed the door open anyway and glanced in. Everything was neat and ordered, the bed carefully made up, its surface smooth and precise. He felt an unexpected wave of disappointment to find the room bare and empty. Some wayward hope, he realized, however improbable, had remained that he would find Cedar there.

Elly glanced at his expression and, obviously not liking what she saw there, tugged anxiously at his arm.

"Mine is the next room," she told him.

"Whose room is this?" he asked, wondering what she had been told to say and, perhaps more telling, what she had been warned against saying.

"Another girl's," Elly replied evasively. "She's not here any more."

Guy reluctantly let her lead him back into the corridor and pull the door closed behind them. This time she did not release his hand as she led him along the corridor.

He soon found himself in her bedroom. It was substantially like the room next door to it, pleasantly furnished, with a frilly, feminine feel to it, but with a good deal more clutter. Elly was not quite the diligent little housekeeper Cedar was, he decided as he looked around at the lingerie-draped chairs, the disordered dressing table with its jumble of fancy porcelain rouge pots and perfume bottles, the general, not entirely distasteful, female disorder.

169

And then he realized that he had no real idea of **Cedar's** habits, that he'd never seen her own bedroom. He found himself feeling oddly guilty at that, that he'd made love to her as he had on the floor of her father's study, without benefit of the comfort of bed and pillows. She deserved better, he told himself. And now he had no idea if he would ever be able to show it to her.

Once inside with the door closed behind them, Elly immediately put her hands on his necktie and began to loosen it.

Guy, oddly uncomfortable, cleared his throat and pulled back.

"Could we, perhaps, talk a bit first?" he asked.

She cocked her head to one side and stared at him. "If that's what you like to do, sugar," she agreed. She smiled. "But I never would have thought you were the sort to be shy with a lady."

Guy couldn't help but smile. "Usually," he replied, "I'm not."

Elly considered his expression thoughtfully, as she had when Blanche first brought them together, wondering what it was that seemed familiar about him. Then, suddenly placing him, she said, "You're the one who stayed the night with Cedar, aren't you?"

He nodded. "Yes," he admitted.

Elly smiled, and in that smile Guy thought he read dollar signs glowing through the dark orbs of her eyes. Apparently his extravagance the night before had not gone unnoticed. And equally apparent was Elly's expectation that she might manage to charm him out of a few dollars.

"Well, I know I can make you just as happy as she did," Elly told him as she moved close once again, letting her torso brush slowly against his. "I can do anythin' for you that she did, and more, much more."

Guy grinned at that. "I'm afraid I must confess to doubting that," he said, remembering just how he and Cedar had spent the night. Whatever Elly might have in

170

mind, he knew, it would in no way compete with that.

Elly pouted. "I can," she insisted. "You just let me show you."

She pressed her lips against his neck, then bit his ear playfully.

Guy put his hands on her shoulders, firmly pushed her to arm's length, and held her there.

"I thought we were going to talk," he said.

She made her eyes grow round and wide and stared up at him with a fair imitation of an innocent, ingenuous smile.

"What shall we talk about?" she asked sweetly. She let her tongue slowly lick first her top lip, then her bottom lip, and, the tour complete, smiled provocatively at him. "I'm all ears."

I'll be damned, Guy thought when he saw the smile. She thinks I'm the sort of man who likes to whisper dirty words to a woman.

"Cedar," he said.

He wasn't surprised to see the smile disappear.

"I don't want to talk about her," Elly said sharply. She pulled back from him, the come-hither look suddenly gone now.

Whatever she'd expected to get from him, she seemed to have lost her interest in working for it, Guy thought. There was fear in her eyes now, and a hint of slyness.

"I'm the customer, remember?" he told her.

"Go tell that to Blanche," she hissed at him. She darted a look at the wall, and then quickly looked away when she saw him staring at her.

But the quick glance was enough for Guy. He realized the wall that had been so interesting to her was the one that faced the room he'd been in the night before, realized that the narrow secret room lie between. And she knows, he thought with a mild wave of revulsion. She knows how Blanche uses that room.

"Do you think she's there now?" he whispered. "Or maybe she's sold the chair to one of her paying guests."

Once again Elly's eyes grew wide, only this time with shock.

"You know about that?" she asked.

He nodded. "And I know that she's done something with Cedar. And you know it, too."

She shook her head. "I don't know any such thing," she said. "And I don't want to talk about it."

She started for the door, but Guy grabbed her arm and pulled her to face him.

"You do know," he said.

"If I do, I don't care," she hissed back.

"She told me you were her friend," he said.

Her eyes grew hard with anger. "Then she was lyin' to you the same way she lied to me. She pretended she was my friend and then she used me. And all it got me was this." She pointed to the bruise on her cheek. She tried to get away from Guy's grasp, but he held her firm.

"She did it for a reason," he told her. "Her father is going to be tried for Mary Farren's murder. She knows he didn't do it. What she did, she did for him."

Elly's anger ebbed suddenly, and her resistance seemed to crumble. Guy released his hold of her arms, but this time she made no effort to turn away from him.

"I know," she said softly. "I liked her. She looked so lost, innocent even. It's been a long time since anyone around here seemed innocent to me." She laughed suddenly, a loud, short burst of bitter laughter. "Can you imagine, innocence in a whorehouse?"

"Help me to help her," Guy said. "Help me find her."

Elly's eyes drifted back to the wall and a touch of fear returned to her eyes.

"I can't," she said.

Guy put his hand on her arm and pulled her across the room with him, lifting the lamp and handing it to her as he passed the dresser. He released her when they were finally beside the place where he assumed the secret door would be. He knelt down and groped along the floorboard for the

172

release, surprised at how quickly he found it this time. He pulled the latch, and the section of wall fell back. He stepped quickly inside.

"Empty," he told her. "Not quite time for Blanche's more peculiar customers, I guess."

"You shouldn't do that," Elly whispered in a voice made hoarse with fear. "If Blanche finds out . . ."

"She won't find out," Guy said, dismissing her objection. "Not unless you tell her. I won't. All I want to do is find Cedar."

Her expression grew hard. "I have to live here," she said. "You don't know what that's like."

He nodded. "You're right. I don't know what it's like. But you can always leave."

"You don't know anythin'," she hissed. "I been tryin' to save enough to get out of this place for more than a year. But Blanche makes sure there's always somethin'. Somehow she makes sure you can't get away from her until she's ready to let you go."

"Maybe I could help you," Guy suggested softly.

Her eyes narrowed with suspicion and she started at his. "Why would you do that?" she demanded after a moment of silence.

He shrugged. "Quid pro quo," he replied.

Her brow wrinkled in confusion. "What?"

"Something in return," he told her. "You help me, and I'll help you."

"Just why should I trust you?" she demanded.

"Because you know that whatever she did, Cedar did it for the right reasons." Now it was his turn to grow contemplative. "And you know her father didn't kill Mary Farren," he said, relying once again on his reporter's intuition and hoping he wasn't wrong.

He wasn't.

Elly looked away and swallowed. Guy realized she was inwardly fighting with herself, her desire to escape from Blanche at war with her fear of the madame. When she finally turned back to him, he realized that the thirst for freedom had outweighed even her fear.

She licked her lips nervously. "You don't know what you're askin' for," she told him. "You don't have any idea of what your little Cedar has gotten herself into."

"It really doesn't matter," he told her. "We neither of us have any choice."

Elly swallowed, obviously not anxious to speak, but aware that she would, that she'd made her decision and was now looking for the courage to go through with it. Guy stood silent, waiting, aware that prodding wouldn't help now, that it might even frighten her off.

When she finally spoke again, Elly's voice was so low he had to lean forward to her to catch the words.

"You ever hear about a town in Massachusetts called Boston Four Corners?" she asked.

He thought for a moment, and then remembered the rumors he'd been hearing for the previous few months.

"That's the town that's been petitioning the New York Assembly for annexation?" he asked.

She nodded.

"That's the one. You know why the good citizens of that town are doin' that?" she asked.

He shrugged and shook his head. He'd heard something, something he'd meant to look into when he'd had the chance, thinking there might be a story in it; but somehow the opportunity never came up, and now he really couldn't remember.

"It's because that town lies on a point of land that's cut off by a ridge of mountains from the rest of Massachusetts. It's so hard for the Massachusetts marshal to get there that he just stopped goin', leavin' the place with no law at all. It is a little town that's been taken over by cattle thieves and horse thieves and all like of villain who cross the state line with their booty and stand there and thumb their noses at the New York marshals knowin' that the Massachusetts law, if they ever decide to come lookin' at

174

all, will come after they're long gone."

"What's that got to do with Cedar?" Guy asked, but even before she answered he somehow knew. And what he knew left a dull ball of fear inside him.

"Michael McNaughton owns a place there, a ranch he calls it, where he buys stolen horses and sells them again," Elly told him. "And that's the place where they've taken your Miss Cedar." She turned away again, and her shoulders drooped. "That's all I know," she said. "Except that if you intend to go there after her, you better bring a gun. McNaughton has a dozen men workin' for him, and they're there to make sure nothin' interferes with their employer's business."

# Chapter Eleven

Cedar strained at the ropes that bound her wrists, even though she knew they were impossible for her to loosen. She continued doggedly, even though she was well aware that the effort was entirely useless and would serve only to rub the skin there more raw than it had already become. Still she twisted and turned her hands, trying to free herself, afraid that if she gave up trying, she would let herself give in as well to the fear that was gnawing at her just the way some creature was gnawing at something in the far corner of the car.

That sound, the diligent gnawing and the sharp little scratching noises that accompanied it, frightened her almost as much as the thought of what was going to happen to her. She refused to let herself consider that the car was about to be invaded by rats, refused to let herself think that she was alone and completely helpless in the totally darkened car. If she did, she knew she would certainly become hysterical.

She wondered how long it had been since Willy had left her there alone and in the dark. An hour, perhaps? Maybe less. She had lost all sense of time. Every minute in the darkness seemed eternal to her. And the fear of being abandoned, of being left alone in an enclosed place without any light, started to gnaw at her with the same sort of persistence as the creature working its way into the car. She told herself it was foolish, nothing more than a childish fear of the empty darkness, but telling herself could not keep it at bay. The terror she'd felt too many times in the preceding forty-eight hours returned to her and left her trembling and with a sick feeling in the pit of her stomach.

For a while after the train had stopped, she'd heard voices and knew there were people around. As the guard had removed the bags of mail, joking and laughing with the man outside as he tossed the bags out and onto a waiting hand truck, she'd been unable to do anything more than watch despondent at the knowledge that there was help there and it was just beyond her reach. But all the while, Willy had carefully kept himself and her from the view of any curious eyes that might care to stray to the interior of the car.

When the guard had finished unloading the mail, he'd jumped down from the car, pushed the door closed, and disappeared into the darkness, acting as though nothing were unusual about his evening run. For all anyone could see, he was leaving the car as empty as it appeared from the exterior to be.

Once the voices had disappeared and the place seemed deserted, Willy had slipped out of the car and left her there alone. All that seemed to have been a long while before to Cedar. He'd told her nothing, and the fear of not knowing what was going to happen to her was almost worse than anything he might actually have done to her.

She finally recognized that she was totally exhausted and realized she had to accept the simple fact that her vain attempts to loosen the ropes were getting nowhere. She finally gave up trying to work her hand loose, for her wrists were raw and painful now and her continued struggling against the ropes only sent a shaft of pain through her wrists and up her arms. Weariness was beginning to overpower even her fear. Cedar quite willingly gave herself up to it, thankful for whatever moments of escape the prospect of sleep might offer her.

She was just dozing off when she heard movement outside the car. She came immediately and sharply awake, and listened to the sound. It was human, she realized, it was a voice, a man's voice, humming a bit tunelessly. She felt herself filling with a surge of hope that it was a watchman out there, making his rounds of the empty cars. All she need do was make him hear her and she would be free.

She kicked her feet against the wooden wall of the car and tried to cry out despite the gag. And all the while she offered up a silent prayer.

A moment later she could hear the sound of the side door of the car being drawn open. Her heart began to beat sharply with relief. She was about to be found, about to be saved from Willy and whatever McNaughton had intended for her.

The door was pulled open and she turned to it, watching as a face appeared and beside it an arm holding a lantern high. The man peered inside.

He was small and wiry, with dark, round eyes and a thick stubble of dark beard on his chin. He appeared to be dirty, but Cedar told herself she was hardly in a position to be choosy about who it was who saved her. She kicked furiously at the floor of the car until he turned in her direction.

Despite the racket she was making, he seemed a bit muddled as he stared into the shadows at the far end of the car. "Hallo?" he called softly. "Somebody there?"

Cedar answered as best she could, again banging her feet against the wooden floor and making what was, at best, a weak and muffled noise—all that escaped through the thick gag. But still, it was enough to catch his attention. He leaned forward and stared into the corner where she was still tied to the foot of the heavy safe.

"What's this?" he muttered.

He put the lantern on the floor of the car and pulled himself clumsily up until he was sitting with his feet dangling outside. It took him a moment to organize himself, to get his feet beneath him and then to stand, for his movements were inordinately uncoordinated and fumbling. Finally, though, he was on his feet, and he lifted the lantern again and slowly approached the place where Cedar lay tied.

He wasn't just dirty, Cedar realized when he was standing over her staring bewilderedly down at her. He was filthy, and there was a distinct and thick odor of alcohol that hung in a thick cloud around him. Obviously confused at the sight of her, he seemed to have no idea as to what he should do.

Cedar shook her head and tried to speak. All that was audible was a thick, meaningless mumble, but it seemed to be enough to stir him to movement. He carefully set the lantern on the floor, then took pains as he bent his knees and slowly knelt beside her. That feat finally accomplished, he reached out with unsteady hands, pulling away the thick cotton gag.

Cedar moved her nearly numbed jaw and took a deep breath which she immediately regretted. But she forgave her rescuer his less than fastidious condition and smiled up at him in thanks.

"You've come just in time," she began. "There's this man Willy, he works for Michael McNaughton and they've kidnapped me and until you came I didn't think I'd ever get away. We have to get to the police, someone . . ."

She stopped. His expression, which had been virtually blank save for a dim bewilderment, grew sharply disturbed at the mention of the police. He was decidedly drunk.

"Police?" he repeated, clearly less than delighted at the suggestion. It seemed to be the only word he'd understood of what she had said. "I ain't done nothin'. No need to call the police."

"No, no, certainly you haven't done anything," Cedar was quick to assure him. "You've saved me, and I hardly know how to thank you. If you could untie me, that's all. If you don't want to talk to anyone, you don't have to." She looked up at him expectantly, but he gave her no indication that he was about to do as she asked him. She saw what could only be uncertainty in his eyes as he stared back at her. She decided a bit of incentive might be useful to induce him to untie her. "I could see you got a reward," she told him hopefully.

That, at least, held his attention. "Reward?" he asked.

Cedar nodded. "Yes, of course. As soon as I get back to New York. I could send it to you. Just untie me." She nodded at the ropes that held her ankles. "Just untie my hands and feet."

He stared for a moment at her bound ankles, seemingly unable to focus on them while his mind was still occupied with other more interesting matters.

"What kind of reward?" he demanded.

Cedar wanted to cry with frustration. It was more than obvious to her that he was totally drunk, that he was too befuddled to make any sense out of what she had told him or even the position she was in or what she was asking of him. Still, the mention of reward had caught enough of his interest to make her hope she could use it.

"Ten dollars," she told him firmly. "Would you like ten dollars? Or twenty? I'll send you twenty dollars just as soon as I get back to New York. All you have to do is untie the ropes."

"Ten dollars," he mumbled, considering in his alcoholic haze to just what use he might put such a sum. "Ten dollars. Or twenty."

"Yes," Cedar said. "Twenty. Just untie me."

She kicked her bound feet against the floor again. She breathed a sigh of relief as he turned and looked at them, then, apparently still under the spell generated by the mention of a reward, started to attack the ropes with less than perfectly steady hands. She watched as he slowly worked the knot loose, nodding and offering words of encouragement when he seemed to lose interest or become muddled.

But finally he managed to untie the knots. He sat back on his haunches, his hand resting on her foot, and stared at the piece of rope that had fallen to the floor.

Cedar flexed her feet and pointed them, feeling the stiffness begin to ease. A few minutes more, she told herself, a few minutes while he untied the last of the ropes that bound her hands together and tied her to the foot of the safe and then she could get away. She could find the authorities, and she would be safe. All she had to do, she told herself, was insure that his mind didn't wander, that he finished untying her despite his inebriated haze.

"That's wonderful," she told him. "Now my hands and I'll be free." She twisted around as far as she could, which wasn't very far at all, hoping to hurry him in his task.

He seemed temporarily more interested in other matters.

"My reward?" he mumbled.

She turned back to face him and nodded. "Yes, yes, of course. I'll be free and you get your reward. I promise. As soon as I get back to New York, I'll send it to you. Twenty dollars."

But the mention of the money suddenly had far less effect on him than it had had a few moments before. "Send it," he muttered, repeating her words. He looked up at her, and his eyes narrowed and his expression grew sly. "How do I know I can trust you?" he demanded.

"I promise," Cedar told him. She heard the catch in her voice, and realized she was on the edge of tears. She was so close now to getting away, but still so far.

He was still looking at her, his eyes still contemplatively narrowed. "You're real pretty," he said. "Prettier than the girls up at Slade's."

She had no idea who Slade was, and she really didn't want to take the time to discuss it.

"Thank you," she said primly. "Now, please, untie my hands."

But he was intent on his own thoughts now.

"They don't pay me no mind," he told her. "They can't even be bothered to spit in my direction. They only bother with the ones what got money. They're real friendly to the ones with money."

"You'll have money," Cedar told him firmly. "The sooner you untie me, the sooner I can send you the money. Then they'll pay attention to you."

He licked his lips slowly, apparently considering her words, apparently thinking of what those twenty dollars would buy for him. But then his gaze fell from her face to slowly take in the shape of her body.

Cedar shifted uncomfortably as she began to fear what ideas might be forming in his mind. She tried to move, straining against the ropes that bound her hands behind her.

"Untie me," she said again, this time with an edge of desperation in her tone. "Untie me, and then you'll have the money."

He shook his head as though he were settling something inside it.

"You're real pretty," he told her again.

Then he touched her ankle and slowly began to push his hand up her leg.

She kicked at him, but he leaned forward, putting the weight of his body against her to keep her still. His hand continued its slow slide along the length of her leg.

Cedar jerked and turned, trying uselessly to get away from him. And then she began to scream.


"For God's sake, it's after eleven o'clock, Guy. I want to get out of this damned place tonight. I think I have a wife waiting. That is, I hope I still have one, if I can ever manage to find my way home."

Granger Nichols stared at the face of the large clock on the wall, made a moue of distaste as he turned to consider the pile of papers on his desk, and then leveled another equally unpleasant glance at Guy.

"We both know you like it better here," Guy replied. "There's no place that you find half so interesting, most certainly not your own parlor." He grinned halfheartedly. He usually enjoyed needling Nichols, but just at that moment he found himself less than pleased with himself, and he knew his concern for Cedar was the reason why. "But if you want to leave," he added, "just write out the expense voucher and I'll wish you a fond good night."

"I already gave you all the money I intend to let you wheedle out of me," Nichols told him. "I pay you for writing news stories, not for you to waste your time at a bordello."

"I have a story, Granger, I told you that. I just need a little more information."

"Blanche sells spectator admission to nonparticipants," Nichols said dryly. "You already told me that. Interesting, but hardly worth putting on the front page. And decidedly not worth any more expense money."

"I have to go to this town, Boston Four Corners," Guy said, trying to keep the impatience out of his voice.

"So go," Nichols replied, dismissing him and looking down at the papers on his desk. He was decidedly not in the mood for any further requests for expenses.

"I have to look as though I have enough money to buy a few stolen horses," Guy insisted.

Nichols reluctantly looked back up at him. "You're *flogging* a *dead* horse, Guy," he said. "There have been rumors about this place for months, ever since Massachusetts tried to cede the land to New York State. Supposedly there are horse thieves that use the town as their headquarters. But until New York and the Congress confirm the transfer, Massachusetts has titular jurisdiction. New York authorities all the way to Saratoga complain about stolen livestock. But by the time the Massachusetts authorities get around to making inquiries, they come up with nothing. There are never any animals that even remotely meet the description of those reported stolen, even when the New York marshals guard every road out of the town."

Guy grinned. "Curiouser and curiouser, don't you think?" he asked. "Stolen horses go in, don't come out, and yet for some reason they aren't there when the constabulary gets around to looking for them. Sounds like a good story to me."

"And this all has nothing to do with the story you're

supposed to be writing," Nichols insisted.

"Our friend Michael McNaughton happens to have a little farm up in this town, Granger. It's all tied in, Mary Farren's murder, Magnus Rushton, this town, and the stolen horses."

"How?" Nichols demanded.

Guy shrugged. "I don't know yet. But that's what I intend to find out."

Nichols slapped his hand down heavily on the desk.

"You were supposed to give me a nice juicy story about a holier-than-thou reform candidate being arrested for killing a whore, not some fairy tale about horses that disappear."

"I told you, the girl's murder is linked with what's happening in that town," Guy insisted. "I can feel it."

"You won't come up with anything," he said. "Whatever is going on there, even assuming there is something going on, they've obviously got it well organized and even better hidden. So forget it and find something more promising to work on. A body washed up on the docks on the west side a few hours ago. If you refuse to write the Rushton story, you can cover that."

Guy shook his head. "I intend to write the Rushton story, Granger," he said. "Only I intend to write facts, not the fiction Tweed is having the police department hand out."

"We've been over this before, Guy," Nichols told him. "It would appear that you have somehow contracted a case of temporary insanity with regard to Rushton. It's old news now, anyway. Let's just get on with our lives, shall we? You go down to the morgue and find out whose body washed ashore by the docks, and I go home to my wife and what is probably by now a burnt and/or cold supper."

Guy was less than impressed with Nichols's suggestion. He put his hands down on the desk and leaned forward, staring at the editor's eyes as he neared him. When he spoke, his expression was intent, with a look that said he had no intention of leaving until Nichols gave in.

"Look, Granger," he began, "it's simple. I go to this town

pretending to be a well-heeled tough looking for a few race-horses and not too particular where they come from. I look around, find out what's happening up there." He snapped his fingers. "And I come back with that front-page story you want."

"And maybe you don't," Nichols told him. "Maybe there is no story, or maybe it's too well hidden for even your well-advertised skills to uncover. Frankly, Guy, it's not worth the time or effort. Not to mention the expenses."

"I already know Michael McNaughton is involved in this mess, Granger. And that's just for starters. McNaughton is Tweed's man. This thing might lead anywhere. I promise you, I'll get you your story."

Nichols shrugged. He seemed as determined not to be convinced as Guy was to convince him.

"You know you can't touch Tweed," he said.

"Because no one's done it so far doesn't mean it can't be done," Guy returned.

Nichols shrugged again, and looked down at the papers on his desk in a gesture of dismissal.

"Then go if you want," he said, "and waste your time. But no expenses."

"You know I'll need to show something if they're going to believe me," Guy said.

"Then you'd better find some money, hadn't you?" Nichols asked. He looked up and smiled innocently at Guy.

Guy straightened. "Look, Granger," he said. "I've been making a few quiet inquiries on the street about this place. It seems there's a bit of gossip going about that there's to be a prizefight up there, a big one. Every shark in the city is going up to this little hole-in-the-wall town."

This, at least, seemed to interest the editor.

"Prizefight?" Nichols asked. "They're illegal," he added with a grin that said that he considered this, at least, a story worthy of a front-page column or two. "Where did you get it?"

"Harry Tricks," Guy told him.

"The bookie?"

Guy nodded. "None other. I happened on him on my way up here. You know as well as I do his word is always gospel."

"You do have an odd assortment of friends, Guy," Nichols mused with a grin.

"Every good reporter needs them," Guy said.

"And this fight?"

"Bare fists and blood," Guy told him with obvious relish. "Gentleman John Morrissey versus Yankee Sullivan. There'll be enough money in bets in that little town to fund a bank." He seemed to be gauging Nichols's interest, weighing the most advantageous tack, convinced he'd finally found the key to the expense strongbox. "I'll get it all for you, Granger," he said, "the fight, the horse thieves, all of it. You can splash it across the front page: the wild West, right here in the civilized East. And you'll be able to throw in McNaughton, the real murderer of that whore at Blanche's, and, if I'm lucky, tie it all to Tweed and some local corruption as well. Think about it. Expenses will be a bargain for a story like that."

"Extremely extravagant expenses," Nichols scowled. "You're always doing this to me, Guy," he muttered angrily.

Guy pushed the expense voucher across the desk, lifted Nichols's pen and dipped it in the ink, then handed it to him.

"And I always bring back a story, Granger," he said. "You know it as well as I do. So why do we always have to go through this little game over a few paltry dollars when you know you'll give it to me in the end?"

"I should fire you," Nichols said as he began to write out the voucher.

"And lose the best reporter you've ever had?" Guy asked. "Besides, you know that you'd miss me. I make life interesting for you. That's more than McBride and the rest of your flunkies do."

Nichols finished the voucher, signed and then blotted it.

"Just keep your mind on your work," he admonished as he handed the slip of paper to Guy.

"When have I ever done anything else?" Guy asked as he pocketed the voucher.

Nichols scowled again.

"At least you're getting away from the city and Magnus Rushton's daughter," he muttered. "Maybe I'll finally get some copy out of you."

Guy paused and stared at him a moment, and then turned away. Hopefully, he thought, he was doing just the opposite from what Nichols expected, hopefully he was going to find Cedar. Because if she wasn't in Boston Four Corners, then there was no place left for him to look.

And if he didn't find her, he realized, and soon, she would probably end just as Mary Farren had, with a bullet in her heart.


Cedar didn't see anything, or hear anything either, when Willy entered the car. A huge shadow simply suddenly appeared out of the night, and a dark arm fell sharply against the side of her attacker's face. The blow sent him sprawling. The drunk fell back on the floor of the car and lay still.

Cedar stopped screaming and looked up, bewildered, at Willy's glowering face.

"I shoulda let him have his fun," he told her. "Serve you right."

She opened her mouth again, but the threat of Willy's raised hand was more than enough to still the scream while it was still in her throat. He knelt down beside her and put his hand on her cheeks, grasping them firmly between his fingers, letting them bite into the flesh.

"Now you listen to me, missy," he said. "You can scream all you like and not one soul in this town will lift a finger to help you, you understand?"

She nodded.

"Good," he said, and released his hold of her. He put his

187

hand to his pocket and brought it out again, this time holding a knife, which he flicked open. "Now we do this easy or we do this hard. It's up to you."

Cedar watched the light glinting from the steel of the blade as he brought it slowly closer to her face. He was grinning at her, enjoying her fear.

He pushed her roughly forward and used the knife to sever the rope that held her tied to the foot of the safe. Then he rose, pulling her to feet.

As he started to leave the car, pulling her along with him, Cedar stared at the prone body of the unconscious drunk. He'd seen her, he knew she was being held against her will. Maybe he'd tell someone.

Willy seemed to read her thoughts. "Don't you waste a thought on that one, missy," he said. "He's so drunk that when he wakes up, he won't remember what happened. He'll just think he came here to sleep it off."

With that he jumped out of the car, carrying her with the same sort of care he might bestow on a sack of potatoes, then set her down and pushed her forward in the darkness. When she stumbled and nearly fell on the uneven ground at the side of the track, he grunted angrily and caught her with a hand under her arm.

"This way," he told her. "It ain't far."

She stumbled through the darkness of the night, darkness that seemed far more complete than night had ever seemed to her in the city. Save for a thin crescent of a moon and a handful of stars, there was no light at all that she could see.

But as Willy had told her, it wasn't far. There was the sound of a horse snorting and then an uneven patch of totally black shadow. Willy pushed her against it, then fumbled in the darkness for a moment. A few seconds later there was the flicker of the match he struck, and then the narrow globe of light from a lantern. The shadow turned into a small carriage and a horse as he adjusted the flame.

"Get in," Willy told her.

But with her hands still tied behind her, that wasn't quite

so easy a feat as it might have seemed, even were she anxious to accommodate him. In the end, he swore, lifted her, and dropped her onto the seat. Then he climbed up beside her, settling himself to the squealed accompaniment of the springs that protested his weight, and took up the reins.

The light the lantern cast was just barely enough to give Cedar a rough impression of a dirt road in front of them and a line of dark, oblong shadows—empty train cars like the one she'd been in, she assumed—behind them. Willy turned the carriage, and they started up a fairly steep hill. From what little Cedar could see, they passed a small station house on the side of the rise.

At the top of the hill the road straightened out, and Cedar realized they were in the town proper. There were a half dozen darkened buildings, then one large one with light and noise, more than she would have suspected from the darkness and silence that had surrounded the station and the empty cars at the foot of the hill. She found herself staring as they passed what might have been once a quiet, small town hotel, complete with a long front porch lined with rockers. The rocking chairs were empty, though, and it was quite obvious to Cedar that this hotel was not currently accommodating visitors from the city seeking the peace of a few quiet days in the country.

Lanterns filled the place with light, and there was a good deal of rough laughter and a sporadic shriek that made Cedar wonder if someone might not be crying out for help or simply issuing an exaggerated expression of merriment. To this was added the sound of a tinny piano being played by someone who was more interested in noise than music. Cedar had heard about dance halls—the less elegant versions of Madame Blanche's establishment that catered to the less well-heeled members of society—but had never, until that moment, seen one.

Willy drove the carriage into the yard at the side of the place and drew the horse to a stop. He tied up the reins, leaped down, and reached up for her.

"You're not taking me into that place?" Cedar asked.

"What's the matter?" he asked with a smile that ended with a sneer. "You too good for it, missy?"

He laughed then, but once he had lifted her from the carriage, she realized that it wasn't towards the dance hall that he pushed her but to a small farmhouse at a small distance further along the road.

Here, too, there were lights in the windows, and Cedar could see a man in his shirtsleeves leaning over a desk. It was to that man that Willy brought her, pulling her up the steps to the front porch, then entering the house without the nicety of knocking.

"Here she is, Slade," Willy said as he pushed Cedar before him through a small hall and into the front room. "With McNaughton's compliments."

Cedar couldn't help but stare at the desk top, momentarily mesmerized by the sight of the money that nearly covered its surface. But her glance was soon drawn to the man who had been busy counting it, the man Willy had called Slade.

He was large, with a huge barrel chest and a short, thick neck topped by a head that was graced with a good deal of dark, curling hair, thick matching beard and mustache, and piercing dark eyes. But in contrast to the physical grossness, there was a strange fussiness about his dress. His white shirt was spotless and his collar stiff and pristine. Dark bands kept his sleeves pulled up neatly so that his cuffs wouldn't become dirtied by contact with the money he'd obviously been counting. His trousers sported an unexpected sharp crease.

An even more oddly, the look he leveled at her made Cedar feel decidedly uncomfortable. There was something about his glance that made her feel as though she ought to cover herself.

He pushed himself away from the desk and stared at her silently for a moment longer, taking in her now rumpled and torn dress and the generous streaks of dirt that decorated both her face and her clothing, and considering her condition with obvious distaste. Then he grunted, apparently satisfied that what lie beneath the dirt would prove acceptable to him.

"You might have mentioned, Willy, that the young lady was so attractive. Cleaned up a bit, she could be useful."

Willy shook his head. "McNaughton's orders is to keep her here until you hear from him. Nothin' else." He smiled and pulled Cedar to face him. "Besides, I don't think she'd be exactly willin' to cooperate, would you, now, missy?"

Cedar's expression filled with disgust. She tried to shrug away from Willy's grasp, and he laughed.

"So it would seem," Slade told Willy. "I must admit, it is a shame, though. There are two gentlemen just arrived who've brought down some really fine horseflesh from Saratoga. They'll want to spend a few days celebrating with what I will be forced to pay them for their booty, and it would please me enormously to return a few of those dollars to my far more deserving pocket."

"Well, I done my job," Willy said. He removed his knife from his pocket again and slit the rope that held Cedar's hands. Then he pushed her roughly into a chair. Startled by the shove, she landed clumsily, but pretended to ignore Slade's sly glance at her half-exposed legs. She steadied herself and settled her skirts properly, then sat rubbing her raw wrists.

"I think I'll go next door and find me some beer and maybe some company for the night," Willy announced as he pushed the knife shut against his leg and returned it to his pocket.

Slade nodded. "Enjoy yourself, Willy," he said. "Let's make this evening on the house, shall we? Tomorrow night, I'm afraid, will be your own."

Willy grinned. "I'm goin' back to the city first train in the mornin'," he said. "But I will take advantage of your hospitality tonight, Slade, and with great pleasure."

Slade seemed less than pleased with that, but he said

nothing as Willy left. Then he turned away, quickly and carefully stowing money on the desk into a thick canvas bag that he carefully locked away in a desk drawer.

His more pressing business completed, he turned his attention back to Cedar, crossing the room to stand over her. He put his hand to her hair and fingered it for an instant before Cedar pulled her head back and it fell through his fingers.

"Don't touch me," she hissed at him.

"Superior, are we?" he asked. He leaned forward, bringing his face close to hers. "I might just decide to take offense at your manners, Miss Rushton."

Cedar shrank back and away from him. His eyes were hard and cold, and she quickly realized that her position with him was tenuous at best.

"Shame," he mused softly, more to himself than to her, and touched his hand to her cheek. "But orders, I'm afraid, are orders." He straightened up, put his hand on her arm, and pulled her up out of the chair. "Let's make you comfortable, shall we?" he said as he pulled her toward the stairs. "A night in a nice comfortable bed might serve to make you a bit friendlier."

Cedar paled at the insinuation she heard in his voice. Slade saw it, and he laughed.

# Chapter Twelve

Cedar couldn't believe that she had actually slept. But the relief she'd felt when Slade had left her alone, locking her in the small attic room, had been enormous. Temporarily relieved of the fear of what he might intend to do, she'd simply fallen onto the narrow cot and, despite the chill in the room and the closed and locked shutters at the window, curled up and slept as though she'd been drugged.

With the morning, however, and the clearer perception that the hours of rest had given her, she recognized that her position was precarious at best. Whatever McNaughton was planning for her, it was quite obvious that he intended to see to it himself. In the meantime she might be safe enough, assuming, that was, that Slade didn't decide to ignore his employer's instructions. Still, she realized she had absolutely no idea how long the meantime would be, nor did she know what would happen to her once that reprieve had expired.

Nor was her present situation even remotely comfortable. The attic room was cold and, save for the narrow cot on which she'd slept, unfurnished and dirty. Added to that was the fact that she had been in the same clothing constantly for more than twenty-four hours. They were rumpled, dirty, and torn, and, she was certain, about as wretchedly miserable looking as she herself felt at that moment. Never before in her life had the simple pleasures of a bath, clean clothing, and warmth seemed much beyond the daily routine of ordinary life to her. Now, when she found herself for the first time without them, such mundane basics grew in importance, no longer just mean necessities, but luxuries whose value seemed beyond price.

More than that, she was hungry, hungrier than she'd ever before been in her life. She'd eaten nothing at all the day before, and very little the day before that. Her hunger had finally outgrown even the temporary intermission her worries about her father and fear for her own safety had given it. Her stomach was beginning to groan in protest at its own emptiness, and she found herself beginning to fantasize about the taste of such mundane fare as one of Mrs. Kneely's cinnamon muffins.

As she was in possession of the means to remedy neither the condition of her inside nor that of her outside, she forced herself to consider her possibilities of escape. The attic room, although shuttered, was dimly lit by early-morning sunlight that worked its way through gaps in the boards. There was more than enough light for her to search the room with a fair amount of diligence.

It was, she realized after a short inspection, certainly a far less secure prison than the basement of Blanche's house had been. The door was a flimsy batten affair, with a wide gap between the side that was latched and the frame. If she could find something narrow enough to slip through the gap, she thought she might manage to dislodge the latch and open it. It was, at that moment, the only heartening thing she had found in a situation that had done nothing but deteriorate during the course of the previous few days.

She looked carefully around the dingy little space and found the bare room offered nothing she could think might be useful to pry open the door. There was not even a loose nail in any of the beams. Save for the cot on which she'd slept, there was nothing.

That left the cot as her only possible source of something she might use as a tool. She turned up the thin mattress and considered the springs. After a moment's thought, she decided they could provide her with the means out of her attic prison. They didn't seem like much, but she decided to remove one and try to straighten a bit of one end, hoping it might serve as a pry she could slip beneath the door latch. She shoved the mattress onto the floor, pulled at one of the springs, and gingerly began to remove it from the cot's frame.

She'd just pulled one end of a spring free, succeeding in the process in scratching an ugly, jagged line on the side of her hand, when she heard footsteps on the bare wooden floor outside her room. She hurriedly pulled the mattress back onto the cot, sure her jailer would not be pleased to find that she was trying to escape, and was standing in front of it when the door was pulled open.

Much to her surprise, it wasn't Slade. The woman who stood facing her was a harridan, a wrinkled, black-clad horrid old thing that might have stepped directly from the witches' scene of *Macbeth*. Although she gave no appearance of being feeble, still the word *ancient* came immediately to Cedar's mind as she stood and stared at her.

There was, strangely, no hint of what she might have looked like when she'd been young, not the slightest vestige of the smooth skin that now clung, wrinkled and dried, on her face and neck, nor even a ghost of gaiety or humor in her dark eyes. But still Cedar found herself seeing Blanche's just-fading features somewhere behind the dreadful mask of wrinkled flesh, and thinking that this crone might be, perhaps, the image of what Blanche might become after another thirty years of greedy debauchery and selfishness had wizened and dried her.

The woman eyed Cedar with the sort of jealous look that only one who was old and ugly could offer someone young and still blooming. Then she stepped forward, moving only a few steps into the room, and set down on the thick dust of the floor the jug of water she was carrying in one hand, and a heap of clothing that she carried over her arm.

"Slade said you'd need these," she croaked. "Clean

195

yourself up and be quick about it."

Cedar was so surprised by her, by both her appearance and the necessities she offered, that she stood, numb and mute for a moment longer, simply returning the woman's stare. She knew she was thankful for the opportunity to wash and change her clothing, but she was too taken aback by the woman's manner to shake the feeling that she was rooted, frozen in the spot where she stood.

"I said be quick about it," the old woman repeated, snapping out the words angrily as she motioned to the jug of water and the pile of clothing.

"All right," Cedar murmured.

She realized she had no desire to further ire this woman, and managed to stir herself. She shrugged as she stepped forward and picked up the jug and the clothing.

Her arms full, Cedar stood for a moment, waiting for the woman to leave her alone to wash and change. When she didn't, when it became obvious that she had no intention of moving, Cedar turned, dropped the clothing onto the cot as she passed it, and carried the water to the far side of the room. Resigned that the woman was not about to leave her alone to her ablutions, and aware that she'd rather be clean than shy, Cedar turned her back on the woman, set the jug down, and quickly unbuttoned and removed her dress. Clad in her shift, she shivered from the chill in the air, and then, as she hurriedly began to wash and found the water was cold as well, shivered even more.

Despite the discomfort, she managed to scrub herself reasonably enough to satisfy herself. She returned to the cot and lifted the clothing the old woman had brought her—a white cotton shirtwaist and a dark blue skirt, both plain and a bit wrinkled, but mercifully clean. She pulled them on. The blouse was a bit large, and the skirt rather short, but still, once she was dressed in them, she found herself feeling remarkably better.

The old woman didn't leave her much time to consider her renewed spirits.

"Come along," she said, and directed Cedar back down the steep and narrow flights of stairs she'd climbed the previous night at Slade's urging.

Once again on the ground floor, the old woman directed her into a small dining room across from the room in which she'd first encountered her unwanted host. It was a surprisingly pleasant room, with large windows that opened onto a splendid view of a wide field just beginning to turn a luxuriously burnished fall gold. The furnishings were plain, sturdily solid oak, but the room had a feeling of neat order about it, the same sort of feeling one had when offered tea in the home of a maiden aunt. It told her that, in this room of the house at least, the normal rituals of hospitality and domesticity would be strictly observed.

Slade was sitting at the table, a large white linen napkin tucked around his neck and covering the impressive expanse of his shirt, his interest apparently completely occupied with a plate heaped with a huge slab of ham and a healthy pile of scrambled eggs.

"Well," the old woman hissed at him as they entered, "I brought her."

Slade looked up from his ample breakfast.

"Most kind of you, Mrs. Fretts," he told the old woman. He turned his attention to Cedar, offering her what appeared to be a sincere smile. "Good morning, Miss Rushton," he said, brightly jovial. He motioned toward the chair opposite the one where he sat. "Won't you join me?"

Part of Cedar wanted to tell him that she wouldn't sit at the table with him even were the alternative to be starvation, but her stomach was insisting she do something entirely different. She hesitated for a moment, undecided, but her hunger, strengthened by the odors emanating from the platters of food on the table, won out in the end. She pulled back the chair and sat, ignoring Slade's satisfied smile as she lifted a spotless white napkin and spread it on her lap.

"Please, help yourself," Slade directed, and he pushed the platters toward her.

In for a penny, in for a pound, Cedar thought as she helped herself from the platter of eggs and the basket of bread. Deciding that remorse over her own weaknesses was futile, she set about addressing the food.

The first bite was like ambrosia in her mouth, and even better as it settled comfortably into her stomach. She hungrily took another.

"It's a pleasure to see you find my hospitality to your liking, Miss Rushton," Slade told her. "Would you prefer coffee or tea?"

She looked up at Slade's decidedly smug smile.

"Your hospitality is far from my liking," she told him after she'd swallowed the bite of bread in her mouth. "I simply do not intend to save you the expense of my board. I'll have a cup of tea, if you please."

Slade laughed and waved the old woman toward the kitchen door to the rear of the room. "A pot of tea for Miss Rushton, Mrs. Fretts," he told her, and watched her scowling retreat. Then he turned back to Cedar. "I see that your humor hasn't improved," he told her pleasantly as he forked a huge bite of ham.

"I can assure you it would improve immeasurably if you were to let me return home to New York," she suggested.

Slade shook his head as he chewed. "I'm afraid I couldn't do that," he said when he'd finally swallowed.

"Why?" she demanded. "Afraid Michael McNaughton might not like it?"

Slade shrugged.

"I have a very profitable arrangement with Mr. McNaughton," he replied. "And quite frankly, I have no intention of imperiling that arrangement, not even for one so lovely as yourself, by not honoring a minor request he has made of me."

"Which is?" she asked.

"To keep you here until he decides what he wants to do with you," Slade told her. He took a slice of bread from the basket and slathered a thick coat of butter on it. "I regret

198

that I will have the pleasure of your company for only a short time. He'll be here in a few days' time. There's going to be little excitement and he'll be coming up to enjoy the spectacle."

"Spectacle?" she asked, intrigued by this unexpected development.

"A prizefight, Miss Rushton. Between two of the best bare-fisted boxers in the country." He put down his knife and brought the piece of bread to his mouth, biting off nearly half of it and chewing it with obvious enjoyment.

She nibbled a bit of bread crust thoughtfully. "Prizefights are illegal," she said finally.

"Precisely," he told her with a slightly greasy smile.

"Where is this place?" she demanded. "What sort of a town allows illegal prizefights?" She lifted a brow. "For that matter, what sort of a town allows people like you to do whatever you do when you're not kidnapping innocent women?"

"Kidnapping?" he objected. "Really, Miss Rushton, I must object. I certainly haven't kidnapped you."

She shrugged, then smiled at him.

"I'm willing to amend *kidnapping* to *illegal imprisonment*," she said. "Does that suit you better?"

He lifted his napkin, wiped his lips, and returned her smile, this time showing some real amusement.

"Touché, Miss Rushton," he replied. "I do enjoy the company of a sharp-witted young woman, especially a *pretty* and sharp-witted young woman. That combination is, I'm afraid, sadly rare these days. But in answer to your question, this is the sort of town that isn't quite either beast or fowl."

"What does that mean?" she asked.

He shrugged, then put down the remaining half slice of bread on the table beside his plate.

"That is, really, of little consequence. What does matter is that you recognize just how important your actions while you are here are to your personal safety."

199

"Which means?" she demanded.

"Which means, Miss Rushton, that should you remain reasonably tractable and not transgress on the rules, you may enjoy your visit in the peaceful tranquility of the countryside."

"Rules?" she asked. "What rules?"

"Why, my rules, of course. There are no others around here," he told her. "If you give your word you will be reasonably cooperative, I am willing to allow you to remain much to your own devices. You may have the freedom of the grounds and enjoy the scenic beauty of this lovely valley." He spread his arms in an expansive gesture. "The farm here, I find, is quite idyllic this time of the year."

"How remarkably kind of you," Cedar muttered with clear sarcasm.

Slade returned his attention to his food, forking a substantial mound of eggs and lifting it to his lips.

"I see no reason why we can't maintain a spirit of conviviality as long as you do not transgress on the boundaries I have set for you," he said before he put it into his mouth.

"And if I should happen to stray?" Cedar ventured.

Slade chewed contentedly, his eyes on Cedar. He didn't speak until he'd swallowed and wiped his lips again with his napkin.

"I would not advise you to do anything of that sort, Miss Rushton," he told her. "You see, I have given my men a detailed description of you. Should you decide to wander beyond the confines of the farm, they are under orders to bring you back using whatever methods they deem necessary."

His eyes narrowed and he stared at her with the same searing glance he'd used the night before. Once again Cedar found herself uncomfortably enduring that glance, wondering just what it was he saw when he stared at her that way, just what he might be capable of doing were he to find her guilty of an infraction of his rules.

"Which means?" she prodded.

Slade's lips turned up in a smile, but it had no hint of humor about it.

"Let me simply suggest to you that I am unfortunately forced to hire these men for certain talents they have, but I fear these talents preclude the possession of even the more basic refinements. In short, these are not men of great breeding, Miss Rushton. They are, in point of fact, for the most part ruthless and on occasion might even be thought brutal. The whores next door try to avoid them when possible, because even in moments of playfulness they tend to lapse into violence. Need I make myself any clearer?"

She shook her head. "No," she murmured. "You've made yourself entirely plain."

"And lest you think you might appeal to one of the local populace not directly in my employ, I shall warn you right now that you needn't be bothered. My word is law in this town, the only law there is. Those who do not like the arrangement or profit by it are quite simply in no position to oppose it."

The old woman, Mrs. Fretts, returned to the room bearing the requested pot of tea, a cup, and a saucer, which she plunked in front of Cedar. Slade scowled as a bit of the tea sloshed from the pot's spout and spread a dark spot on the white linen of the cloth.

Cedar stared at Slade's scowl as he eyed the stain. She could not understand him, couldn't understand his concern with a spot on a tablecloth after the words he'd just spoken to her. His bizarre manner, his polite speech combined with his thinly veiled threats, totally bewildered her. All she understood for certain was that she was no safer in his care than she had been back in McNaughton's and Blanche's. Perhaps even less, for she doubted she would be able to tell what his reactions would be, or when he would drop his veneer of courtliness and become as brutal as the men he had just warned her about.

For he could be brutal, of that she was somehow certain. There was something in his eyes that suggested unspeakable

201

acts lurking behind the carefully cultivated image of a country gentleman he seemed so intent on maintaining. Despite the image, he was certainly no gentleman. A petty tyrant, perhaps, but no gentleman. And from what he had told her, he seemed to rule the town as though it were his own personal fiefdom.

That thought was chilling to her, far more than the morning cold had seemed upstairs in the drafty attic. She had to get away from this place, she told herself. And she had to do it quickly or it would be too late.

Guy climbed down from the train to the small platform of the Boston Four Corners train station. It wasn't much of a station house, he noted, a small, rectangular building, its dark green paint beginning to peel here and there on the clapboard. It didn't even sport the usual fancywork trim that most towns added to their stations, probably, Guy thought, as a show to the arriving visitor, to make the place seem more inviting that it would, in all probability, prove to be. This town, it seemed, felt it need not bother with misrepresenting itself to even the most naive traveler.

Guy looked around. The day was windy and dry, and small whirlwinds of dust danced in the air above the dirt road that wound up the hill behind the station. To the far side of the station were a half dozen cars on side tracks. A small commotion had begun in one of them and Guy turned, his interest roused, to see what was happening.

The car, a mail-car, was apparently being readied to be attached to the train he'd just vacated, which would continue on, heading northward to Boston. There was the sound of angry shouts coming from its interior, and the muffled sound of a scuffle.

Guy quickly realized that a guard, while inspecting the car, had apparently found a derelict asleep inside. The noise that had roused Guy's interest came as the guard booted the derelict out, accomplishing the feat with a fair number of heartily voiced oaths that left little to the imagination as to his opinion of the derelict's physical and moral condition.

Guy grinned. Unlike the train guard, he was delighted at the sight of the derelict. A town drunk, he knew, was often more helpful than an army of righteous citizens could be when one was in the market for a bit of information.

He crossed the tracks to where the derelict was carefully lifting himself from the dirt into which he'd been thrown. He raised a fist to the guard inside the car, but he said nothing, and quickly turned aside to make a vain attempt to slap the dust away from the seat of his pants.

"Good morning, friend," Guy called out as he approached him.

The man turned and stared suspiciously at Guy with red-rimmed eyes.

"I ain't your friend," he muttered, and made an even more theatrical show of trying to rid his filthy trousers of the dust.

Guy took a silver dollar from his pocket and tossed it casually in the air.

"I wouldn't dream of arguing that fact," he agreed. "But there's always the possibility that you might become one."

That last, Guy knew, was a lie. He ordinarily had a strong stomach and had been known to keep up acquaintances with an odd assortment of New York's lesser underlife as a means of finding the answers to questions more respectable citizens were often unable or unwilling to provide, but the odor emanating from this particular drunk was strong enough to make him hope he could get his information quickly and then get away.

The drunk eyed the silver coin, swallowed, and licked his lips. Guy noted with satisfaction that the implication that the coin might be his was not lost on him.

"What do ya want?" he asked.

Guy shrugged. "Just a little friendly talk," he said.

"Talk about what?" the drunk asked.

"Just talk," Guy answered. "I might be interested in

203

finding a woman, if you've seen her."

The drunk offered Guy a lecherous, knowing smile.

"There's women up at Slade's, if ya got the money."

Guy shook his head. "Not just any woman," he said. "A special woman. Pale blond hair and green eyes. Very pretty. You wouldn't have seen anyone who looks like that, would you?"

The drunk put his hand to his forehead as though he were trying to steady something that might be just the tiniest bit loose inside, then turned and darted a glance at the car from which he'd just been ejected and which was now being attached to the line of cars that would make up the Boston train.

"What is it?" Guy demanded sharply. "Have you seen the woman I've described?"

The drunk shook his head slowly. "I dunno," he said. "Maybe. I dunno." shook his head once more. "Seems like last night . . ."

"What about last night?" Guy asked.

The drunk shrugged. "She weren't there now, anyway," he said. "You need a woman and you can pay, you go to Slade," he advised. He held out his hand for the dollar, obviously expecting to be paid for his efforts.

Guy realized it was fruitless to pursue the issue. If the man had actually seen Cedar, he presumably had lost the memory to alcohol. There was little doubt but that he would have been glad to convey the information in return for the dollar, that was more than obvious. He dropped the coin into the man's hand, but before the drunk could pocket it and turn away, Guy produced another.

"What about horses?" Guy asked him. "I've heard tell that a man can find some prime horseflesh hereabouts."

The drunk eyed the coin in his own hand, then the one Guy held up in front of him.

"It's all one stable," he answered with a sly smile. "Slade has the women, and he's got the horses, too."

"This man, Slade," Guy asked as he dropped the second

coin into the man's outstretched hand, "he's important around here?"

The drunk's smile disappeared. "I'll give you this for free, mister," he said. "You cross Slade, and you'll end up findin' a bullet in your back."

"And how do I locate this paragon of capitalism?" Guy asked.

"Huh?"

"Where do I go to find this Slade?" Guy interpreted.

"The Black Grocery," the drunk replied. "Or the hotel. You just follow this road," he said, pointing to the dirt road that wound its way up the hillside. "You can't miss neither."

Then he turned away, carefully placing the two coins in the pocket of his pants, then patting the leg, assuring himself that they were still there. He started off toward a path through the undergrowth at the far side of the tracks, but turned back when he'd gone only a few feet.

"If you're smart, mister, you'll forget all about the horses, the woman, and this place. If you're smart, you'll go back where you come from."

That message delivered, and apparently considering he'd earned what he'd been given by offering it, he turned again and ambled away. Guy watched his stumbling progress until he'd disappeared, then turned and started in the opposite direction, up the winding road that would, he hoped, lead him to a horse trader and whoremonger by the name of Slade.

Cedar shivered slightly. The morning air had been warmed a good deal by a bright sunshine, but there was a stiff wind blowing. It ruffled the leaves that were already beginning to show their bright fall colors, tearing a few of them loose to carry them in a wild dance before finally releasing them to let them drift to the ground.

Despite the fact that she was cold, however, she had absolutely no intention of returning to the house. Slade might

205

think his threats were enough to hold her in rein, but she intended to use the opportunity he had given her to get away from this bizarre little town and back to New York and her father.

She wandered, pretending idle curiosity to any eyes that might be diligent enough to watch her, across the front yard and the slightly overgrown flower beds and toward the hotel. The hotel itself was quiet now, in the morning seeming far more what its outward appearance would make it seem than it had the night before. Whatever festivities occurred there, like the activities at Madame Blanche's house, they apparently ended before the sun rose.

But it was not what went on in the hotel that interested Cedar. She'd already seen more than she ever cared to see of such matters. What interested her were the establishments besides Slade's whorehouse that were situated along the main street of the town.

She glanced back at the house and assured herself that no one was watching her. And then she quickly edged past a large lilac bush that edged the far corner of the hotel, hoping the branches and foliage would block her from Slade or any of his men who might happen to glance in her direction.

She stared out at the length of the dusty road. It wasn't much of a town, she decided. Just down the road from the hotel, there was a store with a large sign proclaiming it to be the Black Grocery, but the roughly painted mug beneath the words convinced her that more beer than groceries was sold there. Besides those two unsavory-looking establishments, there was a small storefront offering feed and farm implements for sale, a fair-sized schoolhouse painted the obligatory red, a blacksmith, and a half dozen small houses, none looking either prosperous or inviting.

Of them all, she decided, the farm store was the most likely to provide the prospect of help. It would, after all, cater to the local farmers, not Slade or his toughs. At that moment, just as though its appearance were meant to confirm her thoughts, a wagon pulled up in front of the store. A bearded farmer wearing worn overalls and a ancient hat pulled the horse to a stop, climbed down from the wagon, and strode into the store.

Cedar darted across the road, ran up the steps, and followed him into the store. She paused for a moment, breathless from the run, listening to the dull tinkle of the bell attached to the door as she looked back to see if she had been followed. Satisfied that no one had noticed her, she turned to see that both the farmer and the shopkeeper were staring at her with expressions that suggested she might have been an alien appearing from another world.

"Can I help you, miss?" the shopkeeper asked, his tone as much as implying that he knew he couldn't but that custom dictated he ask.

Cedar crossed the store, passing by large sacks of seed and animal feed. The storekeeper, she told herself as she eyed the two men. He seemed the most sympathetic of the two.

"Please," she begged. "I need help to get away from here. Slade is holding me against my will. I don't know what . . ."

She stopped. The two men were staring at her now with blank eyes, with expressions that suggested they thought she might be seriously deranged. And then, acting as though she simply weren't there, the farmer heaved a sack of feed from the counter between him and the shopkeeper and dropped it onto his shoulder.

"I'll be seein' you at meetin', Dave," he said to the shopkeeper before he turned and started for the door.

Cedar darted in front of him, blocking his path.

"You don't understand," she told him, and she put her hand on his arm. "I desperately need help. Slade—"

But the farmer obviously had no intention of listening to her. He shook off her hand.

"It's you who don't understand, miss," he told her. "I'm sorry for your trouble. But I have a wife and three little ones. I can't afford to cross Slade."

He tried to edge by her, but Cedar refused to budge, and the clutter in the shop left no way for him to get around her.

"Please," she begged softly. "At least help me to get out of this town. I could hide in your wagon."

He shook his head. "I can't, miss. That's all there is to it. Now will you let me pass?"

Cedar stared at his fixed expression for a moment and realized that there was nothing in his eyes that even remotely suggested he might be swayed. She had, she realized, little choice but to let him leave.

She didn't turn to watch him go. Instead, she stood staring at the shopkeeper as the door banged shut behind her and the small bell made a forlorn little metallic sound. A moment later there was the dull plodding noise of the horse's hooves against the dry dirt of the road and the thin whine of the wheels as the wagon pulled quickly away.

"If there's nothing else, miss," the shopkeeper told her, "I think it best if you leave."

Cedar didn't move. "Isn't there anyone in this town who will help me?" she asked him.

He shook his head, his expression forlorn, but as determined as the farmer's had been.

"No, miss, I'm afraid there isn't," he told her.

"Surely there must be someone who isn't afraid of Slade and his men," she said with a tone that did nothing to disguise the disdain she felt.

"You have no right to condemn us," he told her sharply. "Our lives are here, and for the time being Slade has power over them."

"Then fight him," Cedar countered.

The shopkeeper shook his head. "He has men and they have guns and they're willing to use them. All we can do is mind our own business and wait him out."

"But there are laws . . ." she objected.

A short burst of bitter laughter escaped his lips. "Laws?" he asked. "Don't you know there are no laws in this town, at least none that Slade hasn't made?"

Cedar shook her head. "I don't understand," she murmured.

"Neither do we," the shopkeeper told her. "Now I think you better leave."

Beaten, Cedar turned to the door. Just as she did, the bell sounded a third time as the door was pulled open.

Mrs. Fretts, Slade's horror of a housekeeper, stood in the doorway facing her. An unpleasant smile parted her lips and revealed a mouth of crooked, darkened teeth.

"I told you," she hissed. "I knew she'd tried to get away."

Then she stood aside to let a tall, burly man enter. Once inside, he stood and looked at Cedar for a moment.

"Mr. Slade don't like that," he said.

"No," Mrs. Fretts agreed. "Mr. Slade don't like that at all."

Satisfied with that justification, he started forward, his arms extended, as he reached for Cedar.

# Chapter Thirteen

As he watched the wagon approach, Guy could almost feel the farmer's eyes on him. Dark and knowing, they stared out at him from beneath the worn and ragged brim of the old hat. Guy knew instinctively that those eyes missed nothing, knew they noted the city tough's clothing he had specially chosen, the too loud suit, the stiff collar that had wilted just a bit during the train ride, the expensive leather boots whose shine had grown steadily dimmer with each step that he'd taken since he'd set out from the station, thanks to the thick layer of dust on the road.

What was more meaningful to Guy than the farmer's awareness of him was the fact that he could not miss the look of disgust that filled those eyes as the wagon drew close. This farmer has seen more than his fill of the sort of man I'm pretending to be, Guy thought. And what he's seen of them he hasn't liked.

"I'm lookin' for the Black Grocery," Guy called out to him as the wagon drew near. "Am I headin' in the right direction?"

The farmer didn't so much as turn to him, let alone answer. But once the wagon had passed, Guy heard an angry mutter drift back to him. "You can go to hell. And you can take Slade with you."

Guy stopped at the side of the road, turned, and watched the man's stiff back as the wagon moved down the hill. The local populace, he decided, was not exactly

210

friendly and welcoming to strangers. But then he reminded himself of what he'd heard had been going on in
the town during the previous months, and he told himself
the farmer probably had more than sufficient cause.

He finished his climb and then stood staring down the
length of the road where it straightened out and ran
through the center of the town. Hardly impressive, he
thought. It looked much like any number of small towns
in the area, or perhaps even a little less affluent than
most. No really fine, big houses like those in Lakeville
and Millerton to the south, houses built with the money
made from the iron mines in the area. This was strictly a
farming town, a small handful of structures along this one
stretch of road, and behind them wide fields that ran
right up to the edge of the forested side of the mountain,
virtually empty save for a population of a few groups of
cows and horses grazing in the tall fall grass and punctuated by the occasional barn.

No wonder the Massachusetts authorities had been so
willing to turn their back on the place when the trouble
started, Guy thought. Even tight New Englanders
wouldn't think it worthwhile to bother to try to hold onto
a few hundred acres of gravel and grassland. And it was
no greater wonder that the New York Assembly was drag-
ging their heels about annexing the town. It hardly must
have seemed worth their while.

It is pretty, though, he thought as he stared past the
handful of buildings at the rolling fields of hay swaying
with the force of the wind as it swept over them. Guy felt
himself warming to the view in the way only a city
dweller can appreciate the countryside, with the remote
objectivity given him by the knowledge that he would
never find himself in a position where he would be forced
to struggle to coax a living from those fields.

Guy's moment spent communing with nature was short-
lived, however. Now that he was no longer in the protec-

tion offered by the hillside below, the wind was stronger, sweeping down from the mountain in thick, noisy gusts. He could not ignore the fact that it was stinging his skin as it swept past him, nor that it was covering him with a fine coating of the dust it swept off the road. The taste of it, not a pleasant taste at all and made only worse by the thirst the hours on train had left with him, made his tongue feel thick and dry in his mouth. He set off again along the side of the narrow road, looking for the hotel and the Black Grocery, the two establishments the drunk down at the station had mentioned to him.

It only took him a few minutes to locate the sign that advertised the presence of the Black Grocery. It was literally calling out to him, its rusted hinges squealing as the sign swung erratically in the brisk wind. Guy strode up to the small, unpainted clapboard structure, then crossed the narrow, slightly sagging porch at its front to reach the door. He was, he realized as he pushed open the door of the grocery and entered, glad to be indoors and out of that wind.

He was greeted by an envelope of warm air and a scent with which he was only too familiar, a sharp aroma composed of yeast and malt and barley—in short, the not entirely unpleasant aroma of stale beer. It was an odor Guy associated with the lesser sort of public houses he frequented with his fellow reporters from the *Sun*. It was not what he had expected to find when he'd opened the door.

His first glance around told him that the place had quite obviously once been the usual sort of country general store that one found in a small town, with long rows of shelves lined still with all manner of goods, from sacks of flour to bolts of cloth. But the shelves and the goods they held were mostly thick with a coating of the dust that obviously found its way inside on the heel of that whining wind. There was absolutely no sign that anyone had bothered to dislodge it for months. The only area that seemed to have received much attention of late was a bar at the far side of the room, and that, he realized, was the source of the scent that was making him feel with growing discomfort the dust coating his tongue.

Despite the fact that it wasn't yet noon, there were a half dozen men idling and drinking near that bar. Guy momentarily wondered at that, that there would be so many men lazing in a small country town in the middle of the day during what ought to be the harvest time. But a quick glance told him that these men were not farmers. In fact, from their clothing and the way they suspiciously eyed him, he assumed each was the sort of tough he himself was pretending to be.

Not a friendly crowd, Guy told himself as he crossed the room and made his way to the bar.

"What'll it be?" the tall, bearded, bald-headed and shirtsleeve-and-apron-clad man behind the bar asked him.

"A beer would taste just fine after the dust outside," Guy replied.

The bartender nodded. "It's always blowin' like that hereabouts come the fall," he replied as he lifted a mug from a row of them he had drying on a towel. "But then, it's always blowin' like that hereabouts in winter and spring, too."

Guy laughed. "A real garden spot, eh?"

"Oh, summers the winds stop," the bartender replied, warming to his subject as he filled the mug from a tap. "Summers are just hot. Hot as hades. Sometimes in summer you actually find yourself wishing for that damned wind."

"Can't satisfy human nature, I guess," Guy said with a grin.

The bartender nodded agreement. "Some nights it sounds like there's witches up on that mountain, screamin' and laughin'," he said. He pushed the mug across the bar toward Guy.

"Can't say as I blame them," Guy said. He lifted the mug and took a thankful swallow. "This is one dull-lookin' town. Those witches are probably just happy to get a night out." He drank again, delighted to find the beer was not at all unpalatable.

The bartender laughed. "Yeah, you're probably right. Up from New York, are you?"

Guy nodded. "And beginnin' to wonder what I'm doin' here," he said. "All I need is another mouthful of that dust and I'll be cryin' for the train home."

"Can't say as how I'd be here myself if there wasn't a penny or two to be made," the bartender agreed.

Guy put the mug down on the bar and wiped his lips with the back of his hand.

"Which reminds me that I'm here on business, myself," he said. "I don't suppose you could tell me where I could find a man named Slade?"

"I figured you to be the sort who'd be askin' that question eventually," the bartender told him. "You lookin' for work?"

Guy shook his head. "I got an employer," he said. He gave the bartender a conspiratorial smile as he leaned across the bar. "It was him who sent me here. What I'm lookin' for is some horseflesh, and word is that Slade might be able to provide it."

The bartender nodded. "You come to the right town after all, mister," he said. "Mr. Slade, he just left. You go down the road, pass the hotel, and there's a small house just beyond. He'll be there before long. Likes his meals on time, does Mr. Slade, and I'd say it's nearly noon."

Guy lifted the mug and drained it, then dropped it back on the bar. He fished in his pocket and drew out a few coins, which he deposited beside the mug without bothering to count. It pleased him inordinately to be able to squander a bit more of Granger Nichols's expense money.

"I'm obliged, friend," he told the bartender.

The bartender scooped up the coins, realized the tip was larger than the price of the beer, and smiled.

"Oh, mister," he said as Guy was turning towards the door. "If you plan to stay around a few days, you might find this little town a bit less dull than it looks right now. We're going to have us a real fine prizefight here."

Guy smiled. "I heard word of it in New York," he replied. "Fact is, thought of that fight was the only thing that kept me from turnin' around and gettin' back on that train the minute I set foot on the station platform. Word is, the smart money's on Yankee Sullivan."

"Well, if you want to place a bet, I'll be holdin' 'em the day of the fight."

"I'll keep that in mind," Guy assured him, then he turned and crossed to the door.


"Thank you, Duane," Slade told the man who had dragged Cedar back into the house in Mrs. Fretts's wake. "Your diligence will be duly noted."

"Thank you, Mr. Slade," Duane replied. His expression took on a hint of wheedling greed. "Just doin' my job, that's all."

"Well, you've done your job quite well," Slade told him. "You will find your reward with this week's pay. Now, you may release our guest and get back to your other duties."

Duane released his hold of Cedar's arms, ignoring her as she darted away from him as soon as she was freed and then stood glowering at him. He seemed about to say something further to Slade, but then reconsidered that decision, turned, and left.

"I told you what would happen if you let her walk around loose," Mrs. Fretts hissed at Slade after the hand had gone. "You mark my words. You keep her locked up or she'll be at it again."

"And your recommendation is duly noted, Mrs. Fretts," Slade replied. He considered his housekeeper with a look of modulated distaste that turned to outright vexation when his stomach made a loud rumbling sound, reminding him of that fact that it was nearly his lunchtime and food had yet to be placed on the table. "Now, I suggest you get back to the kitchen," he directed. "It is nearly lunchtime, and I believe I've mentioned to you that I do not appreciate being forced to wait for meals."

Mrs. Fretts darted a smug glance at Cedar, then turned on her heel. "You mark my words," she muttered as she crossed the room. But she didn't stay to argue the point further with Slade just then, thoroughly aware that a late meal would doubtless ire him a good deal more than had Cedar's aborted attempt at departure.

Once she had left the room, Slade turned his attention back to Cedar.

"You are, I'm afraid, quite a disappointment to me, Miss Rushton," he told her, his tone waspishly sharp. "You realize your little pilgrimage will cost me money, as I will have to appropriately reward Duane for his diligence in returning you to me. I dislike that sort of thing immensely."

Cedar rubbed the sore places on her upper arms where Duane's grasp had bruised her.

"Anything I can possibly do to make you even the slightest bit unhappy brings me great joy, Mr. Slade," she replied with a smug little smile.

"Tsk, tsk, tsk," Slade clucked. "Such cheek." His tone had changed and he seemed to be willing to enjoy the opportunity to fence with her. "And I had thought you to be a well-mannered young woman. I was, obviously, mistaken."

"So it would seem," Cedar replied. "Frankly, I must admit that it's never been a matter that has given me much concern. Life provides one with far greater matters to

216

consider than one's relative lack of manners."

"Manners or no, I would not have thought you the sort to be a liar," Slade told her. "You will recall that before I allowed you to leave, I asked you to give your word to me that you'd not try to roam beyond the confines of the farm, and you most willingly complied."

Cedar shook her head. "If you will recall, I gave you my word that I'd behave as you expected me to behave," she said. "If you'd given it the least thought, I should think you'd have expected a prisoner to try to escape. It is, after all, only reasonable under the circumstances."

Slade grinned at her, amused with her logic. "I fear I have made the error of underestimating you, Miss Rushton, a mistake I shall try to make an effort not to repeat in the future," he told her. He watched the way she continued to massage the sore places on her arm. "It would seem that Duane has hurt you. I hope the pain will serve to remind you that such escapades as this are entirely fruitless."

Cedar shrugged. "It will, at least, remind me to be aware of the sharp-sightedness of your watchdogs." She smiled sharply. "In the future I shall take greater pains to avoid them." She dropped her hands from the sore spots on her arms and let them fall to her sides. Her smile faded as she remembered the fear she'd seen in the farmer and the shopkeeper when she'd asked them for their help. "The experience has, I must admit, given me an idea of how very much the local populace respect and revere you."

The sarcasm of that last statement did not escape Slade. But rather than disturbing him, it seemed to provide him with a perverse pleasure and actually brought a pleased smile to his lips. He strode across the room to her and put his hand on her arm.

"It is a great pity you are here under such unpleasant circumstances, Miss Rushton," he said. "It is tiring to deal all the time with the sort of element I am forced to employ here. I think I would find your company most enjoyable were the situation different."

Cedar shrugged away from his hand. "And I am quite sure that regardless of the circumstances, I would find your company just as unpleasant as I do now," she told him.

If he'd seemed irked before to learn that she'd tried to escape, he'd completely hidden it. But now, with her words of open insult biting him, an angry flush tinged his cheeks and his jaw grew taut.

"I would not make the mistake of rousing my ire, Miss Rushton," he told her sharply.

Cedar darted a glance at his eyes and realized that his warning was not mere bluster. Her pluck might amuse him, but outright insults, she was beginning to realize, would only push him to do something she had no doubt would prove unpleasant for her. She told herself she was behaving like a fool by risking his anger for a reward no greater than the satisfaction of being rude to him. She resolved to think before she said anything further to him that might enrage him.

"What do you intend to do with me?" she asked.

"I suppose I shall have to shut you back in the attic room," Slade told her in a thoughtful tone that said he was still pondering that very question himself. "A circumstance which pains me deeply," he added, although he did not sound in the least bit pained. "Aside from the fact that it will deprive me of your conversation at lunch, I must admit to a weakness for the sight of a decorative female, one that is unfortunately lacking in this rural wasteland." He touched his hand to her cheek and began to stroke it. "I could, of course, be persuaded to overlook your transgression were you to give me the slightest incentive."

Cedar pulled away. "I would prefer the attic, thank you," she hissed.

218

"It is such a nasty place," Slade told her dolefully. "But I suppose these things can't be helped." Once again he put his hand on her arm, this time holding it with a grasp that could not be shrugged off. "Come along, Miss Rushton," he said as he started toward the door of the room. "I have no further time that I can afford to waste on you this morning."

Momentarily defeated, but already beginning to consider how she would use the springs of the cot to get out of the attic, Cedar pretended defeat as he led her up the stairs and pulled open the door to the small attic room. A waft of thick, warm air greeted them. The morning chill had long been dispersed by the bright sunshine falling on the dark roof just above, and with the window closed and shuttered, the closed room was heating in the way attic rooms tend to. In an hour or two more, Cedar thought, it would become unbearably close.

"Perhaps a few hours considering these rather unpleasant and uncomfortable surroundings will make you more reasonable, Miss Rushton," Slade told her as he looked around the dim, miserable space. "I shall look forward to your change of heart."

Having uttered that pronouncement, he backed out, slammed the door shut behind him, and secured the latch.

Cedar stood still and tense, listening to the dull thud of the latch as it fell. Even then, when she was sure that he thought her securely locked in, she still didn't move for a few moments longer, fearing he might decide to return and not willing to give him an idea of what she intended to do. It wasn't until she heard the heavy sound of his footsteps on the stairs that she felt secure and turned to consider the cot.

Finally sure she was alone, she quickly pulled the mattress away from the cot and set about working one of the springs loose from the frame.

Slade was just coming down the stairs when Guy appeared at the door. He descended the last few steps and opened the door before Guy had the opportunity to knock, and then stood, staring at his unannounced visitor, his expectant look not so much asking as demanding the reason for the presumption of the disturbance.

Guy pretended not to notice Slade's show of displeasure. In all truth, he found himself more interested in the man's general appearances—the starched white shirt and collar, the flowered vest and the neat, dark suit. This was hardly what he'd expected when he set out to find the notorious horse trader of Boston Four Corners.

"I'm lookin' for a man named Slade," he announced by way of explanation.

Slade looked him over one last time before he responded.

"What business would you have with him?" he asked.

Now was the moment, Guy realized, when he would earn his way into the man's confidence, or it was the moment before the one when he would find himself expelled, most likely in an extremely painful manner.

He grinned pleasantly, with the sort of conspiratorial look that said they both already knew why he'd come.

"I'm told he might be able to sell me some prime horse-flesh," he said. "I'm told he has access to the best animals in the whole of the Northeast."

Slade warmed to the flattery. He pulled the door back to allow Guy to enter.

"Well, sir, you've found him. I am Robert Slade."

Guy held out his right hand. "Glad to meet you, Mr. Slade. My name's Marler, Guy Marler. I've come a long way to find you. A long, uncomfortable way."

Slade considered the hand fastidiously for a moment, apparently deciding if it were clean enough to be touched, before he took it.

"A man with the finest goods to offer has no doubt but that discriminating buyers will eventually make their way to his door," he replied in a professorial tone as he shook Guy's hand. "And my goods will more than compensate you for the small inconvenience of your trip, I assure you." He stood back, waving Guy toward his office. "Won't you come in?"

Guy strolled into the room. Like the man, Slade's office surprised him. It had an air of fussy, almost obsessive, neatness about it, everything from the precise arrangement of the half dozen prints of famous racehorses on the walls to the brightly polished brass fender in front of the fireplace. The desk was neat, the few papers on its surface arranged in a precise, ordered pile. There were even fussy antimacassars on the backs and arms of the upholstered chairs, and an embroidery covered footstool in front of a huge wing chair, obviously Slade's own favorite.

"Nice, snug little place you have here," Guy ventured.

"I feel a man has the right to make himself comfortable if he can," Slade replied. "We must take what little bits of civilization we can into the wilderness." He waved Guy to a chair. "May I offer you some refreshment? Some coffee, perhaps?"

Guy shook his head. "Thanks, no," he said as he sat. "I just had a beer at that place down the road a bit. They serve good beer. What with the wind and the dust in this place, though, I suppose any beer would taste good."

Slade's face momentarily turned in a moue of distaste at the mention of beer. It was obvious that he considered such fare plebeian.

"No doubt," he murmured. He waved his hand, pushing aside the subject, as he seated himself in the wing chair across from Guy, the chair that Guy had taken to be Slade's. "Now, suppose you tell me just what it is you're looking for, Mr. Marler, and I'll tell you if I can be of any help to you in your search."

Guy leaned forward, putting his elbows on his knees and staring directly at Slade.

"I can tell you're a shrewd man, Mr. Slade," he said. "So I won't waste time on pretense with you. I'd intended to come here and dicker with you, pretending that I was looking for a horse to race myself. But I can see that wouldn't work with you. You'd probably see through it in any event, because despite my own expertise in the area, I am sure yours far outweighs it." He had let drop the coarse accent he'd been using at the start of the interview, aware that Slade would think it an acknowledgment of his own shrewdness to admit that he was not simply a street tough.

Slade fairly glowed with the flattery.

"I pride myself on my judgment of both men and horses, Mr. Marler," he interjected.

Guy grinned slightly, just enough to look agreeable, but not enough to show his satisfaction at having found at least one of the man's weaknesses.

"Just as I thought," he said. He leaned forward and quickly reviewed the story he'd concocted that morning during the long train ride. "It's like this. A man, a very rich man, whose name I am not at liberty to divulge and for whom I have on several occasions conducted business that he is unable to perform himself because of his social position, has hired me to find for him a horse, a very special horse. He suggested that I come here, to you, for help."

Once again Slade grinned, this time at the suggestion that his name had found his way to the notice of the sort of man Guy had mentioned.

"And just what sort of a horse would that be, Mr. Marler?" Slade asked.

"A thoroughbred racehorse, Mr. Slade."

"May I ask why, if your employer is such a wealthy man, Mr. Marler, hasn't he pursued the more usual avenues to acquire such an animal?" Slade asked.

"He has," Guy told him. "But there are very few horses that he knows of that meet his requirements, and he has been unable to convince the owners of any of those animals to part with them."

"And he expects me to find an animal of which he has no knowledge?" Slade asked.

Guy nodded. "Or, failing that, find some expedient to procure one of the animals he has so far been unsuccessful in his attempts to obtain."

"I see," Slade said softly. "Such matters can be arranged, but they are very expensive."

"My employer is aware of that fact," Guy replied. "Money is of secondary importance to him. You see, he has made a wager with an associate of his, a wager he does not wish to lose. He told me it was a matter of honor." He grinned. "Rich men can afford to have honor," he added. "At least just enough of it to extend to wagers, but not quite enough to preclude the purchase of stolen horses."

Slade's brow furrowed, and Guy realized he had made a mistake, that although they were both completely aware that they had been discussing the purchase of a stolen horse, still Slade was not pleased that he'd spoken it aloud.

"And just what might your employer's requirements be for this animal, Mr. Marler?" Slade asked.

"To be precise, Mr. Slade, he is looking for an animal capable of winning a race against Prince George."

Slade raised a curious brow. All hint of disapproval disappeared from his expression.

"Commander Vanderbilt's stallion?" he asked. "Your employer is an associate of Commander Vanderbilt?"

Guy shrugged and frowned, pretending confusion but not missing the awed tone that had crept into Slade's voice.

223

"I am afraid I cannot answer that question, Mr. Slade," he said.

Slade nodded knowingly. "I certainly understand, Mr. Marler," he murmured.

Guy had to keep himself from smiling as he realized that Slade was all but apologizing to him for the interruption.

"My employer," he continued, "has told me that he believes that if such an animal exists, you would know where it is and how it might be expediently obtained."

"Prince George has quite a reputation," Slade said thoughtfully. "It might prove an interesting commission." He put his fingers beneath his chin and looked at the ceiling. "There was a young animal that raced this past season in Saratoga who shows great promise. In fact, he wasn't beaten even once—a monumental feat for a yearling. And Prince George is getting fairly old, five years racing. I should say that a spirited youngster such as the one I've just mentioned might be able to match him. It would, at least, be an interesting race."

Guy grinned a conspiratorial grin. The combination of a healthy return for his efforts added to a challenging commission from what he believed was a socially prominent client had completely erased any hint of suspicion that Slade might still have been harboring. Guy just hoped he hadn't precipitated a wholesale raid on the better stables in Saratoga, where the finest horses in the area were raised.

"Sounds like just the sort of animal my employer is seeking," Guy said. "Under the circumstances, I feel sure he would prefer an animal that has not yet become well known."

Slade's lips turned up in an expression of smug assurance.

"I feel sure I can arrange something that will satisfy your employer, Mr. Marler," he said. "Assuming, of

# TO GET YOUR 4 FREE BOOKS WORTH $18.00 — MAIL IN THE FREE BOOK CERTIFICATE T O D A Y

Fill in the Free Book Certificate below, and we'll send your FREE BOOKS to you as soon as we receive it.

If the certificate is missing below, write to: Zebra Home Subscription Service, Inc., P.O. Box 5214, 120 Brighton Road, Clifton, New Jersey 07015-5214.

## 4 FREE BOOKS

**FREE BOOK CERTIFICATE**

**4 FREE BOOKS**

### ZEBRA HOME SUBSCRIPTION SERVICE, INC.

**YES!** Please start my subscription to Zebra Historical Romances and send me my first 4 books absolutely FREE. I understand that each month I may preview four new Zebra Historical Romances free for 10 days. If I'm not satisfied with them, I may return the four books within 10 days and owe nothing. Otherwise, I will pay the low preferred subscriber's price of just $3.75 each; a total of $15.00, *a savings off the publisher's price of $3.00.* I may return any shipment and I may cancel this subscription at any time. There is no obligation to buy any shipment and there are no shipping, handling or other hidden charges. Regardless of what I decide, the four free books are mine to keep.

NAME

ADDRESS _____ APT

CITY _____ STATE ___ ZIP

( )
TELEPHONE

SIGNATURE _____ (if under 18, parent or guardian must sign)

Terms, offer and prices subject to change without notice. Subscription subject to acceptance by Zebra Books. Zebra Books reserves the right to reject any order or cancel any subscription.

course, he is prepared to provide the usual security for such a purchase."

Guy patted the breast pocket of his jacket. "I am instructed to offer you one thousand dollars as retainer against such a purchase, Mr. Slade, conditional only upon my findings that the horse stands a better than fair chance of winning against Prince George." He removed his wallet from the pocket and carefully fanned out ten crisp one-hundred-dollar bills which he then placed on the low table between them.

Slade's eyes fairly glowed as he watched the bills fall from Guy's hands to the table.

"That would be more than reasonable," he agreed.

"My employer would, of course, want to be assured that any striking markings, any means by which the animal could be identified, would be adequately altered," Guy added.

Slade's expression became suddenly prim, as though he took offense at the suggestion that he was anything less than expert in his work.

"Such details are handled as a matter of course," he said.

"Then I believe we have a deal, Mr. Slade," Guy said.

Slade beamed, the picture of a pleasant-faced burgher as he reached for the bills.

"A great pleasure, Mr. Marler," he said. He pushed himself to his feet, removed a key chain from his pocket as he crossed to his desk, and unlocked one of the drawers. Once he'd deposited the money in it and relocked the drawer, he looked back at Guy. "And now that our business is concluded, Mr. Marler, could I persuade you to join me for lunch?"

"There's still the matter of discussing the final delivery," Guy said cautiously. He didn't want to scare Slade off, but it seemed prudent to get as much information out of him as he could as fast as he could.

"We can discuss the details of how you take possession of your property over our meal," Slade suggested. "But you needn't be concerned on that matter. I can assure you that I see that all transfers are made with extreme discretion and without any possible embarrassment to my clients."

Guy grinned. "I should have known, Mr. Slade."

It seemed impossible, but he was about to learn just how the stolen horses that were brought into the town were so miraculously spirited out of it, and he was about to do it over what promised, from the look of Slade, to be a pleasantly substantial lunch. If only, he mused as he wondered how he could approach the subject of the real object of his visit, finding Cedar would prove as simple a matter.

Slade motioned to the door. "The dining room is this way, Mr. Marler. I do hope my housekeeper will provide us with something befitting the wine I've decanted." He put a beefy hand on Guy's shoulder as they started out of the room. "Do you appreciate a decent Burgundy, Mr. Marler?"

"One of life's greatest pleasures, Mr. Slade."

Slade hummed with delight. "Just so, Mr. Marler," he said. "Just so."

Cedar smiled as she felt the thick wire of the spring push against the latch. She had been right, she realized. There was more than sufficient space between the door and the jamb to manipulate the wire. And with just a slightly harder push, the latch should slip up and out and free the door.

It wasn't that easy, of course. It took her three attempts before she could get the uneven wire to sit firmly on the bottom of the latch without sliding, but once she did, it was only a matter of an instant until she heard the latch slip free. She dropped the wire and pushed the door open.

She could hear the muffled sound of voices below—from the direction of the dining room, she realized. She felt a wave of smug knowledge. If what she'd seen at breakfast was any evidence of his habits, Slade would be too involved with his meal to waste a thought on her. All she had to do was avoid the housekeeper as she slipped out of the house. And then . . .

She paused, momentarily unsure. Her experience of the morning had proved only too well that she would find no willing help from any of the local farmers. She was on her own, and if she was to get out of the town, she would have to do it entirely on her own.

The only logical course, then, she told herself, was to try to reach the barn at the rear of the house, find a suitable horse, and ride it to the next town, where she would, hopefully, be able to locate a town marshal.

The prospect was far less odious to her than she might have expected it to be. Riding bareback through the open countryside—assuming, that was, she wasn't chased or stopped by any of Slade's men—had the same allure for her that a fancy dress ball might have for another woman her age. She hadn't been allowed to ride her Uncle Bradford's horses bareback for the last several years on her summer visits to Saratoga. ("A lady simply doesn't ride that way, my dear," she could almost hear her Aunt Felicia chiding.) She found herself beginning to relish the opportunity, even forgetting the possible danger in her enthusiasm for what was beginning to seem to her much like a storybook adventure.

Her plan made, Cedar removed her shoes and, holding them firmly, tiptoed down the stairs slowly, taking great care to make no noise. She knew the most dangerous part would be passing the door to the dining room, but she hoped the food and whoever Slade's company might be

227

would be distraction enough to allow her the chance to slip out the front door unobserved.

Once at the foot of the stairs, she darted a quick look toward the dining room. From where she stood, she could see only Slade's large hands, which were reaching for a glass of wine, and his visitor's back. Slade was speaking, his voice low, as though he didn't want the conversation to be overheard, and aside from the dull drone of his indecipherable words there was only the clatter of cutlery against china as the two men ate.

Cedar took a deep breath, swallowed the lump that had formed in her throat, and darted toward the door.

Luckily Slade had left it unlocked when he'd admitted his guest, and it made no sound as she pulled it open and slipped out of the house. She pressed herself against the wall beside the door and waited, half expecting to hear a shout or find the door pulled open and Slade chasing after her.

But neither happened. She took a quick look around and thankfully found the yard empty. She filled her lungs with a deep breath to steady herself as she pulled her shoes back on, and then darted off the porch, down the front steps, and around to the side of the house.

She felt safer there, out of sight thanks to a thick stand of overgrown forsythia. After a moment to collect herself and assure herself that the barn and the yard just to the front of it were empty, and another deep breath, she started off at a run. When she reached it, she yanked the barn door open and darted inside.

It was dim inside, and there was the smell of hay and animals and manure to greet her. But Cedar was pleased more than anything else by the scent (after all, she'd never had to shovel any of the stuff), knowing that it meant there were horses there.

She started slowly down the row of stables, startled at the sight of the animals she found there. They were fine horses, not the sort one would ever hitch to a farm plow. About half way down the row, she stopped, gaping at the horse that was enclosed in the stall.

She knew this animal, she realized. At first she thought she might be mistaken, but when she whispered "Pridey" and the horse turned and looked at her, she knew she wasn't.

She'd watched this horse when it had been born the spring before the previous one, and had grown much attached to him. When he'd seen how fond Cedar was of the animal, her uncle had named him for her, Cedar's Pride, and the previous summer he had been hers to ride. There was no possibility, she knew, that her uncle would ever have sold this particular animal, and yet here he was, in this little town and in Slade's barn.

"Pridey," she called again softly, and the horse whinnied and put his head over the gate of the stall in response. He stamped his hooves against the wood floor, delighted to see her, expecting the usual treat of an apple or the sugar cubes that she inevitably brought him.

It took her a moment to associate what she'd heard Slade tell Willy the night before about some of his boys returning from Saratoga, but when she did, she understood what Cedar's Pride was doing there, what Slade's real business in this small town was. Cedar's Pride had been stolen, and Slade was dealing in stolen horses.

Cedar patted Pridey's nose and smiled when he nuzzled her.

"We both have to escape, Pridey," she told him as she put her hand to the latch on the gate of the stall. "This is hardly the sort of place where either of us belong."

But she did not even get the opportunity to pull open the stall gate.

"I wouldn't be in such a hurry if I was you."

A ball of dull, sick fear formed in the pit of Cedar's stomach as she turned and found Duane standing not ten feet from her. He was glowering at her, and the expression she saw in his eyes told her quite clearly that this time he would not be content to simply drag her back to Slade.

"A few dollars, that's what he'll give me when I take you back," he muttered angrily. "Not even enough for an hour with one of his whores."

He started forward, his hands reaching out for her.

Cedar turned and started to run, but it was no good. He darted after her, throwing the weight of his body forward, grabbing her, bringing the two of them falling down to the hay-strewn floor of the barn.

Cedar screamed.

# Chapter Fourteen

Guy dropped his fork onto his plate and looked up. "What was that?" he asked.

Slade swallowed the mouthful of wine he had been thoughtfully savoring, then wiped his lips with his napkin.

"What?" he asked. "I didn't hear anything."

But Guy had not waited for Slade. He was already on his feet and starting toward the door.

"I heard a scream," he shouted back at Slade as he darted out of the room, ignoring the other man's obvious reluctance to move from the table.

Guy didn't know why, but the sound of the scream had left a thick, smoldering ball of fear deep inside him. Logic told him that there were probably a fair number of women in the town, and that with the number of toughs either directly employed by Slade, or who passed through the town to buy from or sell to him, the sound of a woman's cry was probably fairly commonplace. He really had no reason to assume that it had been Cedar who had cried out, but something inside him told him it was her.

He cursed himself as an idiot, told himself he should have thought of some other way to be accepted by Slade than by wasting precious hours with the fictitious nonsense about a racehorse. Anything might have been going on while he had been inventing plausible untruths for Slade, while he had been congratulating himself for his ability to manipulate people. He felt sick at the realization that she had been in danger while he had been obliviously sitting at Slade's table. The food he'd eaten grew leaden in his stomach.

"But certainly you must be mistaken," Slade called out after him as he watched Guy dart from the room. He dropped his napkin and pushed his chair back from the table.

He realized it was useless for him to hope to stop Guy, a fact that was only made more obvious to him when a second scream, this one louder than the first, again shattered the calm of the midday quiet. Mrs. Fretts came running into the dining room, her hands wet and dripping, her expression smugly filled with an I-told-you-so look that could not be mistaken. Slade waved her to silence before she could speak, then pushed himself to his feet and started after Guy, who was by now out the front door.

"I'm sure it's nothing over which we need concern ourselves," he called, trying one last time to salvage the sanctity of his lunch despite the fact that by now he knew the effort was useless.

Guy was certainly not about to be assuaged. He was running now, toward the rear of the house where he was certain the cry had come from, and Slade was forced to content himself to plod along, muttering to himself, after him.

Once behind the house, Guy stopped for an instant and considered the empty barnyard and the equally deserted field beyond. Everything looked exactly as it ought to look, calm and peaceful, totally quiet save for the constant moan of the wind sweeping down from the mountainside.

"You see," Slade called out to him as he came panting and huffing up behind him. "There's nothing wrong. You must have been mistaken."

But Guy was not quite ready to allow himself to be placated. He pointed to the barn. "I'd like to look there, if you don't mind," he said, then started off before Slade had the chance to give or deny him leave.

Slade scowled as he considered the sight of Guy's retreating back. He wondered what the chances might be that Guy, were he to find something unpleasant going on in the barn, would decide to back out of their bargain. That, Slade noted, would be a real loss. He had, after all, been quite pleased by the feel of those hundred-dollar bills in his hand.

He had little choice but to follow Guy into the barn. As he did, Slade told himself that this man might represent a social scion, but that he was probably little better than a common tough himself. He assured himself that no matter what might be going on in the barn, his deal was surely safe.

For despite his protestations to the contrary, Slade was as sure as Guy that something unsavory was occurring in the barn; and although his reasons for his deduction were decidedly different from his guest's, he was also equally as sure as was Guy, even without stepping inside the barn, that it was Cedar who had cried out. He also had a sneaking suspicion that the cause for the cry could be laid at the feet of the slow-witted and thickly muscled Duane, whose task at this time of day was to clean out the stalls.

Guy was completely oblivious to Slade by now. He reached the door to the barn, pulled it open, and darted inside. What he found was more than ample to justify his fears. Twenty feet in front of him Cedar was on the floor, struggling with a brute of a man who held a hand over her mouth to keep her from crying out again.

Guy didn't even stop to think that he might be more effective in a fight against a man of Duane's size were he holding a weapon. Despite the fact that there were more than ample objects to hand that he might use, he flung himself forward, using only the weight of his body to am-

233

plify the force of his bare fists as he struck at the completely oblivious Duane.

The blow caught Duane on the side of his cheek, momentarily stunning him. He didn't move, other than to shake his head slowly as though clearing away cobwebs that had settled inside. That feat accomplished, he turned to look up and saw Guy standing over him.

"Get away from her," Guy snarled at him.

Duane put a tentative finger to the cut on his cheek, then stared dully up at Guy as he considered the thin warm trickle of red he'd wiped away from his face. Realizing that he had been hurt, he finally released Cedar. He rolled away from her and up and onto his knees.

"I like fightin', too," he laughed.

Then he pushed himself to his feet as he eyed Guy, measuring his opponent's strength against his own and deciding he was not about to be bested by a man he outweighed by at least fifty pounds. He stood, hunched forward, his hands rolled into huge fists. He was actually smiling, pleased with the prospect of doing battle, as he stared at Guy.

"In fact," he added as he took a few sideways steps to better his position in the narrow alley between the horse stalls, "I think I like fightin' best."

"Then let's have it," Guy hissed back.

Duane lunged forward, his hands striking out. Had he taken the time to aim more carefully at his target, had he had a bit more skill, the force of one of those blows would doubtless have flattened Guy. But he fought blindly, like a huge animal who depends solely on his strength to win out for him. He struck wildly, and his fists found only air as Guy stepped quickly aside and then planted one swift, sharp blow to his abdomen. He made an odd deflating sound as the air was suddenly forced from him, and then he doubled over in pain that was only made worse by his surprise.

234

Guy didn't give him the chance to recover, but followed with a second blow that sent Duane sprawling on the floor.

Cedar had rolled away the moment Duane had released her, and was now hunched over, gasping for air and weeping silently as she leaned against the gate to Pridey's stall. As soon as he saw Duane fall to the floor, Guy darted a look at her, and his heart seemed to stand still inside his chest.

He stepped over Duane, blind to everything except the sight of Cedar, crossing to her and kneeling beside her as he reached out for her. He put his hands on her shoulders and pulled her close. He filled with relief and a wash of thick warmth as he realized that she was safe in his arms.

But he knew he couldn't allow himself to hold her this way for very long. It would hardly improve either his situation or Cedar's were Slade to realize that they knew one another. Even if his own position seemed relatively stable at that moment, he knew it would not take much to topple it. And it was all too apparent from the circumstances in which he'd found her that Cedar's situation was far from ideal.

He put his hands on her shoulders and pushed her to arm's length.

"Are you hurt, miss?" he asked her, hoping that when she looked up at him she would see the warning in his eyes, that she wouldn't give either of them away to Slade.

She seemed numb for a moment, as though she weren't at all sure of what was happening, or even where she was. Then she looked up at him and stared at him through the watery veil of her tears.

"Guy?" she asked softly. "But how . . . ?"

Luckily her words were muffled, lost in a wave of emotion. He'd come after her, saved her. She was completely bewildered by his presence and confused as to how he had found her, but she was far more thankful for it. She fell forward, pressing once more against him, more comforted by the simple contact with him than she could have thought possible.

But Guy shook his head and pressed his fingers sharply into her shoulders by way of warning her. He pushed her gently back and away from him.

"Are you hurt, miss?" he asked again, hating the way she winced when he dug his fingers into her flesh and knowing he had hurt her.

This time she seemed to understand. She darted a quick glance to the door of the barn, where Slade had stood watching what had happened from a safe distance. He was just now slowly walking forward, and his expression was strange, oddly rapt, as though he was somehow personally involved with what had happened to her even though he'd only stood by and watched. Even now, as he approached them, he seemed not quite in control of himself, and that realization somehow terrified her almost more than Duane had.

If nothing else, what she saw in Slade's expression sobered her and helped her regain control of herself. She turned back to stare up at Guy. This is another of his masquerades, she told herself, he's pretending the way he did at Madame Blanche's. And it was more than obvious from the way he was holding and talking to her that it was important that she not give him away, that she act as he was, as though they were strangers.

She wanted to throw her arms around him, to cry out with the relief she felt at the sight of him, to thank him for having come after her, to tell him that this time she would do as he told her, that she would do anything so long as he got her away from Slade and this place. Instead, she forced some calm on herself, raising her hand to brush away the hair that had fallen into her face and allowing herself only a fleeting touch of Guy's hand before she let the hand fall back to her lap.

"No, no I'm all right," she murmured. "I don't know how to thank you, sir," she added, and stared directly into Guy's eyes, not missing the look of relief that filled them as he realized she understood.

Meanwhile, Duane had regained his senses. He stared at the two of them for a moment, then his gaze filled with sheer fury as it settled on Guy. He pushed himself unsteadily to his feet. He was not yet ready to accept defeat at the hands of this smug-looking city slick, not while he could still show him a thing or two. He reached for the pitchfork he'd left leaning against the side of a stall and raised it.

Guy was helping Cedar to her feet when she caught a sign of movement behind him from the corner of her eye. She darted a look at it and saw Duane approaching with the raised pitchfork in his hand.

"Look out!" she cried.

Guy swung around to find Duane about to strike at him.

"Drop it, Duane!"

The boom of Slade's shout was shattering. Spurred by the decidedly unpleasant thought of losing a highly profitable commission, he bellowed with a force that even the huge barrel of his chest seemed incapable of producing. It startled the horses and left them neighing and stamping their feet on the wooden floor of their stalls.

It also stopped Duane cold in his tracks.

He swung around to stare at Slade. It took only one glance at the expression in his employer's eyes to sober him. He let go of the pitchfork, and it dropped to the floor with a dull clattering sound. He looked down at his feet, suddenly a huge and hulking schoolboy, shamefaced at being caught tugging at one of the girls' braids.

"He had no right to come in here like that," he sputtered, motioning angrily at Guy but making no further threatening moves. "She was tryin' to get away again and I was just doin' my job, stoppin' her."

"That will be enough, Duane," Slade told him sharply. "Get back to your work."

The big man's cheeks colored with anger, but he was apparently too intimidated by Slade to go against his orders. He bent over and picked up the pitchfork once again, then stalked out of the barn.

Slade had already dismissed him, even before he was gone. Although both Guy and Cedar stared after his retreating figure, Slade's interest had turned in a new direction, one that couldn't be distracted by thoughts of one of his less manageable employees. He reached forward and grasped Cedar by the arm and pulled her away from Guy.

"You will have to excuse this unfortunate episode," he said to Guy as he started out of the barn, pushing Cedar along with him. "The young lady has been placed in my charge, and has not quite resigned herself to that fact. It would seem Duane misinterpreted the circumstances, assuming she was trying to run away."

"Let go of me," Cedar said, twisting but unable to free herself from Slade's grasp. She turned then to Guy, surprised that he made no move to help her. "I *was* trying to get away," she hissed at Slade.

"Nonsense, my dear," Slade told her in a pleasantly even tone, but as he spoke he tightened his hold of her arm, pulling it to her back and letting his fingers bite cruelly into her. He gave her an angry, warning look. "You wouldn't want my guest to have a wrong impression, now, would you?"

"It wouldn't be a wrong impression," she countered, trying to ignore the sharp hurt in her arm. "You're holding me here against my will. And the horses in that barn are stolen."

Slade's expression grew even more perturbed. "That's

238

enough, Miss Rushton," he told her. Then he turned to Guy. "Once again I must apologize that you were forced to witness all this unpleasantness, Mr. Marler," he said. "I do hope it won't in any way interfere with our business arrangements."

Guy shook his head. "I don't see why it should," he said with what appeared to be an amused smile curling up the corners of his lips. "After all, the young lady seems unhurt."

Guy's smile was pure ruse. He could see the way Slade was handling Cedar and knew she was not entirely unhurt. But there was little he could do to change matters just at that moment, and he dared not rouse Slade's suspicions, for he knew it would mean losing completely what chances he had to get her away.

He walked along blithely at Slade's side telling himself that nothing untoward was happening to Cedar at that moment and that he must ignore the relatively minor injury now being done her dignity in hopes of lulling Slade into a carelessness that would enable him to move freely through the town. Even so, he could not push aside the desire to force Slade to unhand her, and his hands ached as he clenched them to keep them still. At least he had found her, he told himself. At least she hadn't been seriously hurt.

"Domestic disturbances are always disagreeable," he said in what he hoped Slade would consider a tone of friendly patter. He darted a quick glance at Cedar. "And it's true, isn't it, that there's nothing worse than a thankless child?"

Slade offered him a smile that was tinged with relief of his own, relief that stemmed from the disappearance of the fear that he might lose the thousand dollars Guy had so willingly handed over to him.

"Just so," he agreed. "Thankless, and unable to see what is best for them."

That comment made, they walked the remainder of the

distance to the house in silence. Cedar could not help fuming at Guy for the way he seemed able to separate himself from her, the way he seemed so indifferent to her. She had to remind herself that he had just saved her from Duane, that he had come here after her and would somehow get her out of this horrible little town. As hard as it seemed to her, she would simply have to hold her tongue, be patient, and trust him to do what he thought best even if she didn't understand why he was doing what he was doing.

When they returned to the house, Slade waved Guy back to the dining room.

"Please, Mr. Marler, don't let this little interruption ruin your meal," he said. "Sit down, and I'll rejoin you in a few moments."

He started to push Cedar toward the stairs.

"Won't the young lady be joining us?" Guy asked before Slade reached the stairs.

Slade turned back to face him. "I'm afraid this unfortunate episode has upset Miss Rushton," he said.

"All the more reason why some pleasant company might distract her," Guy suggested.

But Slade shook his head and again pushed Cedar toward the stairs.

"A few hours rest, alone in her room, and I'm sure she'll be just fine," he said in a tone that told Guy that it would be wise were he to mind his own business.

Guy watched as Slade roughly urged Cedar up the stairs, then turned and went back into the dining room, trying to figure out just how he was going to get her away from Slade and his men.

"So this is how you got out," Slade muttered as he lifted the piece of twisted metal wire from the floor by the open door where Cedar had let it drop on her way out. "It

240

would seem I'll be forced to take greater pains with you, Miss Rushton."

Cedar edged her way back and away from him. She stood by the cot and stared at him.

"Is that all you have to say?" she demanded. "After what that—that person almost did to me, that's all you have to say?"

Slade shrugged. "I warned you about Duane," he said. "If you refused to heed that warning, you can hardly expect me to blame myself for the repercussions of your own foolhardy actions." He considered her rumpled condition and glowered at her. "Frankly, were it not for the fact that it seemed to disturb my customer, I would have let you deal with the consequences of your actions."

But as he spoke, Slade's expression changed from one of aloof objectivity to something a good deal more involved. Cedar realized she had seen before the look that was slowly filling his eyes, realized she had seen it in the eyes of John Sutton and the other men who had come to Madame Blanche's house. And she also realized that it was the look that had been in Slade's eyes a short while before, while they'd been in the barn and she'd looked up to see him approaching her and Guy.

Better to face his anger, she thought, than what she realized Duane's attack had precipitated in him.

"Animal," she hissed at him, disgusted and terrified at the same time. "You're no better than he is."

But at that moment insults seemed incapable of shattering the mood of mellow anticipation that had come over Slade. He found himself remembering what he'd seen in the barn, the sight of Duane's hand on the pale flesh of her bare leg, the look of terror in her eyes. He began to feel what he'd felt then return, to feel himself warm with an unaccustomed excitement. It would not do to rush it, he told himself. It was an excitement that would only grow stronger with a few hours anticipation. He began to step back, out of the room.

"I'll deal with you later, Miss Rushton," he told her. "Just now I have other, more lucrative business to complete."

"Business?" she asked sharply. "I don't suppose that business would have anything to do with the horse you stole from my uncle's stable?"

Slade's expression changed suddenly. When he turned back to her, Cedar saw that his brow was arched in wary consideration.

"I fear you are taken to imagining things, Miss Rushton," he told her, his tone low and sharp.

Cedar's eyes narrowed thoughtfully. She was, she thought, beginning to understand him. Regardless what other passions might move him, his business was still the greatest one. If she could keep his mind on that, perhaps she would be safe from him.

"I'm imagining nothing," she countered. "I know that horse. And I know my uncle would never have sold him. The fact that he's here could only mean that you stole him." Her expression turned smugly knowing. "You deal in stolen horses," she said. "That's what your customer downstairs is doing here, isn't it? Buying stolen horses from you?"

Slade shook his head. When he spoke again, his tone was coldly threatening.

"I'm afraid, Miss Rushton, these accusations of yours can only get you into more trouble than you can possibly imagine."

"I'm already in trouble," she replied. "Just being here, under your thumb, is more trouble than I care to consider."

The edges of Slade's cheeks colored slightly with anger, and he reentered the room, crossing it to her. He reached out suddenly, putting his hand in her hair, wrapping it around his fingers, and pulling her head back sharply. Cedar uttered a yelp of pain. He ignored it as he placed his free hand on her throat.

"I suggest you consider just how easy it would be for that thumb to press down and squash you, Miss Rushton," he told her as he looked down at her upturned face and increased the pressure of his fingers against her throat. Cedar felt the pressure against her windpipe and gasped softly as she drew in air. "I might remind you that I may very well be all that is standing between you and an unpleasantly short future when Michael McNaughton arrives. If you have an ounce of sense, you would consider how you might convince me to protect you, rather than going to the pains you seem to be determined to take to ire me."

Cedar swallowed, frightened by the look she saw in his eyes as well as by the realization that he could easily press those thick fingers into her neck a bit harder and simply snap it. She'd been wrong, she realized. There was no way she could possibly manipulate this man, not in the least. He was dangerous and she would have to be nothing short of a fool to think she could control him in the slightest way.

Slade saw the fear in her eyes, and a tremor of satisfied pleasure washed through him. He lowered his face to hers, pressing his lips against hers. The feel of them, thick and soft and damp, revolted Cedar, but she was too frightened now to move, too frightened at that moment even to think of fighting him. Even Duane's outright brutality had not frightened her the way Slade did. She had no choice now but to depend solely on Guy.

"Have I made myself clear to you, Miss Rushton?" Slade asked when he'd lifted his lips from hers.

"Yes, Mr. Slade," she replied, her tone weakly submissive. "You've made yourself completely clear."

Her docility, like her fear, seemed to please him.

"There will be no more of your foolish little games," he

told her, giving her hair a final, sharp tug in warning. Then he released his hold, taking his fingers from her neck and unwinding her hair from his hand. "Unfortunately, I have no more time to waste on you just now." Cedar saw the hint of want return to his eyes. "We will have to continue our discussion later."

He smiled once more at her, a smile that promised a good deal more than Cedar wanted to consider. She was left to watch him silently as he stepped out of the room and pulled the door closed behind him. A shiver passed through her despite the heat of the enclosed attic.

This time, when he locked her in, he took the piece of spring she had used to open the door, twisting and placing it so that it firmly secured the latch.

"You will not be able to repeat your previous method of escape," he called in to her. "Under the circumstances, were I you, I would spend the next few hours considering my sins, Miss Rushton." He emitted a brief, sharp bark of laughter. "And ways you might atone for them."

Cedar rattled the door, but the noise only seemed to amuse him. He laughed again as he descended the stairs.


Guy was sitting at the table, his glass in his hand, when Slade returned to the dining room.

"Now, Mr. Marler," Slade said as he reseated himself at his own place, "you must tell me how to get in touch with you in New York. I will set events in motion here. Once the details have been handled and your merchandise is here and available, I will send word to you. I shouldn't imagine it would take more than three or four days."

"You do certainly seem to have the matter in hand," Guy said, taking pains to sound agreeable. "But I hadn't decided to leave your scenic little hamlet just yet."

Slade raised a questioning brow. "I would think a man of your tastes and habits, a man habituated to the diversions New York has to offer him, would be glad to rid himself of the dust of this place," he said.

"Under other circumstances, I would agree most whole-heartedly with you," Guy replied. He swirled the dark red liquid in his glass and held it up, pretending to consider the color of the wine. "But it would seem that your little community is soon to provide a distraction that even New York City cannot offer."

Slade grinned in sly acknowledgment. "You mean, of course, the fight between Morrissey and Sullivan," he said.

Guy nodded. "I thought I'd spend a day or two admiring the scenery and attend that most intriguing event," he said.

"I can't say that I blame you," Slade replied. "I must confess to a certain sense of anticipation with regard to that particular contest myself. Sullivan has been vocally proclaiming his dominance, but I find myself not entirely convinced by mere rhetoric."

"The talk in the city is that Sullivan will win," Guy said. He brought the glass to his lips and took a swallow of his wine. "In any event, and aside from the boasts, time will answer all questions on the matter." He licked a drop of wine from his lips and smiled at Slade. "And I dare say that a few days in the country could not prove detrimental to even the most jaded among us. The fresh, clean air, the sunshine, the beauties of nature to admire."

Slade laughed and nodded his agreement.

"If you wish to remain, I hope you will do me the honor of staying here," he said expansively. "I daresay you will find the accommodations at the hotel a bit rudimentary for a man used to the finer things life has to offer."

Guy smiled. "You are too kind, Mr. Slade." He lifted the glass appreciatively. "And your hospitality is most appreciated."

"Please," Slade said, waving away Guy's thanks and re-

245

turning his smile, "it is the least I can do for a client who admires and appreciates the simple pleasures of the local scenery."

Guy cleared his throat.

"Apropros of simple pleasures and local scenery, Mr. Slade," he said, "it is my habit, whenever possible, to enhance the immediate landscape with the presence of a pretty woman." He put the glass back on the table and grinned at Slade. "I don't suppose there might be a young lady whose time I could appropriate? In exchange for a suitable remuneration, of course."

Slade nodded. "Why certainly," he said. "There are a dozen accommodating women next door, at the hotel."

Guy leaned forward. "I had taken a bit of a fancy to your fiery young charge," he said.

Slade shrugged and gave Guy an apologetic look.

"I'm afraid that particular young woman might not prove quite as appropriate for your purposes, Mr. Marler," he said. "She is not quite as" — he paused for an instant — "shall we say, accomplished? Yes, accomplished. She is not quite as accomplished in such matters as a man of the world would ordinarily find desirable. Besides," he added, rather sharply, "she is apt to invent rather wild stories to boot."

Guy grinned a wide, slightly lecherous grin.

"It's not her talk that interests me, Mr. Slade," he said. "Let me assure you that I would be inclined to treat any stories she might care to share as the fantasies I'm sure they are." He lifted the wineglass again and fixed Slade with a meaningful glance. "And I frankly admire a touch of innocence in a woman. It adds to the challenge."

"Perhaps this one might prove a greater challenge than you'd find worth the effort, Mr. Marler."

Guy pretended to consider a moment, his lips pursed in apparent thought. "I think not," he said finally. "I feel quite confident that, with the proper incentive, she could be convinced to be amenable."

"The proper incentive?"

"I do not wish to appear immodest, Mr. Slade, but I have found that I have a certain knack when it comes to the ladies. Given the opportunity, I have found that a man can always find some way to rouse a woman's more tender emotions." He grinned slyly. "Surely you know what I mean."

Slade cleared his throat, and nodded. "Indeed, Mr. Marler," he replied.

"It is a shame that brute out in the barn didn't understand that it is never even remotely necessary to treat a woman coarsely. But that's neither here nor there. I must admit that he did me a small favor. Considering the young lady's experiences this afternoon, I feel sure I could provide her with the degree of comfort and understanding that would provide all the incentive she needs to become quite pleasant a companion."

"You are a marvel of confidence, Mr. Marler," Slade said.

Guy saw the look of incredulity that Slade leveled at him. He wondered if he hadn't perhaps boasted a bit too much about his abilities. Hoping to still any hint of suspicion that might be forming in Slade's mind, he reached into his breast pocket and for the second time that day removed his wallet. He glanced at the two hundred-dollar bills and the half dozen small bills that remained in it. They were the last of the money he'd wrung from Granger Nichols's tight fists. He hoped it was enough.

"And this, I hope, will provide the incentive to induce you to be willing to honor my whim," he said as he withdrew the two hundred-dollar bills and placed them on the table beside Slade's hand.

Slade looked down at the bills. He hesitated for a moment, his greed battling with his desire to keep Cedar for himself. That desire, which had sprung up when he'd seen

Cedar on the floor of the barn trying vainly to push Duane away and had only grown stronger during the moments he'd spent with her in the attic room, would probably have won out had Guy not put the bills so close to his hand.

The proximity of that money to his hand seemed to heat his fingers, to make them itch. He edged his hand closer to the bills, until the tips of his fingers were on top of them. While his first inclination was to reject Guy's offer, the crisp feel of those bills beneath his fingers subtly and smoothly reversed that inclination. After all, he told himself, she would still be his when this most generous customer left town. It was foolish to turn away good money, very good money, when the only cost to him would be a few days' wait for what he wanted. And the wait, he told himself, would not diminish his pleasure. On the contrary, it would only make it better for him in the end.

"As you like," he said finally as his fingers closed around the bills. "She's yours until after the fight." He lifted the money and put it discreetly into his pocket. "I'm always willing to accommodate a paying customer's whims."

Guy smiled, more than satisfied with the arrangement. He lifted his glass and took another taste of the wine.

"Your hospitality, Mr. Slade," he said, "is as fine as your wine."

But despite the words and the smile, Guy felt far less complacent than he wished to appear. He might have found Cedar, he might even have managed to insure that she would be close to him for the next few days, but that did not in any way affect the fact that he had no means of getting her away. Nor had he found all the answers to the questions he had come to Boston Four Corners to find. He still had no idea how the stolen horses were gotten out of the town. Nor did he have any answers to the identity of Mary Farren's killer.

248

In short, he'd come with his pockets full and a long list of questions that needed answering. His pockets were empty now, and he still didn't have many of the answers he'd come seeking.

If he simply took Cedar and left—assuming, of course, that he could get her away in reasonable safety—he would be returning to New York empty-handed as far as Granger Nichols was concerned. If he didn't go back with either a damn good story or at least the total of the money he'd extracted from Nichols for expenses, he knew he might just as well not return at all. He would most certainly be out of a job. And Magnus Rushton would have lost what little hope remained to him that he might be acquitted.

No, Guy thought, as he emptied the glass of the last of the wine in it, things were not going as well as he had hoped. And at that moment, he didn't see them getting any better.

# Chapter Fifteen

"How kind of you to join us, Miss . . ."

Guy had been seated at the dining table with Slade, but now he leaped to his feet to greet Cedar as she entered the room. "Miss Rushton, is it?"

He smiled at her smugly, giving every indication that he was inordinately pleased with himself.

Cedar had no idea what was going on, but Guy's presence assured her that nothing unduly unpleasant was about to happen to her. And she had to admit that she was more than a little bit relieved at the early reprieve from the heat and discomfort of her attic-room prison.

All of which left her the freedom from fear that allowed her to consider more mundane matters, the most immediate the recognition that she was hungry. Her stomach growled softly as she darted a glance to the platters of food on the table. Their contents had been seriously decimated by Guy's and Slade's meal, but more than enough remained to rouse the empty rumble inside her and make her mouth water.

"Yes, Rushton, Cedar Rushton," she replied absently. She returned his smug smile. "I'm sorry, I don't believe we have been properly introduced."

Once again he flashed a smile, this time a smile with a hint of real amusement in it, as he held out his hand to her. "How thoughtless," he said. "You're right, of course. My name's Guy Marler."

"I'm afraid my joining you has nothing to do with kindness," she added, darting another glance at a plate of roast beef and then turning her eyes accusingly on Slade. "I had no choice in the matter." As though to punctuate the point, she turned to Mrs. Fretts, who had once again escorted her from the confines of the attic room and stood now just behind her wearing what Cedar assumed must be a perpetual expression of disapproval.

"Really, my dear," Slade rasped.

Cedar turned back to face him and found his expression was sharp and intimidating. He was warning her, she realized, telling her that she should behave in the presence of his client or later she would suffer the consequences. She smugly told herself that Guy would see to it that there would be no later, at least not with Slade. But prudence also told her it wouldn't be wise to overstep her bounds, that doing so might get both her and Guy into unnecessary trouble.

"Does this mean I'm to be given a final meal?" she asked brightly. She nodded at the platter of roast beef and potatoes.

Slade pretended surprise. "Are you hungry?" he asked. "I'd thought Mrs. Fretts brought you your lunch in your room." He looked up at the housekeeper. "Really, Mrs. Fretts. How could you be so negligent?" He pointedly ignored the scowl on the housekeeper's face. "Fetch a plate for Miss Rushton, if you please," he ordered, then turned his attention back to Cedar. "Please, sit, my dear."

Guy quickly pulled out a chair, and Cedar settled onto it while he held it for her. Her curiosity was more than a little roused by the amount of attention and consideration she was suddenly being shown. Most especially she was bewildered by the change in Slade. The threatening brute had totally disappeared, supplanted by a good-humored burgher. Whatever had caused the change—and she had little doubt but that Guy had had

251

his hand in it—she was not about to object.

"I hope you've recovered from that unfortunate incident earlier," Guy said as he pushed her chair up close to the table.

It wasn't only Slade who seemed to be a changeling, Cedar mused. Guy's tone was so greasily solicitous that she raised a bewildered brow. Whatever had happened during the half hour she'd been locked in the attic room, it seemed to have transformed both men to a degree that completely baffled her. Especially after the cool way Guy had acted when he and Slade brought her back to the house, this excessive show of regard for her feelings rang decidedly false to her.

This was not at all like him, she mused. She had thought him many things during the previous day, and most of them were decidedly uncomplimentary, but it would never have occurred to her to think of him as the sort who would waste his efforts with shallow pretense.

She turned her face toward his as he leaned close over the side of her chair. She began to feel overwhelmed by a haze of bewildered curiosity.

"Yes," she murmured, "I'm much better now."

He seated himself on the chair beside hers and again leaned toward her. Cedar didn't quite understand why, for she'd thought herself quite under control, but his mention of Duane's attack and his show, however false she might think it, of concern for her, made her feel suddenly weepy and helpless. When it had happened it had somehow seemed remote, impossible, the way a bad dream is remote even when it is terrifying. But now the memory returned to her with a reality that had evaded her while it was actually happening.

The thought of what Duane might have done to her had Guy not come when he had left her trembling inside. She wanted to feel herself close to him, wanted to be enclosed by his arms, wanted him to hold her and assure her that he

252

would get her away from this place, that he would keep her safe.

It was, certainly, a childish reaction, a weakling's reaction. She told herself that it was foolish to feel so dependent on him, that she'd prided herself for having sufficient wits to keep her from ever feeling useless, and yet that was exactly how she felt at that moment, useless and inept and needing him more than she could ever have imagined herself needing a man.

"It must have been terrifying for you," he said.

"It was," Cedar answered, truthfully enough.

She looked at him and then at Slade, still wondering what was going on. Slade's passivity was enough to tell her that whatever it was, it happened with his approval.

There must have been a tremble in her voice when she'd spoken, for Guy put his hand on hers and pressed it.

"I can't tell you how sorry I am it happened," he murmured.

This time Cedar knew that the words weren't forced or false, knew that his concern was real. She looked down at his hand on hers and felt herself go weak inside. So simple a thing, the touch of one hand to another, and yet it sent shivers of warmth and comfort all through her. And with the warmth came a flood of memories, memories of what it had been like to lie with him, of how he'd made her forget everything save his body and her own.

The memory startled her, for she'd determined to purge it completely from her mind, to never allow herself to think about it again. Yet it flowed through her unbidden at that moment, and she welcomed it.

When she glanced up and saw Slade's smile as he noticed Guy's hand on hers, she was tempted to pull her own away. There was something about his expression that made her own thoughts seem dirty to her, vile and base.

"I hope you will give me the opportunity to make you forget it," Guy said, returning to the same question-

253

ably solicitous tone he'd used before.

Cedar forced herself to push aside the thoughts that had filled her at his touch, forced herself to ignore Slade's nasty, knowing glance. Guy was acting this way for a reason, she told herself. Whatever the game was, it seemed only prudent that she play it with him. And that meant she must use her wits, not let herself become maudlin and useless.

She let her eyes grow wide in preparation for the role, then turned them to meet Guy's. She sighed audibly.

"If you hadn't come when you did, I don't want to think what might have happened," she said in a breathily adoring tone that she could see made the corners of his lips twitch in amusement. She wasn't at all sure she liked that. After all, what she'd said was perfectly true. "I don't know how to thank you."

"Mr. Marler had hoped you'd be willing to spend a bit of time with him," Slade interjected.

"I thought I might induce you to show me around this beautifully pastoral setting," Guy added. "I had hoped for a long walk with you through those rolling hills at the foot of the mountain."

So that's what this is all about, Cedar thought. Somehow, he's convinced Slade to let the two of us out of the house alone together. It would seem that Slade was in the business of selling more than stolen horses and the whores at the hotel next door. Well, she was hardly in a position to object to the transaction. In fact, it was more than she could have dared hope for, because it meant she and Guy would be able to get away.

Guy dropped her hand and sat back as Mrs. Fretts deposited a plate, cutlery, and napkin in front of Cedar. He pushed the platter of beef toward her, then helped her to a substantial piece.

Cedar politely smiled her thanks to him, then lifted her fork and knife.

"It would be the least I could do," she agreed. "Certainly

254

my debt to you far exceeds so small a recompense as the one you ask."

"Ah, but a few hours of your company I would think are beyond price, Miss Rushton," he replied.

Cedar was forced to fight to keep herself from laughing at that. She pretended to be distraught. "However meager your request," she sighed, "I fear I find myself unable to honor it." She looked across the table at Slade, fixing him with an accusing glance. "Apparently you haven't been told that I've been confined to the farm," she said, then returned her attention to Guy as she cut a bite of the meat. "Much as I would love to explore the countryside with you, Mr. Marler, I'm afraid that would constitute a transgression of Mr. Slade's rules."

She looked down, busying herself with the task of cutting a bite of the beef, pleased with the uncomfortable choking sound coming from beneath the napkin Slade lifted to his lips.

He recovered and was about to speak when Guy cut him off.

"I've assured Mr. Slade that I would not for an instant take my eyes off you," he said. "And I've promised to return you to him safely and in time for dinner."

He refilled his glass from the bottle and placed it between them, nodding in approval when she reached for the glass. She noticed that he turned slightly and winked at Slade.

It was the wink that angered her, the unspoken conspiracy between men with regard to their ability to handle a woman. She hesitated only an instant, telling herself that if she was acting a part, she might just as well act it to the hilt and give him everything he seemed to want. She lifted the glass and brought it to her lips.

The wine was excellent, that was obvious, even to one of her decidedly limited knowledge of the subject. It felt thick on her tongue, with a rich, heady taste that lingered even after she'd swallowed. She told herself that she oughtn't to be surprised at that, that Slade would deny himself little that brought him pleasure if it were possible for him to avoid the deprivation.

When she returned the glass to the table, she noticed Guy's sharp glance, and she nearly laughed aloud at the way he took the glass, drinking from it and placing it in front of himself, just beyond her reach. She wondered if he thought she might become drunk the way she had that afternoon in her father's house. She returned her attention to the slab of beef on her plate, yet even as she did she realized that that was precisely what she wanted to do — become drunk again as she had that afternoon, drunk enough so that she could let herself repeat the actions of that afternoon without being assaulted by so much as a hint of guilt.

She was, she found, suddenly without any appetite at all. She dropped her knife and fork to the plate and pushed it aside. She felt a dull numbness in the pit of her stomach, and she told herself there was no reason for it, that she was, if anything, doing what Guy wanted her to do, feeling what he wanted her to feel. It was all part of the game he was playing with Slade, part of what they must do to get away.

But it wasn't that, she knew, that had suddenly placed that hard ball she felt in the pit of her stomach. It was the realization that she did feel guilty about that afternoon, that no matter what, she knew it was wrong to do what she had done with a man whose interest in her was little more than a sidebar to his real concern — getting a news story. The last thing she ought to want, she told herself, was Guy Marler's attentions. In fact, her only interest in him ought to be the help she needed in finding a way to clear her father's name. But despite the rational arguments she gave herself, still she knew she did not feel that way, knew she couldn't ever feel that way.

"Excuse me?" she murmured.

She had no idea what Slade had asked her, nor how long she had been sitting in mute, oblivious thought. From the

256

look he leveled at her, she assumed it had been long enough to seem excessive to him.

"I asked you if you weren't hungry?" Slade repeated, this time with a shade of pique in his voice. He nodded toward her plate with its burden of nearly untouched food.

"I suppose the thought of a last meal isn't quite as appealing as I thought it would be," she replied.

"That wasn't funny, my dear," Slade told her.

"And there is no need to think of a last meal," Guy quickly interjected. "After all, I've promised Mr. Slade that you will be perfectly safe in my charge. I wouldn't dream of allowing any harm to befall you."

"I didn't mean to suggest that you would, Mr. Marler," she told him. "I suppose I just wasn't as hungry as I thought."

"Well then, if you've done with your lunch," Guy said, "I assume Mr. Slade has business matters to attend to. It is cruel of us to flaunt our idleness in front of him." He pushed back his chair and stood with his hand extended to her. "Shall we remove our indolent selves from his presence before our example exerts an unduly negative influence over him?"

Cedar stared at his extended hand for a moment, then placed her own in it and stood. Guy tucked it into the crook of his arm.

"We leave you, then, Mr. Slade," he said.

The two men exchanged smugly knowing glances.

"Enjoy your afternoon," Slade grunted as they started for the door.

"What just happened in there?" Cedar demanded once they were out the front door. "Am I to assume that Slade is now playing the role Madame Blanche played two nights ago?"

"I knew the moment I first met you that you were most perceptive, Cedar," Guy replied.

"So you've bought me again?" she asked.

He grinned. "I have purchased exclusive rights to you for a full forty-eight hours," he said. "I should think a short walk through one of those fields will be all that Slade would consider a proper courtship."

"And then?" she asked.

"Let's get away from here before we talk," he said.

He turned toward the wide hay field that led to the forested side of the mountain, crossed the road, and the two of them began to walk through the tall, golden spikes of thick grass.

"How did you find me?" she asked. "Or am I to assume this is simply another coincidence, that you just happened on this place?"

"No," he told her, "I followed you. When you didn't return home, I went back to Blanche's and talked to your friend Elly."

Cedar stared at him a moment, wondering what else he'd done besides talk with Elly. Then she shook her head.

"I don't think she considers me a friend any longer," she said. "Not after what happened. Not after the way I lied to her."

"I think she may have reconsidered that point once I explained why you did what you did," Guy told her.

Cedar fell silent at that, and they walked through the field, listening to the hum of the insects in the hay and the sweeping flow of the wind. It felt remarkably good to her to feel the bite of the wind and the warmth of the afternoon sunshine on her face. After everything that had happened in the preceding days, it seemed impossibly wholesome and innocent to be walking through this field, to turn and glance back at the valley with its half-harvested fields. The small groups of cows seemed to her to be dark-spotted and ungainly dowagers who stood chatting at a tea party, quietly murmuring their secrets to one another while they consumed their afternoon dainties.

But it wasn't innocent, she reminded herself. Slade was there, and so were his men and his whores and the stolen horses. Nothing about it was innocent.

When they had reached the far side of the field and stood staring down into the valley, Guy finally broke their silence.

"You might try to act a little happy to be in my company," he told her. "After all, I told Slade I had a way with the ladies."

She turned to face him and found him grinning at her.

"Do you?" she asked.

He shrugged and sobered. "Perhaps you should tell me," he suggested. "For a while I thought I did, but now I'm not so sure."

They stood for a while, facing one another, staring at one another in silence. The wind tore at Cedar's hair and pressed her skirt against her legs, while the edges of the material were free to billow and snap. Guy felt a thick edge of want as he stared at her. She was more beautiful to him at that moment than he could ever have imagined a woman might be.

He held out his arms to her and Cedar found herself falling into them, wanting to feel them close around her, wanting to feel herself safe again, not caring if that want meant she was weak, not caring about anything save the need she felt for him. And once she felt his arms close around her, everything that had happened since she'd last seen him came flooding back to her in painful accusation of how little she had done on her own, of how useless she had been without him.

"What's this," he asked, and she could hear the amusement in his tone, "the indomitable Miss Rushton on the verge of tears?"

He was right, she realized, she was on the verge of tears. And she was, she knew now, decidedly far from indomitable. Everything she had done since she'd made him leave her at Madame Blanche's had been precisely wrong, and she was only too painfully aware of that fact.

"I should have done as you told me and gone with you," she murmured. "I shouldn't have thought I could deal with them alone. You warned me. I just didn't listen."

"It's over, Cedar," he whispered. He stroked her hair, losing his fingers in the soft, blond curls, wondering why the feel of it pleased him so. "We go on from here."

"Yes," she said, "you're right." She swallowed the lump in her throat and pushed herself away from him. "It's stupid to linger over mistakes, especially when there's still so much to be done."

But the primly resolute mask she was trying to maintain, she realized, was the act now. At that moment she felt neither strong nor ready to march forth into battle, even battle for her father's cause. At that moment, she wanted nothing but the feel of Guy's arms around her.

"Perhaps those things could wait," he told her softly, "at least for a little while."

And then he brought his lips to hers.

It was something Guy realized he had feared he might never know again, the feel of his lips touching hers. He had buried the fear deep within himself, not even wanting to let himself think about it for fear the thought might somehow encourage reality to follow. But despite his efforts, he'd known that deep inside he'd feared he might not find her in time, feared he might never again hold her in his arms. And that fear had eaten into him, filling him with a pain and a sense of loss unlike any he'd ever known before.

But now she was in his arms, safe, close. Since he'd walked into that barn and seen her, all he'd wanted was this, to hold her close, to know that he hadn't lost her after all, to swear to himself that he would always keep her safe. It had been the hardest thing he had ever done to act cavalierly with Slade, to pretend she meant nothing to him, while every thought he had was of her. And now he knew he never wanted to release her.

He pressed his lips to hers hungrily, and then to her ear and her neck. He felt the press of her lips against his neck, felt the warmth of her breath and heard the thick choked catch in her throat.

When he finally released her, he knew that they couldn't simply return to Slade's house, knew that he wanted her beyond all reason. He stared at her eyes in silence, wondering if she'd say something, wondering if she'd give him a hint of what it was she wanted from him, or tell him she wanted nothing at all.

But she didn't. Instead, she stood staring up at him, and her lips, those full, soft lips that had seemed so incredibly enticing to him the first time he'd set eyes on her, were still. They'd become flushed with the heat of their kiss, and were slightly parted. And all he could think of was the taste of them, and how much he wanted more.

He motioned toward the woods.

"Perhaps we might explore?" he suggested, knowing a walk in the woods was not really all he wanted to do at that moment and equally sure from the way she looked at him as she nodded that that was not all she wanted, either.

They walked along the edge of the undergrowth until they found what appeared to be a fairly well worn path. They turned onto it, walking in a solemn silence. Once they were away from the open field, they found the wind had far less of a bite, and even the sound of it seemed a good deal more remote.

They followed the path for a while, then turned off it onto a narrower one, a game path, Guy assumed, and then realized he was right when they came upon a thick stand of tall pines under which was a smooth, worn place where some deer had once made a bed.

He removed his jacket and laid it on the bed of pine needles. Then he sat and held his hands up to Cedar.

There was no pretense now, Cedar realized, and no need for it. If she pretended, it was to herself, and the pretense

261

was that she didn't want this, that she could turn away and dismiss the thought of him from her mind. But even the thought, she knew, was meaningless.

She moved close to him and let him put his hands to her waist and pull her down to him.

Lying on the soft bed of pine needles, staring up at him, seeing him framed by a lacework of greenery on a bed of clear blue sky, it seemed to her as though they were alone in all the world, that they were remote enough so that no one and nothing could come close enough to them to touch them. And that, she realized, was just what she wanted, to be free from thoughts of anything and anyone save him, to simply lose herself to him.

He leaned forward to her, his lips inches from hers, his fingers splaying her hair out around her face, turning it into a silken golden halo. He wanted to lower his lips to hers, to touch them and taste them again, but for a moment he didn't. He simply stared down at her, letting the dull ache of want grow thick inside him.

But Cedar reached up to him, putting her hands to his neck and pulling him down to her, letting the contact fill her, thankful for the fire it set free inside her. Let it burn, she thought. Let it consume every memory of what had happened in the previous days. Let it sear away everything until she felt empty and clean again, clean from Duane's touch and Slade's, clean of the unwanted knowledge she'd gained at Madame Blanche's, clean of those things Magnus had told her that she never wanted to hear.

And it did. The waves of liquid heat rose up inside her until it seemed there was nothing else. Guy's lips fell from her lips to her neck and then followed the exposed V of flesh that grew slowly larger as he unbuttoned her blouse. She let herself drink in the feel of his lips and his hands against her skin as the waves grew higher and hotter.

After that it was all a dim haze, the remote sense of reaching for his belt, the lost, slightly dazed realization that she was shedding the wrinkled skirt, the only sure thing the fact that she was reaching for him, spreading herself beneath him, welcoming him when he pressed himself to her, and the sweet surge of fire as he entered her.

There was nothing else, not even the memory of how it had been the first time. There was only this, this moment, this burst of joyous fire within her, this shattering wave of feeling that pushed away everything else, leaving her breathless and wanting only that it go on forever. The waves throbbed within her, each one supplanting the last and in turn being buried beneath the crashing assault of the next, until suddenly she felt as though she were crushed beneath them, as though she were shattered into a million pieces, as though there were nothing left of her but a great soothing wave of peaceful contentment.

Guy was taken by surprise by the way she clung to him, the way she pressed herself to him, the way she held him close inside her. Her eagerness for him, the realization that he'd awakened this need in her, pleased and excited him more than he could have thought possible. And when he felt her shuddering, trembling release, he could not contain his passion. No amount of skill or practice could have prepared him for the intensity of the sudden and uncontrollable sweep of it as it sent him following.

"What happened?"

Cedar was clinging to him, her breath ragged and strained, as she stared up at him.

Guy smiled. "We made love," he told her.

It startled him to realize that his own breath was as pantingly ragged as was hers. He was as bewildered as she seemed to be, only what he did not understand was not what had happened but how it had happened that way, how it had been so quick, so powerful, so completely beyond his ability to control it. He found himself smiling foolishly and thinking that for all his touted ability with women, she had managed to completely disarm him.

"Is it supposed to be like that?" she asked.

He nodded. "When you're very lucky," he said.

She was silent for a moment, and he held her close to him until her breath became less labored. Then she let her hand drop from his shoulder to his shirt.

"Like this?" she asked.

He grinned. They were both still half-dressed. Those objects of clothing they wore — his shirt, her blouse and chemise — were wrinkled and disordered.

"Disgraceful, isn't it?" he said. "I guess we were in too much of a hurry to think about those things."

But he wasn't in too much of a hurry now, he thought as he pulled aside her blouse, slipping it down her arms and then letting his hands slide slowly along the smooth flesh of her back as he lifted away the chemise. He ought to be sated with that startlingly powerful release, and yet as he touched her he could feel the hunger starting to grow again inside him. He stroked her skin gently, seeking the reward of a slow heated rush to her skin and soon finding exactly what he sought.

He could see from the coy smile on her lips that she knew precisely what he was doing. He realized he didn't mind. He pressed a kiss to each of her rosy nipples and one to her lips before he pulled away from her to shrug off the remainder of his own clothing. Then he returned to her, lowering himself to her, pressing his lips to her breasts and her belly.

The second time, they made love slowly, almost carefully, as Guy took pains to prolong it for her, to bring her to the edge again and again until finally the release that took hold of her was too strong to be denied.

It seemed to last forever, that moment. For the two of them it was an instant that was almost timeless, an eternity encompassed by the space of a sigh and a kiss.

Cedar had never dreamed of anything like this, never thought she could feel so much a part of him. She thought him a magician, thought he had bewitched her, and for a fleeting moment wondered what other powers he might have. But she let the thought pass, not really caring what power he held over her as long as he made her feel the way he did.

It was contagious, that thought of magic, for Guy found himself wondering what sorcery she might possess that wakened such odd feelings of tenderness in him and gave rise to so much want that it seemed to overwhelm him. He had begun by wanting only to touch her, to kiss her. But he'd felt that desire many times and for many women, and always, before, the desire had fled quickly, the fire always being consumed by the spark that lit it. With her it was different, for there seemed to be no end to the want. That difference baffled him, and would, he knew, soon enough force him to wonder where it might lead. But for that moment, as they lay quiet and close, he wanted only to hold her in his arms and feel her body close to his.

They lay still for a while. Cedar realized she'd even dozed when she found herself suddenly sharply awake, staring up to a darkening sky that she had not even noticed growing dimmer. Despite the warmth of Guy's body next to hers, she shivered from the late-afternoon chill.

Guy pressed his lips to her forehead.

"It's getting late," he said softly. "And cold. We should dress and go back."

Startled, she pulled herself away from him, sitting up on her haunches and staring down at him.

"What do you mean, go back?" she demanded.

"I mean it's getting cold. It'll be dark in an hour or so. We can't be wandering out here in the darkness."

She shook her head. "We can't go back there," she insisted. "We have to get away from here, get to the next town, find the police, tell them what is going on here."

Guy pushed himself up to sit facing her. "It's more than twelve miles to the next town, Cedar," he told her. "You

265

don't expect to walk that way in the darkness, do you? Or are you suggesting we sleep out in the cold?"

She smiled smugly at him. "We could keep ourselves warm," she said.

He grinned. "I suppose we could. But the cold aside, I don't think we'd get very far on foot before Slade and his men caught up to us."

She thought about that for a moment, forced to agree that he was probably right. But his expectation that they return to Slade was absurd. She could not understand why he would so much as consider it.

"Then we can go back down to the barn and steal some horses," she said. She felt herself being blanketed by an oddly determined confidence as she spoke, a certainty that they could do anything. "One of those horses is my uncle's anyway, so it wouldn't really be stealing." She stopped and laughed. "What am I saying. What difference does it make? And it can't be wrong to steal horses from a horse thief. We just take horses and get away and find the police and—"

Guy shook his head, putting his fingers to her lips to still her words.

"No, we can't, Cedar," he told her. "We can't leave just yet. And as for going to the police, it wouldn't matter. They don't have jurisdiction over this town."

Cedar's brow wrinkled. "What do you mean?" she asked.

"It's like this," he said as he handed her her chemise.

He began to tell her what he knew about the town, and they were both nearly dressed before he was finished. Cedar was pulling on her shoes when he fell silent, and she sat, thoughtful and confused for a moment before she looked up at him.

"But what has all that to do with us?" she demanded. "We still have to get away from this place." She felt herself shiver and knew it was not the cold that had caused it. "Slade might do anything—"

"You don't have to be afraid of Slade," Guy interjected.

"I've seen to it that he won't go near you for the time being. The man seems to have an exceedingly highly developed sense of greed."

She couldn't keep from laughing at his expression. "How much did you pay him?" she asked.

"More than I care to think about," he replied dryly.

"Well, am I worth it?"

He grinned. "So far," he said, and leaned forward to her to plant a firm little kiss on her lips.

Cedar had to force herself to concentrate on the subject at hand.

"But Slade isn't the only one," she insisted. "Michael McNaughton is coming up here; Slade said he was. And there's no telling what orders he has from Tweed. He could do anything."

But Guy was not about to be intimidated by the possibility of what Tweed's man might or might not do.

"As long as I'm a highly valued customer," he told her, "Slade won't let him do anything that might anger me. I told you, you don't have to be afraid."

"I'm not just thinking about myself," she said. She couldn't understand why he was arguing this way, and her tone was beginning to grow a bit strident. "I'm thinking about my father. We have to get back to the city. We still have to find Mary Farren's killer."

"Just try to have a little patience, Cedar."

She shook her head. "I don't understand you. Why would you want to go back there?"

Guy knelt down beside her and took her hand in his.

"Look, Cedar, I've already told you why there is no law in this town. And you've already figured out that Slade is a horse thief. But he's worked out a way of getting his stolen horses out of the town without taking them back into New York State where he could be caught and prosecuted. If I can find out how he does it, I'll have one hell of a story."

That revelation seemed to momentarily still her.

"Story?" Cedar repeated finally in a dull, unbelieving tone.

Guy nodded. "And if I happen to be able to give a first-hand report of that prizefight McNaughton is coming up here to see, so much the better."

"That's what this is all about?" she asked. "That's why you came here? To get a story?"

"Of course not, Cedar. I didn't say that."

"And my father?" she demanded. "Have you forgotten that we were going to find the man who did the murder he's accused of having committed?"

"It's all tied in," he told her.

"How?" she demanded sharply.

"I don't know yet," he admitted. "But I know it."

"You're just saying that," she accused. "My father has nothing to do with this town. You're refusing to leave simply because there's a story here, a better story than who might have murdered some whore back in New York. And if my father hangs while you go ferreting around looking for your story, then that's just too bad."

"It isn't like that, Cedar," Guy countered. "I didn't say anything like that."

"You didn't have to," she nearly shouted back at him.

He wanted to put his hands on her shoulders and shake her, wanted to explain to her that he had a hunch about her father and the things that were happening in this town, to tell her that for some reason he knew they were somehow linked. But there was no logical way to explain a hunch to her, nor could he force her to believe in him. She would have to do that on her own.

"I think you owe me a little trust, Cedar," he told her sharply.

"I owe my father more," she returned. "I owe him everything I can do to get him out of prison, and that certainly does not entail staying here."

She scrambled to her feet and started to take a few steps

along the game path. Guy darted after her and caught her by the arm.

"Where do you think you're going?" Guy demanded.

"I'm getting away from here," she replied. "If you want to stay and get your damned story, that's your business."

"You can't go wandering alone through the woods at night," he told her.

"You have nothing to say about what I can and can't do," she retorted.

Guy's expression hardened. "I have to go back," he told her, "and like it or not, I need you to go back with me."

Cedar stared at him in an icy, angry silence. He hadn't come after her after all, she told herself. He didn't care what happened to her. All he cared about was his damned story.

And what had happened that afternoon between them was nothing more than a little entertainment for him.

"You can go to hell," she hissed.

"I most likely will," he replied.

He tightened his hold of her arm and turned her back in the direction from which they'd come.

# Chapter Sixteen

Cedar scowled in anger as she walked into the bedroom. She stood for a moment, staring at the neatly turned down bed. With its cheery patchwork cover folded down to the bed's foot, and what appeared to be two or three thick wool blankets as a line of defense against the night cold, Slade's guest room provided a good deal more animal comfort than the attic had offered Cedar the night before. But it wasn't the warmth of the bed that interested her at that moment, nor was it the allure of a soft, thick mattress.

She turned and faced Guy.

"You really don't expect me to spend the night here with you, do you?" she demanded.

"I'm afraid so," he told her, then pushed the door closed behind him and locked it.

"Well, I won't," she hissed. "I never want to see you again, never mind sleep in the same bed with you."

Guy shrugged. Her humor had not improved in the least since their argument that afternoon, and she had made absolutely no effort to hide that fact at all during dinner. Slade had seemed a bit amused by the situation, and on several occasions offered Guy a knowing smirk, as much as to say that only a fool pays a fortune for a woman who is not only unwilling, but openly antagonistic. Nonetheless, he'd made no offer to put an end to their arrangement nor to return Guy's money, obviously more than willing to let his smug and self-assured customer sleep in the uncomfortable bed

270

he'd made for himself. As a result, the evening had progressed, despite Cedar's rancid humor, to its expected end.

An end, it was only too obvious, that did not quite meet with Cedar's approval.

"Much as I would love to oblige you, Miss Rushton, I'm afraid my reputation won't allow me to accommodate your wishes," he told her. "Your rather less than adoring manner at the dinner table has made our host doubt my manly charms." He smiled at her ruefully. "I'd hate to think that it led to him doubting my word in general, for that could be decidedly unpleasant for us both. Perhaps you might give him another impression come breakfast."

"I think not," she countered. "I don't care about your reputation, and I don't care about Slade or what he thinks or anything else."

"Well, I suggest that you do start caring," Guy told her. He lowered his voice. "What would you do should Slade offer to return my money to me and cancel our arrangement? Would that please you more?"

Cedar swallowed. She hadn't thought about that. But she wasn't about to admit to him that the possibility might be any more unpleasant to her than their current situation.

"The only arrangement that would please me is getting away from here," she told him.

Guy leveled a clearly annoyed glance at her.

"I told you, Cedar, have a little patience," he growled.

"I've run out of patience," she retorted, her tone steadily rising. "If you won't get me away from this horrid place, I—"

Guy put his arm around her shoulder, held her firmly, and clamped his hand over her mouth, stopping the flow of her words.

"For God's sake," he hissed in a low whisper, "watch what you're saying. We don't need to have you overheard just now. This little pique of yours can get us into more trouble than I can handle. Or need I remind you that horse thieves

271

are not notorious for the kind and considerate way they treat people who get in their way?"

She pushed his hand away. "It's not a little pique," she returned, but she had the sense to keep her voice down. She could not argue the fact that were Slade to overhear them there might be decidedly unpleasant repercussions. "You can stay here and get your damned story if you want, but I intend to leave."

"Well you can't leave tonight," he replied with an exasperated sigh. "Even you must be aware that Slade will post a guard, so you might just as well behave reasonably. We'll talk in the morning."

She glared at him. "I'm not going to sleep in that bed with you," she hissed.

Guy felt a wash of regret. It occurred to him that both times they'd been intimate the conditions had been something less than idyllic. He realized he'd actually looked forward to spending the night with her, even hoped that during the course of it he might convince her to be a bit more trusting of him. But the look in her eyes told him that any attempt to sway her would be as ill received as his verbal arguments seemed to be. Best to let her stew, he told himself.

And hopefully try to keep her from getting them both killed.

"Suit yourself," he told her. "You can have the bed. I'll sleep on the sofa."

He nodded toward the small, horsehair-covered sofa between the two windows. Even were it not far too short for his frame, it would hardly have provided a comfortable bed for him. The horsehair looked itchy and the upholstery lumpy and hard.

Her first reaction was to think that he deserved such a bed, that the more uncomfortable he was, the more it would please her. But then she told herself that she wouldn't give him the satisfaction of thinking himself superior to her by pretending he was behaving gallantly.

"I wouldn't dream of allowing you to put yourself to any discomfort, Mr. Marler," she said. "You can have the bed. I'll sleep on the couch."

As soon as she'd uttered the words, she realized that she had really assumed he would insist, realized that the couch was not only too short for his frame, it was even too short to allow her to stretch out. But much to her regret, he didn't so much as try to dissuade her. Once it was made, he seemed to be perfectly satisfied with her suggestion.

"If that's what you want, Cedar," he said with a shrug.

Resigned to sleeping in the bed alone, he began to remove his clothing.

Cedar swallowed as she watched him drop his jacket over the arm of a chair and begin to unbutton his shirt.

"What do you think you're doing?" she demanded.

"I should think that's obvious," he said. "I'm going to bed. It's late. I've drunk some of Slade's wine, and it's made me groggy. Is that explanation enough for you?"

She scowled, but didn't respond.

"And if you have an ounce of sense," he continued, "you'll get some sleep as well."

Instead, she stood where she was, staring at him, watching as he quickly shed his clothing, telling herself that she hated him. No matter what she told herself, however, she couldn't turn away, couldn't keep her eyes from the rippled movement of the muscles beneath the skin of his naked chest, or, more embarrassing still for her, from the sharply protuberant member with its neat frame of thick, dark blond curls.

He went about his task with a businesslike precision, arranging his clothing neatly on the chair before he drew back the blankets and climbed into the bed. Covering himself to the waist with the blankets, he heaped the pillows and made himself comfortable before he put an arm lazily behind his head and turned to stare at her.

273

"Aren't you about ready?" he asked. "You can't sleep like that."

She told herself she hated him, detested the smug smile he wore as he watched her kick off her shoes and then pull off her stockings.

"You can turn off the light now," she told him.

Guy grinned lasciviously.

"That would be a shame, Cedar," he replied. "I was so enjoying watching you disrobing. After the small fortune I paid Slade for your company, you at least ought to allow me that small pleasure."

She scowled at him. "I don't care what you paid him. Turn off the light," she snapped.

He laughed, then leaned forward to the bedside table and blew out the lamp.

"There," he said in a slightly forlorn tone. "Anything to oblige a lady, even if it causes me serious suffering."

She turned her back to him and removed first the skirt and then the blouse. She was totally oblivious to the fact that the moonlight that streamed into the room left him with more than ample light to see by, or that it gave her body a silvery glow, a fact that did not escape Guy's eyes.

"It's a shame you're determined to sleep on that lumpy couch," he said, "when the bed is so comfortable. Should you change your mind, I am more than willing to share."

"I will be just fine, thank you, Mr. Marler," she said.

He shrugged. "As you like," he said. Then he pulled the top blanket free and tossed it to the far side of the bed.

Cedar glared at him as she balled up the blanket into her arms. Then she turned her back to him and started across the room to the couch.

"Pleasant dreams, Cedar," Guy murmured before he turned on his side.

Cedar grunted something indistinct but sounding suspiciously unladylike in its intonation. Guy chuckled softly, a fact which only infuriated Cedar. She ignored him as she

274

sat down, swung her legs up onto the couch, then spread the blanket over herself.

It didn't take her long to realize that she would be forced to keep her knees bent because there wasn't sufficient room to stretch them out, and the couch's arm was hard and ungiving beneath her head. She turned, trying to shift her position to one that was more comfortable, and failing completely.

"Is something wrong, Cedar?" Guy asked her after he'd listened to her toss uncomfortably for a few moments.

If she'd been able to see his face, she'd have found he was grinning smugly.

"A gentleman would have at least offered me a pillow," she sniffed.

"I thought we'd agreed at the very start that I'm not a gentleman," he said with a laugh, but he stood and crossed the room to her, pillow in hand. "But seeing you in pain is more than I can stand," he added when he stood over her.

Cedar turned and looked up at him. The moonlight streaming through the window illuminated him completely, revealing in glowing detail ample evidence that he wasn't at that moment all that interested in sleep. She realized he had been just as able to see her a few moments before when she'd undressed as she was now able to see him.

She snatched away the pillow and turned her back to him as she threw it onto the couch and batted angrily at it.

"Gentleman, ha," she sneered as she resolutely made a concerted effort to show him just how indifferent she was to his presence.

Guy shrugged and returned to bed, wondering how she could be so totally oblivious of him when he felt so very far from indifferent to her.

Despite the show, however, Cedar was far from oblivious to him, nor was she likely to sleep. A dull pain had been steadily growing inside her since their argument in the woods, and it would not go away. The realization that his job meant more to him than she ever would left some core deep within her shattered and bleeding. That first moment she'd seen him, she'd felt such relief to know he'd come for her, such certainty that he would help her, and it was more than she could bear to realize that she was simply a minor adjunct to his real interests.

The horsehair cover of the sofa was itchy and uncomfortable beneath her, but she was determined not to give him the satisfaction of seeing her tossing uncomfortably on the couch, just as she refused to let him see the silent tears that stole down her cheeks. She held herself still and choked back any sound of a sob that might have threatened to escape.

Guy lay for a while staring at her still, stiff back. It seemed almost eloquent to him, saying more about her than she might have wished to have spoken. She was narrowminded and ungiving, he told himself. It irked him more than he could have expressed to her, had he made the effort to speak, that she could not understand that he was doing everything he could, that without his job and the access it gave him he would be of little use to her father, and unless he returned to New York with a story he would most likely have no job. Whatever physical charms she might possess—and they were, he knew, more than ample—she would never be anything more than a stranger to him, never mean more to him than the dull hurt of want that filled him each time he thought of her. Never, that was, unless she somehow learned to give a little, and to trust him.

He pushed aside the desire to go to her and reach for her and try to make her understand, fully aware that the effort would probably be useless. He whispered the single word "Damn" into the darkness and turned away, hoping to will himself to sleep.

"What?"

Cedar came to a hazily uncomprehending wakefulness. She didn't recognize anything she saw, not that there was much—the dark brown upholstery of the back of the couch, the carved rosewood roses at the crown, a narrow glimpse of a pale-colored, slightly faded, flowered wallpaper.

She didn't have the time to either place herself or look further for a few more clues as to where she might be. The movement of a hand on her shoulder, probably, she realized, what had wakened her in the first place, was firm and insistent.

"Hurry up, Cedar," Guy whispered softly to her. "We've got a little bit of investigating to do."

"Investigating?" she murmured, still drowsy and not quite in full control of her faculties.

"Look," he whispered, and pointed to the window. It was located a few feet from her head, just past the side of the couch.

Curious, and for the moment not thinking about how indifferent she was to him, his story, and everything it entailed, she pushed herself up and leaned over the arm of the couch so that she could see out the window.

It was early, not long after dawn, she assumed, seeing the thin fingers of light that were struggling into the sky. But it was obviously not the sky that had drawn Guy's interest. She looked down, toward the barn to the rear of the house, and saw what he had seen. Three of Slade's men were busy leading a half dozen horses out of the barn and into the yard.

She turned and looked up at Guy.

"So?" she asked.

"They're taking those horses someplace," he told her.

She sighed in exasperation, not understanding why he seemed to find that fact so interesting.

"So?" she repeated.

Guy knelt down beside her, obviously not wanting to be seen should one of Slade's men look up toward the window, for he was taking pains to keep himself from being directly in front of it.

"Look," he whispered. "Slade told me that when the arrangements are completed, I can collect my merchandise from a small place just to the south of Sheffield."

More puzzles, she mused.

"That's in Massachusetts, isn't it?" she asked.

He nodded. "On the other side of those mountains. What he didn't tell me — and he made a point of letting me know that it wasn't my concern when I asked — was how he got the horses moved from here to there."

Cedar stared at him and shrugged. Her mind was beginning to feel a good deal less muddled, but not enough to make any real sense out of what he was telling her, or even give a hint as to why he thought the situation so intriguing.

"It's hardly a mystery," she said. "They must take the horses over the mountain."

"No," he told her, shaking his head. "That mountain is too steep. I've made a few discreet inquiries and checked the maps. There are only a few rough, rudimentary paths. No one in his right mind would risk a valuable thoroughbred that way. There are too many places where an animal could stumble and break a leg on that sort of path."

"Then they take them around the mountain," she suggested.

"The only way around would mean they'd have to go back into New York State," Guy replied. "If they did that, they'd be caught in possession of the stolen animals and subject to arrest." He shook his head. "No, Slade has some other way. And we're going to find out what it is."

"We are?" she asked.

He nodded. "We are."

"How?"

"Easy." He snapped his fingers. "We're going to follow after them."

"We are?" she asked.

He nodded as he picked up the heap of her clothes from where she'd let them fall to the floor the night before.

"We are," he said. "Get dressed. And hurry."

Cedar was surprised at the speed with which he dressed. She was still pulling on her shoes while Guy was standing, staring out the window with an anxious expression on his face.

"They've got them all haltered and they're starting out," he told her. "Can't you hurry?"

"I am hurrying," she told him. Her shoes finally donned, she stood and stared at him. "I would have appreciated the chance to wash, at least," she muttered.

"You can wash later," he told her. He put his hand on her arm and hurried her to the door. "If you're a good little girl, I'll find you a nice cold stream to wash in. Make you realize what a spoiled, city-soft person you really are."

With that he unlocked the door and pulled it open. After a quick look to make sure the hall was empty, he darted out, pulling her along with him.

"Be quiet," he whispered. "We don't need Slade asking us what we're up to," he told her.

"I know, I know," she muttered. But she kept her voice low and made an effort to walk as silently as possible.

It occurred to her that she'd told him the previous day that she didn't care about him or his story. Still, since the moment he'd wakened her, it hadn't even occurred to her to dismiss him, to tell him she didn't care what he did, and go back to sleep. He'd managed to rouse her curiosity, and she knew she wouldn't have turned back even had he suggested it.

They walked down the front stairs and reached the front door without making any discernible noise or rousing any attention. Guy drew back the door latch and slowly pulled the door open. Miraculously, it didn't squeak or groan. They hurried outside, Guy pulled the door closed behind them, and they ran down the stairs and around to the side of the house where they could get a protected view of the now slowly retreating caravan of horses and their three herders.

The horses were being led along a hedgerow at the edge of the very field Guy and Cedar had walked through the previous afternoon, moving toward the thick forested edge of the mountain.

"You see?" Guy said. "I told you they were taking them across the mountain."

"So now what do we do?"

"We follow," he told her. "And we make sure we're not seen."

He took her hand and started off at what was, for him, an easy lope, but it was more than fast enough to require Cedar to run as fast as she could to keep up with him. At first she feared that one of Slade's men would appear as Duane had that first morning when she'd tried to escape, but then she realized that they were busily occupied herding the horses, and that Slade was probably depending on Guy to keep an eye on her. In any event, she saw no one, and no one appeared to challenge them.

They crossed to the edge of the field, following along the hedgerow on the opposite side from that taken by Slade's hands and the horses. Guy cautioned her to keep low so that in the event one of the hands glanced back, he wouldn't catch a glimpse of their heads over the top of the bushes. Although Guy set a strong pace, there was still a good distance between themselves and the small caravan. He made no attempt to shorten it, something that was quite easy considering the head start Slade's men had on them.

When they reached the far end of the field, Guy stopped to let Cedar catch her breath. She was less than pleased to find that she was breathless and already aching from the run. She dropped down to the ground and began to rub her sore calves as Guy darted a cautious glance over the top of the hedgerow.

When she looked up at him, she found he was frowning. "What is it?" she demanded.

"I don't know," he replied. "They've disappeared."

"That's impossible," she told him. "They can't just vanish."

Guy nodded in agreement. "There must be a path into the woods somewhere up there. You stay here. I'm going to try to see where they went."

As she scrambled back to her feet, Cedar made a valiant, if unsuccessful, effort to hide the grimace that crept to her lips at the thought of more running.

"You're not leaving me alone here," she told him.

He grinned. "I thought you were the one who was going to take off alone, on foot, in the darkness," he teased. "Surely such an intrepid outdoorswoman can't be afraid to be alone in an open field in the middle of the day."

She scowled. "It's just after dawn, not the middle of the day," she corrected. "And I'm coming with you."

He shrugged. "Then come on."

He pushed his way through the hedgerow, opening enough space so that she could follow close to him without being permanently caught in the brambles. He had been right, she saw as soon as she was through the row of bushes. There was absolutely no sign of the horses or Slade's men now save for the trail of prints in the dark, damp dirt that edged the hay field.

Guy took her hand again.

"This way," he told her.

They followed along after the trail of prints, moving a good deal more slowly now as Guy realized Cedar wouldn't be able to keep up their original pace indefinitely.

But they hadn't gone very far when the trail of hoof marks in the dirt suddenly disappeared. As far as Cedar could see, there was nothing even remotely resembling a path into the forest there. She stared at the last thick confusion of tracks, then at what looked to her to be a completely undisturbed growth of underbrush.

"They couldn't have gone through there," she said. "There's no path. Even if they just went through the undergrowth, those branches would be broken and squashed down."

"So common sense would make it seem," Guy murmured thoughtfully.

He looked thoughtful, but not nearly as bewildered as she felt, and Cedar had to admit that fact disturbed her. At least he could have the common decency to admit he was as baffled as she was.

"They couldn't have just flown away," she said.

He laughed. "No, I don't think that would be possible, either," he agreed.

"Then just where did they go?" Cedar demanded in an exasperated tone.

"Logic says through there," Guy said, pointing to the underbrush.

More games, Cedar thought. He'd just a moment before agreed that the undisturbed brush meant that horses couldn't have gone through the woods there.

"I don't suppose you'd care to explain how they could tramp through that without so much as disturbing a pine needle?" she asked.

Guy only shrugged, then began to prowl into the edge of the undergrowth.

"Stay here," he told her. "I'll be right back."

She wasn't happy about doing as he told her, but he slipped into the undergrowth before she could object and she found she'd didn't have much choice. It wasn't easy to stand there alone, feeling as foolish as she did, and, moreover, aware that she was in more or less plain sight of the house. But there was little she could do about it save shrink down into the hay to make herself less visible should Slade or Mrs. Fretts decide to rise early and take an appreciative glance at nature before going about the business of the day. Guy had disappeared, and she was afraid to call out to him for fear the sound of it would alert the hands. She would simply have to content herself to wait quietly for Guy to return.

Waiting quietly was not the uppermost thought on her mind, however, when she heard the sound of movement in the pine branches just in front of her. She found herself wondering what sort of large animals might inhabit these woods, if bears might venture this close to cleared land. Had fear not rooted her to the place where she was standing, she would certainly have bolted.

"Guy?" she whispered hopefully.

When there was no answer, Cedar began to cast about for a place to hide. If it wasn't Guy back there, she knew for certain that she didn't want to be seen by whoever or whatever it was. Again she considered the possibility of bears, sure nothing as harmless as a deer could possibly make so much noise. A bear or Slade's men—in either case she would rather not greet whoever was moving that limb. But then the branch began to shift and then slide backwards, and common sense returned, telling her that trees simply don't move of their own volition, nor do bears usually bother with rearranging the flora. If it wasn't Guy, she told herself, it must be one of Slade's men.

She darted a glance along the edge of the field wondering how far she could get, but before she had the chance to go more than a half dozen paces, a two-foot section of pine branches simply fell back and away, revealing a narrow path. Guy was standing in the middle of it, holding a very thick and obviously heavy bough.

"Well, don't just stand there," he told her. "This is heavy. Come on."

Cedar turned back and skirted through the opening, then stood watching as he pushed the bough forward. There were a half dozen huge limbs, she realized, all newly cut so that the needles remained thick and fresh. They were laid out so that their greenery made what appeared to be a thicket, nearly five feet tall, that filled in the space beneath the lowest limbs of the pines on either side of what she now saw was a well-worn path.

"Great way to hide a path, huh?" Guy asked as he pushed the bough back into place. "Just make it look like more of the forest."

When he was finally satisfied that he'd returned the bough to the place he'd found it and then dropped it, the opening was completely obscured. Cedar was sure there would be no sign of the path from the other side.

"You might have answered when I called," she said. "You frightened me."

Guy shrugged. "Sorry. Mea culpa. I didn't hear you."

That said, he dismissed the matter. It was more than obvious to Cedar that he wasn't one for heartfelt or extensive apologies. She told herself she'd be a fool to expect anything more from him.

"Perhaps I ought to have screamed," she suggested.

He ignored her.

"Come on," he said. He took her hand and started along the path.

"We're still following?" she asked.

He nodded and pointed to the fresh tracks on the path.

"We're still following," he said.

"How did you know that they obscured the path that way?" she asked.

"Hunch," he replied. "Divine inspiration, if you like."

She looked up at him, her brow furrowed with confused disbelief.

"How did you know?" she insisted.

"I just did," he said. One look at her skeptical expression was enough to make him start to think the matter out, to put words to it. In fact, it *had* been simply one of his hunches, but now he forced himself to think of some reason that would satisfy her more than by trying to tell her that he just had somehow known. "It stood to reason. As you said, they couldn't have flown away. Short of simply vanishing into thin air, they had to have turned off onto a path. It's lucky Slade's men were careless enough not to obscure the tracks, or we'd probably have taken hours to have found it."

The explanation seemed to satisfy her, and they continued on along the path, walking in silence for a short while. The way soon began to cant upward, the slope growing steadily sharper, and Cedar found the climb a good deal more taxing than what would ordinarily be considered a pleasant stroll through the countryside. Had Guy made an effort to slow his pace, or even to decrease his long stride to match her shorter one, it wouldn't have been nearly so difficult, but he was so rapt in the pursuit of his story that he seemed almost unaware of her. She trotted along at his side, telling herself she'd sooner fall down in a dead faint from exhaustion before she'd beg him to slow down on her account.

"I told you they were just taking the animals over the mountain," she said after a prolonged silence.

He motioned to her to keep her voice down.

"Not on this path," he told her in a whisper. "Farm horses could go all the way up and over on a path like this. Maybe. But not racing animals. They'd be risking injuries. A thoroughbred with a broken leg is worthless. They wouldn't want to take that kind of risk. There'd be no real profit."

"Then where are we going?" she demanded.

She was becoming exasperated, she realized, thoroughly tired of his smug assurance that every suggestion she made was just so much nonsense.

The path turned sharply to the right just then, and they followed it, only to find themselves in a small clearing.

"Here, I think," Guy murmured.

Cedar made a slow survey of the edges of the clearing. Once again they seemed to be facing a solid wall of undergrowth all around them save for the path to their rear.

"Another hidden path?" she asked.

Guy looked down at the tracks.

"I don't know," he admitted slowly.

He released his hold of her hand and slowly circled the edge of the clearing, carefully inspecting the ground as he moved.

Cedar considered the floor of the clearing, staring at the tracks that seemed so intriguing to him. To her, it was nothing more than a confusion of hoof marks, hundreds of them. From what she could see, they were going in every direction. She could get no hint whatsoever as to which direction Slade's men might have taken. Logic said they'd go on up the mountain, but logic, especially hers, did not seem to find much acceptance.

As she looked eastward, toward the summit, she realized that the rock face of the mountain grew suddenly far steeper. The undergrowth that clung to the pockets of earth among the rocks was a good deal thinner than it had been further down the mountain. Not a dozen feet from the place where they stood it was ragged and sparse, and just beyond that a thick wall of stone rose almost straight up for nearly thirty feet.

Guy was right, she realized. There was no way a horse could continue to climb anywhere from this place. It would seem her logic was as worthless as Guy had suggested it would be.

She moved closer to the edge of the clearing and peered into the brush. And, surprisingly, she saw something glowing a short distance away.

Now what could that be? she mused. How could there be a light coming from what ought to be the solid rock of the mountain side?

She pushed her way into the brush and found that it moved far more easily than it ought to have. It was cut, she realized, and set there to hide something, the same way the branches had been left to disguise the path leading from the edge of the hay field.

Her thoughts were interrupted by the sound of muffled voices, and it didn't take more than a few seconds for Cedar to realize they were coming closer.

Slade's men, she thought. If they found her and Guy there, she had no doubt that something altogether unpleasant would follow.

She darted a look at Guy, wondering if he had heard, too. He had, she realized, for he was running back across the clearing toward her.

"Come on," he whispered.

He grasped her arm and pulled her backwards, downhill, into the undergrowth. They stumbled through a thick stand of bushes, then Guy pushed her roughly down to the ground and fell to his knees beside her.

The voices were growing steadily louder, there was no mistaking that. Slade's men were getting closer very quickly.

"What's going to happen?" she whispered in a low, panicked voice.

"Nothing, I hope," he whispered in reply. "If there is, I'd rather not think about it."

# Chapter Seventeen

Cedar pressed herself close to the ground. She lay with her cheek touching the dirt, her head turned toward the clearing, as she strained to see what was happening. She ought not to move, she told herself. If she did, Slade's men might notice some movement in the bushes or hear any careless noise she might make. She'd be as good as giving herself and Guy away.

The ground was damp with dew, and spongy soft beneath her. She could smell the thick, sharp odor of rotted leaves and pine needles, and even caught a taste of the dirt on her tongue. Once she was still, the hum of insects seemed abnormally loud, an industrious drone that filled the air around her.

Had she not felt Guy's hand on her shoulder, had he not been close enough beside her for her to feel the radiated heat of his body, she knew that she would certainly have been terrified. But as it was, she felt only an odd detachment, as though she weren't really lying there but somewhere else, somewhere safe where she could watch the play of events with no more at stake than the appeasement of her curiosity.

That sense of detachment surprised her, especially when she realized that it was nothing more than Guy's presence that gave her such a feeling of security. They were little more than five or six feet from the edge of the open clearing, with only a few twigs and leaves to obscure them from view, and still she felt absolutely confident that nothing and no one could hurt her. She was forced to keep reminding herself that she mustn't move, that she and Guy really were in danger.

The sound of the voices grew louder until Cedar realized that Slade's men were very close. She dared to lift her head a few inches, inching her hands up so that she could rest her chin in them. She calmly lay, staring through the welter of leaves and branches of the bushes, watching the three men who had entered the clearing.

They were joking loudly with one another as they set about work, hefting large branches to the side of the clearing that faced the mountain, at the very place where she'd stood only a moment before when she'd seen that odd light from what had seemed the inside of the mountain. At first she thought they were trying to cover another path like the one that led from the hay field, but then she realized that no path would go up to the solid, nearly vertical wall of stone of the mountain face. There had to be something there, something embedded in the side of the mountain.

There had to be a cave.

The thought was intriguing enough to her to make her forget the need for caution. She turned to face Guy.

"What do you suppose they're hiding?" she whispered.

Guy clamped his hand over her mouth.

"Shh," he hissed at her, his expression an angry enough warning to her to make her regret her mistake.

He took his hand away, then turned back to stare at the men, as curious as was she. Cedar realized he was being far more cautious than she, realized that he would not so much as whisper lest they give themselves away. She would have to content herself to sit motionless and watch as well, at least for the time being, a situation that hardly satisfied her.

The hands finished moving the branches, leaving the far edge of the clearing looking as though it were completely impenetrable, a wall of thick brush fronting a wall of solid rock. Whatever they were hiding, Cedar thought, they had done a good job of it. If she were to wander into the clearing and see it as it was now, she would never think to so much as glance behind that heap of brush.

Slade's men now each took up small bunches of branches and began to sweep at the dirt floor of the clearing, a task that would have seemed ridiculously useless to her under any other circumstance. Just then, however, it didn't take her long to realize that they were removing the tracks the horses had left to further obliterate any trace of their passage.

The horses, she thought with a start, only now realizing that the men were on foot and that the horses were nowhere to be seen. Whatever lay behind that heap of brush, it was becoming more and more intriguing to her now. Her curiosity was eating at her, and she knew she would not leave without finding out what was behind the wall of brush that the three hands had so carefully erected. Even were Guy to suggest they start back to the city at that very moment, she would not have given up the opportunity to satisfy that curiosity, not even were he to promise to spend every waking moment from that instant trying to find Mary Farren's killer. She had caught a hint of the disease that made him so involved with his job, and was beginning to realize that it was curiosity far more than any burning need for success that motivated him to do what he did.

Sweeping away the prints in the dirt was not a task the hands seemed especially delighted to perform, and there was a good deal of very vocal cursing as they swatted at the surface of the clearing with their makeshift brooms. There was a short period when they stood not six feet from where Cedar and Guy lay motionless, huddled against the ground, but there was no indication that they so much as suspected anyone might be there. The three slowly worked their way out of the clearing, backing onto the path, sweeping away the tracks as they went.

For what seemed a long while after the clearing was empty, Cedar and Guy remained silent and motionless. They could still hear the hands' voices as they made measured progress at their housekeeping task, eradicating all evidence of their passage. Guy made it clear when Cedar tried to move that it would be foolhardy to leave their hiding place until they were well out of earshot.

It was nearly a half an hour before the last rumble of the hands' rough talk faded completely away. Only then did Guy push himself to his feet and stare at the silent clearing.

"Don't move," he told Cedar firmly. "I'll come back for you."

Cedar decided against making a protest. She didn't, she realized, really want to face Duane or another of Slade's men. Instead, she nodded, then watched as Guy carefully edged his way back into the clearing and disappeared along the path the hands had taken.

He returned a few minutes later.

"They're gone," he told her, and held back the branches of the bushes to let her walk through them more easily. "They're heading back down to the farm."

Cedar scrambled to her feet and stepped back into the clearing. She hastily dusted away the bits of leaves and twigs that clung to her clothing, swatting absently at her skirt while she spoke.

"Why didn't they do that on their way in?" Cedar asked. "Why didn't they cover over their tracks on their way in?"

"Lazy, probably," he replied. "I suspect that Slade wouldn't appreciate the laxity. Still, they did put some brush over the path on their way in, so it would seem they made at least a halfhearted effort to hide wherever it was they went. I guess they thought no one would be roaming around at this hour of the morning and decided to save themselves some work. In any case, if they hadn't been so negligent, we'd probably never have even found the path from the field. We ought to thank them." He turned then and stared at the heap of brush the hands had pushed against the rock. He was smiling when he spoke to her. "What do you suppose they were hiding?" he asked.

"What they were hiding is a cave," she suggested in a tone that implied she was already certain and the question was totally unnecessary. Apart from that, there was also a hint of something else, something that said clearly she was more than willing to do a bit of exploring.

He grinned as he sensed her interest, recognizing the itch of curiosity that was so familiar to him.

"Sounds reasonable," he agreed, his own tone more jovial than anything else. "And why would they want to keep the opening to a cave hidden, do you suppose?"

Cedar looked up at him and returned the grin she saw turning up the corners of his lips.

"Because they're hiding something inside?" she suggested.

He nodded. "Something important, I'd say, considering the effort they've been to to make sure they're keeping its hiding place secret," he told her. His eyes were glowing in pleasant anticipation. "Let's find out, shall we?"

Cedar nodded, and he made a flamboyant gesture as he offered her his arm. She laughed as she took it, and they set out across the clearing.

She darted a glance at his expression as they crossed the clearing. As intrigued as she was at that moment, still he seemed far more rapt in the expectation that he was about to unravel a secret that was being so painstakingly hidden. He was, she realized, enjoying himself immensely, as though this was the sort of thing he considered the highest form of entertainment.

He loves this, she told herself. That thought was suddenly daunting to her, dulling even of the edges of her curiosity. He loves this, she thought. And she couldn't keep herself from wondering if he could ever love anything, or anyone, more. The answers she provided to that question were less than comforting to her at that moment, for she was sure that a woman would never take better than second place in importance to him. She told herself that she oughtn't to care, that a man like that was the last thing she wanted, but a part of her knew she was lying. She found herself feeling hurt and resentful and more than a little sad.

"They did a damn good job," Guy muttered as he dropped her hand and inspected the thick wall of brush. "There's no way anyone would think of looking behind that."

"I saw something before," Cedar told him, realizing that she hadn't yet told him about the light. "It looked like there was a light somewhere back in the darkness in there."

Her comment made Guy's smile broaden.

"You don't say?" he mused softly.

His tone, Cedar realized, was nothing short of delighted.

"It *is* a cave, isn't it?" she asked.

"I think it's better than that," he told her. "I think it's Slade own private little pathway to fortune."

"Will you please speak English?" she demanded in a tone turned suddenly petulant. "And stop looking so pleased with yourself."

He laughed. "If you insist, Miss Rushton." He composed his features into a decidedly theatrical version of abject depression. "Is this suitable?"

She darted a glance at him and couldn't keep from laughing.

"All right," she agreed. "Be pleased with yourself if you must. Just tell me what you're talking about. What's in there?"

"My guess is, it's how Slade gets those stolen horses into Massachusetts without having to face the New York law."

"A tunnel?" she asked. "All the way through the mountain? That's not possible. People would know about it. They couldn't dig anything like that without anyone knowing about it."

Guy shrugged. "Maybe they didn't have to dig it," he suggested.

"I thought you agreed to speak English, not gibberish," she said.

"These mountains are filled with caves," he said. "And what's more, until recently, there was a good deal of iron taken out of them. Anything's possible."

"So you think it might be a mine shaft?" she asked. "All the way through the mountain?"

"Only one way to find out that I can think of," he said.

He began to pull away some of the brush Slade's men had so carefully arranged.

They pulled aside only enough of the brush to allow them to edge their way through, and once past it found themselves facing a hole in the mountain's rock face some four feet wide and at least six feet high. It was dark inside, like looking into a bottle of ink, but there was a lantern set on the ground not more than three feet from the entrance, just at the edge of the arc of daylight that filtered inside.

"Nice of them to leave this for us, don't you think?" Guy asked her as he fished a small tin of matches from his pocket, removed one, and ignited it on the heel of his boot, then knelt by the lantern and lit it.

"I doubt they were really thinking of us," Cedar commented in a dry tone as she watched him adjust the flame.

"Well, I think it would be uncharitable of us to hold that against them," Guy admonished.

He straightened out and held the lantern up so they could see inside. It was a cave, not a mine shaft, that was obvious, with solid rock walls that nature had carved without leaving the rough edges caused by picks or shovels, and without the support of timber beams. The light picked out flecks of mica in the dull gray granite on either side of them, while directly in front of them the circle of light reached forward and then faded into blackness.

Cedar took Guy's hand. "Do you really think it goes all the way through?" she asked in an awed whisper.

"Only one way to find out," he replied. He pressed her hand, then once again tucked it into the crook of his arm. "If you would do me the honor of a promenade, Miss Rushton?"

She laughed softly. "With pleasure, Mr. Marler," she replied.

They walked forward, into the darkness, Guy holding the lantern aloft to create as wide a circle of light as possible. The darkness formed behind them as they passed. It seemed to creep up behind them and devour the small fingers of light that edged their way between and around their two moving forms.

The floor of the cave sloped gently downward, and with each step downward and away from the outside the air seemed to grow just a bit cooler. It wasn't long before Cedar felt a dull chill that she thought could only emanate from the stone itself.

For a while the stone walls and the black hole in front of them seemed endless, and Cedar began to wonder impatiently if they would find anything or if they would go on walking through the darkness forever. And with that thought came memories of stories about people lost in caves, unable to find their way out. She felt a sudden wave of panic. Suddenly the air seemed heavy with the weight of the mountain of rock above them.

"Do you think this is wise?" she asked Guy. "I've heard of people going into caves and never coming out."

"You should have thought of that before we started, Cedar," Guy told her. He didn't seem unduly concerned. "However, I must admit the prospect of being trapped here to the end of our days, alone together, is not altogether unappealing."

"Appealing enough to eradicate all thoughts of a short future and an imminent death from thirst?" she asked.

He grinned. "If it meant that we met that end in one another's arms," he replied.

There didn't seem to be much fear in either his expression or his tone, and Cedar assumed he didn't really think there was much chance that they'd meet such an end. Still, she was beginning to grow hungry and thirsty just realizing that there was no food or water available to them.

"I'd rather not, if it's all the same to you," she said.

He dropped her arm and turned to face her. "You're breaking my heart, Cedar," he said, and he put his arms around her. "What could be more romantic than such an end?"

She pushed his arms away.

"Living to get out of here," she replied.

He nodded solemnly. "Happily-ever-afters are appealing, too," he agreed.

He was laughing at her and she knew it. Still, she felt a bitter wave of hurt at his words. At that moment a happy ending for her and her father seemed beyond her imagination.

"If you believe in such things," she muttered.

"Which means you don't?" he asked her.

She shrugged and turned to look back into the darkness through which they'd just traveled. "I'm not sure what I believe in any more," she replied. "I used to think I knew, but that seems a long time ago now."

"Well, you can believe that we're not in any real danger of getting lost in here," he assured her. "There hasn't been a single turnoff from this tunnel. If worse comes to worse, we just go back." He stared into the darkness in front of them. "But I don't think we're quite ready to do that yet," he said softly.

"Speak for yourself," she objected.

"Shh," he whispered, and put a finger to her lips. "Listen."

Cedar darted a confused glance at him, and then one into the circle of darkness of the tunnel that fell down and away from them. She stood stock-still, listening to the thick silence of the cave. It was strange, she thought, that silence, so deep, so unlike the forested mountainside they'd just left, a place that, even when still, was full of bird and insect sounds.

She shook her head, hearing nothing, not understanding why he'd told her to listen.

"What . . . ?"

Before she had the chance to finish the question, she heard. It was distant, and muffled, but she had no doubt that it was unquestionably the sound of a horse neighing.

"The horses?" she murmured. "Do you think they're still in the cave?"

Guy only shrugged and took her arm. They continued on through the long winding tunnel of the cave.

Cedar couldn't quite believe she was actually seeing what she thought she was seeing. At first it was little more than a dull glow that she told herself she was just imagining, but as they moved closer to it, she realized it was real, that there really was some sort of light not far ahead of them.

"Look," she said. "There's a light—"

Guy put his hand to her lips, stilling the rest of her words. She suddenly realized that a light could mean they were not alone in the cave. She bit her lower lip, angry with herself for the stupidity of her mistake, aware now, as Guy so obviously was, that if there was someone there, it would be dangerous for them to give their presence away to him.

Guy peered down the tunnel, considering the pale glow. He blew out the flame of their lantern and pushed her against the stone wall of the cave.

"Stay here," he told her in a whisper as he pressed the handle of the lantern into her hand. "Don't make any noise."

He started down the tunnel, his movement stealthily silent despite the speed with which he moved. If the dark shadow of his form had not been outlined by the pale glow that slid into the tunnel, she would have thought he'd simply disappeared.

Cedar didn't like that, not the way he left her alone in the near darkness nor the fact that he could be walking into anything, alone and unarmed. She started after him, her fear for him outweighing her logic, not stopping to think that if some of Slade's men were there, she'd be of less than little help to him.

She kept her eyes on the shadow she had to keep telling herself was really him and not some ghost, trying not to let it get any further away from her than it already was, but realizing that it was growing steadily smaller with the distance between them. She dared not run after him, dared not take the chance that she would make noise, that the lantern in her hand would scrape against the rock wall or clatter if she dropped it or she'd let a scream escape her if she fell. And then she saw him stand framed for a second by the glow before he simply disappeared.

She stopped and stared at the place where Guy had been, at what was now just an irregularly shaped oval that seemed to glow with a cool, bluish light. More than anything she wanted to scream at him to come back, not to leave her alone there, not to be such a fool as to walk straight into . . . into . . .

Into what? She stared at the pale glow and she wondered. The light did not seem to be the sort cast by a lantern. The color of it was somehow wrong to be the light caused by a flame. Yet she could think of nothing else that it might be.

She waited a few seconds longer, listening, trying to separate the sound of the beating of her own heart from any other noise in the cave. After a moment, she realized that she could hear only the sound that had first alerted Guy a few moments prior, the neighing of a horse, distinct now, and much louder than it had been before, and a strange, irregular plopping noise that completely baffled her.

Logic told her that if it was safe, if there was nothing up there but the horses, Guy would have called out to her or come back for her. But he'd done neither. What if he'd fallen, she asked herself, what if he'd hit his head and was lying senseless on the cold stone floor of the cave? Or worse, what if some of Slade's men were up there, lying in wait?

She started forward again, not knowing what else to do. She was terrified that something had happened to him. The thought that he might be hurt, that he might need her, blotted out any suggestion that if Guy had walked into a trap, she was about to follow.

When she was only twenty-or-so feet from the opening, he suddenly appeared again, framed by the oval of bluish light behind him.

"Guy?" she cried softly.

It wasn't really a question, for it was undoubtedly him, but simply a gasp of relief. She realized that she hadn't really thought he'd fallen or been set upon. She realized that some irrational part inside her had feared he'd simply disappeared into that pale light, that he'd stepped into it and fallen away into some bottomless chasm.

"I thought I told you to stay back there," he chastised.

"You did," she agreed as she fell into his arms.

He chuckled softly and wrapped his arms around her. "I suppose I ought to be angry with you," he said, but it was obvious that he wasn't.

She glanced over his shoulder and then pushed herself away from him.

"And I suppose I ought to tell you that you have no right to tell me what to do and what not to do."

"I suppose," he agreed as he released his hold of her and then stepped aside to let her see what he had seen. "What do you think?"

Cedar had no words to answer him. She'd heard of places like this but never seen one, never thought to see one. She stood still, dumb and rooted, and simply stared.

It was a huge space, as large as the interior of Trinity Church, she thought, or even larger. The ceiling was fully thirty feet from the floor, and it was incredibly beautiful, decorated with hundreds of hanging stalactites that glowed with color. Drops of water were slowly forming on the ends of many of them, and Cedar realized they were the cause of the strange plopping noise she'd heard from outside in the tunnel. Beneath them, cones of the same softly glowing color reached up, some actually touching the downward-hanging shafts, even fusing with them and making strangely shaped columns that reached from floor to ceiling.

At the far side was a pool, and it, too, glowed, a luminous, clear blue, the eerie, pale luminescence the source of the strange light. Near to the pool a pen had been built, and at that moment it held the horses Slade's men had taken earlier from the barn.

"What causes that light?" she asked, too awed by the place to pay much attention to the horses at that moment.

He shrugged. "I've heard of such things, phosphors, substances that glow this way," he said. "The whole place must be filled with it."

Cedar moved dazedly forward, reaching out to touch one of the cones, touching it with tentative, unsure fingers. She was surprised at the solidity of the thing, at the unexpected smoothness of it beneath her fingers.

"Is this all real?" she murmured, quite in awe of the place.

Guy came up to stand behind her. "It's hard to believe, but I suppose it is," he said. He, too, put his hand to the damp, smooth stone, and leaned forward to her.

A horse whinnied loudly, and Cedar turned to face the pen. She smiled when she recognized Cedar's Pride was among the others.

"Pridey," she called, and she darted forward.

And immediately slipped on the damp stone underfoot, falling in a graceless, splay-legged heap.

Guy hurried up to her and knelt at her side.

"Are you hurt?" he asked as he offered her his hand.

"Only my pride," she muttered. She grasped his hand

with both hers and allowed him to help her back to her feet. She rubbed her sore rump. "Well, almost only my pride."

He laughed. "Take it slowly, Cedar. I don't relish carrying you out of here."

She tossed her head. "You needn't be bothered," she told him. "I'm sure Pridey won't mind."

As though he were being cued, Cedar's Pride whinnied loudly, stamping his feet against the stone and tossing his head with impatience as he recognized her voice.

Cedar turned back to the pen and started forward once again, this time a good deal more careful about the way she stepped.

She stopped when she was still several feet from the pen, and stared at the horse. He looked different, and she was bewildered.

"What is it?" Guy asked.

She shook her head. "I don't know," she admitted. She continued to stare at Cedar's Pride. "It's Pridey, all right, but he's different."

"Different?"

It took her several seconds more to realize what was wrong, but it was only when it struck her that she answered.

"His blaze," she said finally. "There's something wrong with his blaze."

Guy shook his head.

"Wrong? How can there be something wrong?"

Cedar started to walk again, covering the last few feet more quickly.

"I don't know," she admitted. "It's just wrong, that's all." When she was beside the pen, Cedar's Pride nudged her shoulder, and she reached up and patted him. "And his fetlocks," she said. "He had stockings, and now he doesn't."

Guy shrugged. "Maybe it isn't the right horse."

Cedar turned to look up at him and scowled. "Do you honestly think I don't know this horse?" she demanded.

Then, as Cedar's Pride began to nuzzle her, she added, "Or that he doesn't know me?"

Guy had to admit that she was right. There was no disputing the fact that the animal knew her. He considered the horses, and the pen. It was supplied with a goodly quantity of hay, and at the far side was a trough filled with feed. Beside the closed gate was a large bucket with a brush hanging by a thin leather thong from its side.

He walked to the gate, then knelt beside the bucket, considering the remnants of thick, dark liquid that clung to its side. He touched it with his fingers and then sniffed at it.

"What is it?" Cedar demanded. She'd followed him, and Cedar's Pride had followed along after her on the far side of the pen fence.

Guy wiped away the mark on his fingers by rubbing them against the stone floor, then he looked up at her.

"I would say it's the reason why your horse looks different," he told her. "Dye. They bring the horses here and disguise any distinguishing marks with dye before they deliver them."

"Then Slade's already sold Pridey?" Cedar asked with a pang of loss.

Guy nodded. "Most likely. He's probably just waiting for his customer so he can make delivery."

Cedar looked around at the strange cavern. It seemed an odd place to hold the animals.

"But if this is a path through the mountain," she asked him, "then why have they left them here? Why not take them all the way through?" She counted the animals in the pen. All six of the hands they had taken from the barn were there.

"I don't know," he admitted. "Whatever the reason, they're well tended. And it would seem they're to be kept here for a while." He pointed to the heap of clean hay and the well-filled trough. "Maybe Slade's buyer isn't ready to take delivery, but he doesn't want them to remain in town tomorrow."

302

He grinned.

"What, may I ask, is so amusing?" Cedar demanded. "And what's so special about tomorrow?"

"Tomorrow's the fight," he reminded her. "And it just seems funny. Slade afraid that his stolen horses might be stolen from him by one of the toughs who'll be showing up for the fight."

"Oh, the fight," Cedar murmured. She felt suddenly bitter, and couldn't keep what she was feeling from creeping into her tone. "I'd almost forgotten that was why you came here."

Guy looked at her in silence for a moment, then put his hand on her arm. "I came here to find you, Cedar," he told her sharply.

Cedar stared into his eyes. She wanted more than anything else to believe him, but somehow she realized she couldn't. His job, that's what really interested him, she told herself, doing his job and satisfying his curiosity. She pulled her arm away from him.

"If that was so, then why didn't we leave yesterday?" she demanded. When he opened his mouth to answer, she shook her head and waved her hand, stilling him before he had the chance. "It doesn't matter any more," she told him. She stared up at him, imploring him, begging him silently, wishing more than anything else that what he'd said might be true. "We can leave now," she said. "We can take Pridey and one of the other horses and get out of this horrible place."

"How?" he demanded. "Back through town? Don't you realize that Slade has all the roads guarded?"

Cedar scowled in frustration. "Then through the mountain. You said that was how Slade got the horses into Massachusetts. We could go out the way he takes the horses."

He stared at her in silence for a moment, then he turned away to scan the strangely formed forest of stone around them.

"All right," he said in a forced, hard tone. "Let's see if we can find Slade's path out of here."

They spent the next half hour exploring the walls of the cavern, searching for the way out. Their progress was slow, for they had to take care not to slip on the wet stone as they made their way around the writhing, climbing, and hanging formations. But eventually they found it.

"This is it," Guy told her.

He pointed into a narrow shaft, and Cedar looked in. It wasn't at all like the tunnel they'd taken into the cavern, for this was man made, a roughly hewn narrow slit in the stone that was bolstered with heavy wooden beams to keep it from collapsing.

"Stay here," Guy told her. "I'll get the lantern."

Cedar watched him make his way to the far side of the cavern, all the while thinking how much she hated the coldly distant tone he'd taken with her and the set line of his features when he'd looked at her. She was forcing him to do something he didn't want to do, she realized, and he didn't like that in the least.

Well, she told herself, she didn't care what he liked and what he didn't like. She had to get away from this town if she was going to help her father, and if that fact didn't please him, it was no concern of hers.

He returned carrying the lit lantern, and he walked right past her without speaking to her, holding up the light as he stepped into the narrow shaft. Cedar scrambled along behind him, not wanting to be left behind.

But Guy hadn't gone far when he stopped. Cedar nearly bumped into him.

"What is it?" she demanded.

"That's how Slade's kept this secret," he said. He pointed to the walls of the tunnel just in front of them.

Cedar stared. Just beyond the place where they were

standing, the tunnel grew much wider and the beamed supports were far better built than that just behind them.

"Why does it change?" she asked.

"I'd say Slade had his men cut this short piece, from the cavern to this old mine shaft," Guy told her.

Cedar considered the tunnel as they walked a few feet further. It was, indeed, a mine shaft, complete with a rail on the stone floor to hold the cars that would carry out the mined ore.

"Fools," Guy hissed suddenly. "How could they be stupid enough to leave the remainder of their explosives lying around like that?"

Cedar turned to the heap of wooden crates he was staring at and saw what he saw: the letters *TNT* stenciled on the sides.

"Isn't that dangerous?" she murmured.

"That it is," he agreed.

Cedar began to hurry past the pile of crates, wanting to get away from them as quickly as she could. But Guy put his hand on her arm and halted her.

"I think we can safely say this is a path out," he told her. "Let's go back and get you a horse."

Cedar furrowed her brow in confusion. "Get me a horse?" she asked. "We both need horses."

Guy shook his head. "You're going, Cedar. When you get out of the tunnel, just ride as fast as you can. If there's a guard on the far side, he won't be expecting you, and you shouldn't have any trouble. Get to a town and find a sheriff. You'll be safe."

All the time he was speaking, Cedar was slowly shaking her head, not quite believing what he was saying.

"But you're coming with me," she insisted.

"I can't," he told her.

She balled her hands into fists and stamped her foot in anger. "You can't mean to tell me you intend to go back there to watch that damned fight for your paper?"

"That's precisely what I intend to do," he said.

"You're insane," she hissed at him. "How will you explain to Slade my disappearance?"

He shrugged. "I don't know."

"He won't be happy, Guy," she said. "There's no telling what he might do."

"No, he won't be happy," he agreed. "But I don't think he'll do anything to me. He won't want to lose a customer."

"And what if he figures out you really aren't here to buy a horse after all?" she asked. "Your job can't be that important to you."

"It isn't," he said.

That response baffled her. For a moment she stared at him, wondering if he was simply saying it, wondering if he was lying. It didn't take her more than a glance at his eyes to realize that he wasn't.

"Then why go back there?" she demanded.

He inhaled deeply, then took a long time to release the breath. He seemed at a loss, unable to express himself, or unwilling to.

"Why?" she demanded once again.

"Look, Cedar," he said finally. "You want answers, and I can't give them to you. Not that I don't want to. It's just that they won't make any sense to you."

"Try," she insisted.

"All right," he agreed. "Michael McNaughton owns that farm back there, not Slade. And we know McNaughton is mixed up with Mary Farren's murder. What we don't know is why. I just have this feeling I'll be able to find some answers if I stay here. I can't explain to you why, I just have this feeling."

Cedar thought about that in silence for a moment.

"Answers that will help my father?" she asked softly.

He didn't answer, just nodded. He couldn't explain matters any more clearly than he already had. It was up to her now, to trust him or not. And if she didn't, he realized, if she left, it would make what he intended to do a good deal more dangerous for him.

Staring into his eyes, Cedar suddenly wanted more than anything to accept what he had told her, to believe it. Not that any of it made any real sense to her, but still, she wanted more than anything to believe. It wasn't easy for her to admit it to herself, but she realized it wasn't only because he had mentioned he hoped to find something that might help her father. It was simply that something inside her wanted to trust him.

She swallowed. She wasn't at all sure she liked what she was about to say, but she knew she couldn't do anything else.

"Then I'll stay, too," she told him.

# Chapter Eighteen

Cedar was panting from the effort of the run back through the tunnel to the clearing and then along the forest path to the edge of the hay field. Once there, she stood for a moment as Guy returned the brush he'd moved so that they could pass, catching her breath. She stared down as the early-morning sunlight lit the small village nestled in the valley below her and brightened the colors of the leaves that still clung to the trees. It looked so peaceful and calm, she thought, so sleepily wholesome, so much like any of a thousand other farm towns that dotted the countryside. As she considered the rolling, windswept hillside of the hay field and the town beyond, she was almost surprised by the sense of dread she felt at the prospect of returning to so pleasant looking a place.

Guy didn't give her long to admire the scenery. He hurried her along, and they skirted the far side of the field quickly, then hurried down the hillside, keeping close to the shadows of the long hedgerow just as they had when they'd followed Slade's men and the horses earlier. Once they reached the bottom of the hill and were approaching the farmhouse, Guy raised his hand, motioning to her to stop. Cedar came to a halt at his side.

"Damn," he muttered as he stared across the remainder of the field at Slade's farmhouse.

"What is it?" she asked as she peered at the empty farmyard. She could see nothing at all out of the ordinary or in the least alarming. It was quiet and peaceful, still void of the activity that would mark the beginning of the farm's workday.

"We must have taken longer than I thought," he replied, and pointed toward the house. "There's smoke coming from the kitchen chimney. Mrs. Fretts must be starting breakfast."

She followed his gaze to the rear chimney and realized that he was right. Thick puffs of pale smoke snaked their way aloft from it.

"What do we do now?" she asked.

Cedar didn't need to be told why Guy was so concerned about the housekeeper being up and about so early. She was as aware as was he that Mrs. Fretts would not keep silent about their morning ramble were she to catch sight of them. And that, Cedar realized, would surely bring unpleasant repercussions. There was no question in her mind but that Slade would quickly realize it wasn't a love of birdcalls and the mist of dew on the grass that had taken them out into the morning chill so early.

"We hopefully keep out of sight," Guy told her.

He didn't sound hopeful, and Cedar wondered what their chances of avoiding Mrs. Fretts's sharp eyes might be. The words *let's go back* leaped into her mind, and she wanted, more than anything, to say them. But Guy's expression was fixed, and she knew he wouldn't even consider leaving yet.

They hadn't any real choice, she knew. Once she'd accepted the fact that Guy had no intention of running away instead of returning to the farmhouse, she resigned herself to do the same. She was glad that she hadn't suggested that they leave, knowing it would do no good, sure he wouldn't even consider it and would think the less of her if she had.

The air was crisp and dry and just beginning to be warmed by the morning sun that had risen while they were inside the cave. A stiff wind was blowing, bringing with it the scent of wood smoke from the fire Mrs. Fretts had lit in the oven in preparation for the breakfast biscuits. Despite herself, Cedar found the scent set her stomach groaning with hunger.

They kept low and close to the hedgerow all along the last of the field. Except for the smoke, there was no sign that anyone was up and about yet. Cedar assumed that the hands, once finished with their peculiar morning task, must have returned to their beds for a hour or two of rest before their workday began.

"So far, so good," Guy murmured when they reached the end of the hedgerow without any sign of having alerted anyone to their presence. "Now comes the hard part."

He let her rest for a moment and catch her breath while he considered the empty, open field that lay still between them and the cover of the bushes that edged the house. It seemed quiet and peaceful enough, but he was the first to admit that appearances could be only too deceiving.

He turned to face Cedar. She was still flushed, but her breathing had slowed and she seemed as prepared for another run as he had any right to expect her to be.

"Ready for the real run?" he asked with an encouraging grin.

"The real run?" she asked. "What have we been doing?"

"Practicing," he said.

She laughed. "Then I suppose it's made me as ready as I'm likely to become," she replied with a nod.

Guy scanned the farmhouse and barnyard one last time, decided there was no one immediately apparent, and took her hand.

"Let's go," he said.

They ran the last of the distance to the front porch of the house, stopping only when they were out of the open and in the sheltered obscurity offered by the bushes. Then they stood wordless and panting, trying to catch their breath as they watched for any sign that they'd been seen by one of the hands or by Mrs. Fretts.

Cedar was mildly comforted by the sound of the rattle of pans in the kitchen as the housekeeper got on with the task of preparing breakfast. The feeling of comfort, however, was short-lived. She realized that Mrs. Fretts would be in and out of the dining room, setting the table and laying out food. If they should enter the house while she was there, or if she happened to look up and glance through the open kitchen door at that moment, Cedar knew they would surely be seen. Even if they weren't seen, there was little chance that they could manage to climb the stairs so soundlessly that they wouldn't be heard.

"How do we get past her?" she asked Guy in what she thought was a cautious whisper.

Apparently, it wasn't cautious enough to suit him.

"Shh," he warned her.

But he needn't have bothered instructing her to be silent. She was dumb with surprise when she saw him begin to pull off his clothing.

He removed his jacket, then pulled his shirt free from his trousers and unbuttoned it.

Cedar finally overcame her surprise as he handed her his jacket.

"What are you doing?" she hissed, her mouth close to his ear.

He waited for her to take his jacket from him, then began to pull off one of his boots.

"You take these and run as fast as you can back to the room," he told her. He handed her the first boot and began to tug at the second. "I'll see if I can't create a little diversion to keep your jailers from getting suspicious." He looked down at her feet as he held out the second boot. "Take off your shoes," he instructed. "You'll make less noise."

Cedar was still bewildered, but she did as he said, removing her shoes, bundling up his clothing and adding them to the heap. She was beginning to doubt his sanity just a bit as she stared at him standing there, barefooted and with his

311

shirt loose and unbuttoned, but she diplomatically held her tongue. Had it been later in the day, she might have thought he'd been addled by the sun.

Guy crept silently up the porch steps, staring cautiously through the glass of the door before he edged it open. He looked inside, then signaled her with a sharp, sweeping motion of his arm.

Cedar ran, up the front steps and, with Guy waving her on, into the house and up the stairs. When she was only halfway up, she heard the sound of footsteps coming from the kitchen. Just as she had feared, Mrs. Fretts had heard her on the stairs, she realized, and was coming to investigate. She froze, barely managing to turn to stare questioningly down at Guy.

Much to her surprise, he'd climbed half a dozen steps behind her. He was looking up at her, motioning to her to go on, mouthing to her to be quick. She nodded to him, then turned and ran up the remaining stairs, praying he knew what he was doing. Behind her, she could hear him making a good deal of noise as he descended the steps he'd just climbed.

"Good morning," he called out to the housekeeper as he stepped down into the front hall. His hand on the newel post, he turned and faced Mrs. Fretts as she stormed out from the kitchen, wiping the flour that whitened her hands onto her apron.

"I heard a noise at the door," she said, her tone angry, accusing, and she turned to look up the stairs.

But Guy didn't budge and Mrs. Fretts couldn't look past him far enough to see Cedar as she darted up the last of the stairs and ran along the hall to the door to the room she'd shared with him the night before. Guy stood firm, staring down at the housekeeper. Her expression was suspicious, but she really had nothing of which she could accuse him.

He decided to try charm, and grinned his most boyish grin at her, having often found it smoothed his path with older ladies and hoping it might appease her. When it didn't, he shrugged.

"I just came down to fetch some hot water," he told her with a bland smile. "I thought you'd be too busy with the breakfast to be bothered." He nodded toward the stairs. "The young lady would like a bath," he added by way of explanation.

"Hot water?" Mrs. Fretts asked in a tone that said only too plainly particular requests were unheard of at that hour, and implied his request suggested something she would sooner not consider had happened the night before and, even worse, had occurred under the very roof that sheltered her.

The housekeeper still looked doubtful and Guy knew she was less than entirely convinced. But as she began to realize he was offering to save her the work of fetching the water, a task which might ordinarily be expected of her, she began to mellow a bit.

He nodded and smiled again, this time more hopefully.

The housekeeper pushed past him and darted a final glance up to the second-floor landing. It was empty and still, and she finally turned back to the door leading to the kitchen.

"Well, come along then," she called back to Guy. "You can have a cup of coffee while I set the water on the fire."

Guy grinned and trotted along behind her.


Cedar sat in the tub of warm water, taking an inordinate pleasure in scrubbing herself. It seemed forever since the last time she'd had the luxury of a bath. When Guy had appeared at the bedroom door bearing two large buckets of steaming water and smiling inanely at her, she'd actually thrown her arms around his neck and kissed him. When he seemed willing to drop the buckets and return the favor, however, she had drawn back, not wanting to trust herself to

313

feel his arms around her. She'd told him it had been nothing more than the flush of relief she'd felt as she realized he'd managed to keep the fact that they'd taken a morning excursion from Mrs. Fretts.

"How did you do it?" she'd asked.

He'd shrugged. "I lied," he said, as though that was only apparent enough, and the question best not asked.

She'd stared at him a moment, then murmured, "You do that very well, don't you?" Then she'd turned away, not wanting to think what that might mean about him.

She pushed the thought aside as the flush of relief soon turned to pleasantly warm anticipation at the prospect of a warm tub. She'd even been more than willing to ignore his lecherous smile and laughter when he told her he'd only come upon the idea because it would mean he'd have the pleasure of watching her remove her clothing.

The anticipation had been fully realized, and now she took great pleasure in the task of lathering herself extravagantly with the bar of Slade's sandalwood soap. It pleased her to know that the scented soap was undoubtedly very expensive. She swished the bar in the water, then rubbed it furiously to make a thick foam, delighted that she was not only pleasing herself but putting her jailer to a bit of expense at the same time.

Guy pulled the door to the room open and stood for a moment, staring at her surrounded by the layer of pale white foam that floated on the surface of the water. For an instant she seemed very childish to him, her long hair damp and tipped with white lather as she intently busied herself blowing bubbles with the soap film between her fingers and watching them float for a moment before they burst in the air. But when she turned, reaching for the bucket of warm water and half baring her breasts, he decided there was nothing at all childish about her after all.

He entered the room and crossed it quickly, lifting the bucket before she could pull it close enough to her so that

314

she could lift it. He held it over her for a moment, then poured some of it down her back and onto her arms.

"I didn't know you were there," she told him, not quite sure how she felt about his presence at that particular moment.

It wasn't, she knew, as though she had any right to be shy about being naked in front of him. She was only too painfully aware that he had already seen all there was to see of her. Still, she wasn't all that sure she was comfortable knowing he had been watching her.

"Best entertainment since I can't remember when," he told her.

She looked up at him, and a hint of uncertainty crept into her eyes.

"Second-best, perhaps," she corrected.

He raised a doubtful brow.

"I don't think there is any way I could compete with this morning's entertainment," she murmured by way of answer to his unasked question. She was, she found, surprised at the feeling of regret that fact generated within her.

"Really?" he asked.

He leaned over her, grabbed her wrist and sniffed the bar and the fragrant bubbles that coated her hand, then released his hold, letting his hand slide over the damp, soap-slicked skin of her arm and come to a slow stop at her shoulder. He lowered his lips to touch the back of her neck.

The contact sent a shiver of pleasure down Cedar's spine. For a few seconds she leaned back, lost in the feeling of his touch, wanting more than anything for him to go on touching her, wanting him never to stop. But the moment passed, and she told herself she had no time for such feelings or such thoughts. Even worse, she told herself that feeling as she did only meant she was a fool. She pulled away from him.

"Besides," she added as she dropped the soap into its dish, "we're not really here to amuse you, are we?" Her tone, she

315

realized, had turned arch. "Or were you lying when you told me that you wanted to come back here because you were sure you could find something that could help my father?"

He lied to the housekeeper and convinced *her* of his sincerity, Cedar told herself. He could just as easily have lied to me.

Her words and her tone were enough to dull the edge of ardor Guy was beginning to feel. He released his hold of her and straightened to stand looking down at her, wondering why the suggestion that he'd lied to her left him aching with hurt, why the suggestion that she couldn't trust him pained him so. Even more, he regretted the fact that she'd only come back with him because of her father. That was all that mattered to her, he told himself, her father. There was no room for a man like Guy in her moral, upright life. She considered herself too far above someone who did what he did for a living, someone who twisted the truth to learn what he wanted to learn, someone who might be just a little less than the perfection she saw in her precious father.

"No," he said through tight lips. "I wasn't lying to you, Cedar."

She looked up at him, surprised at the hint of hurt she thought she saw in his eyes. Part of her wished she hadn't said what she had to him, wished he would put his arms around her again. But the look quickly faded from his eyes and she told herself she'd imagined it. She reminded herself of the easy way he'd fooled Slade and, only a short while before, the housekeeper. He was used to lying, she told herself. He did it very well. She'd be a fool to believe him.

She turned away from him and began to rinse the remaining soap film from her skin.

"I don't suppose you'd care to outline to me just what it is we're looking for or how we go about finding it?" she asked.

"No," he confessed. "I don't care to make any predictions just yet. In fact, I don't know what it is we're

316

looking for, much less how to find it."

She turned and looked up at him once again.

"Then why did we come back here when we could have gotten away?" she hissed angrily.

"You could have gone," he replied.

Cedar considered his expression, the cool look of distance that filled his eyes now, and she told herself that save for the bother it would have made for him with Slade, he would have been indifferent if she had gone. Entertainment, that was what he'd called her not a moment before. She was starting to believe he thought her nothing else but a convenient diversion.

She swallowed the ball that filled her throat, afraid she might cry at that moment, surprised with the ache that suddenly seemed to fill her. Sitting there, naked in the tub, thinking of those things they'd been through that morning and all she'd learned about him in the course of it, she realized suddenly that she was in love with him.

The ache grew stronger, and she told herself that what she felt could only hurt her, that the last thing loving Guy Marler could ever bring to her was happiness. He had other needs in his life, other interests, and they would always far outweigh what little she might ever mean to him.

She turned away again, afraid he would see it in her eyes, afraid he would somehow know that she loved him just from the way she looked at him. She didn't want his absent, pitying stare in response. The last thing she wanted from him was pity.

"What do we do now?" she murmured.

"We wait and keep our eyes open," he told her. "With any luck, it'll just fall into our hands."

"Is that the way it usually happens?" she asked. "Information you need just falls into your hands?"

Surely it wasn't that easy, she thought. She'd heard him lie with a tone of absolute sincerity. She wondered what else he would do to get what he wanted.

He shrugged. "Sometimes."

"And if not?"

He hesitated a moment, thinking of the things he'd done in the past to get information he wanted, knowing that she would not approve of much of it, not quite approving of it himself at that moment.

"Then I nudge things a bit," he replied.

He was being evasive, and she knew it. He didn't want to talk about this with her, and yet she couldn't let it go.

"How?"

"By doing whatever has to be done," he said sharply. He turned away from her and crossed to the door. "I should think breakfast's on the table by now," he told her. "I'll see you downstairs."

Cedar didn't look up until she heard the door close behind him.


Cedar silently fumed all through breakfast, telling herself that she ought to ignore Slade's knowing smiles and what seemed to her Guy's overly theatrical pretense of superior male satisfaction. Still, she could not keep but wondering what sort of conversation they'd had before she'd come down. She thought she could almost hear Slade's guarded inquiries and Guy's jovially lecherous responses. She told herself she was disgusted with men, all men, and Guy Marler most emphatically in particular.

In any event, her mood cast no pall on her appetite, and the hunger that her early-morning excursion had generated Slade took as having been caused by other exertions. She took no pains to disabuse him of that supposition or in any way overstep her bounds with him. When she found him staring at her with an expectant, thoughtful expression, she realized that she didn't really have to pretend to act as though she was afraid of him. She realized that she really was.

The meal had just about come to its end when the sharp sound of a train's whistle filled the air. It wasn't startling, for there were a surprising number of trains that stopped at the small train station down the hill. Guy had told her that the station was a switching point, where several lines met and cars were redistributed and transferred to trains going north to Boston, south to New York, or onto the several lines that radiated to the west. It surprised her to realize how quickly she had become accustomed to the sound in the previous twenty-four hours, how she'd grown to be almost oblivious to the intermittent noise of the whistles.

But that particular arrival for some reason seemed to rouse Slade.

He looked up at her and smiled, and then turned to Guy.

"I don't suppose you'd mind waiting in my office for a few moments, would you, Mr. Marler?" he asked. "I have a few words to exchange with our dear Cedar, and when that matter is tended to, you and I can complete our few remaining business details."

Guy seemed startled by the request, but he hid his surprise behind his raised coffee cup. By the time he returned the cup to the saucer, his expression was pleasant and composed.

"I don't think we've left anything that could not be discussed in Cedar's presence, have we?" he asked.

Slade shrugged, obviously unwilling to be persuaded.

"Ladies become bored with these things so easily," he said. "I don't think we need bother lovely Cedar with such mundane matters, especially as they in no way concern her."

Guy realized that any further argument would be not only fruitless, but might possibly be dangerous as well were it to make Slade suspicious. Acting as though the matter were of little interest to him one way or the other, he nodded his agreement.

"As you like, then," he said.

He stood, smiled at Slade, and leaned down to plant a

319

quick kiss at the back of Cedar's neck, grinning knowingly at Slade when she colored from his touch. Then he refilled his coffee cup, pretending complete obliviousness to Slade's growing impatience with the time he was taking about leaving. Only then did he finally leave, taking his coffee with him.

Cedar could almost feel Slade's glance on her once Guy was gone. She hated being in the same room alone with him. She did not quite understand why, but he seemed far more frightening to her than he had before, and far less predictable. Perhaps it was the simple fact that she'd come so close to leaving, escaping from the necessity of being forced to see him ever again. Whatever the reason, she realized that the way he looked at her made her exceedingly uncomfortable.

"I think it would be best if you confine yourself to your room for the remainder of the day, my dear," he told her in a tone that suggested he was not making a suggestion but giving her an order.

"And may I inquire as to why I'm to be imprisoned again?" she demanded. "I don't recall having transgressed on any of your rules."

Slade darted a sharp, warning glance at her, and she found herself looking down at her plate, unwilling to face what she saw in his eyes. She could not escape the fact that he was waiting until Guy was gone, that he expected to have his own chance with her then. And she was also well aware that if he was to continue to believe that Guy would leave her behind when he returned to the city the following day after the fight, she would have to behave as though that was what she expected to happen as well. She would have to pretend that she expected to find herself alone and in Slade's hands, pretend that she was prepared to face whatever unpleasantness that would entail.

"I hardly think *imprison* is the proper term, my dear," Slade told her, enunciating his words very precisely, his manner turning the pleasant words of assurance into something else entirely.

Cedar took the hint.

"Have I done something wrong?" she murmured, this time making the question sound meekly submissive, as though she were begging for some way of righting whatever offense she had inadvertently given him.

Slade smiled a satisfied smile.

"Of course not, my dear," he said, waving away her question in a gesture of benign dismissal. "Mr. Marler tells me you have been a perfectly charming companion, a fact which I must confess baffles me, but also delights me." He grinned at her. "But then, again, perhaps it doesn't present so great a mystery after all. Perhaps you simply hope to charm him into taking you away with him when he leaves?"

Cedar felt a shiver of fear, wondering how he knew, wondering just how much he really knew and how much was simply conjecture. She managed to pretend to ignore his suggestion.

"I've done what you wanted," she told him. "Why am I to be confined once again?"

Slade shook his head emphatically.

"Oh, no, not confined, my dear. I wouldn't think of doing anything so unnecessarily crude as locking you up in the attic again. That is, I wouldn't as long as you behave reasonably. I simply think you would be more comfortable and a good deal safer were you to confine yourself to the room you shared last night with Mr. Marler."

"Safer?" she asked.

"I assume that a woman of breeding such as yourself is unfamiliar with the sort of man who might feel compelled to travel a hundred miles solely to witness an illegal prizefight," he told her.

She scowled. "A man such as yourself and Mr. Marler?" she asked.

She half expected him to anger at that, but he didn't. Instead, he smiled.

"Ah, my dear, there is much you have to learn. There are gentlemen, like myself, who consider such spectacles simply a matter of business, an opportunity to be exploited. Then there are the less intelligent ones, men like Marler, who actually believe there is sport in this act of public brutality, and see it as an opportunity to place an ill informed but hopeful wager. But it is neither myself nor Mr. Marler of whom I am speaking. There will be a goodly number of visitors to this town, come to watch the fight, the common sort who frequent such events for nothing more than the simple joy of the mayhem it creates and their own lust for the scent of blood."

Cedar darted a cold look at him.

"Men like Duane, you mean?" she asked.

He nodded and then smiled as he recalled what he'd seen the day before in the barn. Even the memory seemed to whet his appetite, and he looked at her with hungry anticipation, anxious for the opportunity he knew would soon be his.

Cedar saw the smile, and it served to increase her discomfort with him. There was much about the common sort of man he derided that apparently provided him with more than a bit of amusement; perhaps he did not even realize those qualities were also within himself. She wondered what else he might consider amusement, and to what lengths he might go in order to entertain himself.

"Precisely like Duane, my dear," he said. "Envision, if you will, a whole town, filled to the proverbial rafters with creatures precisely like Duane. I expect they'll begin arriving soon, on the very next train from New York, I should think. They'll make an outing of the event, a sort of brawling, drunken excursion into the country. I should hate to think of you, alone, at the mercy of an untold number of such brutes. As your protector I should not be happy were anything untoward to happen to you."

Cedar heard his words, but more than that she could see his expression, could understand what he was really saying to her, that he had his own plans for her and that he did not want them ruined by the toughs that would be arriving to watch the prizefight.

She shuddered. Neither prospect roused anything but revulsion in her. She thought for a few moments about what he'd said to her.

"Why did you call yourself my protector?" she asked.

He nodded. "Under the circumstances, my dear, it seems quite appropriate. Consider, if you will: Michael McNaughton will be arriving some time this afternoon to attend tomorrow's prizefight. Whatever small indiscretion you might have committed that so ired Mr. McNaughton to cause him to go to the bother of having you sent here, I'm sure it is understood he is not entirely pleased with you. More than that, I don't suppose I need remind you that once our friend Mr. Marler has returned to New York, I will be the one person that stands between you and McNaughton, now, do I?"

"No," she murmured in hesitant reply.

His words and his manner sent an unpleasant chill of fear through her, and she couldn't keep herself from darting an incautious glance toward the door by which Guy had left the room.

Slade watched her, and rather than alerting him, her panicked glance seemed, more than anything else, to amuse him. He laughed.

"I'm afraid, my dear, you are sorely mistaken if you think whatever stories you may have told friend Marler will have in any way convinced him to take you with him. He and I have serious business to transact, business he would not think of placing in jeopardy by being so foolish as to cross me. Do not think him so great a fool as to be swayed by a night or two spent even in your charming embrace."

323

Cedar's fear turned to regret. What he was saying, she realized, was in many respects true. Guy wouldn't leave her behind, certainly, but neither would he be swayed, not by her, not by anything she could do or say.

Slade saw the regret in her expression and incorrectly decided its cause. He leaned across the table to her.

"Come, come, my dear," he said in an uncharacteristically consoling tone. "You have made the effort to be charming to Mr. Marler in the hopes that he would help you. Unfortunately he cannot. But I remind you that I can. Make the same effort with me, and I assure you I will allow nothing untoward to happen to you."

When Cedar didn't move, didn't say anything, he pushed his chair back and stood. He walked around the table until he was standing behind her. Then, as Guy had, he leaned forward and pressed his lips against the back of her neck.

Cedar felt a wash of revulsion fill her at his touch. Every bite of food she'd eaten suddenly seemed to rebel inside her, and she began to tremble.

Slade took no notice of her reaction, or else purposely ignored it. He put his hands on her arms, holding her still as he touched his cheek to her hair. Then he brought his lips close to her ear.

"You'll see, my dear," he said softly. "I promise you I can make matters agreeable for us both. You only need let me. I ask only the smallest bit of encouragement from you."

Then he pressed his lips once again to her neck, mistaking her tremble of revulsion for one of delight, for he was smiling as he released her and straightened.

"Now," he said, "I must leave you to tend to the unfortunate contingencies of rude business. Go upstairs. I'm sure Mr. Marler will be along to see you shortly."

# Chapter Nineteen

Cedar soon found that Slade's predictions regarding what would soon happen in the town had been precisely accurate. Each train north from New York brought more bodies to swell the growing ranks of the ruffians come to watch the fight. She and Guy sat by the window much of the day, watching the town fill with what appeared to be an endless swarm of loud, raucous, brawling humanity.

These visitors were in a holiday mood, and few of them had any thought to allow an unfortunate lack of funds to have an adverse effect on either their mood or their enjoyment of their outing. They simply stole whatever they saw that took their fancy or whetted their appetites. A gang of them swarmed into the general store and nearly emptied it before the shopkeeper had the chance to close and lock the doors, not that locked doors would in all probability have stopped them. They emptied every chicken coop and pigsty in town and then went on and did the same on the surrounding farms, slaughtering the animals on the spot. In the hay fields they started fires over which they cooked their stolen dinners, unmindful of the damage they did to the nearly ready to be harvested hay, then ate, washing down their booty with a seemingly endless supply of whiskey.

Mostly the townspeople simply locked their doors and stayed inside, praying to be left alone. As inured as they were to Slade's rule of force, they were still unprepared for this wholesale invasion. During the months since Slade had taken up residence and brought his own less than legal brand of commerce to the town, they'd at least found they would be left alone if they made no trouble among the horse thieves and whores. Now they could do little more than cower helplessly in their houses, watching as this army of toughs, like a swarm of vicious locust, swept through their town and took what even Slade had left to them.

A few incautiously made the attempt to protect their chickens and pigs, facing down the ruffians with nothing more than their fists and their pitchforks. Vastly outnumbered and outarmed, invariably they soon found themselves nursing bloody noses, cracked ribs, and wounded pride as the band of toughs who had beaten them more often than not laughed when the townspeople were forced to give up and retreat indoors. It quickly became only too apparent that with no marshal to protect them, there was no possible way they could stem the wave of lawlessness that had swept through the town.

Of the whole of Boston Four Corners, only Slade's farm seemed invulnerable to the ravages of their attacks, and Slade's chickens stalked about the barnyard with impunity as though it were an ordinary day. Cedar quickly realized it wasn't respect for one of their own that kept the bands of roving toughs away, but rather Slade's hired hands, armed and on guard, pointedly brandishing rifles in warning to any who dared trespass.

As disquieting as all that was, it wasn't nearly as upsetting to her as was the sight of Michael McNaughton. He appeared, marching along the street not long after the last afternoon train from New York arrived, stalking through the town as though he owned it. The already drunken revelers with whom he'd shared the train staggered along behind him, calling out to earlier arrivals, waving their whiskey bottles by way of greeting.

McNaughton turned from the road and approached the front of the house with the manner of a man who was quite pleased with himself. He seemed pleased, if anything, at the crowd the prospect of the fight had gathered, and completely oblivious to the harm they were doing the town.

Slade, apparently expecting his arrival, was waiting on the porch to greet him. He hurried down the steps as McNaughton neared, calling out a loud "Welcome to Hells Acres Farm!" as he shook McNaughton's hand.

As soon as she realized who it was that Slade had greeted with such enthusiasm, Cedar turned to Guy.

"He's here," she told him in a hoarse whisper.

"McNaughton?" he asked.

She nodded, and pointed downward to where Slade and McNaughton had begun to climb the porch steps.

"Now the fun starts," Guy whispered.

Cedar turned to face him, startled and not quite believing what it was she saw as she considered the glint of anticipation in his eyes. She shook her head.

"I swear I don't understand a single thing about you," she told him. "That man is dangerous. How can you so much as suggest you might find anything that's going to happen even remotely amusing?"

Guy let a crooked smile turn up the edges of his lips. Once again Cedar saw the look she'd noticed in his eyes when they'd stood outside the cave earlier that day. It was only too clear to her that he meant what he'd said, that he really was looking forward to the next twenty-four hours with anticipation.

"I'll give them a chance to get settled into Slade's office," he told her. "Hopefully they'll talk business as soon as Slade finishes dispensing the obligatory drinks to chase away the road dust. I'd be willing to bet next month's salary that those two have something less than legal cooked up."

327

"You're going to listen at keyholes, I suppose?" Cedar asked him.

She heard the note of distaste in her tone and knew Guy could not miss it either. She was entirely mystified as to why she should care if he chose to spy on Slade and McNaughton, but somehow she found she couldn't lose her attitude about an act she could only consider offensive and improper.

Guy heard the edge to her words and immediately recognized its cause.

"I certainly intend to do my damnedest and try." He made no attempt to justify himself, doubting if he could convince her that every base action is not entirely unwarranted. "You stay here, out of harm's way."

She seemed surprised at that.

"I can't come with you?" she asked.

"No," he told her firmly. "You'll give us away and get us both in trouble. I'm afraid I must inform you that you're just too well brought up to be any good at this sort of thing. You will be pleased to know that you have no talent whatsoever for listening at keyholes, lying, and otherwise behaving in the socially unacceptable manner at which I've become so adept through years of applied study and careful practice."

It was only too apparent that he was baiting her, for he layered the words thick with sarcasm. She could tell he was angry with her for the way she'd showed her contempt, but she refused to allow him to make her regret the way she felt. He was the one who was wrong, she told herself. If there was any guilt to be felt, he was the one who ought to feel it.

"You're not being funny, Guy," she muttered.

He stared at her without blinking for a moment before he replied, wondering why her disdain hurt him, why he cared at all, for that matter, what she thought. He told himself that she considered herself above him, that her lawyer father had passed on to her upper-class prejudices that she would never lose, and that those attitudes separated him from her absolutely and permanently. He'd been a fool to let himself become entangled with her, and the sooner he'd done what he'd promised her he'd do, the better for him. He'd get the proof they needed and get her out of the town, and then he could wash his hands of her. He neither wanted nor needed the bother caring for her had caused him, especially as she had made it all too apparent that she wanted no part of him.

"I suppose it wasn't," he said finally. "But then, humor was never one of my stronger assets."

He made no attempt to hide from her the sudden wash of anger that swept over him. Let her keep her superiority, her holier-than-thou attitudes, he told himself. He was thoroughly sick of them.

Cedar reacted to his anger not with remorse but in kind. Only much of her anger, she quickly realized, was with herself for the disdain she felt for what he'd told her he intended to do. After all, she told herself, he was trying to help her father. Even if she had no other motive for trusting him, she ought to have no qualms about anything he did if it would end with Magnus being cleared of Mary Farren's murder.

But she did have another reason, she told herself. If she loved him, she ought not to be able to believe he would do anything wrong.

He waited a moment for her to say something, part of him hoping she'd apologize, part of him sure she wouldn't. Finally, he gave up.

"You stay here, lock the door, and don't let anyone but me in," he ordered. "As you so pointedly noted, I have a bit of eavesdropping to do, and I wouldn't want you to compromise your fine morals by taking part."

With that, he crossed the room, opened the door, nodded to her, and pointed to the lock to remind her to secure it once he'd gone. Then he stepped outside and pulled the door closed behind him.

Cedar followed him to the door and carefully locked it. She stood with her hand on the bolt, trying to convince herself that she didn't feel numb and empty inside, trying to tell herself that she didn't care what he thought of her, and failing miserably.

Guy's timing couldn't have been better. He'd no sooner settled himself with his ear close to the door to Slade's office when he heard McNaughton address Slade.

"Well, do you have it all settled? I have ten thousand on Morrissey, and if I lose it, believe me, I'll see that it comes out of your fat hide."

Guy grinned. He could almost picture Slade's expression at that moment, the look of anger and distaste that would most assuredly be very hard for him to hide even if he had the inclination. Apparently he didn't. His voice was rasping and sharp when he replied.

"I suggest you remember who it is who keeps you living in comfort in that fine new house of yours on Gramercy Park. Without me to tell you what to do, you'd be nothing more than the same petty Tammany drone you were five years ago."

"Petty drone?" McNaughton asked, then punctuated the question with a dull laugh. "Aren't we full of upper-class shit lately? Trying to impress the Rushton girl, are we?"

"I've her well tended to."

Slade had replied quickly, a shade too quickly, Guy thought. He was beginning to realize just what Slade's interest in Cedar was, and he wondered if he had made a mistake by not encouraging her to leave without him that morning. He might need her presence to complete his masquerade, but endangering her was the last thing he wanted to do.

330

"I'm sure you do," McNaughton said. It was only too obvious that he'd surmised what Guy had. "But we'll get back to her later. Just now I'm interested in the fight."

"A bargain," Slade told him, and now he sounded very smug, as though he was quite pleased with himself. "Only five hundred. Frankly, it even surprised me to find how easily Allaire allowed himself to be bribed. I was under the impression referees were hard to corrupt."

"He could be playing you for a mark," McNaughton suggested. "Thinking he can take the money and not deliver."

"No, he's not enough of a fool to think he'd live to get out of town if he did. He's already taken half, and that puts him in my pocket. He'll be waiting, hand out, for the other half after the fight. Don't worry. Morrissey will win, one way or another."

Interesting, Guy thought. From what he'd been told by his street informers back in New York, most of the sure money was on Yankee and the odds being offered on the outcome of the fight reflected the expectation that Sullivan would win. If Slade had managed to corrupt the referee and insure that Morrissey would take the fight, McNaughton's ten-thousand-dollar bet would bring him at least three times that amount in winnings. And if word got out that he'd arranged the outcome of the fight, it would also probably mean his death warrant would be signed by any number of the men who made their living by taking wagers. It was a deadly dangerous game that McNaughton was playing, and it didn't make sense to Guy.

Didn't make sense, he amended, unless McNaughton was so desperate for cash he'd do anything to get it.

"Believe me, he'd better," McNaughton told Slade. "I need the winnings from that bet to make the final payment on the last two parcels."

Whatever the parcels were that McNaughton had mentioned, Guy realized they must be very important. Important enough to involve murder? he wondered. He wished he knew more.

"You have the papers?" Slade asked.

"Right here, in my pocket," McNaughton replied. "Here. You better lock them up now, before I forget."

There was a rustle of paper and the rough scraping sound as one of the drawers of Slade's desk was pulled open. It was an easy sound for Guy to identify. He'd heard it the day before when Slade had opened a drawer to deposit those crisp hundred-dollar bills Guy had given him.

Before he had any more time to consider what he'd overheard might mean, Guy heard the sharp sound of footsteps coming from the kitchen. He barely had time to straighten up and dart across the front hall toward the dining room before Mrs. Fretts appeared bearing a tray with a stack of sandwiches, presumably a small snack for McNaughton after the rigors of his journey from the city.

"Ah, Mrs. Fretts," he exclaimed loudly enough to startle the housekeeper and make her whirl around to face him. "I don't suppose one of those might be for me?" He started to reach for the sandwiches.

"No, they're not," Mrs. Fretts said, and pulled the tray back.

"What's this?"

The door to Slade's office had been pulled open, and McNaughton stood facing them, glowering, not at all pleased to find a stranger in the house. But Guy wasn't interested in McNaughton at that moment. He found it far more intriguing to watch Slade turn a key, lock his desk drawer, and then deposit his key ring into his vest pocket.

"Who are you?" McNaughton demanded.

Guy forced his attention to McNaughton.

"Pleased to meet you," he said, extending his hand, delighted to see that this was the last thing that McNaughton seemed to expect. "My name's Marler. Guy Marler. I came up here to transact a bit of business with our friend Mr. Slade and decided to stay for the fight." He grasped McNaughton's hand and pumped it with enthusiasm. "I suppose you're here for the same reason, eh?" He smiled knowingly. "And maybe a bit of fun away from the disapproving eye of the little woman, eh?" He winked conspiratorially. "You ask Slade. He fixed me up just fine. I'm sure he can do the same for you. Oh, I don't think I caught the name?"

Slightly mystified by the flow of comradely verbiage, McNaughton completed his half of the introduction. But Guy couldn't keep his eyes from straying back to Slade, nor could he do much but wonder how he was going to manage to steal Slade's keys and find out what it was he'd just locked away for safekeeping.

Guy eyed the inside of the Black Grocery with a fresh eye. Funny, he thought, he hadn't noticed how dirty the place was the first time he'd seen it. Or how strong the reek of beer was. Or how the air was thick enough with cigar smoke to take on a dirty gray-blue cast. Or even how the cuspidors that occupied every corner and half a dozen other places near the bar hadn't been emptied recently, or how the areas around them were stained by the good deal of spittle directed at them that never actually reached its mark.

He assumed it was simply habit that made him oblivious to those things. After all, he spent a good deal of his time in saloons in New York, and not all of it was absolutely necessary in the pursuit of a good story. He was simply accustomed enough to the less than pristine condition of such places to be able to ignore what he knew he'd sooner not see.

But with Cedar visibly cringing at his side, he found himself suddenly seeing it all for the first time, and what he saw decidedly disgusted him.

He almost wished he'd insisted she remain in the farmhouse. But she'd wanted to come with him, and he'd had to admit that he wasn't entirely happy with the idea of letting her out of his sight with McNaughton in town. The man had already murdered one woman. Guy had little doubt but that he'd repeat the act should the opportunity present itself.

He could have turned down Slade's invitation, he supposed. But that would have looked suspicious, and he'd decided that going along, and taking Cedar with him, was the least of all possible evils. Now, however, he was not quite so sure.

Just at that moment he was decidedly uncomfortable to see nearly every eye in the large, crowded room turn to consider Cedar as she stood in the center of what was ordinarily an exclusively male enclave. Had Slade not been with them, Guy had little doubt but that there would eventually be serious trouble keeping that attention confined to merely ogling her and smiling lecherously. He told himself that they weren't hurting her, and so he ought to be able to ignore those looks. He wondered why he couldn't and why they generated such rage within him.

Luckily his concerns for Cedar were soon alleviated as John Morrissey entered the bar in the wake of a half dozen of his followers. Not ten minutes later, Sullivan, also surrounded, arrived. Between the two of them, they quickly drew the attention of the crowd who had, after all, come so far to see these men fight. The attention that had seemed permanently settled on Cedar turned to the far more intriguing presence of the two prizefighters, a fact which Guy, more than a bit amused now, thought telling with respect to the attitudes of the men, who seemed to consider the prospect of watching blood being spilled more interesting than the sight of a beautiful woman.

The two boxers took up places at opposite ends of the bar, eyed each other warily for a moment or two, and then pretended to ignore the presence of the other entirely, turning their attention instead to the clamor of admirers that soon encircled them both.

Guy immediately recognized why the odds on the fight favored Sullivan. He was a huge man, decidedly the larger of the two, nearly a head taller and a good deal brawnier than Morrissey. If appearances meant anything, then Sullivan would walk away with the fight.

But Guy knew that appearances did not necessarily tell the whole of every story, and in all likelihood of this one in particular. Morrissey, although the smaller of the two, was by all ordinary criteria still a large and powerful man. More than that, Guy noticed that Sullivan had ordered a whiskey as soon as he'd approached the bar, downed it, and was already well into a second as he loudly and pointedly announced to his fans that he would handily win the fight the following afternoon, adding that he could outfight, outdrink, and outperform any man he'd ever met, claims he was more than willing to prove, either right there or at the whorehouse down the road. This performance was loudly and enthusiastically received by his fans, who rushed forward to him, more than willing to stand him to a drink for the honor of shaking so remarkable a man's hand.

Morrissey, on the other hand, slowly nursed the single beer he'd ordered when he'd entered the bar. His expression as he listened to his opponent's bragging was more than comment enough on what he thought of his opponent. When queried about Sullivan's statement that he could outfight any man he'd ever met, Morrissey only replied that he and Mr. Sullivan had not yet been formally introduced. He smiled, and talked confidently to the men who came to shake his hand, but he was not nearly so loud or boastful as Sullivan.

A cautious man, Guy thought. He would depend on his intellect and his speed to compensate for Sullivan's greater size and strength. Despite the handicap, Guy thought he definitely stood a better than average chance to win in a fair fight with Sullivan.

But it wasn't to be a fair fight, Guy reminded himself. The outcome had already been decided and had nothing to do with the skill or the strength of either of the two participants.

The knowledge of that fact took on a vastly increased importance to Guy as he spotted an old friend of his enter the bar.

Not that Guy would ever have called his relationship with Dublin O'Donnell as personally close or in any way intimate. Still, the pickpocket had often proved to be a font of obscure knowledge about the most unlikely people, which, for a price, he was only too willing to share with an accommodating listener. And Guy was always accommodating. He considered an encounter with the slight, red-haired pickpocket worth far more than the few dollars that changed from his hands to O'Donnell's. And, at that moment, Guy took his presence to be the first genuinely good omen he'd had since he'd arrived in the town.

He raised his hand and called out O'Donnell's name over the uproar in the room. O'Donnell spotted him and waved in response. It took him a few moments to work his way through the crowd, but he soon was standing beside Guy.

Guy smiled at him amiably. "How's business, Dublin?" he asked.

O'Donnell shook his head. "This is a holiday, Guy, me friend," he answered. "No business. I've just come to watch the goings on, have a bit o' booze and maybe a bit o' snugglin' with a convenient trollop, if this piss little town can offer one." He suddenly seemed to notice Cedar. "Beggin' your pardon, miss."

Guy turned to Cedar and saw the same distaste in her expression as she looked at O'Donnell as when she'd considered the less than pristine atmosphere of the saloon. He found he couldn't keep himself from laughing. Whether she knew it or not, Dublin O'Donnell might very well provide them with what they needed to help Magnus, and yet her disapproval of the pickpocket's speech was only a hint of what it would be had she known what it was Guy was going to ask him to do.

"Cedar, may I present Dublin O'Donnell, a friend of mine from the city." He ignored the look she darted at him, one that suggested she might have known he'd consort with such. "Dublin, this is Miss Cedar Rushton."

O'Donnell raised an intrigued brow, recognizing Cedar's name just as Guy knew he would.

"A pleasure, Mr. O'Donnell," Cedar said in a tone that couldn't quite hide the suggestion that she felt something else entirely.

"The pleasure is all mine, miss," O'Donnell replied, then, despite the crush of the crowd around him, attempted a formal bow from the waist, which went sadly askew. He straightened up, then looked at Cedar with sad, puppyish eyes. "I've always wanted to be introduced to a lady," he moaned. "And now that I am, circumstances contrive to show me off as the mannerless hooligan I am." Then, improbably, he winked at her.

Despite herself, Cedar could not quite keep from smiling at him.

"I assure you, Mr. O'Donnell," she told him, "circumstances notwithstanding, your manners are decidedly better than any number of persons I've met of late who attempt to pass themselves off as gentlemen." She darted another look at Guy.

O'Donnell laughed, then turned to Guy. "Come to

watch the fight, have you, Guy?" he asked. "Or maybe just have one of your own?"

Now it was Guy's turn to smile. "Hopefully just watch, Dublin," he said. "But then again, there's no accounting for the unexpected."

O'Donnell glanced at Cedar again and his expression sobered. "I understand," he said softly. "Any help I can offer?"

"As a matter of fact, there is." Guy said.

He lowered his voice and moved closer to O'Donnell, putting his lips next to the pickpocket's ear.


"Well, that was a pleasant evening," Cedar said. She crossed the room to the dresser, where she groped in the near darkness for the box of matches. "Such a charming gathering. And in so magnificent an ambience. How can I ever express my thanks for so memorable an experience?"

"May I remind you, you wanted to come?" Guy asked.

He was right, Cedar fumed silently as she finally found the box of matches. She withdrew one, lifted the globe of the oil lamp, ignited the match, then carefully lit the wick. She *had* wanted to go with him. The thought of being left alone in the house while Slade's men roamed the grounds had terrified her.

"I had no idea you had so many friends among the rabble of New York," she said.

Guy smiled. He'd recognized a good deal more of the saloon's clientele than he'd expected, although he'd only spoken with half a dozen.

"Slade seemed impressed with that fact, too," he told her. "It would seem to verify the old saying that acquaintances make the man."

"It's clothing that makes the man," Cedar corrected.

Guy shrugged. "As you like."

338

"You might have warned me at least," she said as she finished adjusting the flame, then resettled the glass globe.

"Warned you?" he asked.

"What it was like in that kind of a place," she said.

"If I had, would that have made it any more to your liking?" he asked.

She turned around to face him and found that he was beginning to disrobe. He'd removed his jacket and now sat on the bed in preparation to pull off his boots.

"No," she admitted. "Probably not. I suppose I ought to be grateful that you didn't agree to go along with McNaughton to the whorehouse."

Guy looked up at her, his boot momentarily forgotten as he considered her expression.

"Now why do I have an odd feeling you're going to make me regret that particular act of chivalry?" he asked. "I suppose you intend to sleep on the couch again tonight?"

Cedar told herself to ignore his query, but even so, she felt her cheeks heat with the flush she had no need to see in the mirror to know was there. It disconcerted her, far more than she wanted to admit to herself. And the last thing she would do would be admit it to him. Bewildered by the sudden surge of emotion, her reaction was to attack.

"I thought we came back to this horrid little town—"

"Actually, I think it's a rather nice little town," Guy interrupted. "Neat fields, scenic mountainside to look at, lots of nice, clean air to breathe."

Cedar ignored him. "I thought we came back here to find some evidence that will help my father," she told him sharply. "As far as I can see, you've done nothing but drink and smoke and stand around that disgusting bar."

Guy shrugged, unimpressed with her anger.

"I did a good deal more than that," he said.

"Oh, yes," Cedar scowled. "I almost forgot. You also

339

chatted with some of your upstanding friends from New York. What are they? Thieves? Panderers? What other fine members of society do you count amongst your coterie?"

"As a matter of fact," he replied, "two or three of them make their living taking bets, one is an exceptionally gifted second-story man, and O'Donnell — I'm sure you remember him, he was the one who somehow managed to crack the ice in your expression for a second or two — he's a pickpocket by profession."

He returned his attention to his boot, pulling it off and dropping it to the floor.

"Oh, yes, Mr. O'Donnell," Cedar sneered, ignoring the comment about her expression, "I remember him. He was planning the evening around a search for an accommodating trollop, as I recall."

Guy looked up at her sharply.

"You can't blame a man for being human, Cedar," he told her. "Or need I remind you it was a similar weakness on your precious father's part that got you into this little fix?"

As soon as he'd uttered the words, he wished he could call them back. Her face seemed to slowly crumble, her lower lip starting to tremble first, soon followed by her chin, and liquid filled her eyes. She turned away, but even so, he knew that she was fighting the tears.

He stood and crossed the room to stand behind her.

"I'm sorry, Cedar," he said softly. "I shouldn't have said that."

She wished he wouldn't try to be kind to her then, wished he would give her a reason to hate him. Since Magnus had been arrested her whole world had been shattered, everything she'd been raised to believe seemed to have turned into a lie. And Guy was always there when it happened, his very presence pointing out her failings to her, her intolerance, the fallacy of what she deemed right

340

and what she deemed wrong. She wanted to hate him, wanted to convince herself that it was his values, not hers, that were wrong. More than anything, she wanted to go back to the way things had been, wanted to feel as secure and sure of herself as she'd felt before the whole horrible thing had begun.

She sniffed and, for lack of a handkerchief, wiped her sleeve across her cheeks.

"Why not?" she demanded. "It's true, isn't it? Why don't you just say that my father's no better than those ruffians we saw tonight?"

And what was worse, she thought, was that she despised him for it, hated her own father for preaching morality while he practiced immorality. It wasn't even the fact that he had gone to this other woman while her mother had still been alive that caused that anger, she knew. It was instead the fact that he'd told her, that he'd let her believe something her whole life and then taken that belief and shattered it without any idea of what he was doing to her. She couldn't hide any longer from the fact that a part of her hated him, and she hated herself for feeling as she did. She felt herself awash in a misery that seemed unending and impossible to escape.

Guy put his hands on her arms and turned her around to face him. She looked so unsettled, so miserable, and yet so vulnerable. And beautiful. More beautiful than anything or anyone he'd ever seen before. He felt a dull lurch of want inside.

"I shouldn't have said it because it hurt you, Cedar," he said softly.

"Does that matter?" she asked, and tried to shrug away from him.

He held her tight, refusing to release her.

"Yes, it matters," he told her. "It matters because I love you."

He had no idea why he said it. He certainly hadn't

341

meant to. But once the words were spoken, he realized that it was true. The differences between them, those things that had seemed to divide them so completely, suddenly seemed trivial to him, completely unimportant. He loved her and that was really all that mattered.

Cedar stopped struggling, momentarily stunned, telling herself that she hadn't really heard him say the words but had imagined them. And then, when she realized it hadn't been her imagination, she told herself it was a lie, that he lied well enough to say even those words and make them sound real. She stared up at him, searching his face, looking into his eyes, asking herself if she could be so great a fool as to trust what she saw in them.

"Don't," she murmured. "Please don't lie to me."

"I love you," he said again, and he wrapped his arms around her and pulled her close.

"Don't, Guy," she whispered. "I'm too tired to fight you. I'm too lost and too tired to fight myself any more."

"I love you," he said as he lowered his lips to hers. "And you love me, too. Whether you know it or not, you love me."

# Chapter Twenty

From that moment on, Cedar was lost, and she knew it.

She had been foundering during the previous few days, unable to find anything near to firm footing on ground that seemed to be continually shifting beneath her. One moment everything would seem so clear to her, and she'd be certain that she knew what she must do and how she must do it. The next moment she would find herself lost and bewildered, only too painfully aware that every move she made was the wrong one and every step she took only brought her further from where she wanted to be.

At that moment there seemed to be only one solid, sure thing in her life, and that was the way Guy made her feel. Nothing else was real to her, nothing else certain except the secure warmth of his arms holding her and the taste of his lips on hers.

It might mean nothing to him, she told herself. It might be nothing more than a lie.

She ought to care, ought to want to know the truth before she gave herself to him again. She wasn't drunk, as she had been the first time, nor was she so filled with relief at the sight of him that her reason was temporarily dulled by her gratitude. This time she was in full possession of herself, and the intellect on which she'd always prided herself told her she ought to care.

But she knew she didn't.

For this one night, she told herself, she wouldn't search for answers that could only hurt her. She would not turn away from this one comfort that remained in her life. For this one night, she wouldn't let it matter that he might not really love her. For this one night, she simply wouldn't let herself think at all.

It would all be over soon enough in any event. Guy would get the proof to free her father that he had promised her he'd find, or else there was no proof to be found and he wouldn't. Life would go on, resolutely leading from one inevitability to another. Magnus would be tried for Mary Farren's murder, and he would be either convicted or he would be freed. She'd done what little she could to help him and none of it had led anywhere, despite the pain it had cost her. All she'd managed to do was rail ineffectually at an unfair fate; all her attempts to change things had amounted to nothing as far as Magnus was concerned. She had no more ideas, nowhere else to turn. She knew she could do nothing more.

The one thing she had managed to do, it seemed, was fall in love with a man who had other priorities in his life. And that might very well have soured the remainder of her own life.

Even if her future held nothing but the ruins left behind by the events of the preceding days, even if she must eventually face the fact that Guy had simply used her, still there was no reason why she must face that future until she was forced to meet it. She would at least allow herself a few sweet memories to look back on when nothing else remained.

She pressed herself to him, putting her arms around his neck, parting her lips to welcome his, feeling the thick, hot wave the contact ignited, savoring it, giving herself over to it. What did it matter, she thought, what did any of it matter? If she no longer knew what was right and what was wrong, at least she knew what she felt when he held her, when he made love to her. In a world that had grown increasingly mad, at least she felt herself safe when she was surrounded by the circle of his arms.

He kissed her again, his tongue a darting probe that sent out shivers of sweet fire. The heat of his hands on her back drifted outward, radiating through her, growing ever more intense as she felt the hard press of him when he pulled her body close to his.

Guy lifted his lips from hers, letting them drift to her ear and her neck, feeling the heat and the thickening beat of her pulse that sprang up at his touch. It was all the evidence he needed that what he'd told her was true. She might deny it, she might not want to admit it, but she loved him. The verbal fencing, the arguments, the differences that had seemed insurmountable, none of it, he realized, really mattered. No matter what she said, her body could tell him only the truth, and what it was saying to him was what he wanted to hear.

He lifted her and carried her across the room. When he'd lowered her to the bed, he stood for a moment, staring down at her before he followed her, thinking only that from that instant his fate was fixed. There would never be another woman for him, never be anyone who would make him feel as he did at that moment. If he was fool enough to let himself lose her, he might as well tear out his heart, for it would be dead even if it went on beating inside him.

He had always found words easily, always been glib enough to use them to get what he wanted. He made his living with words. But at that moment words failed him. There were only those three, the three she refused to accept, the three she thought to be a lie. And without them, he realized there was nothing he could say.

Instead he kissed her, touching her, caressing her, telling her with his body what she had not wanted to hear him say in words. Then he drew his lips away from hers and put his hands on either side of her face. He lay, staring down at her, looking for the truth and finding it in her eyes.

"You love me, Cedar," he whispered. "You know it as well as I do."

"No!"

It was a lie, certainly. She knew it. And what's more, she knew he knew it, too.

"I told you earlier," he said, "that there are things you don't do very well. Lying was one of them."

She looked up at him, holding his eyes with hers, searching them and, unlike him, unable to convince herself that what she saw wasn't simply what she wanted to see, that it wasn't a ruse meant to manipulate, to take something he thought she might be otherwise unwilling to give. More than anything, she wished she had never heard him lie so convincingly, wished she could simply believe.

"Unlike you?" she asked in a strained whisper.

He flinched inwardly when he heard the words, knowing why she asked, understanding her fear to simply accept words from a man who had shown her how easily words could be used to mislead and misdirect.

"Unlike me," he replied, knowing that there was no defense for him, no way to deny what they both knew was true.

She was silent a moment, staring at him, not wanting to ask and yet unable to keep herself from uttering the query.

"And are you lying now, too, Guy?" she asked.

"What do you want me to say, Cedar?" he asked. "Will it matter how I answer?"

She tore her eyes away from his, looking away, afraid of what he might see in her eyes. The last thing she wanted was his pity. He was right, she knew. It didn't matter what he told her, whether or not he said what she wanted to hear, whether or not he lied.

"No," she answered.

He waited a moment for her to turn back and face him, and when she didn't, he started to pull away from her.

"At least I'm no rapist," he said.

That, at least, along with the bitterness of his tone, was enough to make her turn back to face him. Her decisions were made, she told herself. Lie or not, she didn't care.

"Tell me you love me, Guy," she begged softly. "Tell me and I'll believe."

For this night, at least, she added silently. For this night she could not help but believe.

"I love you," he whispered, and brought his lips once again to find hers.

Cedar put her hands on his shoulders, pulling him down to her and pressing herself close to him. As she knew it would, her body reacted immediately to his, filling with a thick, hot rush, the sweetly heady delirium he released within her. She was grateful for it, for it pushed away the doubt and left her without thought, without suspicion, without the knowledge of just how well he lied. This was what she wanted, and if logic told her she was a fool to want it, then she would simply turn her back on reason.

When he started to undo the buttons of her blouse, she helped him and then sat and shrugged herself free of it. Then, rather than lying back, she pushed him instead down to the pillows and began to return the favor, leaning over him and releasing the buttons of his shirt, letting her fingers trail against his flesh.

Guy put his hands in her hair and pulled away the pins that held it. The thick folds of curls fell forward, touching his naked chest, a soft caress of cool silk beside the warmth of her hands. He stared up at her intent expression and smiled, but his amusement with her quickly van-

347

ished as she leaned forward and pressed her lips against the exposed flesh of his chest. He closed his eyes, letting himself fill with the feeling of his body's response to her touch.

When she reached for his belt and released it, when she began to slowly unfasten the buttons of his trousers, when he felt the touch of her fingers and her lips against his belly and slowly, ever so slowly, lowering, he felt a wave of want unlike any he had ever felt before. This was torture, a sweet, wrenching torture that filled him with a throbbing, aching desire that he knew was more than the need his flesh had for hers.

He reached for her, pulling her to him, quickly sweeping away the remainder of both her clothing and his own. He was filled with the need to feel her close to him, to have his body touching hers. When he pushed her back to the pillows and followed her, he was surprised at how the want seemed still to grow. The touch of her skin, the sweet, soft flesh of her thigh against his, the press of her breast against his chest, the pale, smooth hollow of her neck beneath his lips—she ignited fires within him he'd never felt before.

He let his hands slowly slide over the swell of her hips, then back to the slope of her waist. As he did, he felt her hands, more tentative than his, more curious, as she followed his lead to make a similar exploration of her own. This, too, unexpectedly excited him, this tentative, inexperienced examination. It made no sense to him that she could rouse him with a trembling hand more fully than could any of the far more knowledgeable partners he had had in the past.

When he nudged her thighs with his own, Cedar readily spread herself beneath him in response, reaching her hands to his shoulders and pulling him close to her. She pressed her lips to his neck, feeling the thick, even thud of his heartbeat like the thunder of racing hooves. She knew

348

it was echoed by her own. She waited for him expectantly, filled with a desire that had grown until it now was nothing less than an aching need.

Guy held himself from her for a moment, staring down at her, wondering just what she had done to make him feel this way, wondering how he'd relinquished to her this power he suddenly realized she wielded over him.

"I love you, Cedar," he whispered before he lowered his lips to hers and pressed himself to her.

He made love to her with an intensity that bewildered him, an intensity born of the need to convince her with his body of what he had been unable to convince her with his words. He felt the heat rising in her, felt her trembling response, and knew that despite her doubts, still her body could not dismiss what they both knew, what neither of them could escape.

Cedar clung to the words, telling herself she believed, realizing that even if it was a lie, still she was bound to him and part of her always would be. He touched her and she was awash with liquid fire, he moved inside her and she became lost in a sea of throbbing passion. It lifted her, the waves washing over her, carrying her ever higher until she thought she might be drowned by the tides that throbbed within her.

When it came for her, the release was shattering. She felt as though her body had melted, merged with his, and all there was for her was the feeling of being a part of him, and he a part of her. She heard herself moan, and the sound of it was something alien, as though it came from somewhere and someone else. She clung to him, afraid that if she let go, she would dissolve into nothingness.

He followed her, unable to control himself any longer once he felt her trembling release, and was himself lost in the confusion of the intensity of the climax that claimed him. There was no longer any question in his mind that he would ever feel this way with anyone else. They were fated for one another, and one way or another, he knew, he would convince her of that fact.

But for that moment there were no words, nor was there any need for any. They lay together, bound still in the afterglow of passion, she softly cradled in his arms.

And as he listened to her heartbeat slowly return to normal, as her breathing dissolved into the regularity of sleep, he told himself that he still had a lifetime in front of him, a lifetime to make her believe, a lifetime to hold her in his arms. They need only get past the next day and he would have all the time in the world.

All the time in the world, that was, assuming nothing went wrong, assuming he managed to accomplish what he'd promised her he would and then got them both out of Slade's insane fiefdom while they were still in possession of their lives.


The early-afternoon sun was brilliantly sharp, picking out the bright colors of the leaves that had turned, seemingly almost overnight, to their autumn reds and yellows and oranges. A rustle of wind from off the mountain, the almost ceaseless wind that Cedar had come to realize was ever present in this place, shook a shower of them from the long row of huge maples that lined the road. It startled Cedar to realize how perfectly beautiful the day was. It hardly seemed fitting, she thought, especially considering what the day promised to hold in store.

The anxious flow of men that at that moment crowded what was really more a rutted wagon path than a real road seemed oblivious to the harmless bombardment of falling leaves. They were far more intent on reaching the place the locals called Vosburgh's Meadow, the field where the prizefight was to be held. Nothing, it seemed, was more important to them than finding a place that would afford a good view of the contest.

"I can't believe you're making me watch this barbarian spectacle," Cedar sniped at Guy as they walked along, jostled by the crowd.

"I don't intend to let you out of my sight today," he told her, and he tightened his hold of her arm. "I wouldn't be surprised if all hell breaks out around here in a few hours."

"What does that mean?" she demanded.

But he only shook his head, motioning for her to be quiet when he saw Slade, who was walking a few feet ahead of them with McNaughton, turn to see that they weren't lagging too far behind.

Cedar acquiesced, trudging along silently at his side. They followed the flow of the crowd in front of them, turning off the road and onto a wide, open hay field. At the far side of the field there was a row of trees, and when they reached it, she found that the level field sloped sharply downward just beyond, forming the side of a nearly perfect natural bowl. In the center of the area a ring had been erected and roped off, ready for the fight.

Already a good portion of the hillside surrounding the ring was covered with men who sat patiently waiting for the main event to begin. Some merely idled; others formed intent groups and gambled, playing cards and dice on blankets spread on the grass. Cedar realized that a good number of them must have slept in the open field the night before. There were a number of blankets on the grass, and dark patches that gave evidence to the fires they'd started to keep themselves warm.

There was an aura of pleased expectancy about the crowd. A slightly subdued, not quite sober, vaguely alcoholic haze, no doubt caused by the drinking that had continued throughout the night, seemed to hang in the air over the whole of the place.

"This way," Slade turned and said to Guy.

He pointed to a cordoned-off place near the ring, an area equipped with the luxury of two long benches that had been set aside for the time-keeper, Slade, and his guests.

"Box seats," Guy said to Cedar. "It seems you're going to get to see the whole fight from up close enough to smell the blood."

Cedar scowled. She didn't know if he was being serious, or if he was simply mocking her for the reluctance she'd shown about attending at all.

But Guy didn't seem to have any interest in either her facial expressions or her attitudes at that moment. His glance was suddenly riveted on a man just in front of Slade who was trying to make his way against the flow of the crowd.

She looked up and watched, too, taking only a moment to recognize the man as one of those Guy had spoken to in the saloon the night before, the man who had been introduced to her as Dublin O'Donnell. She watched as he was pushed from side to side by the men streaming past him, his body seeming to bounce as it was struck again and again. And then one especially intent spectator, searching for a place to sit that was as close as possible to the ring, negligently shoved the slight, red-headed O'Donnell and sent him reeling.

For a moment it seemed as if O'Donnell might fall and be trampled by the crowd, but he shifted forward and instead stumbled into Slade. His arms flailed as he tried to keep himself erect. He grasped Slade's jacket and just managed to keep on his feet.

"Clumsy fool," Slade snarled, pushing the obviously inebriated O'Donnell away.

"Sorry, guv," O'Donnell said.

He smiled lopsidedly and then patted at the front of Slade's shirt, apparently attempting to smooth away wrinkles he'd inadvertently left in the course of the mishap.

Slade pushed him aside.

"You're drunk," he hissed with a thick note of disgust in his voice. "Let me pass."

O'Donnell stepped away.

"Certainly, guv," he said, and made a wobbly attempt at a bow as Slade swept past him.

O'Donnell stood watching as Slade moved away, seemingly intrigued by his progress. Then he turned and started forward against the flow again, this time moving miraculously without incident past a half dozen men. He stumbled again only when Guy was in front of him.

He barely brushed against Guy, but still he apologized profusely, offering him a leering "Sorry, guv" just as he had to Slade.

Then, improbably, he turned to Cedar with a smile and winked at her before he melted into the crowd.

Startled, Cedar stared at him. But he gave no further sign that he knew either her or Guy, instead turning and elbowing his way into the flow of the crowd.

In only a moment, he had vanished.

"That man is drunk," she said, not making any attempt to hide the distaste she felt at the public display.

"Is he?" Guy asked her softly.

She considered his smug expression.

"What does that mean?" she demanded.

Guy only shook his head, obviously not intending to offer her a reply. He took her arm and guided her through the ropes that set off the small area with the benches from the rest of the open field.

She sat where Guy directed her, on the bench just behind the one where Slade and McNaughton had settled themselves. Guy seated himself at her side.

"Quiet crowd, isn't it?" he asked.

She hadn't noticed it until then, but once he mentioned it, she realized he was right. There had to be well over a two thousand men in the field, with more still coming, and yet they made very little noise. The sound of their voices was far less than the din she would have thought such a hoard would have raised.

"Yes, it is," she agreed. Then she scowled. "They're probably all too hung over from their harmless revelry last night to be able to talk."

Guy laughed, but he quickly sobered as he looked around.

"Or maybe it's because there aren't any women here," he suggested.

"Am I to take it that means women are the only gossips in your estimation, Mr. Marler?" she asked. "I might have thought a man in your profession might know better."

Guy didn't answer, and from his expression Cedar realized he wasn't simply making a typically superior male comment. There had been no laughter in his tone when he spoke. She looked around the hillside once again.

It was true, Cedar realized. She couldn't see more than a handful of women in the crowd, and from their dress it was more than obvious that they made their living in Slade's bordello. She saw that Guy was not entirely pleased by that fact, that he seemed to be worried about her safety.

But for the moment, she realized, she was more than safe enough. The attention of every man in the field was firmly centered on the ring, riveted on what they had come to watch. She turned and looked around, surprised to see how quickly the hillside around the whole of the bowl had become completely filled with humanity.

And from the appearance of that mass of humanity, she could see that not all the observers were the toughs who had come up from New York. Easily identifiable by their overalls were small groups of farmers from the surrounding area. Obviously they had decided that if they couldn't turn away the hoard of interlopers who had invaded their domain, they might at least benefit from the spectacle that had brought the chaos virtually to their doorsteps. The farmers sat together in small, tight groups. Somehow they managed to appear distinct and separate from the men around them, although there was no obvious distance between them and their neighbors.

Even the limbs of the trees at the top of the hillside now held spectators—farm boys who had climbed up into the line of maples that edged the top of the field and settled there for want of a better prospect from which to watch the fight. They peered out through the fringe of brightly colored leaves like strange-looking, large-eyed fruits nestled among the fall-colored foliage.

While she was still intrigued by the sight of the boys perched on the tree limbs, the relative silence in the field was suddenly shattered. A thick, spontaneous rumble of sound rose up and hung over the bowl, echoing back upon itself. Cheers and the thunder of feet stamping against the ground and of hands beating against one another all combined to make a deafening roar.

The sudden noise startled Cedar, and she jumped.

Guy put his hand on her arm, calming her.

"There," he said, and pointed to the cause of the uproar.

Cedar turned and stared where he pointed, just as virtually every other person in the field was by now staring at the entrance of the two combatants. They walked slowly down the path that opened up in front of them to allow them to pass and then sealed itself in their wake. Each fighter was entirely surrounded by his own entourage, a group of rough and decidedly threatening men who seemed to take very seriously their occupation of keeping any overly anxious fan from expressing his admiration too personally.

The swell of noise didn't lessen during the ten minutes it took for the completion of the slow march from the edge of the hill down to the center of the bowl. Sullivan courted the crowd shamelessly, swaggering, flinging the crimson-lined cape he wore back and over his shoulders, lifting his bare arms skyward in a gesture that said only too clearly he expected to win. Morrissey was a bit less theatrical, dressed as he was in a simple high-necked sweater and wearing a fixed and resolute expression, but he, too, lifted his clasped hands over his head and nodded to the men who called out to him.

Finally they reached the side of the ring. The two groups separated, making their ways to opposite corners. Calm and businesslike, the combatants quickly stripped to their waists and then carefully adjusted the lacings of the high, soft leather boots they wore. Ready, the two men climbed into the ring to join the referee who had entered moments before.

As soon as the two set foot inside the ring, the deafening clamor died completely away, replaced by a silence that was almost eerie after the roar that had come before it. Michael Allaire, the referee, moved to the center of the ring and announced the fight. Although his voice was not inordinately loud, every word carried in the hush to even the furthest spectator. The preliminaries completed, he then grasped both fighters' arms, and the two men went through the ritual of shaking hands before they separated and returned to their respective corners.

Cedar was almost startled by the sound of the bell. The noise was sharp and surprisingly loud in the now nearly silent field. But the fighters were more than prepared for it. They both darted immediately forward, moving to the center of the ring, bare fists raised and ready. They slowly circled, eyeing one another for a long instant as each looked for the first opening.

Cedar didn't see who threw the first punch. It seemed little more than a blur to her. From where she sat, she noticed mostly the four dark-booted feet that danced quickly from side to side and the powerful arms that thrust fists forward in short, tight jabs. One thing was perfectly clear to her, however, and that was the noise, the thick, sharp sound of bare fist meeting belly or shoulder or chin, each blow quickly followed by the sickening liquid sound of breath being forcefully exhaled in a resigned grunt of pain.

One particularly vicious blow brought Sullivan to his knees, and Cedar thought hopefully that it might end the match then and there. But he quickly pushed himself back to his feet, and as soon as he had straightened, he threw a punch, his fist landing firmly against the side of Morrissey's nose. A spurt of red immediately rewarded him for the effort.

The round lasted one minute, and just as the bell rang, Allaire darted forward and separated the two men. Sullivan and Morrissey parted obediently, stepping back and eyeing one another before they turned to return to their respective corners.

Cedar found she was grasping Guy's arm. He seemed hardly to notice, for his attention was, at that moment, firmly centered on Slade and McNaughton, but it startled her when she looked down and saw her hand. She didn't remember having reached for his arm, and the sight of her own fingers, holding on so tightly they were nearly white, made her realize just how tense she was. She had to force herself to release her hold.

"How long does this last?" she asked.

Guy shrugged. "Until one of them can't go on any longer," he told her.

She glanced up and stared first at Morrissey, then at Sullivan. Each sat in his corner, stony-eyed and from all appearances oblivious to the ministrations of their seconds, their faces as set and as unemotional as granite. After only one round, Morrissey's left eye was blackened, and there were still traces of blood dripping from his injured nose. Sullivan's shoulder showed a deep violet welt that she knew must be a painful bruise, and there was a narrow line of dark red on his lower lip. Neither seemed to show any interest in their injuries nor in the hurried nursing their seconds performed.

She wondered what would make men go through such punishment, wondered why they weren't revolted by the fact that their pain was nothing more than amusement to the watching hoard. She felt a sudden wave of revulsion, not only at what the two men were doing to themselves and one another, but at the fact that she was sitting there and watching it.

"Do we have to . . . ?"

She never got the chance to ask Guy to leave. Her words were drowned out by the sound of the bell, and Guy's attention, like that of every other male sitting in the field, returned to the center of the ring. Cedar gave up, at least temporarily, knowing that a request to leave would go, if not unheard, then certainly unheeded. She steeled herself to watch.

The fight went on, round after round. Cedar had soon lost count of them, and she ceased to watch. But turning her head away could not keep her from hearing the sounds of fist meeting flesh and reluctantly exhaled grunts of pain, nor could she avoid the shower of fresh blood droplets that was sprayed on her by a particularly vicious blow.

From what she could gather, neither of the fighters was taking a distinct lead, although when she did glance up and look at them, it seemed to her that Morrissey was the more seriously marked of the two. All she knew for sure was that the relative silence with which the crowd had greeted the beginning of the fight had slowly been replaced by a swell of noise, an occasional shout of encouragement at first, and then more and more shouts and catcalls, until it seemed as though the whole of the valley reverberated with the noise.

If Cedar had thought to ask him, Guy could have told her that the men fought thirty-seven vicious rounds before Allaire halted it and announced a winner. She didn't ask. She didn't even notice when the end of the fight was called. What she did notice was the presence of both men's seconds in the ring, each side angrily shouting at the other, and the change in the tone of shouts from the spectators.

"What's happened?" she demanded as Guy firmly grasped her and stood, pulling her to her feet.

"The referee's given the fight to Morrissey," he told her. "Come on, we have to get out of here."

She didn't understand why he seemed suddenly in such a hurry to leave, but she was more than willing to go. All around them, angry men were standing and shouting. Fists were raised in the air and arguments were breaking out.

Guy threaded his way through the mob, more often than not using pure brute force to carve a path for them, constantly guarding Cedar with his body. Cedar kept close to him, afraid they might be caught in the growing anger of the crowd or, even worse, that she might become separated from him. All around her the air was filled with the odors of sweat and stale beer and was laced with the steadily growing madness that marks a mob.

Somehow Guy managed to maneuver them to the top of the hill and away from the stragglers at the edge of the crowd.

"What's happening back there?" Cedar asked when he gave her an instant to catch her breath.

She looked back and saw Morrissey and Allaire vacating the ring while Sullivan refused to leave, instead shouting at his opponent to return and go on fighting like a man.

"I'd say Sullivan and a few of his fans aren't quite

happy with the referee's decision," he told her. "Come on. We haven't much time."

"Where are we going?" she demanded when he took her arm once again and started across the field to the road.

"Back to the farmhouse," he told her.

Cedar balked.

"No!" she shouted angrily at him.

Suddenly all the rationalizing she'd done the night before, all the reasons she'd given herself to convince herself that she believed in him—all of that vanished. She felt used, felt as though he'd kept her there only to provide himself with the proper accouterments for his masquerade. Well, she'd helped him fool Slade and get his damned story about the fight and the stolen horses. She wasn't about to do any more.

"I won't go back there," she shouted at him. "The fight's over. You have your damned story. I want to leave."

"It wasn't just for the story that we stayed," he retorted.

"Oh, yes, I remember," she spat back. "There was that fantasy about finding something that will help my father." She shot an angry glance at him. "Why don't you just admit it was a lie? There isn't any proof and you know it."

He stared at her for a moment, his eyes finding and holding hers. He saw anger in them, and nothing else. It hurt him to realize that she couldn't believe in him, hurt him more than he wanted to admit even to himself.

"We have to go back, Cedar," he said finally. "Can't you trust me? You've come this far. Is it too much to ask for you to trust me just a little while longer?"

He stood, completely motionless, waiting for her to decide, thinking that in many ways his whole life hinged on her answer.

# Chapter Twenty-one

Cedar stared back into his eyes. As soon as she did, and against all rational laws of logic, she found herself wavering.

She would have to be a fool to go back with him, she told herself. Slade would soon go back there, and McNaughton. At that moment what she wanted most was to get away from the town and those two men in particular.

It wasn't as though she needed Guy. She knew where the path was, knew how to find the tunnel through the mountain. She could leave him, go without him if he refused to take her. She could turn her back on him, cross the field and disappear into the woods. She could get away, without Slade or McNaughton ever even seeing her go. She could turn her back on Guy and forget all the horrible things that had happened to her in the days since she'd been brought to this miserable little town.

But she didn't.

She didn't know why, and refused to allow herself to consider the question, sure that if she did she'd realize how frightened she was to stay, how much wiser it would be simply to turn away from him, ignore what she felt when she looked in his eyes, and go.

She swallowed, working up her courage.

"All right," she murmured. "A little while longer."

Guy breathed a thick sigh of relief. He grasped her hand in his.

"I don't think we'll have much of a head start," he told her. "Dublin and the others will do what they can, but there's a limit to what they'll be able to do."

Cedar scowled. Why, she wondered, was he talking in riddles?

"What can your drunken friend do?" she demanded.

He grinned. "Later," he said, tugging at her hand. "I'll tell you later."

They ran down the now deserted road and then across the yard to the farmhouse. This time they took no care to try to hide themselves. This time Guy simply relied on the hope that all of Slade's men had gone to watch the fight and were embroiled in the havoc he and Cedar had left behind in Vosburgh's Meadow.

They ran up the steps and into the house. Guy darted across the front hall, pulling open the door to Slade's office.

"Now what?" Cedar demanded.

"Now we see what we can find," he told her.

Cedar grimaced. He'd come back, he'd taken the chance they'd be caught, and all for some vague idea he had that he might find something. It seemed nothing less than madness to her, and she told herself she was equally as mad for having come back with him. She found herself wishing she'd gone on without him. When he entered the study, she hesitated, darting a glance at the front door before she followed him.

He put his hand in his pocket and pulled out a key ring. He held it up for a second, turning back to her and grinning, then turned his attention to considering what it held.

Cedar stared at him in disbelief as he selected what appeared to be a likely key and tried to fit it into the lock of the top drawer of Slade's desk.

"That's Slade's key ring," she said in a whisper gone dull with surprise. "How did you get it?"

He darted a look up at her. "With a little help from my friend," he said, and then he grinned.

"You had your friend steal it, didn't you?" she said, thinking aloud. She recalled the incident with distaste, a distaste that only grew as she realized it had been orchestrated to Guy's orders. "That man O'Donnell. He wasn't drunk at all. It was all an act so he could steal Slade's keys."

Guy's grin disappeared. "Before you go all holy on me and preach the lesson about the sin of stealing, you might remember I did it to help your father."

That said, he returned his attention to what he was doing, rejecting the first key when it didn't turn in the lock, and selecting another.

"Now what have we here?" he mused softly as the key turned. He pulled the drawer open and stared inside.

Intrigued now, Cedar realized she was no longer concerned with how he'd obtained the key ring. Despite herself, she was, instead, far more interested in what he might have found. She crossed the room to the desk.

"What's in there?" she asked as she leaned forward, staring into the drawer and watching Guy rifle through the contents.

He was silent for a moment as he considered what he'd found. It didn't take him long. He exhaled a short, disgusted snort, then pushed the drawer closed and began the procedure with the keys once again.

"What was in there?" Cedar demanded again, this time her tone a bit testy as she realized he was ignoring her.

"Nothing," Guy grunted. "Some money, a stack of IOUs, letters. I didn't look at them closely, but they looked personal."

He had by now found the right key for the next drawer.

He turned it in the lock, then pulled the drawer open.

Guy didn't so much as have to inspect the contents to know that he'd found what he was looking for. He could feel the hairs on the back of his neck stand up, could feel the shiver of excitement that preceded the moment when he was about to find the answers to his questions. A sixth sense was telling him that the papers in this drawer were important, the proof he'd promised Cedar he'd find that would free her father.

"But I think we have something now," he murmured as he lifted out a pile of papers and laid them out on the surface of the desk.

Cedar watched him carefully unfold what appeared to be a map. Guy's suggestion that he'd found something left an odd thumping in her chest, a strange feeling of excitement and curiosity that only grew when she saw his lips turn up in a satisfied smile as he scanned the papers he'd found.

She leaned over the desk and looked at the map. It was a city map, she quickly realized, a survey map of a portion of the center of New York, with the familiar street names clearly marked and each block neatly divided, every plot marked with the name of its owner. A good number of those plots in the center of the map were circled with bright red ink.

"What is it?" she asked.

Guy only pointed to the lettering at the top of the sheet. Cedar read the carefully lettered script: *Proposed Site of Pennsylvania Station.*

She looked back up at Guy, more confused now than she had been at the start, and watched him leaf through a dozen official-looking documents. From what she could see, they appeared to be deeds. A map of the proposed site of a new Harlem Railroad station, a thick pile of deeds — that was what he'd found. Whatever it might mean to him, she realized that none of it, as far as she

364

could see, seemed to have any bearing on her father's situation.

Guy's smile became broader as he opened the documents, one after another, and scanned their contents. Whatever he'd found, Cedar realized, it pleased him as much as finding the cave and discovering how Slade managed the magic act that made stolen horses disappear. It was his smugly satisfied smile that ignited the spark of her intuition. She realized that she had once again caught a bit of the madness that kept him searching until he found what he wanted to know.

She reached for one of the documents, but even before she unfolded it she realized that she now had an inkling of an idea of what it was that he found so interesting.

"McNaughton has used his office to get information on land that will become a new railroad station, hasn't he?" she asked.

Guy looked up from the papers in his hands and grinned at her. "I knew you were a very astute woman the moment I laid eyes on you," he said.

"And those are deeds," she went on. "He and Tweed have been buying up cheap plots of land that will very soon become very valuable."

Guy grinned again and nodded. "Precisely. That's why the election was so important."

"Tweed couldn't afford to let my father, or anyone else but Michael McNaughton, win the election," she went on. "Tweed didn't want to lose his source of information." Her mind was whirling now, all the mysteries as to why her father had been so neatly framed for murder no longer so mysterious. "And the only way to do that was to discredit my father and any other candidate backed by the reformists, not by Tammany."

"Right again," Guy told her. "They had to discredit the whole movement. That's probably what saved your father's life and signed the death warrant for Mary Farren."

Cedar nodded, immediately understanding what he was saying.

"If they'd just killed Papa, another candidate running on a reform platform might have won. But if they showed him to be a whoring murderer, that cast a pall on the whole party that supported him. They had to make my father look worse than they are."

Guy began to gather up the heap of papers. "I think you might consider becoming a reporter, Cedar," he told her. "You got it all right, with one minor exception."

"Exception?" she asked.

He nodded, then pointed to the deed she held, open, but as yet unread, in her hand.

"It wasn't Tweed," he said.

She looked down at the deed. Tweed's name wasn't among the three that were listed as buyers. But there was a surprise for her.

The three names listed as buyers were those of Michael McNaughton, Robert Slade, and Chester Bowles.

She looked back up at Guy, her eyes wide with disbelief. Her father's chief political supporter was a member of the conspiracy to frame him for Mary Farren's murder.

"I don't believe it," she said. "Chester Bowles practically funded my father's campaign. Why would he do that if he intended to have him framed for murder?"

"Come, come, my dear. Use that fine wit of yours. It was the perfect way to insure that there would be only one strong candidate. A most astute plan, don't you think?"

It wasn't Guy who had answered her. Cedar realized she didn't have to turn to know who it was who had spoken. A sick feeling of dread began to fill her.

She and Guy both turned to find Slade standing in the doorway, smiling broadly at them.

He was aiming the pistol he was holding squarely at Guy's chest.

366

Guy stepped around the side of the desk, edging himself in front of Cedar, shielding her body with his own. He smiled pleasantly at Slade.

"*Your* plan, I suppose?" he asked in a conversational tone.

Slade nodded. There was a distinct glow of pride in his eyes as he answered.

"Precisely," he told Guy. "McNaughton hasn't the brains God gave to the average alley cat. But what he did have was the connections at Tammany, as well as the means of financing the scheme, although he didn't realize it until I pointed it out to him. He has made a valuable, if uninspired, partner in this business."

"Then you came up with the whole idea?" Guy asked. "You came up here and used the location of this farm to provide you with the financing for those land purchases of yours with the profits from the sale of stolen horses?"

Now it was Slade's turn to smile. "I do so enjoy a conversation with an intelligent man, Mr. Marler," he said as he moved slowly forward, into the room. "It pains me to find you are not quite the person you represented yourself to be. I suppose this means our business dealings were not entirely on the up-and-up? I take it you have no employer in need of a fast horse?"

Guy shrugged. "I'm afraid I don't," he replied.

"A shame," Slade muttered. "I do prefer to be able to trust the men with whom I do business. Lying is such an unpleasant habit."

Guy showed no indication that he was in the least ashamed.

"I suppose that's one of the risks you run when you deal in stolen horses," Guy told him.

Slade ignored him.

"And you, lovely Cedar," he said, turning to her. "You should have told me that you were acquainted with Mr.

Marler. I'm afraid this means I can't place my trust in you, either. And that is a decided shame. I do appreciate the company of a handsome and intelligent woman. It is a combination that is far too rare. I had hoped it would not be necessary to turn you over to McNaughton, but it seems that it will be, after all. That, too, pains me. I'm afraid he can be a very unpleasant man on occasion."

"There's no need for that," Guy told him, his tone still very calm, very reasonable. "She can't do you any harm."

"I'm afraid she can," Slade replied. "As long as she didn't really know anything, I was willing to risk keeping her alive as long as she showed a willingness to make herself amusing and agreeable. If she somehow managed to escape, she couldn't really do me any harm. But you, Mr. Marler, have given her information that could ruin me. I'm afraid even Cedar's charms are not so great as to convince me to run the risk entailed in letting her live."

"She's already gone to Tweed and called him a murderer," Guy told him. "By now anyone who matters in the city government considers her addled, a crank who'll say anything to get her father freed."

"Ah, such chivalry from you, Mr. Marler. I find it touching, if not convincing. But even if Miss Rushton's word is suspect, still she might start the wrong people asking unnecessary questions and looking for answers, answers that could only prove unpleasant for me." He shook his head. "No, I'm afraid the only solution is to eliminate any source of risk. And that" — he gestured with the pistol — "means eliminating the two of you."

"What are you going to do?" Cedar asked him.

"Oh, I'm not going to do anything, lovely Cedar," he told her. "I personally abhor violence and prefer to leave it to others who are, shall we say, less fastidious than I. For now I will merely return you to the attic room along with your friend Mr. Marler. I regret that you find the room unpleasant, but it's the only place in the house that's secure. Once McNaughton returns from that melee out in the field, I'll leave your final arrangements with him." He was suddenly struck with a thought, and he turned his attention back to Guy. "I don't suppose you had anything to do with the way that mob reacted to Allaire's decision, did you?" he asked.

Guy shrugged. "We do what little we can in this world," he replied. "My only question is how you got back so quickly."

"Your rioting friends didn't seem to know I had a number of men in my employ who are paid to see to my well-being," Slade replied. "I suppose they're still exchanging blows with those ruffians, but I, as you can see, escaped unscathed."

"Shame," Guy muttered. "It would have been so much nicer to be able to think you were justly paid by the men who lost money on the fight you fixed."

"Fixed?" Slade raised his brow in mock innocence. "You do shock me, Mr. Marler. Such an insult would, under other circumstances, lead me to address such an assault on my honor."

Guy smiled icily at him. "You don't have any honor, Slade," he said.

Slade's cheeks above his beard grew a deep red, his eyes blazed angrily, and the hand that held the pistol began to shake. For an instant Cedar feared he would use the weapon then and there, despite his proclaimed abhorrence of violence. But the flush faded as quickly as it had come, and his hand grew steady once again.

"Enough of this," Slade said sharply. He motioned to the door. "Upstairs, the two of you."

He stood back, intending that Guy and Cedar pass in front of him. Guy put his hand on Cedar's back.

"Why don't you go first, Cedar?" he suggested. "I believe you know the way."

She glanced at him as she walked past him, and she

369

saw the look in his eyes. He wasn't afraid, she realized, no more than he'd been afraid when they'd entered the cave or the hidden room in Madame Blanche's. He was going to do something, she realized, and this time it could only be something foolish and dangerous.

She did the only logical thing she could think of doing. When she neared Slade, she pretended to stumble. She let herself fall forward, clumsily reaching out toward Slade as though she were attempting to keep herself upright. Hopefully she would disorient him enough to make him drop the pistol and give Guy an opening to deal with him.

It had worked for Dublin O'Donnell earlier, she told herself. It had to work for her.

Unfortunately, she wasn't quite as adept at subterfuge as O'Donnell had been. Slade sensed what she was about before she actually touched him. He stepped aside, letting her fall forward to the floor, while he kept the pistol firmly in his hand.

But Guy didn't let the opportunity pass. As Cedar fell to Slade's side, he lunged forward, directing his shoulder into Slade's chest and reaching for the pistol.

Cedar tumbled to the floor, the landing jarring her knees and her arms. But she didn't have time to let herself consider the pain. She turned and watched the two men scuffle, and then felt herself fill with a wave of cold horror when she heard the sound of a shot.

There was an instant of sheer terror for Cedar as she watched Guy fall backward with a bright red stain sprouting from his left arm. But she didn't allow herself time to stop and think, to let the realization of what had happened sink far enough in so that it atrophied her.

She pushed herself to her feet. While Slade's attention was still riveted on Guy, she grabbed the vase from the table behind her and rushed forward, bringing the vase down on the back of Slade's head.

The porcelain shattered in her hand and fell in a shower of pieces. She stood back, waiting for Slade to fall. For an instant it seemed that the impact had had no effect on him at all. He turned to look at her and started to raise the pistol. She backed away, bumping into the table, realizing that there was no place she could go to avoid a bullet.

And then Slade suddenly seemed to simply crumble as he fell in a heavy heap at her feet.

She stared at him in disbelief for an instant, then stepped past him, completely forgetting about him as she darted to Guy's side. There was a shower of red droplets on the floor and chair and the desk behind him. There seemed to be blood everywhere.

"Don't look so stricken, Cedar," Guy told her. He reached up and grasped her hand. "You haven't gotten rid of me so easily as this."

She exhaled a deep sigh of relief, then helped him to his feet.

"You have to get to a doctor," she said.

"Later, when we're away from here," he told her. "Slade won't stay asleep very long."

He steadied himself, then turned back to the desk and quickly began gathering up the map and the deeds. When she realized what he was doing, Cedar helped him, handing the deeds to him as he stuffed them into the pocket of his jacket. Then he turned and glanced down at Slade.

"After what you said about the fight, I didn't think you approved of violence, Cedar," he sniped gently.

"I don't," she replied. "But extraordinary circumstances call for extraordinary actions."

He grinned. "I don't suppose the circumstances are extraordinary enough for you to take his pistol?" he asked.

She swallowed, then knelt down and gingerly lifted the

371

pistol. But before she had a chance to straighten up and hand it to him, she heard a blood-chilling scream.

Cedar looked up. The housekeeper, Mrs. Fretts, had heard the report of the shot and had come to investigate. She was standing in the doorway, staring in, a look of horror on her face as she saw the still body of Slade and the dark scattering of Guy's blood.

Cedar considered the pistol in her hand, and the look of hatred on the housekeeper's face. Before the older woman could collect her thoughts enough to try to dart off, Cedar pointed the pistol directly at her.

"In here," Cedar ordered. She stood, the act of keeping the pistol steady in hands that wanted to shake taking nearly all her control.

The housekeeper glanced at Slade once again and then slowly walked into the room.

"Sit there," Cedar ordered her, and pointed toward Slade's arm chair.

As Mrs. Fretts sat, Cedar turned to Guy, her expression saying clearly that she no longer knew what to do.

But he seemed to have no problem making a decision. He took the pistol from her and nudged her toward the door.

"We have to get out of here," he told her. He turned to the housekeeper. "Stay where you are and be quiet and we won't hurt you," he said.

They backed out of the room, keeping their eyes on the housekeeper. Once in the hall, Guy pushed the door closed and then threw the latch.

"That won't hold her long," he whispered to Cedar. "Especially when she realizes Slade isn't dead. Let's go."

His hand on Cedar's arm, the two of them darted out of the house and down the porch steps. They were scarcely out of the house before they heard Mrs. Fretts start to scream.

They started across the barnyard and toward the

hedgerow that edged the hillside field.

"Through Slade's tunnel?" Cedar asked.

Guy nodded. "It's safest," he said. "Slade doesn't know that we know about it. When he comes to and finds us gone, he'll think we went to the station to try to catch a train to the city."

They climbed the hillside at a slow run, then edged the woods at the far side of the field. As Guy scanned the undergrowth, looking for the path, Cedar darted a glance back into the valley, toward Vosburgh's Meadow. By now the spectators who had been brawling there were spilling out onto the road, returning to the town. They were shouting angrily, pushing one another, fighting as they went. She was glad she wasn't one of the townspeople, glad she didn't have to stay in the town and endure whatever havoc the ruffians would leave in their wake before they finally left.

"Here it is," Guy told her, returning her attention to their own predicament.

He edged his way into the brush that obscured the path, and Cedar followed, pushing her way past the heap, ignoring the sharp edges of limbs and thorns that scratched and caught at her clothing. Once past the pile of brush, they began to run again. But their pace was slowing, Cedar noticed, and she realized it wasn't that Guy was being gentlemanly so that she wouldn't tire. He was, she realized, simply unable to run any faster.

She glanced at his left arm. It was hanging limp at his side, and a dark red stream was still steadily flowing from it. She realized that if the wound wasn't bandaged, the bleeding wouldn't stop. Guy would either bleed to death or simply become too weak to go on.

"You have to at least let me bandage your arm," she told him.

This time he didn't protest. He, too, realized that he wouldn't be able to go on much longer if he continued to

373

lose blood as he was.

He pulled off his jacket and sat obediently on a stone at the side of the path.

"Be as quick as you can, Cedar," he told her. "I don't like the idea of our roaming around here with Slade's men on the loose."

"I don't like it any more than you do," she told him.

She lifted her skirt and pulled off a long piece of petticoat. It wasn't exactly pristine after the excursion to Vosburgh's Meadow, but she realized neither she nor Guy was in a position at that moment to be too fastidious. The bandage in hand, she turned her attention to his arm.

One glance at it made her shudder. His shirtsleeve was soaked with his blood, and the hole the bullet had made was gruesome with gore. She'd never seen a bullet wound before, and she wasn't precisely prepared to face it. She felt her stomach lurch uncomfortably.

Guy needed only a glance at her suddenly paled cheeks to realize what she was feeling. He reached for the bandage she held in her shaking hands.

"I can do it," he told her.

But she pulled back and shook her head. Swallowing and bracing herself, she reached for his arm.

"No," she told him. "You won't be able to do it tight enough to stop the bleeding."

She pulled away the torn bits of fabric from his shirt that clung to the edges of the hole, and then began to wrap the piece of petticoat around his arm.

"I don't think I told you how very much I admired the way you coshed Slade," Guy told her.

She glanced at his face. She knew he was trying to distract her, to keep her from thinking about the queasiness in her stomach and the unpleasant blossom of red that was already staining the bandage, and she appreciated the effort. He was grinning at her, and she couldn't keep from grinning back. For an instant she had the unsettling feeling that he really had enjoyed the sight of her slamming that vase into the back of Slade's head.

"Well, I didn't precisely enjoy doing it," she told him and tugged the bandage tighter.

He winced but didn't complain.

"No," he agreed. "I don't suppose a properly brought up, moral person would. And never let it be said I accused you of being anything less than proper and moral."

"Unlike you?" she suggested.

He nodded. "Unlike me," he agreed. "I have to admit that as much pleasure as I found in watching you lay out Slade the way you did, still it was superseded by the sheer joy of realizing I'd managed to corrupt you just enough to allow you to perform so unladylike an act."

She'd wound the whole of the piece of petticoat around his arm by now. She pulled the bandage tight and began to tie it.

Guy winced once more. "I don't suppose this is your idea of punishment for that sin, is it?"

Cedar wanted to be angry with him, wanted to tell him that whatever changes he'd made in her were certainly not for the better as far as she was concerned.

Instead she found she was smiling in spite of herself.

"It would seem I've committed a good number of unladylike acts of late," she murmured. A shade of bitterness had crept into her tone. "And, as I recall, you've been the cause of just about all of them."

Guy reached up and grasped her hand, holding it in his as he stood.

"I have, haven't I?" he asked in a low, husky voice.

She stared up into his eyes and nodded. She couldn't help but think of those things she'd done the night before when she lay in his arms. He had been the cause of them, there was no disputing that. She'd never thought of herself doing such things before she met him, and couldn't even think of being touched by anyone else.

"Yes," she asserted. "You have."

He released her hand, putting his good arm around her back and pulling her close. They stood silent for a moment, their eyes lost in one another's, and Cedar knew he knew what she had been thinking about, knew he was thinking about it, too.

A breathless second passed, and then he lowered his lips to hers.

It was more a promise than anything else, that kiss. Cedar accepted it gladly, realizing that whatever corrupting he'd done, still he hadn't lied. There *had* been proof—at least proof McNaughton had a motive to murder Mary Farren, proof that would help clear her father's name—and he'd found it, just as he'd promised. Perhaps, she thought, she could allow herself to simply trust him, without question. Perhaps there were times when the most foolish thing a woman could do was look for reasons and logic where neither might really belong.

Guy released her with obvious regret.

"There'll be time for this later," he told her. "Hopefully a good deal of time. But just now, I think we ought to get out of here."

He considered his bandaged arm for an instant, then lifted his torn and blood stained jacket and pulled it on. He took her hand, and they set out again, moving as quickly as Guy could manage along the path to the cave.

"I don't remember it being this far," Cedar whispered.

She stared into the circle of light cast by the lantern she was holding. All she could see was more of the downward-sloping cave, entirely undifferentiated from that she'd already passed.

A moment's thought, however, made her realize that the reason the cave seemed longer to her was that they were walking more slowly. One look at Guy was more than enough to tell her he was drained, and although she knew he wouldn't admit it, it was all he could do to keep going at all. If they didn't soon get to the huge room where Slade had the stolen horses penned, she feared he might collapse.

But he did keep on, for nearly half an hour longer, doggedly walking on until they could see the strange soft glow that had so amazed Cedar the first time.

"There it is," she exclaimed. "A little bit further, Guy, and we'll have lovely horses to ride out of here."

He grinned gamely. "Am I hearing things?" he asked. "Did you actually suggest we steal horses?"

"Not exactly steal," she replied. "Reclaim for their owners. I for one don't intend to let Slade keep them. Especially not Pridey."

"I think I may have gone a bit overboard with you, Cedar," he chided. "First you indulge your taste for violence, now it's horse stealing. I shudder to think where all this might lead."

"I'll tell you it could lead anywhere if Slade tries to stop us from getting back to New York," she muttered angrily. She turned to Guy. "You're sure he won't come after us?"

"I'm sure of nothing, Cedar," he replied. "Let's just hope. Frankly, I'm not sure just how much I'd be able to do to stop him at the moment."

She looked up at his face. He was pale, and she knew what it had to have cost him even to make such an admission. She didn't say anything, just held his arm a bit more tightly and kept doggedly on.

When they finally reached the opening, she found it looked just as it had the first time, found she had the same dazed reaction to the unexpected beauty of the place. The dully glowing colors of the slowly forming rock pillars left her feeling hushed and awed.

"Let's get a drink," she suggested, and nodded toward the pool. "I can rebandage your arm, and I think we

377

could both use a short rest."

They made their way across the damp and slippery floor to the pool, then sat at its edge. Guy put a hand into the water, lifted it wet and dripping, and sniffed it before he finally tasted.

"It tastes clean enough," he told Cedar. "If it's tainted, we won't know it until it's too late."

Cedar wasn't listening. She was busy untying the bandage on his arm and quickly removing it. It was sticky with blood, she realized, an awful lot of blood. But when she'd removed it, she saw that the flow had slowed to thin ooze, and she told herself that that, at least, was good.

She rinsed out the bloody piece of petticoat and washed the hole as well as she could with it, then tore off another piece and rebandaged his arm. Only when she was finished did she settle herself down beside the pool and reach her hands into the water for a drink.

She lifted a cupped handful.

"Are you still feeling well?" she said before she drank.

"Is that why you've held back?" he asked her with a laugh. "To see if it killed me first?"

She shrugged as she lifted her hands to her lips.

"No need for both of us dying if it is tainted," she murmured.

"Oh, it ain't tainted. But it is goin' to be the death of both o' ya."

Cedar let the water drip through her fingers unheeded. She looked up to where the voice was coming from, to the place where the horses where penned.

Slade's hired hand, Duane, emerged from behind a large bale of hay by the corner of the pen. He was moving toward them, a pitchfork in his hands and a look of dark fury in his eyes.

## Chapter Twenty-two

"I thought I was missin' all the fun," Duane said. He looked at Cedar and his lips turned up in a lecherous grin. "Well, it looks like I'll be gettin' to make a little bit o' fun o' my own now, don't it?"

Cedar gaped at him, openmouthed with surprise and disgust. There was no doubt in her mind about what he intended, no doubt at all that he planned to complete the act he'd been forced to abandon two days before in the barn.

She realized he'd probably been sent to the cave to insure the safety of the penned horses, realized that he must have been sullen and angry to have been forced to miss seeing the prizefight. And from the way he was looking at her and Guy, it was only too clear that he intended to take out both his anger and his frustration on the two of them.

He was moving closer, the pitchfork held threateningly forward, the sharp tines directed toward Guy's neck.

But Guy appeared to be completely undisturbed by the threat. He looked up at Duane and smiled amiably.

"You really shouldn't hold your toys that way," he chided. "Someone might misconstrue your greeting as a threat and react accordingly."

Duane's cheeks flushed red with anger.

"You and me got a score to even up, Mister City Slicker," he hissed at Guy. "And your pretty little friend there, I got me some business with her that never got finished." He darted a look at Cedar. "We're goin' to have some fun, you and me," he told her.

Cedar shuddered, but Guy still seemed calmly unmoved. He continued to stare up at Duane.

"We have no argument with you," he said. "Let me escort the lady through without incident and I'll see that your name is forgotten in the report the authorities receive with regard to Slade's stolen horse deals."

Duane laughed. "You may have no argument with me, but it sure does look like you was havin' one hell of an argument with somebody," he said, and nodded toward Guy's blood-covered left arm. "I wonder who that somebody could be? Slade maybe?"

Guy shrugged.

"You know what I think, Mister City Slicker?" Duane went on. "I think it was Slade who gave you that little nick. I think maybe Slade will be real happy when I tell him how I helped you manage to get yourself killed."

Still brandishing the pitchfork, he leered at Guy, waiting for some reaction to his threat. He was rewarded with little more than a shrug and a dull smile.

"What if I were to tell you that Slade will never be happy again?" Guy asked in the same sort of conversational tone he might have used were he inquiring about the weather.

Cedar darted a confused glance at him. Slade surely hadn't been dead when they left him. There was no way she could have hit him hard enough for that. Guy's expression was completely calm, betraying no hint of what he was thinking. She had to remind herself of how well he lied.

Luckily she kept her wits well enough to hold her tongue, telling herself that Guy was trying to keep Duane occupied, to keep the hired hand's thoughts busy. Her eyes drifted to the hand he was slowly edging into his jacket pocket. She remembered with a sudden flash of understanding that he'd dropped Slade's pistol into that pocket after they'd left the house.

She breathed a sigh of relief. She wasn't a murderess after all. Guy was simply trying to distract Duane enough so that he could remove the pistol from his pocket and scare the hand into letting them go.

It took only one glance at Duane for her to realize that the suggestion that Slade was already dead seemed more to amuse than upset him.

"So you killed the fat old bastard, did ya?" he asked. "I thought o' doin' it once or twice myself. There's some quarters that might think ya deserve a medal for the act. There'll be no mournin' for him, that's for sure."

Guy nodded toward the penned horses.

"In that case, you could take the horses, sell them, and keep the money for yourself," he suggested. "Under the circumstances, I don't think Slade will mind."

Duane smiled at him. "You know, I just might do that," he said. He started forward again. "That is, once I finish settlin' the score I have with you and the woman."

He raised the pitchfork to strike at Guy.

As soon as Duane started to move, Guy pulled back and rolled to the side, away from the pool, pulling the pistol out of his pocket as his back hit the stone floor of the cavern. Cedar heard his grunt of pain as he turned and his weight fell on his injured arm, but it was nearly smothered by the sound of her own scream of fright as Duane ran the last few steps separating them and stabbed downward at Guy with the pitchfork.

The sound of Cedar's scream was quickly lost, muffled by the noise of a shot as Guy fired the pistol.

For an instant the noise in the cave was deafening. It seemed to grow for a moment before it began to fade, and then it echoed through the tunnels, returning again and again to her ears, a repeating reminder of what had happened, of what had almost happened.

She sat unmoving for a moment, staring dully at Guy where he lay, propped on one elbow, the pistol still clenched in his hand. He seemed to have become a good deal paler, and she could see the sleeve of his jacket was once again red with a fresh flow of blood that the impact of his fall had caused. But her concern for him still couldn't keep her from letting her gaze drift to Duane, couldn't keep her from staring as Guy was staring at the hired hand's still body.

He lay facedown on the stone, a red puddle of blood leaking from his chest and pooling around his torso. He was completely motionless, and she would have known he was dead even if she hadn't seen the tine of the pitchfork on which he'd fallen protruding from his neck.

She turned away, sickened by what she'd seen. Had her stomach not been nearly empty, she would certainly have emptied it at that moment. Nothing she'd ever seen was that horrible. And even then she knew that she would be haunted by the memory of it for the rest of her life.

She pushed herself to her feet, running and nearly slipping on the wet stone beneath her feet, skirting Duane's body as she scrambled past it to Guy's side.

He was pushing himself painfully to his knees when she reached him, having dropped the pistol to let it lie on the stone near his hand. She fell to her knees beside him.

"Are you all right?" he asked her.

Cedar nodded. But even as she did, she knew she wasn't all right, knew that she was fighting to hold back a horrified scream and the sobs that threatened to claim control of her. Her hands were shaking, and she couldn't make them stop. She was trembling, suddenly without control of her muscles, unable to stop the heaving lurching inside her stomach.

She gratefully fell against him when he put his arm around her.

"We're leaving now, Cedar," Guy told her gently.

He pushed himself to his feet and urged her up to hers. She started to turn back, to look at Duane's body, but he put his hand on her cheek and turned her face so that she couldn't see it.

"He's dead, Cedar. There's nothing we can do for him," he told her. "I didn't have any choice."

She nodded, knowing that it was true, that Duane would have killed Guy, and eventually killed her, if he hadn't done what he had. Still, the knowledge that it had been Duane's life or theirs did not make the memory of the sight of his body any less horrible.

"I know," she murmured. "I wasn't blaming you."

He stared at her for a moment, wondering what it was she was thinking, wondering if what she'd said was really true. He hadn't thought of it until that moment, not until he'd looked into her eyes and seen the shock, the sheer horror that filled her at the knowledge of the way Duane had died. He had done what he knew he had to do to survive, to keep her safe. Now, measuring himself by what he thought were her standards, he wasn't so sure. Perhaps, he wondered, there might have been another way, perhaps he hadn't really had to kill Duane.

"Let's get out of here," he said.

He began to pull her toward the place where the horses were penned. Cedar moved slowly at his side, telling herself she mustn't think, telling herself that if she did, she'd collapse there and then and they'd never get away.

They opened the gate to the corral and herded four of the six horses toward the mine shaft at the far side of the cavern, shouting and waving until the animals found their way to the tunnel and had disappeared into the narrow passage. Then they returned to the pen, to saddle the remaining two horses.

Cedar watched Guy walk. He was terribly pale now, his breathing labored, as were his steps. She felt a wave of guilt as she realized she had been more concerned with Duane's death than with Guy's life. He was growing weaker, that was only too obvious. She was afraid he wouldn't be able to stay on a horse.

"Are you well enough to ride?" she asked him.

She didn't know why she asked. No matter what he answered, her own eyes told her the answer to her question, and it was that he would soon be far too weak to stay in a saddle.

He nodded, but before he had time to answer, they heard a shout coming from the cave behind them.

"I'm going to get you, Marler. You and the girl will never get out of here alive."

Cedar froze and stared at Guy.

"It's McNaughton," she whispered.

There was more noise from the tunnel, a muffled voice that seemed to be saying "I told you I heard voices." They quickly realized that McNaughton wasn't alone.

Guy nodded. "It's McNaughton, all right. And the other voice is Slade's."

Cedar felt herself fill with a wave of sharp, biting terror. Hadn't they already been through enough, she wondered. How long could this nightmare continue?

"We have to get out of here," she said in a terrified whisper.

Guy glanced at the saddles sitting on the top of one of the rails of the fence. It was far easier to cling to a pommel than a horse's mane, to remain astride with feet resting in stirrups, but there was no time to think of saddling the horses now. He pointed at Cedar's Pride. The handsome animal was standing just behind her, nuzzling her shoulder, begging for the apple and sugar she had always brought him when she stayed at her uncle's farm.

"Can you ride bareback?" Guy asked.

She nodded. "Just watch."

He grinned at her. "Not such a lady after all, are you?"

She scowled, but didn't answer. Instead, she turned and patted the horse's neck.

"Let's show him, Pridey," she said.

She grabbed a handful of the horse's mane. He stood quiet for her while she pulled herself onto his back, from all appearances not in the least upset by the procedure.

Cedar looked down at Guy with a smirk, but quickly lost her smugness. Once again she was struck by his pallor, by the realization that he was growing paler and weaker.

"You can't ride," she told him, and started to dismount, sure he wouldn't be able even to mount on his own.

"Stay where you are," he ordered her sharply. "I'll be damned if I'll be outdone by a prissy little moralist. It'd be the ruin of my reputation."

He drew in several deep breaths, seemingly gathering up what remained of his strength, then put his good hand on his horse's mane and swung himself up and onto the animal's back. He was breathless from the exertion, but much to Cedar's surprise, he looked reasonably steady.

"Get going," he told her. He nodded toward the tunnel that would lead them to freedom.

Cedar kicked Pridey's side and turned him to the tunnel. Obedient, he started out at a fast walk. Cedar looked back to be sure that Guy was following.

And when she did, she saw Michael McNaughton emerge from the cave and enter the open space of the cavern. Another man was behind him. She could just make out Slade's face from the shadows cast by the lantern in McNaughton's hand.

There was no question that she and Guy hadn't been seen. Slade pushed past McNaughton, running forward into the open space of the cavern. He needed only a glance to spot them. When he did, he raised his hand and pointed a pistol, aiming at them.

"You're a dead man, Marler," he shouted, his voice filled with fury. "Both you and the girl are dead."

And then he fired.

The sound of the shot echoed off the walls of the cavern, almost obscuring the sound of the second shot as McNaughton fired, too.

"Get going," Guy shouted at Cedar.

She dug her heels into Pridey's sides and he took off, the sound of his hooves beating a steady, thick throb against the stone. She turned and stared back at Guy, afraid he'd been hit by the gunfire, terrified she was leaving him behind to be killed.

But he was just behind her, his body leaning forward as he grasped his mount's mane.

"Go on," he shouted at her.

She gratefully realized he was still close, that he hadn't been hit. But that thought was not as comforting as it might have been. Both McNaughton and Slade were chasing after them, and they continued to fire as they ran. Luckily their aim was impeded by the forest of stone pillars that littered the expanse of the cavern, but she realized that eventually one of them would fire a shot that would not miss.

There was nothing they could do but try to run. Too late, she remembered the pistol she'd taken from Slade, lying on the stone where Guy had dropped it. It had saved them from Duane, but it could do them no good now.

She knew their lead would not be very great for very long. On horseback she and Guy could outrun Slade and his men in the large space of the cavern, but once they reached the narrow tunnel, even the horses would be forced to slow their pace. And McNaughton and Slade were well acquainted with the tunnel, while she and Guy had never gone all the way through. If there was a branch or a turn off, they might never reach the outside again alive.

She reached the tunnel first and pulled Pridey to a halt until Guy caught up with her. For a moment she sat shaking with fear, hearing nothing but the thick thud of her own heartbeat and the sharp, echoing report of the gunfire behind her.

"Please, Lord," she murmured in a desperate prayer, "don't let them kill Guy, don't let anything happen to Guy."

She was rewarded by the sound of Guy's horse as it entered the cave behind her.

"Go on," he shouted at her. "They're still coming."

Remembering the way the tunnel became narrower and lower, she leaned forward, her head low against Pridey's neck, and urged the animal on. He wasn't quite so anxious to move now as he had been. The light from the phosphors that gave the cavern its strange glow quickly faded, and the two were soon staring into near-complete darkness. Cedar couldn't blame him. She was frightened, too, and nearly blind as her eyes struggled to become adjusted to the lack of light.

And despite the noise of the horses' hooves against the stone floor of the tunnel, still she could hear the sharp pounding of the boots of the men who were running across the cavern in pursuit.

"Guy?" she cried back into the darkness behind her. "Guy, are you there?"

"Go on, Cedar," came the faint reply.

It was only comforting to her for a moment, because she soon became aware that she couldn't hear his horse behind her any longer. She drew Pridey to a stop and listened to the sporadic sound of gunfire coming from the cavern. There was no doubt that McNaughton and Slade were getting closer.

"Guy?" she whispered.

This time there was no answer.

She slid down from the horse's back and started to retrace her steps along the dark tunnel. The faint reflected glow from the cavern was in front of her now, and she was surprised by how much it allowed her to see with her by now dark-accustomed eyes. She realized she could see more than well enough to determine that the horse that was now approaching her was riderless.

She flattened herself against the wall as the animal passed her. He was snorting and shaking his head, and Cedar realized he was probably completely terrified by the dark and the persistent shattering sound of gunfire. But her interests weren't with the horse at that moment. They were with Guy.

She began to run now, feeling terror gripping at her with every step she took closer to the entrance to the cavern, closer to McNaughton and to Slade. There was only one thing of which she was certain, and that was that she was not about to leave Guy behind to be killed.

She could see him when she was still a few feet from him, see he was lying on his back on the floor of the tunnel. A thick, stabbing pain ran through her, and all she could think, seeing the shadow lying there and knowing it was his body, was that he was dead.

And then she saw him move, and she ran the last few feet, dropping to her knees at his side.

"Guy?"

He turned dazed eyes to meet hers. There was a thin line of blood starting at his temple and running in a crease along the side of his head. It was simple enough for her to realize that a bullet had managed to find its way into the tunnel and to ricochet until it found its intended mark.

"Guy, you've got to get up. We have to get out of here."

His eyes steadied, and he put his fingers tentatively against the red line on his head. He winced, drew his hand away, and considered the blood on his fingers as though he'd never seen such stuff before.

"Guy!" Cedar was feeling desperate now. They hadn't much time and she knew it. "You have to get up. We have to get out of here."

He stared at her in confusion for an instant, and then his expression finally cleared.

"Go on," he hissed at her. "Get out of here."

There was a sharp, loud noise, and Cedar bent forward, leaning over Guy as a bit of stone shattered somewhere above her head. Another bullet had found its way into the shaft. The closer Slade and McNaughton got to them, the more bullets, she knew, there would be.

She shook her head. "I'm not going to leave you here," she told him. "So don't even try to order me to. If you stay here, then so do I."

Guy's expression grew sharp.

"If you don't get out of here, Cedar, you're dead."

She swallowed, then nodded. "If *we* don't get out of here," she corrected, *"we're* dead. We leave together, or not at all."

He reached for her arm and pulled himself with difficulty up to a sitting position. Cedar glanced at his arm. The jacket sleeve was drenched with his blood. Her flimsy bandage was doing him no good at all. He needed a doctor to remove the bullet and repair the damage it had done. And if he didn't get to one soon, it wouldn't make any difference if Slade reached them or not.

"Damn it, Cedar, why can't you behave like a normal woman and do as you're told?" he hissed at her.

She was momentarily startled by his pained expression and the provoked sound of his voice. It was almost as if he found her determination to defy him more irritating

389

than he found Slade's threat frightening. She started to giggle at that, irrationally and completely uncontrollably. But she didn't let go of his hand, and by the time he'd pulled himself to his feet, she'd gotten herself under control.

She put his arm around her shoulder and her own around his waist.

"Pridey's up there," she told him. "We can ride him out of here. It's not far. We can still get away."

They walked for a bit, then Guy stopped.

"Wait," he told her. "There. Let me get some of that."

She stared into the murk of the side of the tunnel, only barely making out the dark shadows of wooden crates stacked close to the wall. She remembered they contained the remains of the explosives that Slade's men had used to open the old mine shaft so that it would meet the cavern.

"What are you going to do?" she demanded as she helped him to the side of the tunnel.

"You know as well as I do that we can't outrun them, Cedar," Guy told her. "At least I can't, not like this. If you won't go on without me, then I don't see that we have much choice."

"But—but they could be caught in here, trapped," she objected. "We'd be murderers."

He nodded. He knew what collapsing the shaft might mean as well as she did.

"Have you any other ideas?" he asked.

And as though to reinforce the urgency of their situation, Slade's voice came snaking through the tunnel after them.

"You can't get out of here, Marler," it told them. "You're wounded. Give yourself up and maybe I'll let the girl live."

"Well, Cedar?" Guy whispered.

She swallowed, and then shook her head. Guy was right. There was no other way.

"What do you need?" she asked as she pulled off the top of the nearest crate.

Guy found a roll of fuse, and at his direction Cedar fastened it to one of the sticks of explosive.

"Leave it there," he directed.

She dropped the stick onto the top of the crate and once again put her arm around his waist. They started out again, moving as quickly as they could through the dark tunnel, Guy letting out the fuse as they went.

Cedar was starting to think that Pridey had deserted her after all, for it seemed to take forever before they found him. But the horse was standing as she left him, patiently waiting, and she called out in relief to him when she finally caught sight of him.

Guy had found his pocketknife, and as soon as she released her hold of him, he cut the long piece of fuse.

"Now what?" she asked.

"You get on the horse and get ready to get out of here," he told her.

He began to kneel clumsily on the stone floor of the tunnel, preparing to light the fuse.

But Cedar fell to her knees beside him and took the match he'd removed from his pocket from his shaking hand.

"You get up on Pridey," she told him. "I'll do this."

He stared at her, his eyes sharp in the darkness.

"Are you sure you want to do this, Cedar?" he asked. "You don't have to."

But she did, she realized. He could barely hold himself erect. She had to take the responsibility now if they were to escape. Even if they managed to get through the tunnel, still Slade and McNaughton would be after them. With Guy in the condition he was in, there was no question but that they would be caught. And if they were

391

caught, there was no question at all in her mind now but that Slade would have them killed.

She realized as well as Guy did that this was the only way.

"Yes, I do," she told him.

There was a note of resignation in her voice, but one of determination as well. She had been forced to make a moral decision, choosing her life and Guy's over those of Slade and McNaughton. It wasn't something she'd wanted, but she realized that she couldn't let the responsibility fall completely on Guy's shoulders, realized that she must take her share as well.

He nodded, then pushed himself clumsily back to his feet. She glanced up at him and realized that he was in no condition to mount unaided. She scrambled to her feet and darted to Pridey's side, where she knelt to give him a hand up.

"Some rescue this is," he muttered as he put his hand onto the horse's mane.

"Stop being such an arrogant, egotistical male," she replied.

"I was the one who was supposed to take care of getting you out of Slade's clutches," he said.

He put his foot onto the step she made of her hands, but still tried to pull himself, to keep from putting too much of his weight on her.

"Remind me to remind you of that fact sometime," she told him before she heaved him up, pushing with all her might. She grunted with the effort.

With her help, Guy just managed to get himself onto Pridey's back. Once she was sure he was settled, Cedar darted back to the fuse. She looked at the match she'd taken from him for an instant, then struck it against the stone wall. It flared immediately into flame.

Her hands were shaking when she touched the match to the end of the fuse. As she did, she heard the sound of voices in the tunnel and realized Slade and McNaughton had crossed the cavern and were entering the shaft.

They didn't have much time.

The fuse sputtered, and for an instant she thought her heart would stop as it seemed it wouldn't light. But then the flame caught, and she stood and watched as the fuse flashed into flame that began to slowly crawl along the long snake leading back to the crates of explosives.

"Come on, Cedar," Guy hissed at her. "Now."

She turned and ran to Pridey's side. Guy reached down for her, and she took his hand and grasped Pridey's mane, then pulled herself up and settled herself in front of Guy.

She could hear footsteps against stone. Sounds echoed through the tunnel, she realized, and their pursuers probably sounded closer than they actually were, but still she knew Slade and McNaughton were getting nearer. She shuddered as she realized what would happen to them when the lighted fuse reached the crates of explosives.

"Go back, Slade," Guy shouted into the darkness of the tunnel behind them. "If you want to live, go back now."

She turned back and looked questioningly at Guy.

He shrugged. "At least we tried," he told her.

The only response to his warning was the sound of a gunshot. Slade was telling Guy what he thought of his warning, and what he intended to do once he caught them.

Cedar leaned forward, pressing herself close to the horse's neck.

"Run, Pridey," she whispered into his ear. "For all our lives, run."

Everything turned into a confusion of movement and darkness and the terrifying sound of gunfire. If the past few hours had seemed like a nightmare to Cedar, this was the culmination of that nightmare, the moment when the ogres leaped out of the dream and the monsters became heart-stoppingly real.

There was the scent of horseflesh and the sound of hooves sharp against stone as Cedar's Pride ran, and there was the interminable darkness of the tunnel still in front of them. And there was the now seemingly constant sound of gunfire as Slade and McNaughton fired into the tunnel. Cedar wondered why they continued to fire, wondered if they thought she and Guy would be terrified into surrendering by the constant sound, or if they simply hoped the bullets would strike their marks in the darkness. All it meant to her was that the nightmare refused to come to an end.

Only the feel of Guy's body close to hers, his arm around her, holding her, seemed solid and sure. As long as he was with her, she told herself, she would be safe, but she knew that she was deluding herself, knew that neither of them was safe. As long as Slade and McNaughton were still alive, as long as they were still following, she and Guy were anything but safe.

And then there was a faint glimmer of light somewhere up in front of them. Cedar exhaled a thick sigh of relief, knowing that they were finally reaching the end of the tunnel.

She turned back to Guy.

"We're going to make it," she shouted to him. "We're almost there."

But he didn't respond to her. She realized he couldn't hear. His hand had grown lax and she realized that he was no longer holding her close but simply slumped against her.

As she turned back and stared at the thin line of light in front of them, she heard the shattering boom of the explosion behind them as the lighted fuse reached the crate of explosives.

The floor beneath them rumbled and the walls of the

shaft around them shook. Cedar's Pride stumbled, falling against the side of the tunnel, and Cedar screamed with the pain of his weight pressing against her leg. For a moment she was certain he'd fall and she and Guy would be trapped against the stone by his weight.

The roar behind them grew, and she could feel the rock shifting around them, settling, falling. She knew instinctively that the tunnel behind them was beginning to collapse.

She looked up and saw the thin stream of daylight.

They were so close, she thought. And they were going to die, trapped in the tunnel along with Slade and McNaughton.

Slade had, it seemed, gotten what he wanted after all.

# Chapter Twenty-three

Cedar's Pride neighed and then, snorting with fright, somehow managed to regain his balance, pulling himself away from the wall of the shaft and freeing Cedar. He would have reared, but there was no room in the tunnel. Instead he steadied himself, stamping and pawing at the ground with his hooves as though he wanted to assure himself that he was still on solid footing.

The walls of the tunnel were shaking now, visibly moving, and a thick cloud of dust was rising around them. Behind them, the rumble was growing louder. Cedar could literally feel the shaft's advancing collapse as it came closer and closer to them. There was no more time. If they didn't get out now, there was no chance that they would ever escape.

She leaned forward, pressing herself close to the horse's neck.

"Come on, Pridey," Cedar urged him. "You can do it. I know you can."

Cedar's Pride had spotted the wedge of light to the front of them, and he seemed to sense as Cedar did that safety was within his reach. He pulled his head back and neighed. Then he began to run with all of the speed for which he'd been bred.

They emerged from the mine shaft with the tunnel collapsing with an earsplitting roar just feet behind them. A thick wave of stone dust followed them, settling on the grass of the small open space in front of the old mine's entrance.

Cedar's Pride stood, snorting and panting, then shook himself with fear and exhaustion. Unbalanced by Guy's dead weight leaning against her, Cedar lost her hold and the two of them fell.

The ground even there, outside the shaft, Cedar realized, was shaking, and a tearing, wrenching noise emerged from the mountain as the rock resettled itself, filling in the space of the collapsed shaft. Cedar lay with her body beside Guy's, trembling with a strange mixture of nearly overwhelming relief and horror. Her heart was thumping wildly, and one thought filled her mind—the triumphant realization that they were still alive.

When the noise stilled, she turned and glanced back at what once had been the mine shaft. It was nothing but a heap of rubble protruding from the mountain now, with only a scattering of rotten wood that she realized must once have been a gate barring entry to the shaft. Afraid that any change might be noticed and investigated, Slade had doubtless left the old gate as it had been before he began to use the mine as his back door for his stolen horse deals.

It was very lucky for her and Guy that the wood had been old enough and rotted enough so that the horses they had sent through the shaft earlier had been able to push down the gate. For if Cedar's Pride had been slowed by the wooden bars in his way, even if he'd just hesitated, they'd surely have been trapped inside the collapsing tunnel.

She looked back at Guy. He seemed improbably pale in the last of the afternoon sunlight, and far too still. She was stricken with a horrifying fear that it had all been for nothing, that he had died in that last race for freedom. With the fear came the knowledge that without him she would sooner have died as well than go on living without him.

She put her hand on his cheek. It was trembling, she saw, as was the whole of her body, trembling not with fear now but with a wrenching misery unlike anything she'd ever known before.

But at her touch, his eyes fluttered open. A wave of uncontained, joyful relief swept through her.

"What's this I see, Cedar?" he asked in a hoarse whisper. "Could those tears I see in your eyes actually be for me?"

He seemed pleased by the possibility, entirely too pleased, Cedar thought, but she was not in the position at that moment to deflate his smugness.

"I thought you were dead," she told him.

"It's a wonder we both aren't," he murmured. "Or are we?" he asked softly. "Are you an angel?"

She shook her head and smiled down at him. "No," she told him. "No one has ever suggested I even remotely resemble an angel."

He stared up at the blue of the sky through the tracery of limbs branching over them, then turned and looked around, realizing what had happened after only a glance at the rubble filling the entry to the mine. He turned back to stare up at her and raised a stiff arm to wipe away the moisture at the edges of her eyes.

"Now that I consider the matter, it occurs to me that you consider me too unscrupulous to die," he said with a pained smile.

"I have never so much as implied that death was beyond you," she returned.

"Then may I accept this unprecedented display of concern as an indication that you might in some small way regret my passing?" he asked.

"You'll take it as you like regardless of what I say," she said, but she could not help but grin slightly. She lifted her hand to his and pulled it from her cheek to press a kiss to it.

He returned her grin. "I suppose I will." The grin faded and he turned his head and looked once more at the still rumbling shaft. "Slade and McNaughton?" he asked.

She shook her head. "They didn't come out," she told him. "We barely made it."

He began to struggle to push himself up from the ground. "We have to get back to New York, Cedar," he told her. "We still have to see Chester Bowles, force him to come forward and clear your father. It won't be long before he learns what happened to his partners and takes to the hills."

She helped him sit up. "There's time for that," she told him. "What we have to do right now is get you to a doctor."

As if her words had summoned them, three men dressed in overalls appeared at the edge of the clearing, obviously drawn by curiosity to investigate the deep rumbling sound coming from the mountain. They stood for a moment, frozen as they stared at the collapsed shaft. Then the oldest of the three, a gray-haired, grizzled man, whistled.

The sound woke the two others from their reverie. They ran up to Cedar and Guy.

"What happened?" one asked. "Easy there, man," he said to Guy after a glance at his arm and the line of blood on his temple. "You're hurt."

"Them horses that came runnin' out a while back yours?" the other demanded.

Cedar nodded. "Yes," she replied. Then she shook her head. "Not exactly." But horses were not uppermost in her mind at that moment. She nodded towards Guy. "He needs a doctor. Can you help?"

The older man had, by now, joined them.

"Looks like the both of you could stand to see Doc

Sherwood." He turned to one of the two younger men. "Don't stand there like a damn fool askin' questions, Davie," he said. "Go get the wagon so's we can get these folks to town." He motioned to the other. "And you, you see about getting those horses rounded up," he said with typical New England practicality. "That's valuable horseflesh, there. Don't want it wanderin' round the county untended." He leaned forward and gave Guy his hand. "Name's Westfall," he said as he practically lifted Guy to his feet. "My land's just down the hillside. Lucky we come up here to take a look-see at that noise. You take it easy there. If that fool of a boy doesn't take all night harnessing my nag to the wagon, we'll have you to the doctor's before you know it."

Cedar sighed with relief, then scrambled to her feet. This loquacious old man obviously had matters well in hand.

"What were you doin' in there?" he asked her. "Must have been frightenin' being in that shaft when it started to collapse."

"Yes," Cedar murmured as she helped him help Guy. "It was worse than frightening."

"Don't look so worried, miss," Doctor Robert Sherwood told Cedar after he'd taken a look at Guy's wounds. He'd cleaned up the line of blood on Guy's head and quickly bandaged it, then turned his attention to the bullet hole in his arm. "The bullet hit an artery and he's lost a lot of blood, but it's not beyond fixing."

Cedar nodded to let him know that she understood, but she wasn't all that convinced. Seeing Guy lying on the white table, looking almost as pale as the surface beneath him, she wasn't at all sure the doctor's assurances were anything more than words meant to comfort her.

When she'd helped strip away Guy's jacket and shirt

400

and remove the sodden bandage, she'd seen the blood continuing to flow from the hole in his arm in a sickening stream. All that blood, she'd thought, wondering if there was enough left inside him to keep him alive.

Now, as she watched the doctor arrange a row of unpleasant-looking instruments on a metal tray in preparation to remove the bullet and repair the damage it had done, she felt a sick dread at the thought of watching but knew she could not turn away. She felt an irrational fear that something horrible might happen if she didn't.

Sherwood paused in his preparations, went to a cabinet at the side of the room, opened it, and removed a bottle and a glass. He handed them to Cedar.

"Fill this half full, and let him drink it," he said.

Cedar took the bottle and stared at the label doubtfully.

"Whiskey?" she asked.

"Purely medicinal," he replied in a gruff tone that implied he didn't like his directions questioned. "Painkiller." The matter presumably settled, he returned to organizing his tray of instruments.

"A doctor after my own heart," Guy murmured. "Don't waste his time arguing, Cedar. Be a good girl and just follow orders for once."

His words forced Cedar's attention away from the tray of scalpels, clamps, and tongs. She scowled, but didn't reply. The truth was, she was simply too frightened to rise to the bait Guy was offering. Instead, she went about the task of half filling the glass.

When she held it to his lips, he lifted his hand, weakly reaching for hers. She grasped his and pressed it between her own. He stared up at her then, considering her worried expression, her pale cheeks.

"I thought we agreed that I was too unscrupulous to die, Cedar," he said softly.

Sherwood turned back to face them.

"Which leads me to ask if you'd care to explain just

how you got this bit of unnecessary metal in your body," he interrupted.

He glanced first at Cedar and then at Guy, his sharp gray eyes peering out of the wrinkled flesh of his face and telling them that it wasn't a casual request but a matter of law, and he meant to have his answer.

Cedar swallowed, and turned her eyes from Sherwood's to Guy's and back to meet the doctor's. There was no way of telling just a part of it, she decided.

"Perhaps you might send for the sheriff," she suggested. "I don't think either of us has the strength to tell it all twice."

"Like that, is it?" Sherwood murmured. He rolled up his sleeves and washed his hands in silence, then turned back to face her. "I suppose it can wait," he told her. "He's not going anywhere for a while, and from the looks of you, neither are you."

Cedar nodded gratefully. She wasn't quite ready to talk about it yet, not with her mind too filled with worry about Guy.

Sherwood darted a look at the glass she was still holding and then turned his attention to Guy.

"You'd better take another good pull of that whiskey," he ordered. "This is going to hurt."

It had been a seemingly endless night. First she'd spent a gruesome hour watching the doctor remove the bullet from Guy's arm and then sew and bandage the wound.

After that, there had been the visit by the local sheriff. She'd haltingly begun by telling him about the prize-fight, but once started, the story seemed to flow out of her, and she found herself talking about the stolen horses and the flight through the cave and the mine shaft almost impersonally, as though it had happened to someone else.

But after the first telling, there had been questions and

402

she'd ended by repeating just about all of it, not once, but several times. When the sheriff had finally been convinced that no crime had actually been committed in his jurisdiction—he'd told her several times that Boston Four Corners was decidedly outside his authority—and then agreed that the collapse of the tunnel had doubtless killed the villains in any event, he'd told her he'd himself inspect the mine shaft and see that the horses, including Cedar's Pride, were properly stabled until arrangements could be made to return them to their owners. Then he'd left, leaving her to spend the remainder of a long and uneasy night watching Guy's fevered and restless sleep.

By morning, however, Guy had much improved. Despite Cedar's fears that he wasn't strong enough to leave, the doctor had pronounced him sufficiently recovered for the train ride back to New York. Guy had been anxious to go, and at his urging Cedar had to admit that she wanted to get matters finally settled as well.

She'd sipped a cup of hot tea and watched while Guy had bolted down an enormous breakfast prepared by the doctor's sympathetic wife. ("A good sign," Sherwood had assured her. "Healing makes a man hungry.") After that, Guy paid the doctor for his services and then hurried Cedar off to catch the early-morning train to the city.

And now she was sitting beside him on the dark maroon, coarse velvet coach seat, her head back and her eyes closed, but unable to sleep. Instead she listened to the steady droning throb of the engine and the wheels on the track. Every few minutes she turned to check on Guy, but he slept deeply and peacefully at her side, and she had to admit that he probably was a good deal the better for the rest and the breakfast.

Still, it seemed impossible to her that he could sleep so peacefully, especially knowing what it was they intended to do once they reached New York. She sat upright and stared at him through hollow, dark-circled, sleep-starved eyes and thought it all through one last time.

They'd gone over it while waiting for the train, quietly, with Guy reviewing their options before they'd made their decision. What they had, he'd told her, was proof that Chester Bowles was involved in an arrangement to buy up, along with Slade and McNaughton, land the owners had no way of knowing would soon become very valuable. Strictly speaking, it was fraud, because they had knowledge of privileged information. But fraud was not murder, and what they didn't have was anything concrete to tie him to Mary Farren's death. And more than that, Bowles could claim ignorance of any arrangement, could claim he'd invested in the land purely to develop it. After all, that was what he did for a living. Some might even consider his part made him an astute business man and nothing more.

She'd protested, reminding him that Slade had said he'd been part of the scheme from the start.

To which Guy had replied that they still had no proof he was linked to the murder, which, in any case, he most probably hadn't actually taken any active part in. That, they both agreed, had doubtless been McNaughton's job. They could go to the police with their story of a conspiracy including fraud and murder, and hope they were believed and Magnus freed. Or they could instead go to Bowles and offer to trade what proof they had of his involvement in the fraud for a statement from him to the police that Magnus was innocent and naming Michael McNaughton as Mary Farren's killer.

"But what if he laughs at us?" Cedar had asked. "What if he realizes that we really have nothing and tells us to go ahead and go to the police?"

"There's something there, Cedar," he'd replied. "I can't quite put my finger on it, but I know it's there. If they hadn't had something to hold over him, Bowles would never have agreed with Slade and McNaughton to become

404

involved with murder. He hasn't the courage for that."

"Well, then, what is it?" she'd demanded.

"I don't know yet. It's there, I know it's there, but I haven't been able to put my finger on it yet. Hopefully it'll come to me by the time we get to New York."

Cedar hadn't been pleased with that, neither with the prospect of going to Bowles nor with Guy's admission that he wasn't quite sure yet how they could force him to give them what they wanted. What she did know was that by surrendering the deeds into Bowles's hands they were allowing him to get away with what he'd done without any real punishment, and that was what Guy was telling her they must do.

In the end she'd reluctantly agreed with Guy's opinion that the police would most likely not be as open to theories as they would to a sworn statement. They would have to offer to deal with Bowles. There was simply no other way.

They would go directly to Chester Bowles's home, present him with the documents they'd taken from Slade's desk—the map and the deeds—and give him the choice: go to the police and name Mary Farren's murderer, or else face some unknown threat Guy assured her was real—the threat that had made a spineless man like Bowles willing to become involved in murder. He'd do it, Guy had assured her. A man like Bowles would trade a fortune for his partner's name without even blinking.

None of her thoughts at that moment in any way pleased Cedar, and she decided that dwelling on what they must do would not in any way improve her opinion of it. Instead, she turned and stared at Guy, watching him sleep. It all seemed so cut-and-dried to him, she thought—we do this, and Bowles does that. But it wasn't cut-and-dried to her. She felt they were trading justice for their own ends, and although she knew there was no other way that she could be sure her father would be cleared of the charges against him, still she was not at all sure that what they were doing was right.

In a few hours, she told herself, the whole horrible mess would be behind her. Her father would be freed and she could go back to her own life. But at that moment her old life held little charms for her, and the thought of returning to it left her filled with dread. She'd changed from the person she'd been the night—could it only have been little more than a week before?—when she'd first met Guy. It seemed like a lifetime had passed since then, and in passing it had completely transformed her. She was sure she could never go back and become once again what she'd been that night.

She quite simply couldn't go back and pretend she hadn't fallen in love with Guy Marler.

But that was what she'd have to do, she realized. He'd made no promises to her, and she'd be a fool to expect any from him now. His life would go on, and so would hers, and they would drift apart as quickly as they'd come together. Whatever had been between them, it was over now, and she would simply have to resign herself to that fact.

She sighed and told herself that whatever was to happen, there was nothing she could do to change it. She might just as well do as Guy was doing—close her eyes and sleep. After all, she was tired, more tired than she remembered ever being in her life.

And if she slept, she told herself, at least she wouldn't have to think any more . . .

The hand nudging her shoulder was nothing more than an unwanted, bothersome intrusion, and Cedar pushed against it without opening her eyes, wanting only to return to the empty peace of sleep. The hand, however, refused to go away. It kept nudging her, and she was forced finally to open her eyes.

And when she had, she fervently wished she hadn't.

At first she told herself it was a dream, part of the nightmare she thought she'd left behind in the mine shaft.

She rubbed her eyes and stared with disbelief.

And the nightmare stared back at her, its beard bristling around a satisfied smile, its dark eyes filled with hate and a perverse pleasure as it watched her slowly come to the realization that it wasn't a nightmare after all, but real.

"You're dead," she mouthed in a hoarse whisper.

Slade leaned closer to her and pressed the pistol he held beneath his jacket against her side.

"In that case, it would seem I've come back to haunt you," he hissed at her.


Cedar darted a frightened look around the car. There were few other passengers on this early train — half a dozen drummers wearily playing cards in the front, a scattering of others throughout the car . . . none close enough to see the pistol in Slade's hand or hear what they were saying.

But if she cried out, Cedar thought, surely someone would help her.

"Don't even think about it," Slade told her even as the thought was still forming in her mind. "One word and both you and your friend are dead. Do you understand?"

She nodded.

"Good. Now wake up Marler. Gently. We don't want to attract any unnecessary attention."

Cedar did as he told her, putting her hand on Guy's shoulder and gently pushing until he came sharply awake. He started: when he saw Slade standing beside Cedar, smiling at him, but when Slade motioned to him with the pistol, he quieted, immediately aware of the threat.

Slade smiled. "Very good, Marler. I knew from the very first you were an intelligent man. Now the three of us are

407

going to take a little walk to the next car. A very quiet, uneventful walk, you understand? One move from you that I don't like, and our dear Cedar will be forced to pay for your recklessness."

He pressed the barrel of the pistol into Cedar's side and she flinched as the metal bit into her skin.

"Leave her be, Slade," Guy told him. "We can finish this, just the two of us."

"We've already been through all this, Marler, yesterday, back in my study," Slade told him. "Besides, she is my insurance. As long as I keep her close, I know that you'll be docile and manageable, now, won't you? You wouldn't want anything unpleasant to happen to her."

"I'll give you my word, Slade," Guy said. "We leave her here, and I'll give you my word."

"She comes with us," Slade hissed angrily. "Now move. You first." He smiled. "And remember, I have a pistol pressed against her back, so do be careful not to do anything that would force me to do something unpleasant."

He stepped back, pulling Cedar to her feet with him, and the two of them stood aside as Guy got to his feet and slid past their seats and into the aisle.

One of the drummers at the front of the car looked up for an instant but saw nothing interesting about the two men and the woman who had decided to stretch their legs and take a little walk. It was a common enough practice on train rides. He returned his attention to his cards and the pot he was certain he was about to win.

Guy went first, as Slade had ordered, leading the way to the rear of the car. They walked through the coach to the far end silently, without incident and without rousing the least attention. Guy pulled open the door and walked through.

Once they were all standing between the cars, he turned around and looked at Slade.

"Now what?" he asked, shouting above the sound of the

wind and the throbbing drone of the wheels against the tracks.

"Now you go into the next car," Slade told him.

Guy looked at the door. "It's a freight car," he said. "There's nothing in there."

Slade smiled a humorless smile. "All the better for us to have our little discussion in quiet without worry about being overheard, don't you think?" he asked. He motioned with the pistol. "Open it. Move."

Guy pulled the door open and stepped into the car. Cedar, with the press of Slade's pistol against her back urging her forward, followed close at his heels.

Once they were inside, Slade kicked the door closed behind him. Out of the noise of the wind, the car seemed unnaturally silent.

"There, isn't this cozy?" Slade asked as he motioned them forward.

Guy backed into the car, bumping himself against the crates that nearly filled it.

"Well, we're here," he said to Slade.

"Yes, we are, aren't we?" Slade agreed. "Take a seat, Cedar, my dear." He pushed Cedar toward a crate, and she stumbled, then sat heavily where he'd pushed her. "You, too, Marler. I want the two of you where I can watch you both."

Guy sat beside Cedar, and then Slade settled his bulk on a crate a few feet away, all the while keeping the pistol pointedly aimed at Cedar's heart.

"It would seem you escaped the mine collapse," Guy began, amiably enough, although his eyes showed no indication that he felt the least bit friendly.

Slade smiled at that.

"Ah, yes," he nodded. "I can only assume you'd be interested in my unexpected second lease on life. It's a shame Michael McNaughton can't be here as well."

"Yes," Guy agreed. "A real pity."

"I actually owe my deliverance from that unfortunate accident to you, Marler," Slade went on. "After you called out your warning, I sent McNaughton on alone and, quite prudently, I think, turned back. I was in the cavern when the explosion brought down the mine shaft. It wasn't exactly an experience I'd care to relive, but at least the roof didn't cave in. So it seems you saved my life."

"As I said," Guy murmured, "a real pity."

"And you also did me the favor of ridding me of the need to go to the expense of sharing the proceeds of this little endeavor with one of my partners," Slade went on. "All in all, a rather felicitous event, that mine collapse. I really ought to thank you."

"Right now I think a simple goodbye would be more than sufficient, thanks," Guy told him. He touched his bandaged arm. "You've already given me a most generous gift."

Slade chuckled. "I must admit I do enjoy your company, Marler," he said. "And don't think I wouldn't like to accommodate you. But that would be out of the question, I'm afraid. I've gone to a good deal of trouble to make sure you don't get to New York with the belongings you stole from me—"

"*Stole* is such a harsh word," Guy interrupted.

Slade ignored him. "And I don't intend that effort to be wasted."

"I've heard it said that no effort is ever wasted in the eyes of God," Guy interjected.

Slade scowled. "Your wit is growing suddenly stale, Marler," he hissed.

Guy shrugged. "And here I thought I was being so charming."

Cedar couldn't understand why Guy persisted in baiting Slade as he was doing. She could see the anger simmering just beneath the surface, could see Slade's growing rage.

"Guy?" she whispered, trying to warn him.

But he ignored her, instead keeping his eyes firmly on Slade's.

"It must have been really painful for you to turn tail and run, leaving your partner behind to die, Slade," he said. "Don't believe anyone who tells you that you aren't a fine and sensitive man. And I'm afraid you're a big disappointment to me personally. I'd always accepted the adage that there was honor among thieves. It would seem there isn't any after all."

Slade slammed his hand down on the top of the crate on which he was sitting.

"Enough of this!" he shouted. "Get up and pull open the car door. And remember, I have my pistol on your pretty little friend. Make one suspicious move, and I promise you, I'll kill her."

As Guy stood, Cedar darted a look at Slade's eyes. She needed little more than a glance to know that he intended to kill them. Whether or not they did what he wanted, gave him what he wanted, he intended to kill them.

She looked up at Guy and grasped his arm.

"Don't, Guy," she begged. "He's going to murder us."

Slade laughed. "*Murder* is such a harsh word," he said, mimicking Guy.

Guy pressed her hand, then pulled it away from his arm. "Don't worry, Cedar," he said. "We're going to be all right."

He edged past the piles of freight to the door at the side of the car, darting occasional glances at Slade as he moved.

"That's it," Slade directed. "Just pull it open."

Guy did as he was told, pulling down the heavy metal latch, then pushing the door. With his wounded arm useless, it was a more difficult task than it otherwise might have been, but he managed, holding firmly onto the long metal latch of the door all the while so that he wouldn't lose his balance and fall out.

A sharp wind pulled at him, and he stared out at the steep drop and the churning water below as the train skirted the banks of the Hudson River. He stood for a minute and considered the nearly vertical fall beneath him. It didn't take him very long to realize just what Slade was intending for them.

"Ah, I see we're right on schedule," Slade said, his tone impersonal, carefully cheerful once again, but raised now to carry over the sound of the wind tearing into the car. "Pleasant view I've chosen for you, don't you think?"

Guy edged his way back from the opening.

"Let's get on with it, Slade," he said.

"I suppose it *is* time," Slade replied with a complacent shrug. "You and our dear Cedar took some papers that belong to me, and I must ask for their return."

He raised the pistol, just enough to remind Guy of its presence in case he'd forgotten.

"And assuming I choose not to honor your request?" Guy asked.

"Then I shall be forced to kill the two of you," Slade replied.

"Just as you'll be forced to kill us after you have what you want," Guy returned.

Slade shrugged. "I hadn't intended to dwell on that, at least not just yet. But you're right. The unfortunate contingencies of business, I'm afraid." His eyes narrowed speculatively as he stared at Cedar. "Regrettable, but necessary. Believe me, I'd have arranged matters to allow me a bit more time with lovely Cedar had you not forced my hand." He smiled unpleasantly. "But don't worry. It should be over quickly. The fall should kill you before you ever reach the water."

"Somehow I don't find that thought terribly comforting, Slade," Guy replied.

Slade stood and held out his hand.

"I'll have those deeds now, Marler," he said.

"You can go to hell, Slade," Guy replied.

Slade's cheeks colored above the dark brush of his beard. One glance at him and Cedar knew that Guy's words had pushed him far enough to lose the control that had kept his rage bubbling just beneath the surface.

To her horror, she saw him press his finger against the pistol's trigger as he swung his arm to turn the weapon on Guy.

# Chapter Twenty-four

Cedar was literally frozen with fear. She was sure she was about to see Guy killed and knew she was unable to stop it. She looked up at Slade's eyes and recognized the rage and hatred in them. They'd been through so much, and now it was all for nothing. Slade would kill Guy, and then she would die as well.

But Slade's rage was what Guy had been waiting for, what he had been hoping to see. As long as Slade had kept his weapon aimed at Cedar, he hadn't dared make a move that Slade didn't tell him to make. But in the seconds it took Slade to turn the pistol from her to him, he had a chance, a small chance, but the only one he knew he would get.

Guy lunged forward, his hand reaching for the hand in which Slade held the pistol, pushing it upward even as Slade fired.

There was the sound of the shot being fired, followed by the dull thud as the bullet hit the wooden roof of the car. Then there was a thick liquid *oomph* as Guy's shoulder struck Slade's chest, forcing the air out of him, and his own groan as the contact sent a stabbing throb of pain through his wounded arm. And finally there was the metallic clatter as the pistol fell from Slade's hand and struck and slid along the floor.

Guy tumbled forward, bringing Slade down with him

as he fell. They struggled, rolling on the floor of the car, bumping against the heavy wooden crates, striking out at one another. It was hardly an even match: Slade far outweighed Guy, and Guy was further handicapped by a painful, nearly useless arm. What he did have was a strength born of desperation, for he knew he was fighting not only for his own life, but Cedar's as well.

He knew that strength would not last long, however, knew he was already beginning to feel it flag from the constant assaults of pain as his arm struck the floor or the side of a crate. He didn't know how much longer he could last.

When he saw the opening, he took advantage of it. Slade's hand slipped and Guy managed to strike him squarely on the chin. For a moment Guy thought he might have knocked him unconscious. He started to push himself to his knees, hoping to scramble to the side of the car near the open door where the pistol had finally settled and retrieve it before Slade regained his senses.

But Slade had only been stunned. He reached up and grabbed Guy, pushing him aside, striking at his wounded arm, taking advantage of the numbing pain the blow caused to gain the upper hand. Guy struggled, but he knew that he was still weak from the bullet and the loss of the blood, knew he no longer stood any chance of overpowering the much larger Slade. His one chance had been to get hold of the pistol quickly, and now he had lost that chance.

"Cedar!" he cried.

It had seemed to Cedar that it all happened at once, in a single instant. She remembered seeing the pistol in Slade's hand, remembered watching as Slade turned it on Guy. After that, she saw only the two men, struggling wildly on the floor near her feet, and the pistol, a dozen feet away, not far from the open door and the frightening drop just beyond.

But Guy's cry galvanized her, shocking her out of her terrified daze. She realized that Slade was overpowering him, realized that there was only one chance left for them.

She darted toward the open door, falling to the floor just before she reached the empty, gaping hole in the wall of the car. She felt the cold rush of the wind and looked out to the empty space just a few feet beyond her. She realized how close she was to falling, but she didn't allow herself to think about that, knew she couldn't allow herself to become lost in fear if she and Guy were to survive. She grabbed the pistol just as she heard another sharp blow and Guy's groan of pain. She turned to see Slade pushing himself to his feet and Guy lying motionless on the floor.

Her hands were shaking, but she managed to keep her hold of the pistol. Grasping it with both hands, she put a finger on the trigger.

"Don't move," she shouted at Slade. "You stay right where you are."

Slade turned to face her, his expression more bewildered than frightened as he saw the pistol move in her shaking hands.

He recognized her fear and smiled, sure of himself. He held out his hand.

"You might just as well give that to me, Cedar, my dear," he said. "You won't shoot me. You won't shoot anyone. A woman like yourself, you couldn't kill. You simply aren't capable of the act."

"I will," Cedar shouted back at him.

He shrugged, obviously unconvinced.

"I want those deeds," he told her. He kept his eyes on hers and took a step forward, moving toward her.

She stepped back, knowing she was getting closer to the open door, but afraid enough of him to keep herself thinking about the possibility of falling.

"Stay where you are."

Slade stopped and looked at her, hesitating as he weighed the determination he saw in her eyes.

"None of this is necessary, Cedar," he said slowly. "Just give me the deeds and you and Marler can go. It's a fair trade. And no one will have to die."

She shook her head.

"I don't trust you," she told him. "And I don't believe a word you say."

"As you like," he said. "Marler still has the deeds on him, doesn't he?"

He knelt beside Guy and began to rifle through his pockets. Cedar said nothing. Numbed by the feeling of the pistol in her hands, she was wondering if he was right, wondering if she could actually pull the trigger after all. But Slade finished his search of Guy's pockets and, having found nothing, turned back to face her.

"You have them now, don't you?" he demanded. He pushed himself heavily back to his feet. "Don't you?"

Cedar saw it in his eyes even before he moved, knew that he would come after her and that her only chance was to use the pistol. Her hands shook, and despite the orders her brain sent to her fingers, they refused to pull the trigger. It was one thing, a voice inside her told her, to light a fuse when you weren't facing your enemy, when they were something distant, when they were firing bullets at you. It was something entirely different to look into a man's face and pull the trigger that would release a bullet to kill him.

"Give them to me," Slade hissed at her.

Then he reached out for her and lunged.

Cedar threw herself backward and onto a pile of crates stacked behind her just before Slade reached her. She realized with horror that she'd let the pistol fall, that it was no longer in her hand, but in that instant there was nothing she could do but try to stay out of his grasp.

It took Slade an instant to realize he had misjudged the

distance between them, to recognize that he was moving too quickly. He flailed his arms wildly as he suddenly grasped the fact that his own momentum was about to carry him too far, as he realized he was unable to stop himself.

He cried out in fear as he slid forward, through the open door.

Cedar screamed as he tumbled past her, but her horror only grew as she watched him catch hold of the side of the door. He was hanging out of the train, dangling, clinging to the door and trying to pull himself back inside.

He turned terrified eyes to meet hers.

"Help me!" he cried to her. "You can't just let me die!"

Cedar hesitated only a moment. Despite everything he'd done, she realized he was right. She couldn't just let him die. She began to scramble back over the stack of crates.

And then his eyes fell on the pistol lying just a few inches from the side of the door. Cedar felt a wave of sick terror as she realized what a fool she'd been to let it fall, what a fool to think of trying to help him. He glanced up at her, and she saw it in his eyes, knew he intended to get hold of the pistol and kill her.

She slid the remaining distance to the floor from her perch on the crates, knowing she had to get to the pistol before Slade did. But at the same instant, he pulled himself upward and pushed himself forward, reaching for the pistol.

Cedar knew she would never get to it first. She froze.

Slade's hand fell on the pistol, and he darted a glance of triumph at her.

"It seems I win after all," he hissed, and he started to raise the weapon.

But just as he raised the pistol to aim it at her, his hold of the door slipped.

He shrieked as he fell, his cry only ending when his

body hit the rocks on the side of the steep incline and then fell into the rushing water of the river.

Cedar stood where she was for a moment, staring down at the place where she'd last seen Slade's body. But the moment passed and the train quickly moved too far away to allow her to see it any longer. She was glad when it was no longer in sight. She didn't want to remember what she'd seen.

She turned to find Guy struggling to his feet. She ran to him and put her arms around him and relished the feel of the arm he wrapped around her.

They stood silent and close for a few moments, neither wanting to move. And then Guy pushed her away.

"Stay here," he told her.

She nodded and watched him cross to the side of the car, pull the open door closed, and fix the latch.

"I think we'd better go back into the coach," he said once he'd returned to her.

She nodded. They wouldn't want to be forced to explain what had happened if they didn't have to, at least not just yet. They still had to finish what they'd set out to do, and that meant getting to the city quickly and finding Chester Bowles before he learned what had happened to Slade and McNaughton. An inquiry into Slade's death, even if they were believed unquestioningly, would take more time than they had to give.

Guy put his arm around her once more. They started to walk forward, to the next car. Just as they reached the door, it opened and a conductor looked in.

He was obviously startled to see them there.

"You don't belong here," he told them.

He looked around at the stacks of crates as though he half expected to find them open and looted.

"Sorry," Guy murmured. "We wandered in by mistake."

"Passengers in the coaches only," the conductor muttered, then, convinced that they hadn't raided the crates of freight, he stood aside to let them pass. "Don't come back here again," he warned. "Freight cars are dangerous. Crates shift. I even heard tell of side doors openin' and men fallin' to their death."

Cedar looked up at him, startled by what he'd said, but before she had the chance to speak, Guy said, "We'll be sure to stay in the coach for the rest of the trip."

The conductor nodded. "Good. I don't want no trouble on my run."

"That's the last thing we want," Guy murmured. "Trouble."

He pushed the door open and hurried Cedar through it and into the coach beyond.


Cedar wasn't sure if she was half-asleep or simply dazed by the events of the previous days. She walked mutely at Guy's side, standing quietly as he flagged a hansom.

He pulled the door open and ushered Cedar toward it. Then he turned up to the driver, about to call up their destination. But he hesitated, and turned back to Cedar.

"Where does Bowles live?" he asked her.

She pondered the question for a moment, as though he were asking her something gravely philosophical.

"Cedar?" he asked her softly.

She had to force herself back to reality, shake herself out of the daze.

"Gramercy Park," she murmured. She'd been there once with her father a long, long lifetime before. "Number nineteen."

Guy called up the address to the driver, and the two of them climbed into the cab and settled themselves.

"It'll be all right, Cedar," Guy said softly.

She nodded, but didn't answer. The cab drew away from the curb and began its lurching progress through the afternoon traffic. She stared out the window, dully noting the other carriages fighting for place on the street, realizing that she'd had her hopes raised and smashed too many times to simply accept the possibility that everything really would be all right.

Sensing her mood, Guy put his arm around her and pulled her close. She realized he was trying to be comforting, and by way of telling him she appreciated the effort, she snuggled near to him. But she said nothing, afraid that if they spoke the conversation would turn to what it was they were about to do. She couldn't think of that yet, she told herself. She didn't want to think at all.

A glance out the window told her the carriage had turned onto Broadway, and they were passing the ladies stores that lined the avenue. The street and the narrow sidewalks were filled with busy morning shoppers. She stared out at the throngs of intent, bustling women. Two weeks before, she might have been one of them, she realized, her whole interest devoted to finding the proper shade of ribbon or some new kid gloves at a reasonable price. That seemed like a different lifetime to her now; it was as though she'd become a totally different person. If nothing else, the previous weeks had taught her some hard truths about life, truths about the relative unimportance of ribbons and kid gloves.

She was not at all sure she appreciated the lesson.

She turned away from the window, deciding there was nothing on the street that would distract her after all. She put her hand into the pocket of her by now decidedly rumpled and less than pristine skirt. From its substantial folds she pulled the papers she'd taken from Guy's jacket the previous afternoon just before they'd arrived at the doctor's house.

"I think you ought to take these," she told him. "I held onto them, but I'm not quite sure what to do with them any more."

He nodded and took them from her, pushing them into the breast pocket of his jacket. As he did, he looked down at the dark wool. Cedar had managed to brush away most of the dried blood, but there had been nothing she could do about the hole the bullet had made in the sleeve or the dark rust-colored stains.

"More than likely, we won't even need them," he told her with a smile. "Bowles will probably be so terrified when he sees me, he'll agree to anything we ask just to get away from me."

She darted a look at his expression, then at the stained jacket. The dark marks no longer looked like blood, she decided. Violence, she thought dully, was shocking when it was fresh, but faded quickly and then was forgotten.

"Most likely the maid will turn us away at the door," she replied. "We both look like filthy street beggars." She was silent a moment, not wanting to ask, not wanting to think about it any more, but unable to think about anything else. "Have you thought of what you're going to say to him?" she asked finally.

He didn't answer her, but instead asked a question of his own.

"When you went to Tweed and accused him of having your father framed for murder, what was his reaction?"

She turned and stared at him as though she weren't quite sure if he might not have taken leave of his senses.

"He denied it, of course," she replied.

"I know he denied it. But what was his reaction? Did he seem surprised? Bewildered?"

She shrugged. "I don't know," she said. "He told me I was mad. I'm starting to think that perhaps he was right."

Then she turned away, pretending interest in what she saw in the street, unable to think of anything else worth saying.

* * *

They both remained silent the rest of the short trip. Cedar was almost startled when she felt the cab drawing to a halt, for she hadn't really wanted to think about what would happen when they finally arrived.

But they were there, and she knew the time had come to face both Bowles and her own confused ideas of right and wrong and what they were about to do. Guy helped her out of the cab, paid the driver, and then took her arm as they walked the few steps to the front door.

She rang the bell and they stood waiting for the door to be opened. Cedar needed only a glance at Guy's expression to know that he had decided what he was going to say to Bowles. What's more, she could see that he actually relished this confrontation in the same way he'd relished their first venture into the cave, the way he'd reveled in the prospect of eavesdropping on Slade and McNaughton's conversation. He expected the last of his questions about Mary Farren's death to be answered, and that was all that mattered to him.

Cedar wished she could be as remotely distant as he seemed, as completely objective. She knew she couldn't. She knew she hated what they were about to do.

The door was opened by a maid who seemed, after only a quick glance at them, about ready to shut it in their faces. But Guy put his foot on the jamb and his hand on the door.

"Tell Mr. Bowles that Cedar Rushton is here to see him," Cedar told her in a sharply imperious tone. "Tell him it's important."

The maid seemed a bit cowed by her manner, but not so cowed that she was willing to let them enter. She peered more carefully at Cedar for a moment, then stepped back from the door, not inviting them in, but not barring them either.

"Wait here," she said as she turned, crossed to the far side of the entrance hall, then disappeared.

423

Guy nudged the door a bit further open.

"Shall we?" he asked as he took Cedar's arm and stepped inside.

"We haven't been invited in," she objected.

"No, we haven't, have we?" he agreed. "And it wouldn't be polite to enter without an invitation," he added as he stepped inside.

Resigned, Cedar followed suit.

They hadn't long to wait. No sooner had Guy pushed the door closed behind them than Chester Bowles burst out of the room at the far side of the hall, pushing the door open with enough force to make it strike the wall behind it.

He stood for a moment in the doorway staring at Cedar.

And she stared back at him. She needed no more than a glance at his bewildered expression to realize that he thought he was looking at a ghost. That glance was more than enough to tell her that he knew Michael McNaughton had sent her north to Boston Four Corners, to Slade, more than enough to tell her that he expected never to see her again alive.

She felt a wave of sheer disgust wash over her. He was worse than either Slade or McNaughton, she told herself. He was the Judas goat who had lied to her father then led him to be sacrificed on the altar of his own greed. He didn't even have enough honesty or character to face his victim before he plunged the dagger into his back.

He hesitated only a moment, then regained his composure. He started toward her, his short, thick body moving with a churning energy meant to disguise his bewilderment at seeing her there.

"Cedar, my dear," he said as he approached her, extending his hands in greeting. "I can't tell you how horrible all this is, how very concerned I've been for your father. How is he? I've meant to go see him, but—"

She couldn't stand to hear his insincere gushing, to know he was lying.

"Liar," she hissed angrily at him, unable to control herself. "Murderer."

Bowles stopped, half a dozen feet still from them. His face grew blotched with color, and Cedar could almost hear him think, could almost mouth the words *How much does she know?* He managed, however, to maintain his presence of mind.

"My dear, I understand the strain you've been under, and how difficult this is for you," he said in a voice that was obviously fighting to remain evenly controlled. "But, frankly this wild talk cannot help but concern me. You're speaking like a madwoman."

"I suggest you reserve your concern for yourself, Bowles," Guy broke in.

Bowles turned his attention from Cedar to Guy.

"Who are you?" he demanded. "What do you mean by coming here and . . ."

This time he didn't need to be interrupted. This time his words simply faded into silence as he watched Guy withdraw the handful of deeds from his breast pocket. His eyes grew wide with fear as he realized what it was Guy was showing him.

"Perhaps you would rather we leave?" Guy asked.

Bowles's eyes didn't stray from the deeds.

"How did you get those?" he asked in a strained, hoarse whisper.

"More to the point," Guy asked, "how did your name get on them? Perhaps I should introduce myself after all. My name is Guy Marler, and I'm a reporter for the *New York Sun*. And I can assure you that not only my editor but William Marcy Tweed will be very interested in the contents of these bits of paper should Miss Rushton and I choose to offer them to them."

Cedar watched Bowles face pale as Guy mentioned

425

Tweed's name. Now why, she wondered, would he be afraid of Tweed?

She turned to look questioningly at Guy just as Bowles finally tore his eyes away from the deeds in Guy's hands. He cleared his throat nervously before he spoke.

"Should you choose to do so?" he repeated.

"Precisely," Guy replied. "We have come to you with an offer for a trade. Now shall Miss Rushton and I leave, or do we talk?"

Bowles shoulders drooped in defeat. He glanced at Cedar once again, as though he were looking for pity in her eyes, but there was none there for him to find. He turned back to the room he'd just exited and motioned them towards it.

"We can speak privately in there," he said.


It was twilight. There didn't seem to be any passage of time inside the police station, where there was nothing but a continuous dirty lamplight, but once outside Cedar realized they'd been there for hours, that the sun had already set. She stared up at the sky and inhaled deeply, feeling as though she'd been the one who had been freed. Perhaps, in some ways, she thought, she had.

She turned as her father followed her outside. He stood on the step beside her and did precisely what she had done—looked up at the sky and inhaled. That was the first breath he'd taken in freedom for weeks, she realized. She completely understood the contented smile that settled itself on his lips.

"Are you all right, Papa?" she asked.

He grinned at her. "All right?" he asked with a laugh of sheer happiness. "To be out of that place. I can't tell you how good it feels."

He put his arms around her and hugged her, then pushed her back.

426

"I think this can wait until I've had a bath," he said.

Cedar, too, laughed. "I could stand a bit of soap and water myself," she told him.

Magnus turned from her to Guy.

"I don't know how I'll ever be able to thank you," he said.

Guy shrugged. "I was just getting my story," he said.

Cedar turned to look at Guy, too. All the warmth she'd felt inside her was suddenly extinguished by those few words. All it had meant to him was a story, she thought with a tearing stab of regret, a story and nothing more. Although she told herself she ought to have been braced and ready for that, still the words hurt almost more than she could bear.

"And now you have it," she murmured. "All of it."

He nodded. "Unfortunately the best part will never get into the paper," he said, and then he shrugged.

Magnus's expression changed to one of complete bewilderment.

"What part?" he asked. "Why won't it get into the paper?"

"Papa," Cedar began to explain, "What Chester Bowles told the police was only part of the truth. We had to make a deal with him in order to get him to come forward and tell the police what he knew about McNaughton killing that woman."

"It's late, Cedar," Guy interrupted, his tone cutting off any further thought of continuing on with the subject. "And this isn't quite the place for that particular discussion. Why don't you let me take you both home?"

He put his hand firmly on Cedar's arm and started down the stone steps to the sidewalk, forcing her along with him. Too tired to protest, she moved down the steps at his side, with only a glance back at her father to make sure that he was following.

Guy had just put up his arm to hail a cab when Chester Bowles exited the police station just behind them.

"Marler!" he cried, and he ran down the steps to join them at the curb.

When Cedar saw him approach, she stepped away, pointedly making a show of not wanting to stand too close to him. Bowles, however, didn't seem to notice. He was interested neither in her nor in Magnus at that moment. Without wasting so much as a glance on either of them, he put his hand on Guy's arm.

"Turned you loose already, have they?" Guy sneered at him. "Just goes to show you that the police have as little idea of who the real criminals are as they have of the truth. A sworn statement about your ex-partner and their murder case is neatly solved, ends all tied and tidy, and they don't give a damn about your part in it. But then, I can't say I expected much else."

Magnus darted a questioning, bewildered gaze between them.

"What are you talking about?" he demanded.

"I'm afraid this isn't the time, Magnus," Guy replied.

Bowles gave no indication that he'd even heard the exchange. His attention never wavered from Guy. He seemed to be on the verge of rebutting, but he swallowed whatever it was he had been about to say.

"We have an arrangement, Marler," he replied instead. "I kept my part. Now I expect you to keep yours."

"There are some who might argue that a man's not obligated to keep his word to a thieving back stabber," Guy said.

"I warn you, Marler," Bowles sputtered. His cheeks grew a good deal redder and he bared a row of uneven, tobacco-stained teeth.

Guy shook Bowles's hand away from his arm.

"But I am, after all," he went on, "a man of my word."

He put his hand into his pocket, drew out the deeds, and held them out to Bowles.

428

Bowles stared at the handful of paper for a minute, then reached out and snatched them from Guy's hand as if he expected them to disappear at any moment. Once he was in possession of what he wanted, Bowles's look of desperation and anger disappeared.

"A pleasure doing business with you, Marler," he said.

"Our bargain's complete, Bowles," Guy said. "I hope I never have the misfortune of seeing you again."

Bowles smiled at him, then turned to Cedar and Magnus, acting as though he'd just realized they were there. He lifted his hat and even bowed slightly.

"A great pleasure, as always, Cedar," he said. "Good night, Magnus."

Still bewildered, Magnus replied, "Good night," as Bowles turned away and started across the street.

"Can you believe the nerve of him, the smugness?" Cedar muttered as she watched his back recede into the darkness of the street.

Guy shrugged. "He has the right, I suppose. In the end, he'll be rich from the sale of that land. And he won't even have to share what he gets with the others. All in all, I'd say he has a good deal to be smug about just now."

"I don't like it," Cedar hissed angrily.

Guy took her arm.

"I don't like it either, Cedar," he said. "But we didn't have any other choice."

"Is someone going to explain what you're talking about?" Magnus demanded.

"Yes, Papa," Cedar replied. "Just as soon as we're home. For now—"

The remainder of her sentence died in her throat, cut off by a muffled scream. For as she watched Bowles near the far side of the street, a carriage came speeding around the corner. The galloping horse drawing it was headed directly for Bowles and, despite the apparent efforts of the driver, could not be turned aside.

It happened more quickly than Cedar could have thought possible, the racing horse striking Bowles, trampling him, then continuing on down the darkened street.

"My God," Magnus murmured.

Guy pulled Cedar to him, turning her face to his chest and holding her close so that she wouldn't see Bowles's bloodied body. The three of them stood there, numbed by what they'd seen, as a dozen shouting policemen raced out of the station house behind them toward the battered remains on the street.

# Chapter Twenty-five

"I hope I never see the inside of a police station again," Cedar muttered as Magnus helped her out of the carriage.

"A sentiment I can only second," Magnus agreed.

They'd spent two hours telling the police what they'd seen of Bowles's death, two hours repeating the same story, over and over, with none of it changing the simple fact that Bowles had been run over by a runaway horse pulling a carriage that had continued on and disappeared into the dark of the night.

"Can I offer you a whiskey, Guy?" Magnus asked when Guy had paid off the driver. "I know I could use one."

Guy seemed to waver for a moment, but then he nodded.

"I suppose I could use one, too," he agreed.

Magnus took Cedar's arm and started toward the front door. But before they'd taken a dozen steps, a second carriage drew up and stopped by the curb in front of the house. All three of them turned to see William Marcy Tweed step out of it.

"What is *he* doing here?" Cedar asked in a tone that made no effort to hide her antipathy.

Guy could only shake his head. "I suppose we'll have to wait for him to tell us," he said.

"Miss Rushton," Tweed greeted Cedar jovially as he approached them. "How good to see you again."

Cedar scowled. "You didn't seem very glad to see me the last time we met, Mr. Tweed," she retorted.

"I didn't, did I?" Tweed asked. "But circumstances do change." He turned to Magnus. "As have yours, Mr. Rushton, for the better, I see. You are a very lucky man."

"Am I?" Magnus asked. "I've been accused of a murder of which I am entirely innocent. I've been dropped by my party and will not likely be called back. I wouldn't be surprised if most of my law clients decide they really don't want a lawyer who's been involved in this sort of scandal. In all, it looks as if both my political and law careers are essentially over. On the contrary, Mr. Tweed. I would say I'm not very lucky at all."

Tweed shook his head. "Things could be worse," he said. "After all, you have been released from jail and entirely cleared of the charges against you. You could remain, rotting in the Tombs, still facing a long and unpleasant trial."

"How did you know he's been cleared?" Cedar demanded, breaking in abruptly. "We've only just come from the police."

Tweed turned back to face her and smiled. "A man in a position such as mine makes a point of knowing what goes on in the city, Miss Rushton," he told her. "Word comes to me."

"And just how does that happen?" Guy asked. "Or don't you care to admit you have spies among the police?"

Tweed only shrugged. "You must be the reporter," he said. "Marler, was it?"

Guy nodded. "Guy Marler, *New York Sun,*" he introduced himself. His eyes narrowed speculatively as he considered Tweed's smug attitude. "It would seem you really do have spies among the police if you know who and what I am."

"You underestimate yourself, Mr. Marler," Tweed replied. "You've made a start at earning yourself some small reputation."

"That is a shame," Guy said. "I rather enjoy my anonymity. Besides, it makes my job a good deal easier."

Tweed surveyed Guy's condition, taking in the bandage on his temple and the torn and stained sleeve of his jacket.

432

"It would seem you've earned your story the hard way this time," he mused with a smile.

"I don't suppose you'd like to make it all worthwhile and reveal what else you might know about Mary Farren's murder?" Guy asked. "Or Chester Bowles's death?" he added, almost as an afterthought.

Tweed raised one thick brow. "I will gladly reveal to you that I know nothing at all about the whore. You are free to quote me if you like. As for Bowles, it would seem he, like his friend McNaughton, was a very greedy man. It is only just that he died as he did, don't you think?" He smiled a knowing smile. "It would have been unfortunate were he to walk away from the mischief he'd done without having been forced to pay for it. In all, it was a most felicitous accident that took him."

Cedar was completely bewildered. How could Tweed know anything about Chester Bowles's death? Or for that matter, how could he know what Bowles had done?

"But—" she started.

Tweed cut her off.

"But accidents, or fate if you will, have a way of settling such inequities," he said. "Just like the accident that settled Michael McNaughton's accounts. That just leaves the last of the three—Slade. But I have a feeling his own fate will come to him soon enough. There are men in this city who frown on the practice of arranging the outcome of sporting events."

"Intimates of yours, I suppose?" Guy asked.

Tweed only shrugged.

"Slade has already met with his accident," Cedar said softly.

Tweed turned his glance back to her and lifted a brow. "Has he now?" he murmured. He smiled thoughtfully, then shrugged once again. "It would seem that greed has done all three of them in. That should satisfy you, Miss Rushton, to see there is some justice in this world after all."

"I can't help but wonder if justice might have been differently dealt had they come to you at the start and offered you a share," Guy told him.

Tweed's smile suddenly disappeared and there was absolutely no humor in the gaze he turned on Guy. "If I were a less forgiving man, I might find that insinuation offensive, Mr. Marler," he said.

"A reporter's job sometimes leads him to be offensive, Mr. Tweed," Guy replied, entirely unruffled by Tweed's threatening stare.

"I assure you I can be an unpleasant enemy, Mr. Marler."

"I have no doubt but that you can, Mr. Tweed."

"If I were you, I'd hope our paths not cross again," Tweed murmured through tight lips.

"If I were you, I'd hope the same, Mr. Tweed," Guy replied evenly.

Tweed stared at him a moment longer, taking in Guy's determined expression. There was no doubt in his mind that this reporter had the effrontery to think he could do him harm. He shrugged, then let his expression soften. He was, after all, a powerful man, one who could afford to let a nosy reporter chase around, looking for his bits of scandal. He could always be dealt with should the need arise.

Tweed smiled once again and turned to Magnus.

"In any case, I have come to express my regrets and those of Tammany for all the unpleasantness you've been put through, Mr. Rushton," he said. "It was, after all, at the hands of one of our own, a fact that causes us all distress. Michael McNaughton was a misguided fool, one who would have done far better to keep his actions legal and within the bounds sanctioned by his party."

Magnus glared at him. "I'd hoped to prove to the voters that there is nothing that isn't sanctioned by Tammany," he said. "But it seems you win after all, Tweed. I am ruined, and Tammany remains unscathed."

Tweed nodded. "So it would seem, does it not?" He smiled with satisfaction as he turned to Cedar. "And I have also come to tell you, Miss Rushton, how much I regret we had not met under more pleasant circumstances." He put his hand on his hat, lifted it slightly, and nodded his head. "Good night."

With that he turned on his heel and started back to his carriage. Cedar, Guy, and Magnus stood by the front steps, watching him leave in a dazed silence as they considered the fact that Tammany and Tweed were the only ones who had not been victims of the circumstances rising from Mary Farren's murder.

Cedar sat on the edge of the couch, unable to feel comfortable in her father's study with Guy and Magnus both there. She couldn't keep herself from staring down at the rug in front of the fireplace, at the spot where she and Guy . . .

Stop it, she told herself, stop thinking about it. It's past now, and what's past can't be changed.

But it was one thing for her to tell herself she must get on with her life. It was quite another for her to stop thinking about Guy and what she felt. She darted a look at him, watched him sip his whiskey occasionally as he calmly told her father what had happened, what they'd done. Well, most of what they'd done.

His manner was so easy, so relaxed. He felt none of the churning emotion she felt at that moment, she realized. What had happened between them was nothing more than part of his story to him, just another part that would never get into the papers.

Guy swallowed the last of the whiskey in his glass.

"And when we threatened to go to Tweed," he said, "Bowles knew he was cornered. If the three of them had gone to Tammany in the first place and offered Tweed a share, they'd have been safe. But they were greedy and didn't want to be forced to make a fourth split. So they went on with their plan on their own, even knowing that if Tweed found out, they'd certainly be dead men."

"So you traded those deeds for his statement to the police clearing me?" Magnus asked.

Guy nodded. "And what a story he told them, too," he said. "The man wasted his time as a builder. He should have been an actor. He told them that he and McNaughton had met quite by chance in some saloon, and McNaughton had ended getting drunk and boasting about the way he'd murdered a whore, getting rid of his political opponent and fooling the police all in one genius gesture."

"But didn't they ask him why he hadn't come forward before this?"

Guy nodded. "They did. He told them he was afraid of McNaughton, afraid for his life. He even sobbed as he confessed that part, and begged them to forgive him for taking so long to gather up enough courage to come forward."

Magnus shook his head in disbelief.

"And they believed him?" he asked.

"They had no choice," Guy replied. "He told them about the hidden panel in the room in the bordello, gave them details as to how the murder was done, all of which he knew because he was there when it happened. But once the police accepted his tale of McNaughton's drunken confession, they had to believe the rest of it. Presumably there was no way he could know such details unless they'd been told him by the real murderer."

Magnus sat in silent thought for a moment, staring at his own empty glass. Then he looked up at Guy.

"Care for one last drink?" he asked as he pushed himself to his feet.

Guy handed him his glass. "Just a small one, thanks," he said. "It's late."

"It must have been a fine performance he gave the police," Magnus said as he crossed the room to the liquor cabinet.

"He was staking his life on it," Guy said. "Our bargain was your freedom for the deeds. If you weren't released, the deeds would have gone to Tweed and Bowles would have been dead."

"It almost seems as if he was cheated," Magnus remarked thoughtfully. "He delivered what he promised, and he died anyway."

"Papa, how can you?" Cedar cried. "After what he did to you!"

"I didn't say I pitied him, Cedar," Magnus replied. "I just said that—"

"Cedar!" Guy interrupted, cutting Magnus off. "What do you remember about the horse and coach that struck Bowles?"

Cedar turned and looked at him with a look that clearly implied he must have taken leave of his senses.

"Not again, Guy," she moaned. "Haven't we been through all of that more than enough?"

"Just say it," he insisted.

She scowled, but complied.

"Dark green coach. A large sorrel with a white blaze, better than twenty hands. Just like we told the police."

"Precisely," Guy agreed. "Now what do you remember of the horse and coach in which Tweed arrived when he came to pay you and your father that friendly little visit?"

She closed her eyes and thought for an instant, then opened them and stared at him, suddenly very aware of what he was suggesting.

"A dark green coach," she murmured. "And a large sorrel with a white blaze."

It hadn't occurred to her until he mentioned it, but now that he had, she realized that it could very well have been the same coach, drawn by the same horse.

"But that would make Tweed Bowles's murderer," she said in a hoarse whisper.

He nodded at her and smiled a crooked, knowing smile.

"So it might," he agreed.

She stared at him for a moment longer. He was still smiling, and it was that same smugly certain smile she'd seen on his face more times than she really cared to think about in the preceding days. He was on the track of another story, she told herself, and she and Magnus were probably already half-forgotten as he tried to work it out in his mind.

Guy pushed himself from the couch. "I'm afraid I won't have time for that whiskey after all, Magnus," he said as he started for the door. "Another time, perhaps. This can't wait."

Cedar started to stand, but he waved her back to her chair.

"Don't bother. I'll show myself out," he told her.

And with that, he was gone.

Magnus held up the evening paper.

"Look, here's another, Cedar, with Guy's byline. A description of the havoc the mob left behind when they hijacked a train to return them to the city. Was it really that close to a riot?"

Cedar shrugged, then stared down at her sewing as if darning a sock were the most important task in the world.

"I don't know, Papa. I told you. We left the town and escaped through the tunnel into Massachusetts just at the end of the fight. Those men were all still there."

"Of course, of course." Magnus murmured. "I'd forgotten." He looked up at Cedar. "But if you weren't there when the mob hijacked the train, how could he write about it so vividly?"

"I suppose one of his upstanding friends told him what happened, Papa," Cedar replied. "It would seem your friend Mr. Marler has quite a few unsavory types as his close confidants. Pickpockets, burglars, the absolute cream of society are at his beck and call."

"All these front-page stories," Magnus went on, completely ignoring the rancor in Cedar's words, "the fight, the horse thieves, the secret path through the mountain. Guy must be doing very well for himself."

"A man like Guy Marler gets what he sets out to get, Papa," she murmured.

It was true, she told herself. He gets what he wants, and to hell with whomever he hurts along the way.

"He hasn't been back, has he?" Magnus mused. "It's been more than a week. I thought we'd surely see him by now."

"Why should we see him?" Cedar demanded. "He got his story. There's no reason for him to come back here. I'm sure he has far more interesting acquaintances to visit — those burglars, I mentioned, for instance."

"I thought he seemed a little sweet on you, Cedar," Magnus replied.

"Must we talk about him any more, Papa?" Cedar demanded.

She stabbed angrily at the heel of the sock with her needle and only succeeded in sticking her finger because her vision was suddenly blurred by tears she had no intention of allowing herself to shed. She bit her lip, concentrating on the hurt, trying to force the tears away.

For the first time, Magnus noticed the hurt in her expression. He watched her put the heel of her hand to her cheek and rub it, and realized she was on the verge of tears. When it struck him, he wondered how he had not seen it before.

"You're in love with him, aren't you, Cedar?" he asked her softly.

She looked up at him and tried unsuccessfully to swallow the lump in her throat.

"I don't want to talk about it," she murmured as the first hot tear fell to her cheek.

Magnus dropped his paper, rose, and crossed the room to her. He put his hands on her shoulders.

"I think it's for the best for both of us that we're leaving," he said.

Cedar nodded. "Yes, Papa. It's for the best."


"Oh, Mr. Marler."

Mrs. Kneely, Guy noted, seemed distracted — not that

439

that state was entirely alien to her, he thought. She took a step back from the door to allow him room to enter.

"Mr. Rushton's in his study, I think," she said as she started to turn away from him, back to the parlor. Guy glanced in and saw she was in the midst of putting dust cloths over the furniture.

"I've come to see Cedar," he told her.

"The kitchen," the housekeeper replied in a slightly distracted manner as she returned to her task. "Do you remember the way?"

Guy wondered if she'd be willing to leave her dust cloths to show him if he said he didn't, then decided probably not.

"Yes, I remember," he told her.

He crossed the hall and turned into the corridor that would take him to the rear of the house, all the while wondering just what was going on. But when he pushed open the kitchen door and saw Cedar hard at work wrapping pieces of china in newspaper and putting them into a crate, he realized a lot had happened since he'd last seen her.

"Hello, Cedar."

Cedar spun around and saw him, and nearly dropped the plate she was holding in her hands. She stared at him, eyes wide, not quite sure she believed he was there, and not at all liking the sudden sharp throbbing she felt in her chest when she realized that it must really be him.

"Oh," was all that she seemed capable of saying.

"Oh?" he repeated. "I'd have thought I deserved better than that."

She swallowed the lump in her throat.

"Are you well?" she asked, noting the thin red line on his temple, all that remained of the injury there.

"Good as new," he said, then smiled and flexed his arm to show her. He winced slightly as the pressure set the bullet wound throbbing. "Well, almost as good as new."

"I'm glad," she murmured.

She turned back to the crate and carefully placed the dish she'd just wrapped inside it, concentrating on the task as

440

though her life depended on it. Then she reached for another and started to repeat the process.

Guy stared at her back for an instant, then crossed the room, edging his way past a half dozen already packed crates and the newspaper-laden kitchen table. He put his hands on her shoulders.

"Cedar? What's happening? Where are you going?" he demanded.

"We're leaving," she said. "Papa's starting a new law practice, in Saratoga. We're going to live with my aunt and uncle there."

She inhaled sharply in an attempt to settle herself. She hadn't expected this, she realized, hadn't expected ever to see him again. But now that he was here and there was no way to avoid what could only be a painful few moments, she told herself she could at least get through it with a modicum of her pride still intact.

She edged away from his grasp, placing the wrapped plate into the crate, and reached for another.

He watched her busy attention to her work, feeling the tension between them as though it were something thick enough to hold in his hands.

"Isn't this awfully sudden?" he asked. "Neither you nor Magnus mentioned that you might leave."

She concentrated on folding the paper around the plate, refusing to let herself think that she'd heard a hint of regret in his words.

"Papa had more than half of his clients cancel their accounts with him while he was still in jail, and in the last week more than a dozen more have done the same," she said. "He wants to leave, and I can't say I blame him."

"But this is premature," Guy insisted. "They'll come back to him, or he'll get new clients."

She shrugged, then put the plate she'd finished wrapping in the crate. "He wants to go," she said. She reached for another plate and began to wrap. "We've been reading your stories about the fight and about Slade. We've been waiting

441

to read what you found about Tweed and Bowles's death."

"There was nothing," he said in a pained voice. "I checked Tweed's personal stables as well as Tammany's. No dark green coach. No sorrel with a blaze. There's no way to tie Tweed to Bowles's death."

"Oh," Cedar murmured as she reached for another plate. "You must be disappointed."

"I think he did it on purpose, coming here in that coach, knowing I wouldn't be able to trace it. Or maybe he just thought it was amusing, a way to demonstrate how invulnerable he is."

"It must be quite disappointing for you, losing a story like that."

"There'll be other stories," he muttered. "And one day one of them will lead to Tweed. I just have to find it."

"I'm sure you will," she murmured with a hint of bitterness.

He will, she thought. He'll get what he wants, and he'll do anything to get it.

He stood for a moment, the silence between them becoming awkward again, and watched her wrap another plate and deposit it in the crate. The last of the paper she'd had on the counter used, she was forced to turn around to face him.

"Excuse me," she said and pointed to the papers stacked on the kitchen table. "I need some more."

"Cedar, what's going on here?" he demanded as she stepped by him.

She shrugged as she lifted a pile of the paper and carried it back to the counter. "Why, I should think that would be obvious to a man of your fine observational talents, Guy," she replied as she began to busy herself once more with the plates. "Papa's put the house up for sale. We're leaving. I thought I already explained it all quite clearly."

Guy reached around and put his hand on the plate she was about to wrap.

"Cedar, will you put that damn plate down and look at me?" he growled.

Cedar felt a sudden lurch inside herself when he stepped close to her, when she felt the heat of his body close to her.

"I've a great deal of work to do, Guy," she said as she tried to pull the plate back with shaking hands.

"It'll keep," he said, and refused to let go.

She pulled back, assuming he'd release his hold. He didn't. The plate split with a dull crack, breaking in two.

She finally looked up at him.

"Are you satisfied now?" she demanded.

"I'll buy your father another," he said.

"You can't. This was my grandmother's china, from France." She was shaking now, not with passion, but with anger. "Haven't you done enough? A week ago you ran out of here without so much as a civil goodbye, and now you come in, expecting the world to fall on its knees in front of you. You are the most arrogant man I have ever had the misfortune of meeting."

He grinned. "Guilty," he said. "But I was busy."

He *had* been busy, he realized. There had been that useless search for the dark green coach and the sorrel, and all those stories that had appeared in the *Sun* in the preceding days, but that had only been a small part of it. He'd had to find Dublin O'Donnell and collect the winnings from the bet he'd asked the pickpocket to place for him, a sizable bet on Morrissey. There were some, he supposed, Cedar no doubt included, who would not find such a bet entirely legitimate considering he'd placed it while in possession of the information that Slade had made an arrangement with the referee at the time he'd placed it, but Guy considered that a triviality, one of the few benefits his craft provided him. Besides, he'd needed the money to buy a ring.

"Well, I'm busy now," Cedar told him. She started to stack the pieces of broken porcelain on the counter. "If there's nothing else you wanted to say, I'll thank you to leave so I can get back to work."

He put his hand into his pocket and removed the small box. He wouldn't tell her where the money to buy it had come from, he decided, at least not now. Perhaps someday, but certainly not now.

"As it happens, there is something else," he said. He put his hands on her shoulders and this time forcefully turned her to face him. "A few things actually. As I was saying, I was busy—busy convincing my editor that a man can't take a wife if he has empty pockets, convincing him that I needed a raise. And then, I was busy buying this."

He handed her the box.

She stared at it as though it might bite her, then looked up at him, sure she hadn't heard correctly. She swallowed.

"Taking a what?" she asked.

"A wife," he said firmly as he flipped open the box. "A man can't take a wife if he can't afford to keep her."

Cedar didn't move. She stared at the ring with its small but respectable diamond. It felt as if her heart had stopped beating.

"Keep her?" she murmured.

"Really, Cedar," Guy chided as he removed the ring from the box, reached for her hand, and slid the ring onto her finger, "for a woman who never seemed to me to be at a loss for words, you are extraordinarily mute. Surely you can manage a few appropriate words, like 'Yes, Guy, I'll marry you.'"

Her heart was beating again, Cedar realized, beating wildly. She looked down at her hand where it rested in his and smiled.

"Yes, Guy, I'll marry you," she repeated.

He grinned. "That's better," he said as he put his arms around her. "You might add a simple 'I love you,' if it's not too much to ask."

"I love you."

He pulled her close. "And I love you," he whispered before he pressed his lips to hers.

It was a long, passionate kiss, a kiss that left Cedar

444

breathless, more than a little dizzy, and quite decidedly aware that Guy's ardor was sincere. He pushed her back, sweeping the heap of paper from the large kitchen table to the floor, then lowering her to the table and following her.

She lost herself in his kiss, in the feel of his body close to hers, the touch of his hands cradling her head. But when his lips left hers and strayed to her neck, she realized where they were. She put her hands on his shoulders and pushed him away.

"Guy, we can't do this. What if Papa or Mrs. Kneely should come in?"

"We'll just tell them, very politely, of course," he replied and he smiled, "to leave."

"Guy!"

He kissed her again, but this time playfully, teasingly.

"I've been meaning to ask you something," he told her.

"What?" she asked as she reached up and put her hands on the back of his neck.

"Why are you named Cedar?"

She laughed.

He raised a brow. "Is it that bad?" he asked.

She shook her head.

"My parents spent their honeymoon in Saratoga, at my aunt and uncle's house," she replied. "There's a large cedar grove near it, a place where we often go for picnics. It seems they had a private picnic of their own one afternoon . . ."

He laughed. "You were conceived in a cedar grove?"

She nodded. "So it would seem."

Guy looked around the room, at the rows of cupboards and the large stove on the far wall.

"Do you think your father might consider a private sale of the house, Cedar?" he asked. "I've become very attached to it. And there are still so many rooms where I haven't made love to you."

"Like the kitchen?" she asked.

He nodded, then pressed his lips against her neck.

"But I don't think we should name our firstborn Kitchen," he murmured. "Somehow it doesn't sound dignified. Perhaps Study. Or Bath."

"You're mad," she said with a laugh.

He lifted his head and stared down at her.

"I am," he agreed. "I'm madly in love with you."

And this time, when he kissed her, Cedar entirely forgot that they weren't alone in the house, and even that she was lying on the kitchen table.

"Kitchen," she murmured softly as he unfastened the top buttons of her blouse and pressed his lips against the soft flesh of her breast. "Perhaps it isn't such a bad name after all . . ."

# Author's Note

The Morrissey-Sullivan fight actually occurred much as described here, a brutal, thirty-seven-round, bare-fisted battle that left behind questions of an arranged outcome even though no proof of the allegations was ever actually found. Sullivan made a few unsuccessful attempts at a comeback after his defeat, and died several years later, an alcoholic suicide. For John Morrissey, the prizefight was the start, not the end, of a long career. He entered politics, served in the New York State Legislature, and was to eventually join New York's highest society, becoming an intimate of Commodore Vanderbilt.

The town, Boston Four Corners, went on in its lawless state for nearly two years more. Eventually, however, Congress confirmed the transfer of the land to New York State, and the state formally accepted the twelve hundred acres under its jurisdiction in January of 1855.

Today, Boston Corners, New York, is a sleepy farming community, where dairy cattle outnumber the local inhabitants ten to one. There is no hint remaining of the lawlessness that once ruled there. The train station is gone, as are the tracks, which were taken up several years after the last train stopped running. Even the plaque commemorating the prizefight and marking the field where it occurred is gone, mysteriously disappeared.

The wind, however, continues to howl across the hay fields, and sometimes, on a windy night, one of the old-timers will tell the story he heard when he was a boy, about the wild, bad days and the lost tunnel through the mountain through which horse thieves smuggled away their stolen booty.